Praise for Chris Stark's *Carnival Lights*

"Chris Stark is a masterful storyteller, and *Carnival Lights* is an unforgettable novel. Fluid in time and place, flowing between one past and another, offering a heartbreaking portrait of multigenerational trauma in the lives of one Ojibwe family, this tapestry of stories is beautifully woven and gut-wrenching in its effect. *Carnival Lights* is an important book about the treachery and tragedy that so many Native Americans in this country have experienced, particularly women. Read it, and it may change you forever."

William Kent Krueger, *New York Times* bestselling author

"By weaving narratives back and forth through space and time, Chris Stark's newest novel explores the evolution of violence experienced by Native women and girls at the hands of non-Native men – dating back centuries. Simultaneously graphic and gentle, *Carnival Lights* takes the reader on a daunting journey through generations of trauma, crafting characters that are both vulnerable and resilient."

Sarah Deer, (Mvskoke), Distinguished Professor, University of Kansas, MacArthur Genius Award recipient

"*Carnival Lights* is a heartbreaking wonder of gorgeous prose and urgent story. It propels the reader at a breathless pace as history crashes down on the readers as much as the book's vivid characters. A stunning novel honoring murdered and stolen indigenous girls whose stories are too often dismissed. The author's brilliant heart restores their dignity and via the realm of imagination, brings them home."

Mona Susan Power, author of *The Grass Dancer*, Standing Rock Sioux

"It's not every day that one is given an inimitable gift of truth. *Carnival Lights* is that gift. The history books that we've all read throughout time were purposely devoid of the realities of decades of Native genocide, attempts to eradicate our culture, and the horrendous effects of the boarding school era—trauma that continues to permeate the American Indian communities today. *Carnival Lights* is an opportune story of how two young girls navigate these lived experiences and provides a veracity that will reach deep into your heart, creating a new found reflection of the actualities of this historical trauma. Chris Stark, a skilled narrative artist, once again engenders storytelling that ingeniously weaves multi-generational authenticities for not only the Native communities, but also as reflected for so many others. It's time for all of us to embrace this gift of truth."

> Deb Foster, Anishinaabe, MS-MFT Executive Director for
> the Ain Dah Yung Center, a meeting place for American
> Indian homeless youth and families

"There are so many moods and story currents running through this wonder of a novel that I can attribute to individual women whose lives experiences run parallel to Stark's many characters. The two female adolescences in this novel take us to high and low heights, just like a carnival ride. It's overwhelming, irrational and dangerous, and there is no one to help, just as it has been for Indigenous people from the moment colonizers stepped foot on this continent of Turtle Island. *Carnival Lights* is powerful storytelling. Indigenous ancestors are persistently returning, so as not to be forgotten in death and memory, and Stark puts the reader right in the center of their pain and struggles."

> Mary K. Kunesh, Minnesota Senator, Standing Rock
> Lakota descendant, chair of Minnesota Missing and
> Murdered Indigenous Women taskforce

"*Carnival Lights* is a powerful story of resilience, an emotional rollercoaster ride and an expression of the raw truth of multigenerational trauma. Sher, a lesbian and protector, or what we call 'two-spirit,' is particularly connected with the old ways."

> Lenny Hayes, Sisseton-Wahpeton Oyate,
> and Two-Spirit activist

"Chris Stark weaves Native spirituality throughout *Carnival Lights* from the 1960s, before the Religious Freedom Act of 1978. We will lay under a fern, waiting for a drop of water to fall from the tip of the leaf with Em, feel the freedom of fleeing abuse with Kris and get to know the protector Sher who watches over Kris like a wolf. *Carnival Lights* reminds us that we are not alone, and we are watched over by ones we would have never known or seen if it were not for this desperate moment we are in right now. Chris Stark reminds us how important our teachings are, how our memories can comfort us in our darkest hour when we need it the most. Chris draws us into the inspiration and comfort provided to the characters at times guiding their next move."

 Babette Sandman, Ojibwe elder, White Earth Nation
 enrolled citizen living in Duluth

"The novel *Carnival Lights* twirls like a vine between the past and the present. Two Indian girls and their families are bound by the racism and entitlement that have taken their bodies and their land since Columbus. The imprint of culture handed down by the ancestors is the key to survival through constant danger and uncertainty. Chris Stark provides a deeper understanding of Indian culture and oppression. You cannot put this book down. Once read, you cannot plead ignorance about the continuing genocide in America of the First Nation people. The time to act is now!"

 LaJune Lange, retired District Court Judge
 and human rights advocate

"Chris Stark has done a beautiful job of incorporating this story of cousins; Sher and Kristin, within a historical and cultural narrative. The trauma that they experience is a familiar tale for many of us. I did not just read this story.... I felt this story and I journeyed with Sher and Kristin in all directions, and through many emotions. The connection to the story of Native women today is clear and brilliantly written. *Chi miigwetch*, Chris!"

 Nicole Matthews, ED of Minnesota Indian Women's Sexual
 Assault Coalition, White Earth Anishinaabe

"Through the story of two young Indian girls, Chris Stark's poetic language takes us to the white men's annihilation of the Indians through disease, displacement, disappearance, sexual violence, physical and cultural genocide and vicious, malevolent cruelty. An intersecting thread of the extermination of the Jews is woven throughout the context of perpetrators, victims, survivors and the land, in what Stark describes as the 'spiral' and interconnectedness of all Indian stories.

"The narrative crosses generations to unfold the sources of destruction with a sense of place and character that is heart-wrenching. At the same time, Stark evokes the beauty and vitality of Native traditions, beliefs and relationships, and she infuses her writing with the hope that the people will endure despite almost insurmountable obstacles and unbearable grief. This beautifully-written book should enrage us and move us to seek justice for Indian women and men."

Ellen J. Kennedy, Ph.D., executive director,
World Without Genocide

"The Indigenous story is often untold—even though we are the first Americans. Chris Stark has written a powerful and vivid account of the Indigenous experience from 1860 through 2019 and the killing of George Floyd in Minneapolis. She gives a realistic account of generations of Indigenous people and walks the reader through layers of exploitation, abuse, loss and perseverance. Chris does a masterful job of showing the deeply contrasting views of colonizers and Indigenous people and the often devastating outcome of those differences. While not always easy to read, it will capture your imagination and encourage you to learn more and to, hopefully, drive your commitment to make the future a brighter one for all."

Dr. Priscilla Day, professor, UMN Duluth social work
department, Anishinaabe tribal member

"*Carnival Lights* is a terrific read. It's a tough subject matter but brilliantly written. I could feel, smell and taste what the characters were going through while at the fair and throughout the novel. Wonderfully written."

Terri Forliti, Survivor and Executive Director of
Breaking Free, an Afro-centric program helping women
escape prostitution and trafficking

"A remarkable narrative of two very young women's quest for sanctuary, on a continent that others have taken over, forms the axis upon which Ms. Stark pivots history—vertically and horizontally—enabling us to see the young heroines in their ancestral, clan and family legacies. We learn much in the process and abhor much as we come to understand how it is to be perceived as less than human in one's homeland."
Ninotchka Rosca, novelist

"Chris Stark tells a story that raises, to consciousness realities, sensibilities that exist and surround or are within us but most wish to stay hidden, in a way that weaves time, place, memory and spirit. Her voice is unique, courageous and Indigenous. She tells the story of generations of indigenous women that others talk about in intellectual terms of genocide, colonization, sex trafficking and survival, in a way that pulls from ancestral memories and spirit, and makes the journey of *Carnival Lights*, uncomfortably, amazingly familiar and personal. Reading *Carnival Lights* is an unsettling and healing experience."
Brenda Hill, Siksika

"A heartbreaking account of the violence Indigenous women face down every day in this country, even in broad daylight, even now. Predators abound in this short but powerful book but so, too, does love—love of the earth and love of each other. Even at the hour of death, Stark insists on life. That she does is a gift to us all."
Julian Aguon, author of *The Properties of Perpetual Light*

"Chris Stark has done it again—she has provided the context that is so conspicuous in its absence in mainstream literature. In her second novel, *Carnival Lights*, Stark presents us with the missing context behind the lives of two Indigenous runaway girls in 1969. This context has been historically missing because it involves a diligent and artful untangling of dozens of intersecting immigrant narratives that are also tightly interwoven with the histories of Minnesota's Indigenous people. Much of the backstory in *Carnival Lights* illuminates the intergenerational trauma of Native Americans refracted through fragments of ritual, anecdote, rumor and legend. The canon of American road narratives is challenged and enriched by Stark's powerful story."
Carolyn Gage, playwright, author and activist

"I've been hoping and waiting for this book ever since the author's groundbreaking debut novel, *Nickels: A Tale of Dissociation*. Now *Carnival Nights* confirms Chris Stark's place as one of America's most important authors. This is a story of America never before told. Epic in its temporal and geographical journey, and entirely original in its style, this devastating, lyrical and riveting book belongs on every list of great American novels."
    Professor Zoe Trodd, director of the Rights Lab,
    University of Nottingham

"Chris Stark's *Carnival Lights* hop-skips forward, back and across Minnesota from 1860 to 2010, drawing together threads in the connections between three Ojibwe girls and their families. Stark weaves together ancestral blood memory, dreams, family stories, settler history and a river of trauma that runs through the lives of the girls and their women relatives. She shines a spotlight into the dark corners of Minnesota history, focused on events and experiences of Ojibwe people that have become buried, much like the bones she describes as scattered throughout the site of a settlers' massacre of Indian women, children, and elders. Stark tells us that the need to protect and survive forced parents away from the ceremonies that once connected them to the realm of spirits on the land and brought balance to all of creation. And she shows us connections bent and snapped, pushed aside by violence and abuse. But she also writes of circling back, sharing and protecting, remembering and dreaming and, finally, reclaiming those connections to one another and to the spirits of the land."
    Alexandra "Sandi" Pierce (Seneca), PhD sociology, author
    of Shattered Hearts: The Commercial Sexual Exploitation
    of American Indian Women and Girls in Minnesota

"Stark tells us a story—one that's filled with rage and love; connection and separation; shame and pride. This is the story, the heartbreakingly beautiful story, that holds your breath as you read it. For some of us, it's our story, told back to us with all the honesty and nostalgia and horror we remember. For others, it's her story, and you're in it, even if you've never heard of it before. Now is the time to sit with this."
    Cherry Smiley, radical feminist from the Nlaka'pamux and
    Dine' Nations, PhD candidate in communication studies,
    founder of Women's Studies Online"

CHRIS STARK

Modern History Press

Ann Arbor, MI

Carnival Lights
Copyright © 2021 by Chris Stark. All Rights Reserved.
3rd Printing – October 2021.

Learn more about the author at www.ChristineStark.com

ISBN 978-1-61599-577-6 paperback
ISBN 978-1-61599-578-3 hardcover
ISBN 978-1-61599-579-0 eBook
Audiobook edition available from Audible.com and ITunes

Modern History Press
5145 Pontiac Trail
Ann Arbor, MI 48105

www.ModernHistoryPress.com
info@ModernHistoryPress.com
Tollfree 888-761-6268
FAX 734-761-6861

Distributed by Ingram (USA/CAN/AU), Bertram's Books (UK/EU)

Library of Congress Cataloging-in-Publication Data

Names: Stark, Christine, 1968- author.
Title: Carnival lights / Christine Stark.
Identifiers: LCCN 2021029471 (print) | LCCN 2021029472 (ebook) | ISBN
    9781615995776 (paperback) | ISBN 9781615995783 (hardcover) | ISBN
    9781615995790 (pdf) | ISBN 9781615995790 (eBook)
Classification: LCC PS3619.T3734 C37 2021   (print) | LCC PS3619.T3734
    (ebook) | DDC 813/.6--dc23
LC record available at https://lccn.loc.gov/2021029471
LC ebook record available at https://lccn.loc.gov/2021029472

With gratitude for Sam Emory and
niiyawen'ehn Earl Hoaglund

For the Old Ones

"I seek the religion of the tree..."
—George Morrison

My girl, every tree tells a story. The Standing People hold the stories of the land. They grow according to what happens around them. Story upon story unfolding, one story growing from other stories.

A tree is a story! Sometimes a story grows off the trunk into a clump like those big bulges you see on trunks sometimes. Those bulges. They're a part of a story that got trapped there somehow and instead of becoming a branch it just bulged. Who can say how? Who knows? I don't. Humans don't know everything. We don't need to know everything. It's just how it is, my girl. Clumps. Backwards. Forward. The old days. The days that will come. Stories are not straight lines like how the whites think and write. That is not our way. Stories grow zigzag, branches off branches off branches, shooting in every direction, and more branches off those branches and so on until leaves unfold in the spring, until a story is spoken.

Then, like the leaves, once stories are spoken, they fall to the ground to go back to the earth and the next time the same story is spoken, a new leaf grows, and it is similar, but not exactly the same as the leaf from the year before. My girl, this is how it is—as my grandmother once told me stories, I now tell you stories that you must pass on so that the trees will always have leaves. If the stories stop being told, the trees will have no new leaves; they will die and soon after, so shall we, for we have breath because of the leaves.

The old Ojibwe man paused, focused on the branch he was whittling into a pipe stem. *Even in the white world trees tell stories. Crushed flat and bleached. Called leaves! See, my girl. It's as I told you. Even in their world, trees tell stories. Standing People. Stories. Indians. The land! Howah!*

— Clarence Leonard Braun

Prologue

Village of Park Point, Minnesota, August 1860

The carnival came to town, but not until after the Indian bones were excavated. Under the red beam of the Minnesota Point Lighthouse cast by a fourth-order Fresnel lens and illuminated by a kerosene lamp, a motley assortment of Finnish, German, and French men wielding spades and pick axes broke joints, cracked femurs, shattered fingers, and split the skulls of those buried long before Europeans set foot on the shores of the westernmost tip of *Gitchi Gami,* renamed Lake Superior by the French. A former John Jacob Astor agent in concert with the acting mayor of the unincorporated town of Duluth made the decision to build a carnival to "brighten the dour mood" of the sixty-odd dwelling on the shore and the few hundred in the logging and mining camps nearby. Although it was a hefty investment with questionable immediate return, the two men had plans for the port and needed to attract hundreds, and eventually thousands, more European immigrants to build the city. The two men believed once others heard of the grand carnival held there, Europeans would come in droves. The Europeans were sitting on a gold mine of trade prospects now that they had moved the Indians off the shoreline closer to Fond du Lac. The Indian graveyard had been a problem, though. The men worried someone might kick up a bone during the carnival and cause a sensation, frightening business to St. Paul or Chicago. So the bones were hacked out of the soil by criminal castaways and thrown into a wagon drawn by a single draft horse lent by a man who used the horse to clear tree stumps from the burgeoning township. That is how the Indian bones traveled to their new home, nearly three miles down the river that flowed southward out of *Gitchi Gami*, the largest lake in the world.

Two days after the removal, guided by the red beam of light, the Arawak steamer brought in supplies—a large metal wheel that hitched to a horse directly across from a wooden bench such that as the horse walked in circles, patrons rode the bench for four spins a penny around a fifteen-foot-wide path. Called the Sweetheart Ride—it was the center attraction for the first-ever carnival on the spit of land overlooking *Gitchi Gami*. The ride was the motivating factor behind George Washington Gale Ferris, Jr's invention of the Ferris Wheel, which would make its first appearance at the 1893 World's Columbian Exposition in Chicago, commemorating the four-hundred-year anniversary of Christopher Columbus's landing in the archipelago inhabited by the Taino, and designed to be direct competition to the Eiffel Tower of the 1889 Paris Exposition.

Four days later a four-wagon caravan arrived carrying workers, lard, bags of flour and potatoes and dried pork, canvases, rope, tar, shovels, stakes, and wood that transformed into four tents, including a sideshow of Savage Indian Joe and His Squaw—a Ho Chunk Indian man and a Brothertown mixed-blood Indian woman who looked full-blood. For three days they set up camp, washed clothes on the rocks along the shoreline, mended costumes, and cooked. After considerable labor by the carnival workers that extended late into the evenings under torch light, the townspeople gathered for their first carnival on the Indian cemetery. Based on Mark Twain's character, the evil Injun Joe who was the villain of *The Adventures of Tom Sawyer*, the Harvard-educated, well-read, former John Jacob Astor agent created the sideshow he called "Savage Indian Joe and His Squaw," changing the word "Injun" to "Indian" so as to avoid any legal complications with Twain. Savage Indian Joe and his pretend wife rubbed ochre over their faces and arms, donned goose feather headdresses unlike anything any of their ancestors ever wore, and lunged around a tent, waving their hands in the air and screaming gibberish, frightening European women and children alike, who paid a penny to sit on wooden benches and watch the heathens. An old French fur trader familiar with Indian ways looked into the future and knew this wouldn't end well. The rest enjoyed the frightful show—sucking on the sour, birch, peppermint, lavender, and hoarhound candies while basking in the torch lights that removed the cold and loneliness and hunger they endured thousands of miles from their land, on the other side of the Atlantic. The Indians in the carnival made them feel superior not only to the Red Man, but to the squalor they themselves lived in.

One month later, after the carnival slogged westward over rutted paths, an old Ojibwe Indian lady living in a wigwam far enough out in the woods that the English, as she called all Europeans, had not removed her to the Fond du Lac reservation yet, walked seven miles alone to the site of her parents' and her parents' parents' and her parents' parents' parents' graves. Born in 1784, her grandmother had told her one night when she was a girl of nine that their people knew the time would come when more and more English would arrive, first by ships over water and later by ships in the air, bringing great death and destruction, the *Windigo*, the cannibal spirit. The old Indian lady's grandmother told her that the English would make many lights that would guide the ships to the land. One day there would be so many lights they would no longer see the stars and barely know the difference between day and night. "All those lights," the old woman added, "would make it hard for Indians to see the Star People, our Guardians and Guides, and slowly we will lose our ways. Their lights will steal our people."

The old Ojibwe lady, then just a girl, stepped outside the wigwam to look at the Star People, hundreds of bright lights in the black sky. Her dog, *Animoosh*, stood watch at the edge of the clearing. The moon hung full, just over the tops of the bare tree branches, their leaves the size of beaver ears. She couldn't imagine it—what her grandmother said about not being able to see the Old Ones. She bit a piece of maple tree candy her *nokomis* had given her and slipped inside the wigwam, nestling into the warmth of her grandmother's belly and the beaver pelts they slept in.

Decades later, stooped, in a long skirt, with a red willow basket over one forearm, the old Indian lady wandered the shoreline where the carnival had been, occasionally bending over, setting something she picked from the rocky shoreline into her basket. Unseen, except by a curious Finnish boy who watched her, she moved through the Village of Park Point with the boy like a white shadow behind her. Crossing the spit of land into the unincorporated town of Duluth, a stray hound whose Finnish master had died six days after arriving on a ship, leaving the dog to fend for herself, lunged at the old Indian woman and flung the contents of her basket onto the dirt. The old lady yelled words unintelligible to the boy and kicked the dog in the face, scaring it away. Kneeling, she regathered the contents of her basket and slipped behind an English man's tar paper shack. The young boy ran to where the woman had disappeared. Seeing no one, he searched the ground as he had overheard men discussing their quest for rocks that would make them wealthier than the Czar. *Whoever that was*, he thought.

The boy's mother had recently died giving birth to a baby sister who also died. His eight-year-old sister took over cooking and sewing and stoking the fire at night while their father searched for work in the logging camps farther north. The children were starving. Near where the dog bit the old woman, his eye caught a pearly white shape in the dirt. Grabbing it, thinking perhaps it would be the special rock the men had talked about, the boy ran lest one of the men take what he had found. Long and smooth, about the length of the boy's middle finger, he gave it to his sister, who mistook it for a bird bone and boiled it in the water she'd collected from the Great Lake for their dinner that night. And the next night. And the next.

And then, the one after that.

East

*In Ojibwe ways, the east is where the Ojibwe come
from. It is the spiritual direction, a place of mystery
and adventure.*

Pine Township, Minnesota on the Goodhue Reservation, August 1969

The blazing red and blue light from the cruiser careened off the
windows, utensils, and faces of the women and men eating at the
truck stop diner. No one paid much attention. Sher Braun moved
slowly, paid the cashier—a woman in her mid-twenties who looked
ten years older—with one rumpled dollar and some change damp
with perspiration. The woman nodded absently, turning her back
to the girl and the carnival colors lighting up the inside of the truck
stop diner like it was the Fourth of July. Sher took the hunk of
homemade corn-bread wrapped in plastic with a red sticker on the
side holding it together and put it in her pack along with two
damp cans of Coke, some face makeup, a sky-blue Bic lighter, and
a pack of gum. *The important thing,* she thought, *was to not panic.*

The cop was not there for them. Moving slowly, methodically,
she kept her face as impenetrable as those around her: deep
caverns of darkness garishly lighted up by each cycle of lights. If
they knew at all they thought they were on their way to Fargo. If
the APBs were out on them, they would be looking north,
northwest, and they were on the southern edge of the Goodhue
Reservation zigzagging south, southwest headed to Minneapolis
where she knew someone who knew someone, or they could camp
out by the river until they found jobs or moved on. Whenever the

girls had discussed leaving, Sher had always talked of returning by next spring in time to put the seeds in the ground, with the hope her brother, Jack, would have already left for the war. Kris listened to her cousin, older than her by two months and six days, but she did not reply. Kris was not going back.

Sher strapped the pack over her left shoulder and looked at the woman's back. She glanced through the empty convenience store section and then again at the women and men eating Paul Bunyan-sized portions of mashed potatoes, peas, gravy, and roast beef and drinking iced tea and Cokes out of red, dimpled plastic tumblers half a foot tall. She walked in a long stride that belied the actual length of her legs, careful to set her heavy steel-toe boots down softly on the concrete floor so as to not draw attention to herself.

Sher saw the cop through the front pane of glass. He walked around to the entrance and opened the door, alarming the leftover brass Christmas bells swinging above the top, hanging down just far enough to be nicked every time someone came or went. She wiped her arm across her forehead and looked down at her nails short and thick after years of drinking fresh raw milk and baling hay and shoveling manure.

The cop stopped and stood in front of the door, blocking her exit. "Girl."

Sher looked up. The cop met her eyes and looked from her sweatshirt to her jeans to her boots. She saw *Injun* on his face, in the way his eyes tightened and how his jaw set. She shifted the weight of the pack, nodded, stepped around him, leaned into the door, and walked out.

It was raining outside, a light drizzle, the kind that would be good for the crops right about now. They had enough rain that season to keep things green and growing. Too much rain would do in the crops with mildew and weaken the root systems, and too little rain combined with too much sun could still dry up the crops before harvest. She squinted her eyes to the flashing lights and headed off to the right.

Sher strode across the concrete to the other side of the diesel pumps until she reached some medium-length grass and sparse white weeds with heads as soft as the noses of the young cows back on the farm. She cut up under the dogwood and set foot down a slight hill. The moon hung full and ominous, low in the sky. Sher thought of her grandmother, Ethel Mae Braun, passed over nearly a year now. Ethel had told her granddaughter that "moon" and "grandmother" were the same word in Ojibwe—*nokomis*. "A bunch of bunk," her grandmother said when the radio discussed the astronauts' training schedules, or the date of their scheduled flight, July 20, 1969. She swatted the air with her hand. "Yah, sure. They're on the moon now planting their flag. White people say anything and take everything."

* * *

"That you?"

"Yah."

"Did you get it?"

"Sure did."

Sher stepped into an old hunter's shack, the gray boards all but stripped clean of the barn red paint. The door was off and lying on its side. Slivers of moonlight came in all around through the slat boards, warped and cracking apart from one another. She pulled off her pack and set down on an old wooden milk crate turned upside down as a chair. There were the remains of a fire made not too long ago, the circle of small stones and ashes still visible despite the dark.

"Guess someone else had the same idea as us."

"Guess so."

Sher unzipped the pack and dug around until she found the Cokes. She set them on the ground. Then she dug around for the corn-bread, pulled off the red sticker, and peeled off the plastic. She draped it like a picnic cloth over the dirt. She put her hand under Kristin's chin and lifted it up until enough moonlight ran across her face for Sher to see.

"He popped you good this time."

Kristin pulled her chin away. "Did you get it?"

Sher popped a piece of the corn-bread in her mouth, reached into the bag, and pulled out the face makeup.

"Uh huh," she said. "These too." She pulled out the lighter and Trident gum from the pack—a green, stained, army-issued World War II bag that had been their grandfather's.

The day before they left, Sher had climbed into the barn loft one last time to pull the pack down from behind a rafter, where many times she'd witnessed her grandfather stash it along with a buttery smooth beech tree pipe nestled inside a brown leather and black velour pouch, a brittle turtle shell rattle with a frayed red ribbon braided in black horsehair tail, and faded black and white photographs of two young, dark-complected Indian boys. Sher left the photographs and pipe and rattle, knowing better than to disturb them, but took the government-issued pack.

As a child, up in the loft, when she knew her grandfather was out, Sher had fingered the curled, faded pictures many times over the years, always wondering who the other boy was. One boy was her grandfather—despite his obvious discomfort in both photographs, he still had that impish way about him—head cocked slightly, the left corner of his mouth wanting to pull up into a smile, despite his frown, as if it were running away from the thin slanted white scar that zipped up his chin. His eyes were set to unhappiness, but even in that faded black and white photograph Sher could see the dancing light behind his eyes. His aunties said the night he was born the Northern Lights traveled across the sky and left some of themselves in him.

In one photograph the boys sat on claw-foot chairs, a pedestal between them, and a black curtain draped behind them. Unsmiling, hair cut within an inch of their skulls, stiff gray uniforms that made their arms look like boards nailed to their sides, Sher would have believed it an image from World War II, but they were far too young to have been fighting any war. In the other photograph the same two boys were standing on a dirt road, one black leafless tree behind them, railroad tracks disappearing into the horizon, her grandfather with that frowning, half-cocked smile she'd seen him use a thousand times with white people on Goodhue. To her that look said, despite the unhappiness white people caused and despite his need to protect himself from them, he couldn't help but shine. The Lights danced inside him.

* * *

"Cool man." Kristin imitated the white hippie kids she saw on TV or those who showed up at their farm sometimes. Indians called them "wannabes" due to their long hair, factory-beaded headbands and talk of returning to nature where they could be free like the Indians. "Far out. Free as an eagle. Like your people, man," they'd say. "Stupids," Ethel would mutter, but she always fed and watered them when they showed up at the farmhouse high, half-starved, and dehydrated from some trippy wilderness hike in the adjacent state forest. Generous was the Indian way. Ethel would not lose her ways out of bitterness.

Kristin pretended to toke. But she did not need to smoke marijuana to escape. Soon her spirit was higher than the moon and the stars above her and freer than the light shining in through the hunter's slat boards. As she pretended to smoke marijuana, holding the imaginary joint between her forefinger and thumb, she thought of the Mod Squad—the TV show about three hippie youth who escape jail by becoming undercover cops. She watched it if her dad was passed out when it aired. When sober he made her turn off "that damn degenerate hippie show." Kris loved the trios' clothes and hair—the white man and woman's long hair and the black man's afro—and their language. *Outta sight! Foxy! Groovy!* As Kris's spirit meandered above the hunter's shack, she imagined herself as Linc, the black man, chasing a rapist down an alley at night with the lights of the city behind him. Julie and Pete said, "Dig it, man," as they caught up to her handcuffing the man she'd tackled. "Solid," she said, just like Linc always said in the TV show.

As Sher rolled up the sleeves of her sweatshirt, she watched as Kris went far away. Sher was used to it.

"Nah nah nah, nah nah," Kris sang the opening theme song to Mod Squad.

Sher dragged the disengaged front door back to where it should have been. "Okay, Kris," Sher said. "Let's eat."

The girls ate the cornbread and drank the Cokes and did not talk much at all. They slept on their sides, Kris with the pack under her head and Sher with her rolled sweatshirt under hers.

The morning sun woke them like pinpricks. The girls rolled over and over again. Then sat on the dirt floor Indian style and brushed out their long hair with their fingers. Kristin picked up her Coke can and put it to her lips to get one last drink and then crushed it and threw it into the corner. Sher moved the door back to its side lying position on the ground, slipped on the pack, and walked out of the shack. She moved to the west away from the truck stop diner because she did not want to make a second appearance and draw attention to herself. She walked for a few minutes, stepping over molehills and around dead tree branches and bushes until she reached the creek.

A short hike, for sure, but it transported her to the reservation where nearly every day, unless a blizzard or blistering cold or illness kept her indoors, she ran over her family's farmland until she reached the railroad tracks that cut between the farmland and the Goodhue State Forest. The forest and the reservation were both named after Goodhue County, actually located in southeastern Minnesota, by a Washington, DC bureaucrat in 1892 who mistakenly thought Goodhue County was a chunk of land in north central Minnesota. The Goodhue State Forest, as described in a 1912 tourism pamphlet, was 111,680 acres of pristine woodland, with "bubbling brooks, the Grand Mississippi, Big Bear Falls, sixteen lakes, and a plentitude of ponds untouched by civilization except for the six primitive campsites constructed by the state *for your family's exceptional enjoyment!"*

Originally, the land of the Goodhue State Forest had been set aside as part of the Goodhue Reservation. But when the Office of Indian Affairs opened the reservation to white settlement, the area of the reservation (the northwest quadrant shaped distinctly like a bear's head, its snout pointed west) that would become Goodhue State Forest proved too difficult to farm.

"Difficult to farm" was the official reason given by government officials about why all the homesteaders had left. While on the surface true, it was not the whole tale behind the Europeans moving off the land. Anyone within forty miles of what would become the Goodhue State Forest had heard the widespread stories told by homesteaders that the land was haunted by ghosts who harangued them by tapping on their window panes for hours day and night, week after week, and year after year. One German man, with the lettered assistance of his wife, wrote the mayor, governor, congressmen, police, vicar, pope (although he was Protestant) and Office of Indian Affairs repeatedly until they finally sent the sheriff to take a report, hoping this would end his complaints. When the reluctant officer paid a visit to his farmstead, the husband stated that the tapping was a perverse version of "Fünfmal Hundert Tausend Teufel" aka "500,000 Devils". Then he sang a stanza, rapping his knuckles upon the plank board table he'd crafted with his own hands from the oaks that once covered the farm. At the top of his lungs, in slow, broken English with a heavy German accent he sang for the officer:

> Tho' the door is locked and bolted,
> Should it cause us to refrain!
> Has yet lock a demon halted,
> When the keyhole did remain,
> the keyhole did remain.

> This well pleased the thirsty demons,
> who forthwith leaped thro' the hole
> And at once in demon fashion,
> wine by thousand bottles stole,
> And at once in demon fashion,
> Wine by thousand bottles stole
> sang their songs in wildest chorus;
> Shouting praise to love and wine!

"Is infernal Indian devils. Dem deliver to us insanity in this godsaken land," the man's wife blurted out in broken English slathered with such a thick German accent the Swede had to repeat her words three times in his head to understand her. As abruptly as she spoke, she shut her mouth and receded into a corner near the stone hearth. *He was a good man,* she told herself, *didn't beat her like so many of the others treated their wives, but still, she should watch herself lest she intrude too much into the men's conversation.* Head down, she watched her husband. Despite her twelve years of education compared to his four, and her being a High German, and he a Low German, she still deferred to him. He was the man of the house, the king. "*Koenig,*" he'd say after proving himself physically—his way of making him more than his wife.

The *Koenig* stared at the knots in the table, nodded slow. "Ja," he said. "It's dem fine. Dem Indian devils." The presiding officer, a first-generation Swede, wondered how the Indians, with or without their devils, would know the lyrics to some song sung by Krauts, that he, himself, had never heard. The German man glanced at the Swede's face, the German's eyes slitted and hard. His cheeks ruddy. The officer thought them insane drunkards, noting the empty jugs behind the barn, once full with distilled spirits. Upon further investigation, he jotted in his report, he believed the jugs had held homemade whiskey, although two smelled of lager. He ended the report by noting that the only spirits at the farm were the ones the husband and perhaps wife had drunk themselves, most likely permanently addling their perceptions.

Two weeks after the Swede's visit, feeling unheard and disbelieved, the family set loose their two pigs and six one-week-old piglets, two Holsteins, eight chickens, rooster, and three dogs in a frenzy of screaming and clapping. Figuring the animals were tainted by devils, they left shortly after sunrise after yet another

evening of terror at the hands of "dem Indian devils." The only
ones who believed them, as their wagon rattled down the rutted
dirt back roads toward Bemidji, their long hair flying loose (the
husband had stopped cutting his and his wife had not the time to
bonnet hers), the reins snapping the back of their horse, and three
iron pots clanking, were the Indians they passed.

The Indians knew of such spirits, but only Indians living in bad
ways who also had spiritual gifts could summon them. As the
Indians watched the Germans—yet another white family fleeing—
they argued among themselves about whether it was those bad
Indian spirits, summoned or acting on their own, or whether it was
the land ridding itself of the intruders, or whether it was the bad
spirits those English brought over with them. Only two Indians, up
to the point when the German family fled, had been bothered by
bad spirits. Wavering between the old and the new religions, and
confronted with such terror, they'd returned to the Old Ways,
gifted the old Indian doctors, followed their orders, and cleared the
curses put on them and their families. What the Indians did agree
on was that whatever was happening was happening mostly to the
English.

In a twist of fate, the husband's descent into madness did not
end in Bemidji. He spent the remainder of his life in the Fergus
Falls State Hospital, hair forcibly shorn by staff and fingernails
clipped short so he wouldn't scratch at his face and neck.
Forgotten by his family upon his wife's immediate remarriage, she
and her second husband, a second-generation Swede who owned a
dry goods store, raised the two young sons as the biological
children of the Swede. Thereafter, the family believed its line to be
half Swedish until one hundred and eighteen years later a
descendent discovered, upon taking a DNA test, that in fact they
were 89 percent German, calling into question the adoptive
Swedish father as he was the first in their lineage to claim "Swede."
The widow's first husband heard she remarried a Swede, and on
evenings when his pills hit him just so, causing the shadows to
jump at him, he ranted about Swedes, as he'd come to hate them
all. The staff tied him down during his Swedish rants, but they
knew he'd farmed, and when he was lucid they hoped he would
help run the insane asylum's five-hundred-acre farm that fed the
inmates and staff. However, upon bringing him into the fields with
the idea he would drive a team of plow horses, he'd begin to rock

and then sing in German, grasping wildly at the air around his head as if his hair were long as it was when admitted to the hospital or as if he were battling a horde of bees. After a few minutes of this terror, he'd run. The staff grew weary of chasing him and stopped coaxing him to farm. Never again did his former wife set foot in the countryside. She made sure she and her Swedish husband's burial plots were in a cemetery in town. And, she hated all Indians.

Other official reports along with widespread stories about the hauntings also discussed banging on doors, turning of doorknobs, dropping squirrels and birds down chimneys, sucking dry milk cows, sticking pitch-forks clear through barn roofs, and mangled and half-eaten livestock. The white homesteaders believed it was the Indians, demons summoned by Indians, a punishment from their Christian God for excessive drinking and/or merriment, and explainable natural disasters such as the locust plagues of the 1870s in southern Minnesota. Thus, after the last white homesteader left the area in 1899 and the railroad built through the area failed, former Governor of Minnesota, US Secretary of War, and Head of the Minnesota State Historical Society, Alexander Ramsey suggested, in 1902, it be turned into a state forest. He wrote in an editorial in the *St. Paul Globe* about the need to turn the area into a state forest. This was a turn of events from Ramsey's typical newspaper of choice, *The St. Paul Pioneer Press*. Ramsey made a back room deal with James J. Hill, the lumber and railroad tycoon, the Empire Builder, to humiliate the owner of *The St. Paul Pioneer Press* on Hill's urging. The men had bonded after Hill sold two men to Ramsey to satiate Ramsey's lechery, and therefore, in that manner, created an allegiance of secrets between the two powerful men that no one else knew of beside the two men who had lain on their bellies while Ramsey mounted them from behind, thrusting into the men as if they were women.

Hill wanted Ramsey's statement in the *Globe*, which he owned, for the simple purpose of rubbing salt into the wounds of Gerald T. Buckley, whose first and last attempt to build a railroad had failed on that acreage near the Braun's land, and who was Hill's former confidant and now mortal enemy. Ramsey thought, *If this were the old country, we would settle this with a duel.* His grandfather had told him stories of gentlemen quick-drawing pistols on one another and how the Crown ended the practice by making legislation that declared anyone present—onlookers and medical doctors—would also be charged with murder. Instead, Ramsey wrote, "This great swath of virgin land has sat entirely unused and languid for three years now. While there is an element of truth to the statements made by some in positions to know that the land has proven to be difficult to irrigate, any growth in population of the area was stymied by the failure of the Buckley railroad built alongside the western edge only to cross east, rather than continue north, through the aforementioned acreage. The failure to establish townships is largely due to the ill-timed pursuit of this venture and the ill-fated course chosen by Gerald T. Buckley, against the advice of James J. Hill." Ramsey had agreed to focus on the railroad and not on the difficulty of farming the area for Hill's political purposes, which included humiliating Buckley, who had attempted to undermine Hill's railroad monopoly. Ramsey concluded, "Our great state must render this area useful by turning the land into a State Forest. It will take but a generation to return the cleared areas to a forested area, as it has been for millennia. This is the most prudent and wise use of this acreage."

The state forest's immense body began on the eastern edge of the Braun's farm. The campsites that were eventually built were on the far eastern edge of the state forest, nowhere near the reservation. The board of Goodhue State Forest, in 1911, nine years after the land was set aside by the Minnesota State Legislature and the official entity of Goodhue State Forest was founded, believed it would still be too dangerous for white families to camp that close to Indian Territory, as some of them jokingly called the reservation at that time. "Not only would it be undesirable, it would also be unrealistic," Alexander Ramsey boomed across the Minnesota State Senate floor, "to expect the fine citizens of Minneapolis and St. Paul to come within such close proximity to the uncivilized savages." He doffed his hat and died one year later from congenital heart disease.

* * *

Sher knelt by the creek, unzipped the pack and dug around until she found a small stainless-steel cup. She splashed water on her face, took off her sweatshirt and tank top and washed her breasts and under her arms. Then Sher filled the cup with water and drank. She sat by the creek to dry off under the sun, now around

8:00 a.m. in the sky. After a while she put on her tank top, stuffed her sweatshirt into the large compartment of the pack, and filled the cup with water again. On the walk back to the hunter's shack she passed over some buried, pink-veined gray rocks set there years ago to form a walkway of sorts. She adjusted her gait to fit the spread of the rocks, as she'd done when walking and running the train tracks back home. She found a sole surviving wild blueberry bush and plucked some blueberries, most of which were small and still hard. The birds had already picked through them. Sher put them in the other battered tin cup.

"That you?"

"Yah." Sher walked into the hunter's shack and handed the cup of water to Kristin. She set the cup of blueberries on the ground as their grandparents had done for the girls countless times before.

"Thanks." Kris drained the water.

Sher nodded. She took off the pack, unzipped the small compartment on the front, and pulled out a wad of bills.

"The depot isn't far from here," she said as she sorted the bills with all the presidents' faces lined up the same way like her father had done when he got the money from a butchered steer or a crop.

"How far?" Kris picked up the cup and stood next to Sher.

Sher looked up at the ceiling mentally mapping their path from her memory of the times she and her pops had traveled the roads on their horses. "I'd say about two hours if we go along the back roads."

Kristin rocked back on her heels. "It's only a matter of time before they find out I'm not at your house and you're not at mine."

"I'd say another day—tops—if we're real lucky."

Kristin nodded and ate some blueberries, picking through them, leaving the hardest ones in the cup.

"I figure," said Sher, "they'll look for us on the back roads from Goodhue to Fargo, if they look for us at all, and when they don't find us there, they'll put out a statewide APB. On you and me cousin." Sher smiled, but it was empty.

"They think we're criminals," Kris said, as fear of the police and being off the rez rippled through her. The girls were leaving all they knew.

"Some do," Sher replied.

"Plenty," Kris said, and leaned into her cousin's shoulder.

"Yah," Sher agreed, leaning into Kris.

The girls knew no cop would put out an APB on two Indian girls, but they might do other things to two runaway Indian girls. They had heard the stories, whisperings among the Indian teens, and indirectly addressed by the adults through warnings and behavior. Stay away from the police was rarely directly stated, for Indian children learned to fear them based on the beatings and disappearances and upon what Indians did and did not do: adult Indians and teens' words ran silent in police presence. Eyes dropped. Indians never called the police, and they avoided the police in town as if they still carried the white man's plague that had killed so many Indians.

Kristin handed Sher the bottle of face makeup. The girls sat next to each other. Sher pinned the bills under a rock. She smeared the foundation under Kristin's right eye and across her cheek and then down her jawline to her neck where he held her down and left small red marks. *Good thing she's got light skin,* Sher thought with some bitterness regarding all the times white kids and sometimes other Indian kids hassled Kristin over her looks.

"The bruise is hard to cover."

Kristin pulled back. "Good thing it's not you. You'd just have white blotches all over."

"Yah," Sher said. "Sit still. It needs more."

When they finished with that, Sher gave Kristin her hooded sweatshirt to cover the marks on her neck. Kristin gathered their things and put them in the pack while Sher slipped the bills from under the rock and counted them.

"Thirty-four dollars." Sher put the bills in the small compartment of the pack and picked up the empty Coke can Kristin threw in the corner. "Just to be on the safe side," Sher stuffed it in the pack.

The two girls jogged a jagged line north, northeast to get around the truck stop and then headed south until they hit a dirt road and followed that as it wound about toward the southeast. They walked along the ditch through knee high grass, sharp and green and spear-like, and waist-high weeds poking their wheat-like heads up toward the sun. An occasional frog burped, bellying out its call to its mate. Crickets spoke and grasshoppers flung themselves out from under the girls' feet at the last moment.

The land was wide open and free, pretty as a picture book. Sher wanted to save it like this, save herself like this forever. The rolling grasses and weeds bent their necks in the wind like the swans and pelicans and black cormorants that graced the ponds on the rez every summer. That, and the flatness of the fields covered with the dainty clusters of yellow and purple flowers crouching beneath the spear-like grasses and nuzzling soft weeds, made Sher feel an eternity inside of herself every time she looked out at the grass and weeds billowing like waves under a pale blue sky.

A car drove by. A brand-new blue '69 Mustang with a white C stripe. Not the kind of car they saw on the reservation. The kind Jack, who had moved out with their mother for a few years as a boy when she left the family for long-lost white relatives in New Ulm, wanted except he was half a year away from eighteen and saving whatever little money he could for technical college in Fergus Falls to avoid the draft. It was a losing proposition. Everyone knew he could not make enough to go to college. White boys went to college, at least some of them. But not Indian kids. Sher wondered if the people in the car noticed them, and if they did, would they shoot at the girls the way whites shot at Indians on the interior part of the reservation? Were they close enough to being off rez to not get shot at? What did they think about them trudging through the tall grasses? Probably, she decided, they wouldn't care about two teenage Indian girls who ran away from home.

"Sure we shouldn't walk further off the road," Kristin said, mindful of the practice of whites and their guns.

Sher handed the pack to Kristin.

"Yep. If we cut off it could take a couple of days. Or more. We could get lost and we don't have food left. This way we get on the bus and as long as nobody questions us when we buy the tickets, we're in Minneapolis by midnight." Sher rubbed her neck. She looked at Kris for her thoughts.

"I suppose."

"This is what I'm thinking," Sher continued. "Two Indian girls riding a Greyhound into the big city look like we're going to visit Grandma."

Sher had watched her share of Westerns with her grandparents and sometimes her dad, when he couldn't find anything else to do as an excuse to avoid the TV. From the movies she'd picked up a certain cadence and vocabulary which, at times, she unconsciously incorporated into her own such that her style of speaking became a mish mash of long-voweled, lilting Indian-accented English, Minnesota Canadian border white, TV Western, and then, of course, English-accented Indian—what she remembered from listening to her grandparents and other elders talk Indian.

Even though her family watched Westerns, because it was the only place they could see Indians, the TV Indians weren't much like them, seeming stupid and wooden and unjoking, and not at all like the girls' grandparents or great-grandparents who'd grown up in the backwoods, real Indians who only spoke Indian and never learned English or Finnish or German or French—the languages of those who took their land. Not like how so many Indians were now, staying put in one place all year long and living off canned rations and government cheese. "We used to be," the girls' grandmother, Ethel, would say during the Westerns, tapping her knuckles on the chair's curved wooden arm. "Not like this, not like this, so," and she would stare out the window. "In a corner," she would finish, her gaze returning to the living room. Then she muttered in Indian, and stood up to putter in the kitchen or smoke her stumpy pipe out on the porch overlooking the flat, cleared land that opened into verdant rolling hills and the wide skies of the farm and beyond.

The Westerns were the only time Ethel saw Indians on the little black-and-white Zenith her husband had found in the town's dump and fixed up himself, using some wire scrap to create a beat-up-antennae that lopped over like a dog ear. She never missed a *Lone Ranger* episode and thought Tonto good-looking in his fringed buckskin and his thin headband. When teased about that, she turned crimson. "Ehhh," she said, laughing behind her hand. Disappointed when it went off the air in '57, she swore she'd never watch another Western because there could never be another Indian as good-looking as Tonto, but she did watch them on occasion, right up to the night before her and her husband's old white Chevy truck, which her husband called "Scout" after Tonto's white horse as a way to tease her, spun off a gravel road into the woods. Whenever he cranked the powerful engine he'd rebuilt, he would yell, "Get 'em up, Scout," like Tonto said to his horse, as he thwacked the outside of the door before driving off. "I'm as good looking, eh," he would say and pose so his wife could see his profile. "Look at that chin. I shoulda been in the movies." To which his wife would say, "You've always been my Tonto, old man," and then they would laugh, each in her and his own space, chests and bellies rising up and down, laughing at this old joke between the two of them as if it were the first time they'd heard it.

One night the year before the girls hit the road, their grandparents' truck drove off Highway 212 right at the bend near Point Creek, flipping over four times before it burned upside down, its rear landing on the fork of a pine tree, its cab flattened, crushed into the ground. None but her grandparents, the white men in the truck behind them, the stars, trees, earth, and moon knew what really happened that night. To the rest, it appeared as if an old man lost control, colliding with a single tree with four trunks growing up and outward from its base, spread out like fingers on a hand, as if they'd grown that way just for that night—to catch an old Indian man and woman in full flight. To give them a resting place.

* * *

"I guess so," Kris said.

"We ain't gonna get caught."

"I'm not going back."

They walked another twenty minutes until they approached a paved road that hit up against the dirt road making a dog leg that would take them south. Sher paid attention to what was around them—the way the tan gravel spread out across the pavement like a fan from car tires kicking it there, the angle the sun beat down on the girls and roads and the cluster of shimmering cottonwoods in front of them, the shiny silky tassels of the corn field to their left, and the way a lone leaf on a sumac bush to their right knocked about as if a strong wind were about to whip it off its stem, even though the other leaves around it were still. When Sher saw the sumac leaf, she thought of times back on Goodhue when she'd been running and noticed a leaf waving about, sometimes quite violently, despite no wind and no movement of any other leaves. She didn't know if it meant something, and if it did mean something, she didn't know what. She just paid attention. Even as a young girl, Sher always paid attention.

Sher loved the old stories, especially the ones about the runners who went from camp to camp to call gatherings or warn or ask for help. The first time Sher heard stories about the runners was from her uncle Mo. She didn't know if they were biologically related, as in Indian ways those called "uncles" and "aunties" could be biologically related uncles and aunties, great-uncles and aunties, or

not biologically related at all. "Them old Indians," Mo said at
night when everyone was gathered together, "they had runners who
could run faster and farther than any of these…these ah Olympians
in their fancy shoes with the little pokers out the bottoms. Yes. *Ey*.
And this one time a little unarmed group of women and children
and old, old men out near Porcupine Creek was camping one
night, just minding their own ways as the younger men were off
hunting, and along comes those who don't get named and
ambushed them, those women and old, old men and little children.
And then," he smacked his palms together, "they ran every which
way and the unnamed massacred them even though we had a
peace treaty, they did it anyway. They didn't care about our
agreement. That's what they did. Yes. *Ey*. But a few escaped and off
the runner went, see, always ready to run. That was his job, not to
fight, he always had his running shoes, those moccasins, no little
poles on them." He leaned over and waved his hand over the
bottom of his foot. "And off he'd go like the wind. Always ready in
just a second and he ran up that way toward *Gitchi Gami*," and he
waved behind him toward Lake Superior, "to our relatives and
told them of the deeds and brought back warriors with him to save
any who had hidden and to track the group who'd massacred our
people, those Indians, they call them a different name now, those
white men do, but we called them something else and they tracked
them, easy enough to do, and snuck up on them real quiet and got
back our people because, you see, they'd taken a few as," he
searched for the word as English was not his first language "as
captives and then that there was how the old time runners, they
were important to our survival, back then, in the day. Yes. *Ey*. Yes.
Them old Indians didn't run in circles," and he waved his hand
about and chuckled, "like they do now for no reason except the
clock." He stopped and lit up his pipe and smoked a little. "Things
were hard then, but they are hard now too. You see, that is how it
was. That is all. *Miiw*."

Sher listened. It was like she could see it all when he told the
story such that when Sher ran along the railroad tracks and
through the narrow forest paths on Goodhue, she imagined herself
as a runner in the old days, her people's lives dependent on her
speed and endurance over many miles all alone, and her sure-
footed sprinting through snow and ice and heat. And her courage,
the courage it would take for her to complete that journey. Yes,

that was one thing she liked to think of.

* * *

"Your dad sure is going to be mad when he finds out you're gone and so's his drinking money."

"He sure is," Kristin agreed.

The girls laughed.

"Imagine him calling my mom and finding out you ain't been at my house all weekend, then getting mad and going to his Wayne Newton album to buy himself some whiskey and finding out all that cash disappeared, too."

They laughed harder until they bent over and their eyes teared from laughing and the sun and not having any water. Sher's long black hair hung nearly touched the ground as she leaned over. Kristin held her brown hair off her face up in a ball behind her head. After a while of laughing like that, doubled over, Kristin threw up.

"Where," Kris asked as she wiped her face clean with leaves, "is Em?"

Antwatin Township, Goodhue Reservation, March 1893

The girls' great-great-grandparents through Clarence, who spoke only Ojibwe, lost their eighty-acre allotment two years and five months after the passage of the Nelson Act. The Nelson Act turned the tribally-owned Goodhue Reservation into eighty-acre individually-owned allotments. The idea behind it was to force Indians to farm and to force the tribe to sell off the surplus land to settlers. The Office of Indian Affairs (OIA) agent at Goodhue found another way to steal the allotment from the Indians by demanding each family with an allotment show their deed to the allotment. The girls' great-great-grandparents had not been told to hold the papers, at least not in Indian, and burned the deed in a cooking fire the day after they received it. The map that hung in the Office of Indian Affairs, clearly showed their family as the owners of that parcel, but that did not matter. The OIA agent rode his horse out to the girls' ancestors' land. Through a translator, he told their family that due to poor record keeping at the OIA, without papers—no matter the map—nothing could be proven and parcel 84 had been auctioned. All thirty-two living on the land had to be gone by the following day. If not, the Great White Father would bring in the military. That was the official line from Washington, DC; however, the OIA agent knew that before the military were summoned from Fort Snelling, packed their bags and rations, and rode their horses on mud roads 213 miles to the Goodhue Reservation, the nearby settlers would have run off the Indians, shooting any who did not leave. The agent had even heard of a few hangings of Indians down at the St. Croix River, on the shoreline across from Taylors Falls. The white men had let the bodies hang for weeks. After they'd been picked over by crows and turkey vultures, they tossed their bodies on top of the logs floating down the river on their way to Stillwater where the logs were sorted, loaded onto rafts, and sent to sawmills. When the river pigs saw the mangled Indian men, they parted the debarked tree trunks so that the currents would carry the bodies downstream.

Shocked and confused, as this land had been promised to the girls' great-great-grandparents in perpetuity only a few years earlier, the Ojibwe disappeared into the woods to discuss what they would do without being threatened by the agent or settlers. A week later two young Finnish brothers with hair lighter than straw, their words long and lyrical, not unlike the Ojibwe, arrived and set up camp under the trees. A runner from the Ojibwe camp watched them, and reported back to his family deep in the woods.

The Finns moved onto the land, pushing the Indians to the edge of the allotment, but unlike the other settlers, they did not threaten them with violence and force them to leave altogether. The Indians wondered if maybe they let them stay on the edge because both languages sounded like music, swirling and tinkling like water over bits of ice along the shore of Lake Superior. Their languages were unlike the language of the Indians to the south and west whose words sounded like chewed rocks, hard and guttural, rising from their throat in grunts like the words of the pinched, red-faced men born in Germany, who'd built their new lives on Indian land but still spoke in their old way, many more loyal to the Kaiser than the American leader. The Indians could only guess why they were kinder than the other white people. Despite the land passing legally from one lyrical band of humans to another, they co-existed, uneasily at first, in the woods of northern Minnesota, despite the laws created in that faraway land known as the District of Columbia.

The Finns used gang saws fourteen-feet long that needed two or more men to pull the steel teeth through the ten-foot-wide tree trunks. Then they removed the branches and leaves and hauled the eighty-feet-long stripped trunks on a wagon to the Mississippi. The spines of the trees floated down the Mississippi to the Pine Tree Lumber Company in Little Falls, where the Standing People were cut into perfect straight lines to build square houses. The owners of Pine Tree Lumber Company, Richard Musser, and German immigrant and burgeoning lumber baron Frederic Weyerhauser, who two years later constructed another mansion next door to James J. Hill in St. Paul, built mansions next to each other in Little Falls, overlooking the Mississippi, a stone's throw from Charles Lindbergh's home. Unknown to all involved at that time, Musser's mansion would one day become a museum housing memorabilia from *The Wizard of Oz* thanks to family friend Margaret Hamilton who played the Wicked Witch of the West and was a frequent guest at the mansion.

After cutting down the white pines, the Finns ripped out the stumps and roots with an oxen team, leaving the roots lying on their sides to dry like twenty-foot spiders, their enormous root-limbs twisted and frozen in time. Once the spider roots dried, they piled them in the middle of the ever-widening clearing and burned them. The massive orange flames licked the ceiling of the sky, garishly lighting up the charcoal night skies for months.

At first, the girls' family watched the strange English people cut down the trees and rip out the roots. While they were grateful to not be forced off the edge of their land, now owned by the Finns, their grief and sadness over the destruction of the trees and animals who had lived there threatened to overtake them. The Indians began to be sick, like much of their family at Thatcher's Trail, forty-seven miles from Antwatin on the western edge of the Goodhue Reservation, who, they learned by a letter meant for them but delivered to the Finns, had died from "the disease," including the great-great-grandmother's brother and wife, or disappeared like the eldest grandson, Leonard. Four months after Leonard disappeared, his mother married a white man from Bemidji so she and her nine young children didn't starve as they could not survive on their own. The white man took pity, wrote a letter in English, and sent it to "The Brauns, Indians near Antwatin, Minnesota, on the Goodhue Reservation." The Antwatin postmaster, who was more congenial toward Indians than his predecessor, rode his horse out to the land and handed it off to the Finns, who had one among them who spoke English, who relayed the letter to the one Indian teenager who knew enough English to understand their family had mostly died and those remaining now lived in a city that was the Ojibwe word for a lake with crossing waters.

Vomiting and developing fevers and lacking in energy, the Indians watched entire families of Standing People die until one day the girls' great-great-grandmother prayed and received instructions for medicines to give to her family. After searching the woods for the medicines, preparing and giving them to her family as instructed, she said, "Sit here. On this side." So that their family faced the untouched woods, that in twenty-one years would become the Goodhue State Forest. The great-great-grandmother continued to snare rabbits for her family and conduct ceremonies deep in the woods, where no English would see or hear, until her family all returned to health. In these ways, death was not allowed to take up residence in their bodies. As they returned to health, she said, "Look out here. At the forest. Talk with the Standing People. Pray for them. And the animals. And *maamaa akii*, the land. Pray for your relatives. Don't give up, my girl. Don't give up, my boy."

The flaxen-headed Finns worked hard and slow, as they were accustomed, until they cleared the forest and built a farmhouse, cavernous barn, and chicken coop. For allowing her family to stay on the edge of the land, the girls' great-great-grandmother instructed her grandson, who'd just returned from boarding school, to walk over one morning to help the Finns. "To keep things balanced," she said. His work was exchanged in gratitude for allowing the Indian family to stay. In this way, Clarence learned how to run a farm, and learned some Finnish too. The Finns gladly accepted the help but otherwise paid the Indians no mind, going about their business, singing songs in Finnish, the only language they knew. Although in foreign lands themselves, they sang their favorites from back home such as *Wäinämöinen* from the *Kalevala,* a song expressing their people's desire for independence and simplicity over greed, values they retained from their homeland that were the reasons they did not chase off or murder the Indians huddled on the edge of the land formerly theirs that the Finns were now turning into a farm:

Better dwell in one's own country

There to drink its healthful waters
From the simple cups of birchwood,
Than in foreign lands to wander,
There to drink the rarest liquors
From the golden bowls of strangers.

* * *

The bus depot was just a couple of chairs and a round, chipped, red metal table setting outside a one-room drugstore. The girls bought two, one-way tickets to LaCrosse, Wisconsin figuring it was worth the extra $5 to cover their tracks. In all, they parted with seventeen dollars, including money for a Sunkist and a Coke and four hard boiled eggs to keep up their strength. After they bought the goods Kristin washed out her mouth in the bathroom. Sher set out front in one of the chairs peeling the eggs and drinking her Coke. She craved the taste of fresh milk back on the farm, but she needed the extra pop of the Coke to keep her alert. Kristin joined Sher but ate and drank nothing, pushing instead at the places on the table where the paint had chipped, exposing the dull metal beneath.

They sat there for forty odd minutes, watching trucks with hay bales drive by slow and a tottering brown dog sniff around in a parking lot with grass sprouting through the irregular cracks in the pavement. The ancient white man in the faded sky-blue Twins hat who sold them the tickets came out once and leaned against the door frame but did not say anything. His pa had built the place back in the '20s, sure a town would grow there. But none did and the drugstore sat alone along the road, right on the edge of the reservation. His ma said, "Stupid place to build a store. You could toss a stone south and it would land off rez. No one wants to live on the edge of a reservation. Not Indians and not whites." And she was right. The old man went back inside and puttered around. He turned on the radio, an AM station with talking voices the girls could hear but not discern. At last, the bus came, the heat from the black pavement blazing up around it in shimmering clouds. The driver parked the bus in the vacant parking lot where the dog had sniffed earlier and the blazing heat settled under the bus like a pack of dogs lying down to get out of the sun.

Sher swung her boots off the table where she had been resting them. She picked up the pack, handed one ticket to Kristin, and clicked her tongue as if to say *this is it*. Sher thought about when they were young and her dad was still alive and running the farm and Kristin's old man did not seem to slap her around as much. At least that she knew of. Those days, their grandparents kept Kris for days during the summer out on the Goodhue Reservation. Chores, always, but also fishing. Berry picking. Swimming. Stories. Gathering certain plants, the girls were not told the names of—just told find this one that grew around the base of trees with dark green, jagged leaves and don't be fooled by the ones like that with the smooth edges. And then, when the girls returned with the right plant, their grandmother gave them a leaf to chew and the girls shit black for two days. "Clean you out," their grandmother said, smiling and patting their braids. When gathering plants, they were taught to pinch out some tobacco from a cigarette, or if money were low, then shredded willow bark their grandparents gave to them so that they could leave the brown and red flecks next to the plants before they picked them. "To thank them. Never take without giving tobacco," Ethel told her granddaughters. And in the fall, they spent weekends visiting aunties and uncles and cousins from Antwatin—some of whom were related by blood and others who were not blood-related but still considered family. Those relatives still riced full-time, something Sher's dad and the girls' grandparents could only do part-time, and in certain years if the crops were late not at all, because of the farm.

Things were good then. The girls played in the barn, sliding down bales of hay stacked from the loft to the floor as if it were a giant prickly ride at the Goodhue County Fair. They played with the baby pigs so soft and pink, and they dyed eggs bright green and purple like the glass beads their great-grandmother turned into elaborate floral designs on leather and velour bandolier bags which were, in turn, traded with tourists for cloth and fish and needles and more glass beads and needles. The girls searched for the eggs when Grandma hid them around the house and yard—one ritual she retained from her boarding school days because it was one of the few brightly colored activities to come out of the black, drab church.

And some nights, after the dinner dishes were washed and chores done, they played dice and moccasin games and Quist as taught to them by Jorgen, their tall, fiddle-playing Norwegian neighbor two farms down, one of only a handful of white farmers friendly to their family. He and Harald, his bachelor friend who lived with him and helped run the farm, would come over for an evening with a tin of herring their people in the old country sent. They'd play games at the kitchen table and then, as the night wore down, Jorgen would remove the small instrument he'd made himself from its pine box and play, until the sun rose pink and the girls slept in their grandparents' arms or sprawled out on a sheet, the two odd white men who'd never married, and an Indian farming family, sometimes six and sometimes numbering in the twenties with cousins and friends of friends, making stringed music and jigging in the dark. As the night wore on and the Indians felt safer and looser, the jigging Indians transformed into two steppers and side dancers until it seemed the room was filled with hundreds of dancers and drumming—the spirits of the old ones joining in.

The girls' grandparents and other older Indians no longer concerned themselves with a priest knocking on the door, as their grandparents did when they were babies. This was white music, and they were not in the bush. Times had changed. The priests believed most Indians had adopted white ways now, although every once in a while they heard rumors of Indian drums pounding deep in the woods or seeming to come from under the ground, spurring the priests to dust off an old sermon reminding the Indians in the congregation of their savage past, a road that if followed again would lead them straight to eternal damnation, where they would burn in the bowels of hell for all time, where, if they went back to the old ways, they would suffer eternal death and damnation in a pit of fire for the sins of their ancestors and for their sin of reviving the demon ways.

But that was all over now and the girls could never go back to it. Their grandparents gone just over a year in a freak car accident, and Sher's father passed over eight months now. Sher strapped on the pack. She and Kristin walked over to the Greyhound bus and gave their tickets to the bored, road-stunned driver, weaving their way through the exiting passenger until they sat down in the middle of the bus. They set there for a while as the other passengers got off and peed in the drugstore's bathroom and bought various sundries for the rest of the trip.

The girls said nothing to each other, waiting to see if anyone would call them out at the last minute. *Hey, where you from? Hey, Indians can't leave the reservation. Hey, where you going? Hey, you're runaways*. But no one said anything to them. The last errant passenger filed onto the bus and sat down and the driver pulled the door shut in a wide, arching circle. The bus hacked and coughed and then rolled out of the parking lot with the hounds of heat gathering strength underneath.

Thatcher's Trail, Goodhue Reservation, April 1891

Leonard cut through the waist high ferns in the forest. Three new white men down at the clearing were talking about two more wigwams and an abandoned log house that had burned the day before. He didn't want to hear more and didn't want them to see him, so he cut a wide swath around them until he reached the swell in the forest floor on the northeast side of the clearing. Then he could trot upright beyond the clearing to the ferns that, if stretched upright, were taller than he. As his legs whispered through the ferns—still and silent as far as he could see—Leonard swept the horror of the bloated, pus and blood covered faces and arms out of his mind. The lolling heads and rigid limbs that had no one to bury them. Occasionally, he, on his own, had found wigwams and tar paper shacks burned to the ground, the charred shrunken bodies like burned out tree stumps and fallen trunks after fire crumpled the forest into ash, leaving behind limbless, black trees stark against a charcoal sky. In the end, all returned to the earth. Leonard knew that was what the white man's religion taught too, but he didn't understand their irreverence, their greed.

Some said it was white men sent by the doctors in town who set fire to the burned Indians, some said Indians were doing it. Leonard did not know who set the fires. Maybe both were right— he knew some Indians did for the white men, worked with them to get English clothes and the land for themselves. Leonard watched, and he waited, and he prayed they wouldn't all die like that—the people disappearing, without proper ceremonies. What would happen to their spirits?

Indian ways were disintegrating like the white man's papers they burned. "Useless," the old ones said, except for fire starting. Some Indians didn't know what the papers were about; they'd never seen them before. Who would think a piece of paper would equal the earth? What sort of person could believe that? Others knew the papers were about the land and the dead and dying

Indians that the white men and some mixed Indians leered over, their cannibal words buzzing over the wires strung through the trees between Antwatin and St. Paul. The lumber barons on Summit wouldn't live in such an uncivilized place, but they had their emissaries among the Indians, some of whom were breeds. The lumber barons tapped out their directives that traveled year-round at great speed across wires, among shimmering leaves, and over barren, snow-swept fields.

As Leonard stepped over a fallen tree, he wondered how a piece of paper could have anything to do with the land—the trees and the animals and the earth. There was no equation between the land and a sheet of paper with the black markings of crow's feet. He and his grandfather had walked this fern forest many times, the fronds long and wide, like great arms waving in the winds. *Green as,* Leonard thought, but here Leonard's mind stumbled for there was a specific Indian word for this late spring color of the fronds. A bright green like that auto sign he'd seen in town the other day, but not quite. His grandfather had used the Indian word for "green forest ferns at this time of the spring" with him many times as they made their way to the bay. Already he could not remember it. A woodpecker knocked a hole above him, the sound a rat tat tat. The word meant a specific green, longer and more complicated than "bright" or "forest" or "mint" or any other way green was used in English. It was a word that came up from the land, not from a manmade object that was then transferred to describe the land.

His thighs brushed the fronds in his path. How could "forest" mean one green? One glance and his eyes captured many greens. The Indian word also told of the time of year, and the specific plant, and the shape its leaves took at that time, and the place. And growth. Green is life. Leonard remembered his grandfather saying, "My boy. Look. See the tips of these branches at this time of spring?" and he pointed to the tips of a pine branch that were bright light green, against the dark green of the older growth. "The trees grow their fingernails and toe nails now." But even one Indian word for green, Leonard could not recall. Not one.

Leonard pushed aside a small maple with leaves as big as a child's palm that had sprouted up among the ferns. He looked at the back of his hand, just like his grandfather's—same long fingers, bony knuckles, and the same deep brown skin with the rusted shine of dried pine needles. His grandfather lived in him, yet already, Leonard did not have his words or always have the *kinnikinick* to offer during sunrise and sundown prayers or when he took life as his grandfather had taught him. Sometimes, he felt too overwhelmed to fetch willow branches. Other times he went to where his family had been harvesting willow for generations, but they were gone—plowed over, plucked out of the earth like whiskers to make way for yet another path or garden or clearing for a flat wood house, as his grandfather, who hadn't learned any English until his forties and never learned the white man's language well, had called the white man's clapboard houses.

Leonard leapt over a moss-covered trunk and ran up a hill. Just over this ridge of ferns was their favorite fishing spot in Hook Bay. Seeing the water sparkle through the fronds shot panic and fear through his body, as no men were alive in his family to guide him. He nearly dropped to the ground, but his legs held. He must go on. His family depended on him. Their survival was not just for them, but for those to come.

As he surveyed the water for white men, memories of his grandfather's instructions held him up. "Do not mourn the first year," his grandfather had said. "You must go on. Always. Then when it is a year, the pain will be less. No one will go hungry because you mourn too much."

Leonard's moccasins sprang off the ground onto a black boulder pushed by a machine off the recently cut road. He wanted to see if any white men fished in the bay ahead. He wished to be alone. A wide white scrape slashed across the face of the boulder reminded Leonard of a scar on an old man's cheekbone. His mind reeled. "Grandfather," he called out. Grief slashed his chest, despite his best efforts to not allow it.

The day he and his father had found his grandfather in his wigwam flashed into his mind. He saw again, as if he were reliving it, his grandfather's open eyes, the whites yellowing, the pupils fixed like pebbles, the white scar down his cheekbone from a quarrel he'd had as a boy, and the cloud of green-headed flies lifting off his grandfather. "*Awas*," his father had commanded. "Leave!" Just as his feet pushed into the soft sandy earth of the wigwam floor, he saw his father's hand reach out to cover his grandfather's eyes. He'd died seated on the earth with his back against the strong curved willow branch, like a rib. The fern mats hung down from the curved branches like feathers, tied there just days earlier by his wife even as she coughed from the white man's disease. Leonard's grandfather's hand still grasped his staff, white eagle feathers hanging from its tip. His father fell forward across the old man—"*Noos*," he wept. The feathers shook. Those left behind were not to cry like that. It disrupted the dead's journey. Leonard turned, pushed off the dry earth, knowing his father's weakness might have brought back his grandfather's spirit, kept it from walking its path across the sky to return to the old ones. Leonard ran.

The week after his grandparents' deaths, Leonard had trekked up the logging road cut through the forest a month earlier, when the company showed up with the sheriff to throw off an entire family plus six others who had been living on the plot. The company didn't wait for the Indians to clear off. The sheriff and a company man rode up on horses pulling a giant machine—an enormous metal, log-like thing at its front with spikes as long as a man's forearms. Leonard had been there, visiting, preparing to fish with two other boys. They put their shredded willow bark down at the base of a bulky fir, as instructed. Said their prayers. If they had a good catch, they would be able to feed everyone. Day after day, as more Indians died from this pox, a few straggled onto the survivors' land. Some just babies, barely walking, led by a five-or-six-year-old cousin down a footpath or road a dying parent had pointed out to them. *Down to there. Right at the pond. Up the big hill.* That week, a white doctor who spoke Indian came, and told Leonard's mother and father to turn them away. That was how the pox spread. Leonard's parents kept their eyes on the ground, on their hands, on the white doctor's black boots. Nodded. Said yes in Indian when the white doctor asked if they'd heard him, if they'd understood. He mistook their avoidance as stupidity. They waited for him to go. How could they turn away children? Their relatives? They never would. "We will die first," his father had said. And then he did.

On the rock, Leonard shook his head to blur the death images. In a matter of weeks, his grandparents and father died. He could not see the water. He caught the dart of a shiny black crow between the trees and the whip of a green grass snake beneath fallen gray oak leaves so old their skins had thinned, reminding Leonard of an old person's hands—the leaves' veins popping higher than the mottled sunken skin. Trees. People. Birds. Snakes.

All were related. Leonard dropped down off the rock and ran up the hill toward the river bend, where he hoped he would not find the company men.

Antwatin Township, Goodhue Reservation, Minnesota 1955

The girls' auntie, Em, stayed awake at night when she was young to listen to the adults' stories, even as her siblings faded into their dreams at their grandparents' wigwam. Em's only movement was the flutter of her eyelashes, stark as spider legs against the shining whites of her eyes. Em knew how to be still. Her mother and grandmother had pinched her lips as a baby to teach her quiet, like their mothers and grandmothers had pinched their babies' lips to keep them silent in the forests and marshes so their cries would not alert enemies lurking nearby. Em knew how to breathe so shallow that one would have to look for a long, hard time before realizing her belly and chest moved with life. She'd practiced as a girl, hiding from the white social workers. Her fluttering eyelashes were the only thing that could make her grandmother say, "The little one watches," from the other side of the wigwam. The army-issued wool blanket separated the wigwam in two when needed, pinned back to let the heat from the fire creep into the second room where the children slept. Then the stories were told softer, all in Indian— no mixing of English and Indian words, which the girl could figure out—her mind bending in two languages. Or the stories simply ended altogether, the talk moving on to jokes and teasing and gossiping such that Em lost the thread of that which she was not to hear—Indians dying from tuberculosis and influenza and the pock disease. Entire families gone, no one able to bury them—the animals and insects consuming their bodies. Or one left, a child, found alone without food or water for days, snatched up by the English and given or sold to foster homes, farmers, boarding schools, men on ships, or the state where they'd be fed just enough to be kept alive. Many were sexually violated, girls and boys.

When Em did manage to hear the stories, the ones not intended for her young spirit, the ones her grandparents wanted to protect her from, the most alarming of all were how Indians were captured and sold the way white men sell cattle and pigs. And how Indians were taken across the water, *Gitchi Gami*, never to return. Indian bloodlines were spread all across the world now, sold into slavery like the people with wool on their heads.

"The children," her mother sometimes cried when these stories were told. "The children." Em knew her mother had been one of those children and Em, even at that tender age, like most Indian children, knew Indian children were still in danger from the welfare ladies who came in their clippety clop shoes and with clip boards checking off boxes on their papers, looking for Indian children, searching for any little thing to take them away. And sometimes for nothing, sometimes, just making it all up, stealing the children when their mother was at the neighbor's, trading wild rice for eggs, or at the tavern on a three-day bender—the kids left with relatives. Didn't matter the mother sent her children to their grandmother's. The social work lady stole the kids anyway and sold them to a white couple in Sacramento or Dubuque or Philadelphia where no one would tell them who they really were, where they'd grow up never feeling quite right, never at home in their skin. Where one day when they were nine-years-old they would see their shadow on a sidewalk during a game of hopscotch and *know*. They were Indian.

* * *

Sher pulled the thin bluish-green thread around the neck of the pack of wintergreen gum and then slid out a silver-wrapped stick for herself. She leaned toward Kristin sitting next to her, looking out the far side of the bus as it drove away from her past. Kris watched the tall weeds and lone surviving trees scattered along the prairie's edge waving in the occasional breezes of a merciless August sun.

"Gum?"

Kristin unwrapped a stick and let the wrapping flutter to the floor. She put the gum in her mouth and walked to the back, jogging to the right and left as the bus caught its balance and settled into a cruising speed. Kris clicked open the bathroom door and squeezed inside.

Sher heard the door click. She chewed her gum slowly, pounding it into shape between her back teeth while she watched the sky and prairie roll away, a perfect picture framed by the bus window. She glanced at the man across the aisle sleeping with his tan cowboy hat pulled down over his face. Through the cracks of the seats in front of her, she saw an older woman, probably in her fifties, reading a thick paperback book. Kristin appeared next to Sher and sat. Kristin had applied a fresh coat of face makeup to her lean angular countenance in the bus bathroom.

They rode like that for a while neither of them saying anything or doing much at all other than looking out the windows at the passing landscape and the occasional grove of pine trees clustered together against the wind and snow that would soon blow, turning the green landscape white. Sher fell asleep, the gum lodged between her teeth and cheek for safe keeping, but Kristin stayed awake, sensitive to the scraping of feet or loud coughs from the other passengers. When Sher awoke, Kristin had a small pad of unlined paper and a pencil with a chewed off eraser.

"Where'd you get that?" Sher resurrected her gum.

"Some lady in the back. She's got a whole bag of stuff packed for her kid." Kristin shrugged. "He's in Moose Lake visiting his godmother." Kristin opened the notepad and drew a horizontal line and then a vertical line that made an upside-down T and a smaller horizontal line at the top of the vertical line with a little one coming down off that. Sher yawned and stretched her arms above her head while Kristin marked four slashes off, then left a space, then marked three more slashes.

"Guess."

"A."

"Yah." Kristin marked "a" on the third slash in the first group and on the middle slash in the second group.

"E."

"Yah." Kristin marked "e" on the second slash.

"F."

"Nah."

"B."

"Nah."

"How about D." Sher's mind shifted and she tried to remember how to say "Dad" in Indian but couldn't.

"Yah." Kristin marked off the first and fourth slashes in the first set.

"I know what it says," Sher said and took the pad and pencil away from Kristin to make up her own hidden words. "You can't kill him."

They played hangman and other word games until it was dark outside. The moon rose, blooming like an onion over the prairie and the thin line of black trees on the horizon. Small yellow lights popped on inside the bus, running from the front to the back like clean crisp stitching from a sewing machine. Two perfect lines of light above each set of chairs but not enough for the girls to see by for their word games.

Sher set the notepad and the pencil on the floor.

"You can't just kill him, you know." Sher sucked on her gum. "Think about what Grandma and Papa would say." She caught a white flash of headlights in the window next to her and felt a burst of confusion.

Kristin turned sideways in her chair with her back to Sher. "Grandma would probably tell me to do it." The pack set between them. "If it were the old times, someone would set him out, someone would kill him. Grandma told me so once."

Sher knew she was right. Grandma said that. Sometimes in front of Papa. Sometimes after Papa had left the room. Their grandparents had disagreed over issues of vengeance. Papa said let it go. Don't hate. Don't become one of them. Grandma held to her anger. Said he didn't understand. Hadn't happened to him. And the old ways, for that kind of hurt, said you could. Her voice would trail off. After a few minutes, their grandfather would say, "It's not the old days anymore." And he'd duck out, onto the farm, the way of life that had replaced his grandparents' life. Sometimes, he was not sure he'd done the right thing. Putting his family here. Hoping to set seeds in them, keep the old ways alive, even if latent, so that one day, his grandchildren and great-grandchildren would be alive to bring back the old ways. Regrow the forest.

"They'd send you away to jail or foster care or an insane asylum. Take you away like they did to Auntie Em," Sher said and shut down her sadness over Em. Sher didn't remember it, being just an infant at the time, but they'd taken Em for two months, when she was six, right out of school with no explanation, and she returned to her family a different child, an angry and erratic girl. "He's white. You're not," Sher whispered, her words turning into a hiss that rose above the constant flap flap of the tires as they rolled over the moonlit black pavement, shiny as obsidian.

Kristin jutted her right hip out and turned her pelvic bone and then her whole upper body farther away from Sher. "She wouldn't say no," she said. "Like you did."

Sher did not know if Kris meant their grandmother or Em. Both, she realized, would probably agree with Kristin.

"You don't know either," Kris said, her voice tight and low.

"Sorry," Sher said after a minute. "Kris, I'm sorry." She touched her back lightly. Kristin flinched and Sher pulled her hand away. She'd let her fear of losing all she had left—her cousin Kris—guide her words. "I just miss them. Sometimes. I don't know what to do without them."

Sher watched nothing out the window until she fell asleep. She dreamed of disembodied hands, white as parchment paper, moving toward her. As they opened, reaching for her throat, she felt paralyzing terror. The moment they grasped her throat she woke. In the dream, she knew they belonged to a teacher, but not hers. Whose, she did not know.

* * *

The squealing brakes and the lurching of the bus woke up both girls. They looked out the window next to Sher, the strips of black rubber around the outside of the window moist with condensation left over from the heat of the day. They could see very little, only shadows in the dark punctuated by occasional yellow kaleidoscope lights.

"Hinkley," the bus driver's voice came over the PA system. "Diner on the left. We'll be here for thirty minutes, folks. Everyone back on in thirty." The bus driver clicked off the mouthpiece.

"Want anything." Kristin pursed her lips and pushed them toward the diner outside until she realized that she was pointing with her lips, an Indian thing the white kids at school chided her for. She quickly stopped.

"No," Sher said, even though she was hungry. She didn't want to go through their money so soon.

Kristin grabbed the pack near the top, strangling it like a goose, feeling a wisp of guilt, as if her inability to keep the two worlds separate—how she acted around her grandparents and cousins versus how she acted around her white dad and white school kids and white teachers—would lead to her cousins or grandparents being hurt. When alone, with his only child who was a nearly 50 percent enrolled Ojibwe Indian, Kristin's dad called Indians savages, saying the only thing that could save them was an infusion of white blood until it flushed out all the red. He'd done Kris a favor, he said, he'd given her hope she could achieve something, be something other than their superstitious fears and lack of civilization. When drunk, he would go on for hours. "Civilized. See," and he'd pick up one of her school books or point at the place the TV used to sit, before he kicked it in one night. "Higher thought processes," he'd slur. "Now you have 'em." "Thanks to yer old man." It didn't matter Kris's grandparents owned a farm-a coup for sure that any Indian still owned any land on the reservation as most of it had been bought by whites-because he knew, even if they hid it, that they still believed in the old Indian ways. When he spoke ill of Indians, Kris never responded.

His hatred was tangible, heated. His hatred was the burn of fire. The dog skulked out of the room, tail tucked, and Kris went blank, receding inside her body, her skull a barrier between her own thoughts and his words, until she could leave his physical presence and then sort through the pain and confusion and guilt, as if she were responsible for her dad's words, even though she disagreed, even though it was she he hated. At the core of her confusion was her fear that she was responsible for what he did to her mom.

One morning, when she wasn't yet three, Kris was playing with a sock under her parents' bed. She heard feet scuffling as her father pushed her mother into the bedroom, threw her down, and pinned her to the bed. "Quiet," he whispered. "Do you want the girl to hear?" The wood slats holding up the mattress creaked and bent over Kris's head. A glass of white daisies Kris had picked for her mom fell off the side table, their white heads landed like one large white flower next to the baby under the bed. Fearing the bed would collapse on top of her, her body curled. "Stop. I won't leave you," her mom cried. "Shut it," her father commanded and commenced to strangle her to death a foot above their toddler, curled in terror and holding her breath as her mother rasped for hers, pounded her fists on the bed, clawed his back and face. There was one last gasp and then Kris's father said, "Dumb squaw." He pushed inside her one last time, ejaculated, and then pulled out of her, dismounted, and set off to make himself an early lunch. To the little girl under the bed, it felt as if the world collapsed on her, burying her in the hatred and pain above her. It was then the violence entered her, planting itself there, twisting inside her, waiting to bloom, waiting to take vengeance.

After a turkey sandwich and glass of milk, Morgan dragged his wife's corpse to the wood shed. And then, the next morning, he wrapped and tied her corpse in burlap corn seed sacks from Jacques Corn Seed—the hybrid corn seed seller he sowed on his farm—and drove his toddler and his wife's body to a fourteen-acre swamp where he dumped the body with stones from his farm in the bags for the fish and turtles to feast on. *No one'll find her here,* he thought, as he watched the logo of the seed company—a drawing of Jacques's daughter, a young white girl with blond curls—and listened to his motherless toddler scream from his '47 Chevy truck.

* * *

"You sure?" Kris asked when she stopped a few seats ahead to wait for the passengers in front of her.

"Yah."

"All right."

Kristin moved off and was lost in the mix of passengers emerging from their seats to stretch their legs and gather food items and pee in Hinckley. Ivan's, a former stopover for mobsters on their way up from St. Paul to Duluth and Two Harbors, served the dual purpose as a Greyhound bus depot and the only late-night diner between there and the Cities.

Sher stared at the red and brown fabric on the seat in front of her and then into the shadows that made up the town of Hinckley. Her eyesight was raggy and dull from lack of sleep and stress and the dim lights inside the bus. The streetlights illuminated the backyards of the small white houses built after World War II for the returning GIs and their new brides. Monster oak and pine and maple overshadowed the houses that glowed in the dark like teeth.

Much time went by, too much time, and the bus driver did not return nor did any of the passengers except a young woman with big eyes and a small child. Sher looked out the window at the houses shadowed by the trees stitched together by waist high white picket fences, glimpsing what looked to be a child standing by a fence. She blinked and looked again at nothing. Her eyes were playing tricks. She wondered if she had lost track of time in the dark shadows that played off the houses, jumping from a second-story window to a back step down to a tricycle left on its side, or if she had lost track of time because she was disoriented from sleeping on a rolling bus with no food. She strained her neck to the left and saw that most of the scattered passengers on the bus were looking toward Ivan's diner. She could see nothing other than the lit up red sign that should have read Ivan's Diner but because of burned out bulbs merely read *van's Dine.*

Sher stepped sideways into the aisle, careful not to bump the seat in front of her where the woman reading the paperback dozed with the small book laid flat out over her lap. The woman resembled her white great-great-auntie. Sher thought of her and her other distant relatives on her mother's side who lived in New Ulm. More people spoke German than English in New Ulm. She remembered once attending a huge wedding held in a barn where everyone spoke German and talked about the German-American politics she knew nothing of and the boiling tubs of kielbasa and sauerkraut and the thick pies made with sour cream. And the town square in the very center of town where couples were frequently married inside the imported German bunkers from World War II, which were displayed alongside an old canon from the Civil War and other memorabilia.

And how they didn't much like Sher or her father or her brother, or really even her mother, 5/8 Indian, according to the rolls. But according to her family's count, more like 7/8. There'd been some white man who decided Sher's mom's ancestors' skulls were the wrong shape—too European according to their charts—to be full Indians, and so he changed the trajectory of their family by categorizing them as less than full-bloods, and therefore unable to receive a full allotment.

And then, like a snake winding sideways through grass, Sher's mother's grandmother had married a half-breed, and the numbers fell like an acorn bouncing through branches and leaves until it landed on the unlikely fraction of 5/8. Still, any Indian was too much Indian for Sher's mother's German side of the family, down in New Ulm. Some of her white family was polite but awkward in their presence. They were the ones who felt obliged to save Sher's mother from being Indian. Others made pains not to touch them, while others stared with hard eyes or looked away as if they never saw them. Sher and Jack were of them, although just a small fraction, but the Indian made them something else, something Germans, especially from that part of the state, could not tolerate. Indians were Indians, they thought, and it didn't matter that Sher, her father, mother, and brother's people had nothing to do with the Indian wars a century ago that bloodied that part of the land with Dakota and settler blood. Some of the Germans hated Sher and her father and brother on the spot. It didn't matter to them that part of her bloodline was of theirs, nor did it matter to Sher. After her mother left her white foster parents and joined some sort of different Christian denomination Ethel called a cult, Sher's mother moved to southern Minnesota in an attempt to belong to some long-lost white relatives and a place she could not be part of. History had made that impossible.

Sher stepped as discreetly as possible in her work boots past the sleeping woman to the steps that dropped her abruptly onto the pavement. She caught her legs as they buckled when her feet hit the pavement. Sher turned and walked around the front of the bus toward the late-night diner, the steam still rising off the flat front while the hounds lay cooling under the bus.

She stepped inside the all-night diner, catching the screen door out of habit behind her back before it snapped shut. As she let the screen door slip from the tips of her fingers gently into the frame, she faced a crowd gathered around Kristin and two employees in white aprons. Sher felt out of place, like a crust of cold air coming off the prairie hitting hard in the face. Her black hair and eyes, round face with flat cheeks, and brown skin set her apart from the blonde, long-faced people in the restaurant.

People were yelling and pointing fingers and shaking thick arms. Kristin stood in the middle, getting heat from the man and the woman in the apron who was a waitress there. Kristin said nothing, her gray eyes darting from the man to the crowd and back again. She did not look at the waitress who stood with her hands on her hips, her white-blonde hair lifted up off her face into a beehive by a white scarf. The crowd shouted *we have to leave her, call the Sheriff and get it over with* and *let the girl talk.* An old woman, her back bent over like a question mark, sat at a table ignoring the commotion, picking at her plate.

"Kris, did you order my food?" Sher said as she strode forward, breaking into the din of the crowd.

Kristin looked up, a flash of relief running across her face and then hiding itself like the bruise on her face covered over by the makeup. "I told you I thought my cousin was going to pay for it," she said to the man.

The crowd continued to talk, but the man and the waitress in the apron and a few others looked at Sher walking toward them in her tank top and jeans and heavy work boots.

"Cousin?" a teenager asked, visiting from Ames, Iowa, incredulous that white and brown skin could be related.

The waitress shook her head and folded her arms across her chest. *Dirty thieving Indian* trickled from her thoughts to her face.

"Leave her be," the old woman said from the back. "She's just a girl."

"She's one a them," another woman said and jutted her jaw toward Sher.

"All right, break it up," the man said. He looked at Kristin. "You can go."

Kristin bolted toward Sher.

The bus driver emerged from the side of the crowd and said, "Everybody back on. Five minutes." He waved his arm over his head toward the door.

"Did you order my food yet?" Sher asked again, for effect.

Kristin shook her head no and handed Sher the pack. The crowd dispersed, mostly going out toward the bus. The waitress picked up a sea-blue plate with a half-eaten hamburger and the stub of a pickle and left-over coleslaw. She turned her back, disgusted, and the man began straightening the chairs shoved around the room by the crowd.

"Anything I can get to go real fast?" Sher asked the man straightening the chairs.

"Look," he leaned over and placed his hands flat on the table. "I gave you girls a break. Get on outta here and don't come back."

"Just keep going through," the waitress said, lifting up her chin. "We don't need your types round here."

Sher and Kristin knew what the woman meant. Plenty of whites in the towns around the reservation said things like that. Kristin turned beet red. Sher stepped aside and let Kristin pass. She nodded at the man and then the waitress and turned and walked out behind Kristin.

The girls said nothing. They walked to the bus and stepped single file down the aisle, avoiding the faces of the other passengers. The girls felt a bouquet of shame and anger and fear.

"You girls caught a break," a gray-haired white man said. He fluttered his hand at them like a moth.

The girls dropped into their seats. The woman in front of them muttered in her sleep and the engine roared and the headlights burst on, two straight beams cutting through the night. The bus sighed, moving at the pace of a turtle as passengers settled in. The white houses flickered like candlelight fighting shadows.

"I won't do that again."

"Best not."

The bus stopped in three more towns but the girls did not get off. They stayed awake staring out at the flat farms along the highway or at the small towns as they passed through to pick up passengers, or drop them off outside closed buildings that served as bus depots and pharmacies and diners and once—a feed store. As they passed over the land, Sher saw shadows of small children standing alongside the roads that turned into large birds of prey on second look and then on third look were gone.

* * *

"Minneapolis, twenty minutes," the driver said as the bus neared the outskirts of the city. Passengers leaned to the left or right and pressed their noses to the windows to get a better view of the buildings and the lights so different from what they lived. Sher pressed her temple and cheekbone against the window so she could see the cascading street lights and the roads arching and intersecting one another like bike tire marks down a dirt road after school let out. She wondered if the city had changed much since she saw it last.

Four years ago, her father and she had left Jack to travel to the city in their '49 Ford, pulling behind them a borrowed trailer with two liver-colored cattle, Sher's 18 hand thoroughbred Patsy Cline, a 297-pound hog, and a rooster in a wire cage. Thaddeus and Jack had little in common. It was Sher and her father who were so alike in looks and temperament that her mother called them "two peas in a pod. Just alike you two." She'd contemplate Sher for a moment, as if considering whether Sher had come from her. "Youse nothing like me." Sher's father was tall and slight with hair so dark it shined blue under certain lights and his skin a deep auburn acorn and eyes black as rabbit holes. He had a quiet, steady demeanor, except when he teased or played practical jokes. Then he would burst into laughter.

When Sher was young her father had called her a papoose, her shock of thick black hair on her newborn head made it seem she was born older than her actual age. He liked to tell her stories, stories that Jack had no interest in, like the one about when he was a boy and his grandfather chased off a Bureau of Indian Affairs man with a shotgun who'd come out into the woods looking to put the family on the dole. "Didn't want nothing to do with the US government," Thaddeus said. He smoothed his daughter's hair and kissed her forehead. "And holay man was he mad when his son, your papa, went and joined the Airforce." Thaddeus whistled through his front teeth, making a sound like a bomb dropping. He shook his head, leaving Sher to imagine wide-eyed what had occurred between her papa and her papa's pops.

* * *

"Minneapolis in ten," the driver announced.

Sher pressed her cheekbone harder into the cool glass thinking about what her pops had said to her as they sat in traffic on their way home after the fair all those years ago. "This city eats people up," he'd said, one arm hanging out the driver's window. "Nothing to mess with." Sher would have stayed on the farm and reservation if her grandparents and father had not died. Then, to make matters worse, after they'd died, her mother returned and allowed Jack to take over the farm. He'd cut Sher out of the farm work and into the house as he never could stand it that their father treated his boy and girl the same. Sher was built for men's work. When Kris came to her about needing to leave, Sher left.

As the bus looped south on 94, Kris twisted in her seat for a better view of the freeways swooping and arching over one another sixty feet in the air like enormous versions of the rollercoaster ride at the county fair. Skyscrapers huddled together on the otherwise flat horizon. "Holay," Kris said, wide-eyed.

"Foshay" lit up the tallest skyscraper. Built in 1929 by Wilbur Foshay, who at the time of construction was assembling his third utility empire stretching from Alaska to Nicaragua, the tower was designed to imitate the Washington Monument with each successive floor sloping slightly toward the interior. It was the tallest building west of the Mississippi, and featured African Mahogany, Italian marble, three commissioned busts of George Washington, gold doorknobs and Indiana limestone on the exterior. Foshay invited 25,000 people to the 1929 dedication, including cabinet members, senators, and congressman. He commissioned John Phillip Sousa to create a march for the opening titled "Foshay Tower-Washington Memorial March." Six weeks after the opening Foshay lost everything in the Great Depression and never paid Sousa for the march; in response Sousa never allowed the "Foshay Tower-Washington Memorial March" to be played again.

Excitement coursed through Kris. She'd never been in a city before. Red taillights streamed around the bus and bright headlights flashed through the windows from the opposite direction. The city lights shone into the night sky, creating a glow seen for miles that obscured the stars from the city dwellers' vision. The bus rumbled off the freeway and cut east on Hennepin into the heart of Minneapolis.

"That a church?" Kris asked as they passed the marble basilica—the first basilica in the country—that took up an entire block and looked twenty times bigger than the wooden churches in Antwatin.

"Looks it," Sher said.

The bus passed Loring Park on the right, blocks of apartment buildings, and a four-story, red stone Masonic temple squatting on half a city block. Sher noted the Ionic columns and thought of her art and social science teacher, Mrs. Luckstrim, a thirty-seven-year-old white woman who'd moved to Antwatin from Ames, Iowa shortly after her husband died from the flu. Every fall Mrs. Luckstrim related her personal history to her class. Married just three months, her husband was one of the thirty-eight staff and students to die from a tuberculosis outbreak at Iowa State College that took nearly as many from the college as did the 1918 influenza pandemic. Mired in grief, Mrs. Luckstrim completed her Bachelor of Arts in Teaching and took the first job she could find on some "godforsaken reservation" where she whiled away long winter nights in "the middle of nowhere" reading everything she could get from the county library, especially about the "Ancients and their Arts." Sher had been one of her finest students, ever. White or Indian. Sher *applied* her lessons to the world around her, Mrs. Luckstrim was fond of saying.

She had never resolved her husband's sudden death—never dating even once. The thought of his once robust body lying motionless as his lungs ate themselves from the inside out, filling with blood and fluid until he drowned, haunted her. She dreamt of his young, sturdy, smiling face suddenly blue and gasping and spitting up blood. At times, she glimpsed him just around a corner, beckoning her. Or his face condensed in the steam emitted from a pot as she cooked. Or his voice whispered her name—*Vera, Vera*—when the lamp she read by burned alone at night. At first, she told her parents. They said to stop thinking of him. She could not. The more she tried not to think of him, the more he showed up in her daily life, so she tried to counteract the haunting by keeping him alive in her memory, never cutting and tying off the cord between them. His pressed white cotton shirt and black wool trousers hung in her closet, his undergraduate photograph in profile on her wall (they'd not had the money to pay a photographer when they married), his shoes at the front door, and the coins in the pocket of the pair of pants he did not wear the day he died.

For this, other white people shunned her, her family visited but once, and so, isolated and outcast, she imagined herself to be like the Indians. Aligned with them. Except, of course, better. That was a given, she told herself—look at what her people had accomplished—stone sculptures detailing the body's every flexed muscle and vein, permanent dwellings and places of worship that did not blow over or rot away, and the vanishing point that created the ability to render the world in three-dimensional images, not like the childish pictographs the Indians had painted on rocks a few hours north of the reservation. Being full-blooded Irish didn't stop her from claiming greatness with the Greeks. *Oh,* she thought, *how she wished to travel to the land of her ancestors—the ancient Greeks and Romans!*

Sher was one of two or three Indians whom Mrs. Luckstrim believed smart enough for a university. Sher was the exception that proved the rule, she told herself, why the Indian girl had largely mastered foreground, mid-ground, and background. She'd drawn a white farmhouse with two red rocking chairs, whose Mrs. Luckstrim did not know, in nearly perfect line from a bird's eye view. And her drawings of mammals were rather astounding in their detail. The sketch of a wolf or hound dog, Mrs. Luckstrim was not sure which and did not ask, was rather realistic except for the right front leg that was too short and lost all dimension, as if it returned to the childish sketchings of primitive people with no regard for how the actual dog—or wolf—leg would appear bent in that way. This cemented Mrs. Luckstrim's view that the girl needed her, one had to watch over the promising Indians as they were always susceptible to going back to their ways.

Thoughts of Sher often murmured through Mrs. Luckstrim's head, so much more like a boy than a girl, yet astonishingly none of the Indians teased or shunned her. Sher's even temperament, confidence, quick mind, and much to Mrs. Luckstrim's delight, her particular interest in Greek and Roman architecture made Mrs. Luckstrim almost consider her family. Almost, but not quite. At times, Sher appeared in her dreams, caring for Mrs. Luckstrim the way a husband would, the way hers would have. She allowed those thoughts to trail off, thereby never taking responsibility for her life, never forcing herself to think: my husband is gone for good or in my dreams this Indian girl and I kiss and touch the way a man and wife do. Mrs. Luckstrim thought of Sher from the perspective of the young woman she'd never grown out of, the one still longing for a man, even if that man was in the shape of an Indian teenage girl, which did not seem strange or wrong or abnormal to her, as long as she did not think of it.

* * *

As the bus circled downtown Minneapolis, Kristin stared wide-eyed at the all-night, seemingly never-ending street carnival that went on block after block. Tall buildings and huge signs lighting the night sky with bright, flashing lights—Moby Dicks; The Sconce Lounge; Hamm's Beer from the land of sky blue waters; Orpheum, Park Here!; Adam Hats; Aster Theater; Shinders 25c Readers Digest! Coca Cola! Pipes, Cigars, Tobacco! Magazines, Lunch, Candy!; Gopher Theatre; Bridgemans Ice Cream; Williams Bar; Millie Owens Wigs and Things; Adonis Tie Shop $1.50!; The Depot featuring Joe Cocker Live! The streets were packed with white and Negro men and women milling shoulder to shoulder, laughing and smoking and shouting at friends and strangers alike. The girls had never seen such a ruckus.

The bus turned north one block onto First Avenue into the new Greyhound bus depot's parking lot. As the bus rolled to a stop the hounds of heat settled in, lying in wait under the rows upon rows of Greyhound buses.

Kris could not have imagined so many people all in one place. Excitement bordering on mania with a shot of fear hit her bloodstream. "Dang," she said, breathless.

"Well," her cousin said. "Here we are." After seeing the night-time display of lights and crowds, Sher doubted leaving the reservation. Here things would be different. Maybe too different.

South

*In Ojibwe ways, the south is the place when a
person is no longer a child but not yet an adult. A
person is wandering and searching.*

The girls arrived in the city with $12 and two empty stomachs,
their grandfather's World War II pack, two stainless steel cups,
some face makeup, gum, and a lighter. The bus driver turned on his
speaker and announced, "Minneapolis. Ten-forty p.m. Ten-minute
layover. We'll be in Saint Paul in twenty-five minutes." He stretched
his arms, yawned and stepped off the bus. Sher and Kristin stared
at the seats in front of them and then looked at one another.

"This it?"

"Yah." Kristin swallowed, but it turned into a gulp.

"Want to go on to Saint Paul?"

"Nah."

"Okay then. Ready?"

Kristin picked up the pack and stepped into the aisle, setting the
bag against the angled front of her thighs as she stood waiting for
the people in front to move, her body contorted because of the
narrowness of the space. Kristin moved forward a little and then
had to wait for a man three rows up to pull a rolled-over, brown
grocery bag off the rack above the seats. Sher stepped into the aisle
taking up the space where Kristin had been, her body sore and
cranky and locked from the long bus ride and the stress of the day
and the lack of food.

Outside someone shrieked *Johnny!* The passengers moved
forward a few steps, trapped like cattle in a marking chute. Their
grandmother thought cows dull. Out of place. "The old ones
hunted buffalo," she said, tensing her neck the way she did when

she talked of the old ones. "Back in the day. My grandparents. Some of us did." And by this she meant not only the Sioux but some Ojibwe hunted buffalo too, those ones who lived half in the woods and half on the prairie hunted the intelligent, powerful buffalo who ran straight into oncoming storms instead of huddling away from them like cattle do. "Maybe that's our problem," their grandmother muttered. "Indians eating cows. Now we're like them."

As Sher and Kristin stepped off the bus, the hounds of heat rustled beneath the bus, complacent and cooling, sweating out their tongues, waiting for their next run. Sher strode into the bus depot as if she had purpose and a plan so as not to appear weak. She moved like someone used to long hard hours of outdoor work—strong and quick on her feet. Years of chores and running through woods had increased her physical and spiritual strength. She moved like a boy. Kristin followed behind, letting Sher lead the way as she always had. Even when they were young, Sher was the one to push through the tall, lanky alfalfa crops or instigate jumping off the porch to see if the girls' spirits would go up while their bodies descended to the earth, or climb into the doorless '39 Chevy vacated next to the barn. Once in the car the girls pretended to drive to Canada or North Dakota where their family lived—the Canadians on a government reserve and the North Dakota Ojibwe in tar shacks with no electricity, stuck there waiting for the government's promises of running water and electricity and solid houses that eighty years after the treaty had not yet arrived.

In Antwatin, a thirty-minute drive over the roads or an hour walk through the woods, many Indians lived in tar-covered shacks, unlike the girls' grandfather, Clarence, who learned a trade in the Army—mechanic—and then had a white army friend who acted as a cultural liaison between him and the white world to help Clarence use his GI Bill to buy the tools needed to fix automobiles and trucks as a side job on the farm, since they made no real money from the farm. Whoever heard of Indians owning a farm, Indians and whites said alike. Except for a few, the government's goal of turning Indians into farmers had failed.

But the farm was how Clarence kept his family on their ancestors' land. It was how they didn't migrate to the city, become lost, unrecognizable to their people and their ways, to the old ones. The farm was the best choice he could make so as to not drift into whiteness like the snow across the fields where just a few generations before the mountainous trees were clear cut and the forest carved into hunks. Butchering the forest compromised, but did not wipe out, the immense white pines, jack pines, and birches; the exquisite pink lady slippers and the burdock, milk thistle, dandelion, and other plants deemed weeds by the white people; the insects—multiple varieties of spiders, ticks, and worms; and the animals—porcupine, wolverine, soft-nosed and sure-footed deer, and even grizzlies, years back, grizzlies roamed that area once, too.

Along with the outright destruction or the diminishment of the flora and creeping, crawling, flying creatures, a way of life was changed forever. Even so, despite the vast changes wrought by the whites, Clarence had been taught by his grandmother that Indians must stay on their land. Whether conscious of it or not, the loss and diminishment of the land was the grief they all carried. And grief, more so than any other emotion, is heat held inside, rising up and pushing out. Although the girls did not know it, grief was responsible for sending them to Minneapolis. Grief encompassed everything.

* * *

The girls stood at the entrance to the Greyhound bus depot and stared at the people sitting in row after row of pale-yellow plastic seats linked together, one after the other, by steel rods under the armrests. A clerk sold tickets from a window across from them. The only other door was to their right.

"I'm dry," Kristin said.

Sher pushed Kris to the left toward a drinking fountain and a pay phone, the receiver hanging straight down to the floor like a weight on a fishing line.

Kristin pushed in the smooth steel button and drank water until she thought she would float away. Sher set the pack on the floor against the wall and pulled out a bent envelope, the red stamp half peeled off and curling like an October leaf. She opened the ragged top and took out a letter written on thin blue-lined paper. She glanced at it, refolded it, put it back in the envelope and slipped the envelope into the pack.

"Too late to call now." Sher closed her eyes and leaned against the wall, squatting comfortably the way she always did at the farm when she took a break.

"Girls. Very, very pretty girls."

Sher opened her eyes but did not move her body.

A white man leaned against the wall next to Sher but looked at Kristin.

Kristin moved so the water fountain was between her and Sher and the man, the look of a caught animal in her face and in the way her body stood under her clothes.

"Mm hmm." The man stepped around Sher. He leaned over the water fountain and made a show of spreading his legs, sliding his brown shiny flat-bottom shoes out to the side and settling in slow to take a drink.

Kristin darted to the other side of Sher.

The man took a long drink. "Mm hmm," he said. "Now that was some fine-tasting water."

Sher pulled the pack to her but continued to squat. She knew that to get up right then would be a sign of fear and she knew, after years of working with cows and horses and pigs on the farm and hunting deer and watching her father deal with white people he did not trust, which was most, that one must never show fear. She must be steady.

"What's your name, there?" the man asked, using his chin like a finger to point at Kris. His shoes splayed outward under dirty jeans that folded over in ridges around his knees and ankles.

"Kristin," Kris blurted out of fear and anxiety.

"Kristin," the man said like he was playing around with it in his mouth. "That's a pretty name. Can I call you Krissy?"

Kristin froze. Her father called her Krissy when he was drunk.

"Sir." Sher dangled her arms over her knees, using a particular language reserved for interacting with white people. "Excuse us, but we've had a long trip."

"That so," he said, leaning against the wall.

Sher stood and strapped on the pack. "C'mon, Kris, time to go."

"This jackass bothering you?" Another white man appeared out of nowhere.

Sher jerked around, the pack to the wall. The water fountain was now between both men and the girls. The shiny shoe man stepped to the other side of Kristin.

"Get the hell out of here," the new man said. He was older and dressed in navy pants and a clean white, button-down shirt.

"Go to hell yourself," the first man said.

They shoved one another until the new man put his forearm

over the other man's neck, pinning him against the wall.

"All right," the shiny shoe man rasped.

The new man hit him on the chest. "Get out."

He walked out the door the girls came in through.

Sher nodded at the new man. "Time to go," she said.

"Wait," he said. "Are you meeting someone here?"

"No, yes," Sher and Kristin said, their words coming out on top of the other.

"Aha," the new man said. "I think you've got a problem." He nodded toward the glass door at the far end of the room. Two cops stood on the street corner.

Kristin froze. When her father was drunk, he used to threaten to call the sheriff on her grandparents.

The new man watched her. "Does someone hit you, honey?" he asked.

"No. No problems. Sir." Sher grabbed Kristin's arm. "C'mon. Grandma will be here any minute."

"Ah uh yah." Kris couldn't think.

Sher pushed her toward the glass door, figuring it the best choice since the other man had gone out the other door.

The new man followed.

"Girls," he hissed. "One word from me and you two will be in the pen tonight and headed for juvie jail in the morning."

"No, please," Kristin said, turning around. "We haven't done anything."

"One word," and he nodded toward the cops outside at the corner, "and those two pigs will be over here waiting with you for your long-lost grandma."

"We've got to catch our ride," Sher pulled Kristin's elbow.

"Juvenile runaways," the new man said. "You've done plenty on that count alone." He moved quicker than he looked capable of, and put his hand on Kristin's other elbow, sidling up to her so it would not be obvious he was holding her.

"Where are you going, Krissy?" he whispered in her ear. "Have you figured that out yet?" He squeezed her elbow. "Why don't you come with me? I'll take good care of you."

"Get your hands off her." Sher hacked his arm and kicked his kneecap with the sole of her boot.

The man yelped, grabbing his knee.

The clerk yelled, "Hey!"

"Run, Kris!"

Kristin bolted out the glass door, the parking lot to her right quiet now, filled with the Greyhound buses resting in the dark. In front of her was a busy street. The cops were across it. She took two steps to the right and then turned left. Sher pushed out the door and the two girls ran into each other, their feet tangling together. They fell, banging their knees and elbows on the cement.

Sher jumped up, pulled Kris to her feet, and the girls ran to the left alongside the bus depot, hoping the cops hadn't noticed. A middle-aged couple stepped out a door into their path, forcing them to stop and then start again. Sher looked back. The couple stood apart, watching the girls run. Between them, Sher saw the well-dressed man on the sidewalk, looking to his right.

The girls ran. The pack slapped against Sher's back.

"In here." Sher yanked Kris down a narrow brick alley. A cat ran off. Sher cut behind some garbage cans, lost her footing and slid into a pile of bulky garbage bags. Kristin tumbled behind her. The girls froze like the statue game they used to play. The alley smelled like fish and sour milk.

Footsteps approached. Sher peered between the cans and reached back reflexively to touch Kristin's lips. The well-dressed man stopped at the alley, and then continued down the sidewalk, away from the depot. Sher watched the street and Kristin watched her, keeping her head low. The girls did not move. A man trotted by, coming from the direction of the bus depot. Sher thought, but could not be sure, that it was the first man, the one with the shiny shoes, half-running because he could not lift his feet up high enough or fast enough without slipping. After he passed the alley Sher looked at Kristin and lifted her eyebrows as if to say *who knows*.

When the girls were babies, their grandmother had pinched their lips to teach them silence. The girls knew how to be still, not make any sound, thoughtful even of their breathing, until their grandmother found them flat on the floor beneath the homemade, horsehair-stuffed mattress or under the work shelf in the basement over which their grandmother had draped an old wool blanket to hide them from the white lady social workers who came looking to steal Indian children.

When older, if the girls were out in the yard and heard a car different than the rattle of their grandparents' truck they'd run to the house or barn or shed. If in the fields, the girls stood stock still in line with the corn rows or dove into an indentation in the earth where they stayed until the bell on the porch rang four times. Their grandmother only dyed their homespun clothes earth colors, leaving behind the brightly beaded and dyed regalia of the Ojibwe to make sure her babies did not pop out of the browns and greens like red chokecherries, before they ripened into a purple mass hanging heavy off a branch. If in the house when a car drove up unannounced, their grandmother commanded, "Down!" The girls ran, slid, and ducked into their hiding holes, listening, breathing without sound, always waiting for the bell, four times.

Ethel's granddaughters were not going to disappear into the white world as she had, stolen from her family and placed in a Catholic boarding school and then sold to work as a domestic on a farm outside Fargo. Two months after being dropped off by the nuns, and daily beatings by the farm wife with a broomstick and rolling pin, she ran away, finally escaping for good down unknown back roads.

* * *

The girls stayed in the alley for some time, occasionally glancing behind them where the alley doglegged to the right. A silence rose up around them, split by sirens and the squeals of wheels. No bell rang four times so they could come out of hiding, bury themselves in their grandmother's belly and fleshy arms. Sher glanced from the street to the alley behind them, and then back again. Her knee and shin swelled from the crash into the bags. Anxiety surfaced in Kris, popping like welts over her body. She rested her head on Sher's calf. Sher smoothed her cousin's hair and kept watch, breathing through her mouth to minimize the smell, wanting to spit, but afraid of the noise that would make.

Time stilled. The moon edged west. Sher thought of the story about how time was brought to Indians by a big clock. She could see her grandfather telling the story again, his skinny brown legs jutting out of his shorts and off the upside-down bucket he sat on. "Since then," he said, his eyes shining with that light that popped when he told stories, "Indians have been weighted down." He pulled on an imaginary chain around his neck. "Just like the white man, by that tick-tock time machine."

The number of cars on the street lessened. Muffled voices, sirens, and laughing drifted down the alley. Sher shifted, found another crack she could peer through, and then locked her body in that position. Kris moved with her. Two men's voices neared. The depot men stopped and looked down the alley.

"Look down there?"

"No need," the well-dressed man said. "I would of seen them turn into it."

The man with the shiny shoes stared down the alley. "They're gone. For now."

"One's Indian. Maybe both."

"We'll find them. Can't hide on these streets forever."

The two men continued toward the bus depot.

Ice water trickled down Sher's spine. She put her finger to Kris's lips just in case the men were still in earshot. She felt down her knee, tender to the touch on the inside, to a wide flat bump on her shin.

After twenty minutes, hearing nothing, Sher tapped Kris. The girls stood. Sher shook her leg out in an effort to get the blood flowing. She dared not loosen the laces. The girls turned right down the alley that slammed into the one they were in. They walked past ripped garbage bags with chewed out halves of squash and fish bones and milk cartons and butter wrappers strewn about.

"Must be cats and coons."

"Yah. Or rats."

"Yah."

They scanned for their droppings or the animals themselves, hiding out behind bags or scurrying off or looking up from a feast of rotted food, their sharp eyes picking out everything in the dark. But Sher and Kristin saw none. The girls reached a narrow street with no curbs, just wide enough for one car to pass through. No people and no cars, only tall dark buildings rising up around them. Sher motioned for Kristin to follow her away from the street she had last seen the two men on.

"The one who chased us came back looking for us."

"Yah?"

Sher did not see any reason to tell Kristin that the two men had tried to work them over as a team in the depot. It would frighten her too much. Sher's hair flung down over her back and shoulders and onto her chest. The right side of her body had a black dirt streak from the cuff of her jeans all the way up to her shoulder. She walked with a bad limp, but her face showed nothing, not the tiredness nor the hunger nor the fear.

Kristin wondered if Sher was afraid. She was so afraid she thought she would throw up. "Sher?"

"Yah."

They reached a main road and turned east, away from the bus depot.

"We look like quite a pair." Kristin's face makeup had disappeared somewhere between the bus ride and lying in the alley. The bruise was prominent even under the inconsistent lights of the city but the hickies remained hidden by her shirt and hair.

"We sure do." Sher smiled, and then stepped on her foot wrong. She grimaced from the pain in her ankle shooting up the side of her calf. "Wait." Sher bent over and undid the laces on her hurt ankle and then slid out a pocket knife. The knife had been her grandmother's. Her fingers expertly laced up her boot as she stood on one leg.

Kristin looked up and down the street but saw only parked cars at meters. One of the meter heads had been ripped off. All that was left was a jagged steel neckline.

Sher released the blade. It was thick and strong and well kept up. The knife could be used to cut just about anything, including the throat of an animal, if need be. She pushed the blade back inside itself and wiped off a smudge on the steel handle inlaid with a turquoise and yellow, beaded flower her grandmother had appliqued herself. Her grandmother said her beading looked like a child's, but Sher thought it beautiful. Through the knife she felt her grandmother with her. She slid it in her jean pocket.

"Dad had Grandma stitch a pocket on the inside of my boot." She ran her finger over the pocket, right behind the ankle bone. "He said every Indian should carry a knife. Especially a girl." Sher pushed the knife deeper in her pocket and looked around at nothing specific but took in all of it. "Dad got these boots at the state fair. On sale. At a country western stand." She stared at the top of her boot—the black leather scratched and faded to brown in areas. "They sold everything," she said, remembering how grateful and special she felt when he bought the boots for her, instead of having her wear her brother's hand-me-downs as she'd done all her life. She didn't mind. Boys' clothes suited her well. But it was still special to have something brand new.

The girls walked west.

"You wouldn't believe it, Kris. How big it is. Fifty. A hundred times bigger than the county fair."

Kristin said nothing. She always remained quiet when Sher talked about her father. She missed him too. She'd always wished Thaddeus was her pops. Thinking about her uncle made Kristin remember all the evenings spent at her grandparents' farm after her dad went on a bender and Kris ran. The fourth time she ran away she had just turned five and her father had showed up at the farm with the sheriff. Clarence saw them coming up the drive, pulled off his shirt, tied it around Kris's eyes, and carried her into the basement. He opened a hidden hatch and set her in the tunnel that ran between the house and barn. "Don't make a noise, my girl," he said and pinched her lips. "Don't never tell no one." He knew, of course, she could figure he'd taken her in the basement, but not being able to see would help her forget, feel unsure about where he took her. Lives depended on no one knowing about the tunnel. Kris didn't make a sound as the sheriff and her father searched the farm house, barn, and fields for over an hour.

"I know she's here, old man," her father said to Clarence in the kitchen. "Morgan," the sheriff said. "I gotta head out. I don't know where your girl is, but she ain't here." Morgan glared at Clarence. "I'll be back," he said as he left with the sheriff. As soon as they reached the bottom of the drive, Clarence pointed his lips toward where the men disappeared and Sher's dad took off running to make sure Kris's dad didn't double back to the farm. Ninety minutes later, he returned breathing hard. "He's sitting in front of his TV," he said. "Passed out." Clarence retrieved Kris.

"We have to keep her," Ethel said, as she and Clarence sat on the porch watching the girls play tag in the yard. "White men are no good. They have disease in their heart." Clarence kept his eyes on Sher and Kris as they darted across the dirt, remembering that for a week after their daughter had disappeared Morgan had stood at the end of the drive at dusk, the fire from his cigarettes burning through the evening air, his rifle on his hip. Kris stood a foot away from him, frozen, tall as his knees. The first night Clarence approached him, Clarence asked, "Where is she, Morgan?" Morgan took a long drag, crushed his cigarette in the dirt, and stepped to the side so his rifle pointed at Kris's head. "Don't know, old man. Probably ran off with one of those Black bucks that been seen around here." Clarence caught his breath. Morgan continued,

"Be a shame if Sheriff Fink found out about them Negroes someone been hiding." Clarence glanced at his granddaughter's eyes, but they were vacant. "Know what I'm sayin' old man?" Clarence took one last look at the rifle, the absence of his granddaughter's spirit, and turned and walked up the drive. The rest of the week, every so often, Morgan returned and yelled, "Old man, I'll take her from you too," and pointed his rifle at his toddler's head.

Clarence and Ethel knew Morgan had killed their daughter, Josie. But they didn't know how and didn't know where her body was. They'd asked an old Indian doctor, the proper way with tobacco and gifts and food. He said she was in water, somewhere nearby, but that they would never find her. He told them to burn a fire for four days to help her spirit. Then he cast his eyes downward and said the *manidoog* showed him a white man with a fire stick with bright lights spinning around him. One day he'd take Kris away. "One day," he said to emphasize that time did not exist in the spirit world and one day could mean tomorrow or many years.

In effort to avoid or delay that fate, Clarence disagreed with his wife that they shouldn't allow her to return to Morgan once he sobered up, fearful that if they didn't return their granddaughter, he would kill her. They told no one about what the Indian doctor said. Kris went home two days after the sheriff searched for her. After that, when her dad went on a drunken spree, she would run to her grandparents until he sobered up, drove out to the farm, and stood at the end of the drive. Then Kris ran out to him, afraid to make him wait, as her grandparents watched from the porch. She never looked back, afraid somehow it would cause him to kill them.

Through all this was her mother's absence. No one spoke of her mother. Her mind didn't remember what happened to her mother, but her spirit would never forget. The rape, the bed springs, the drive to the swamp with the burlap sacks all buried themselves inside her, erupting in fits of rage and frustration or fits during which she seemed younger than her biological age.

On the girls' first day of kindergarten, the teacher had asked each student to stand and tell the class something they loved about their moms. When it was Kris's turn, she stared at the wall covered in construction paper masks the children had drawn of their faces and then taped to the wall. "Kris?" the teacher asked. Kris's eyes automatically defocused. She stood staring at fuzzy blobs of color. "Kris!" The teacher was losing her patience. *Another retarded Indian kid*, she thought and pushed the girl into her chair. "Too much booze in the belly, if you know what I mean," was a common refrain from the teacher, who grew up in Antwatin, the daughter of a Goodhue County judge.

As Ethel fixed dinner in the kitchen to celebrate the girls' first day of kindergarten, Sher asked, "Grandma, where's Kris's mom?" Ethel's pain flared. She turned toward Sher with a hot frying pan of bacon grease. "Never again will you ask that question!" she snapped. Sher stepped back, absorbing her grandmother's anger and grief. The hot lard popping and spitting in the pan, a foot in front of Sher's face, lit fear in Sher. Sher never asked again. Ethel had not meant to frighten her granddaughter, but her rage and grief escaped, abruptly and violently taking over the kitchen. The family could not survive discussing Josie's disappearance, or any of the others over the generations since the English arrived. Therefore, the absence of Kris's mom was never discussed. Unseen yet palpable, her disappearance filled them all with a grief that could turn into popping, spitting rage at any moment but could never be directly voiced, if they were to survive.

* * *

"This way." Sher pointed straight ahead. "We can swing around the depot and get something to eat." Sher smiled. "Before we end up back in that alley fighting for food with the coons."

"Or rats."

"Yah. Rats."

The girls continued under blinking yellow stoplights. They crossed Second Avenue to Nicollet, passing an occasional bum huddled up against a wall or flung out across some stairs, still clutching a bottle in his sleep.

Kristin feared she would become one of them.

"Come on." Sher grabbed her arm. "Remember how we used to skip around the chicken coop when we were little, making up songs, scaring all the chickens until they practically flew?" Sher's ankle hurt.

"Yah, and your brother." Kristin laughed. "He was so mad. So mad. Slipped and fell in chicken crap. And your dad laughing so hard. He didn't even get mad about the chickens, just laughed at your brother all covered in chicken poop and feathers and dirt."

"Told him his Indian name was Chicken Legs."

The girls hooted.

"He never liked to see us have fun." Sher wiped her eyes from laughter that in the past year seemed to mix up with grief and sadness fast. Often, she had not liked how her brother acted, but she loved him and missed him in his boyhood, before his anger transformed into shame and the shame transformed him into an Indian who did not want to be Indian.

They stepped around a man muttering to himself.

"We're gonna end up like that, aren't we?" Kristin stopped laughing. "Oh, shoot, oh crap, aren't we, Sher? We're gonna end up just crazy like these men." She thought they never should have left the reservation, never should have come to this foreign place where drunks slept outside. Even on the rez, that whites said was so bad, drunks slept inside. Their grandparents had let them crash in the barn, warm, in the hay, until they'd slept it off. Do some work in the fields for food once they sobered up. They'd never leave a drunk on the sidewalk like they did here.

Kristin squatted against a boarded-up building. She dug her heels into a patch of bone-dry dirt.

"We're gonna be okay," Sher said. She sat next to Kris, stretching her bad leg out in front of her.

"Solid?"

"Solid."

They set there like that for a while.

"What about the war?"

"What about it?"

"All those people. On the TV. Dying." Kris sobbed.

She had never seen Kris like this before. She figured it was from her dad. He hurt her bad last time. And Kris had become more concerned with the war shortly after their grandparents died, but not like this, like the war was destroying Kris, too.

"I don't know, Kris." Sher looked at her nails. She wished her dad was alive. She believed he would have taken Kris in, stood up to Kris's dad, kept the farm steady, not sold Patsy to pay off a mismanagement of the cows.

"Sher," Kris cried. "What's going to happen?"

"Kris. Kristin. It'll be okay." She looked away from Kris. Their grandma always said the spirits took four.

"How do you know?"

"I don't. I just believe it."

"What about the war?"

Sher shrugged.

"Someone has to stop it."

"Yah." Sher put her arm around Kristin like she used to do when they were little and posed for the black and white pictures of themselves with strawberry jam smeared across their T-shirts or sitting on the rocks down at the water, their skinny brown legs dangling over a pond on the farm. "We'll figure a way."

Antwatin Township, Goodhue Reservation, 1934

The girls' great-grandparents, their thirteen-year-old grandfather, a great-auntie and great-uncle and their five children lived together in a tar-paper-covered wigwam on the northern edge of the farm farthest from the road, under the boughs of the state forest. Layered headlines from the late 1910s, '20s, and '30s insulated and decorated the walls in the wigwam. Some were from the Finns in the farmhouse as their relative was editor of Duluth's most prosperous Finnish newspaper, *The Industrialisti*. The girls' great-grandparents had also dragged home bundles of other newspapers whenever they found them—an alley in Antwatin, behind the Knights of Columbus in Duluth, and a coup—ten fresh bundles of *Minneapolis Star* in the weeds at the end of a path off 23 that fell off a Sunday delivery truck early one morning. Layer after layer turned the interior of their wigwam into a collage of partial headlines from Minneapolis, Duluth, and International Falls, blending into text from a Canadian or Virginia or Aitkin newspaper along with occasional pictures of white, fat-bellied men in dark, three-piece suits, baseball players in baggy, knee-length pants sliding cleats up, and thin-waisted white ladies in dresses down to their feet smiling over steel cast cooking stoves.

The girls' great-grandmother, when sewing or cutting onions for porcupine stew or scraping leather, made up story after story based on the pictures inside her house until she had enough vignettes to fill many books. She spoke in Indian with a smattering of English to keep up with the language she learned a bit of in the boarding school and to stay connected with her children, who were learning English at the day boarding school in Antwatin. Her stories from the newspapers nearly always ended with Indians getting their land back. "My boy," she would say, "stories have power. It matters, the words that come out of our mouths. My girl," she would say. "Words have power. Our thoughts have power. Our prayers have power." Indeed, every day since they'd been kicked off their land and allowed to live at the edge of the Finn's farm and the government's forest, which meant that to the white world they legally lived nowhere, she put down *asema*, tobacco, at the base of the oldest white pine she could find, and asked the *manidoog* and *Gitchi Manidoo* for the return of the land her people had lived on and their bones buried in for generations. "One day," she would tell her family, "the land will be returned to us. The land wants us back." They said, "Mmmmm," to show they believed her. She had never lied. She refused many offers to move into town, or St. Paul, or another reservation. "One day," she would say, "one day. *Minogizhigad*. That is the day it will be when we return to the land. A good day."

One time, a visiting English friend who spoke some Indian said, "You could put those stories in a book." The girls' great-grand-mother handed her a needle, sinew, and rabbit skin. "Mitten," she directed. "*Miigwetch. Gawiin*. Thank you. No," she said. "Stories are circles." She finished the sentence in Indian because she was unsure of the English translation. "How to say that?" she asked her friend while making a downward twirling motion with her hand. "Spirals," the white friend. "*Eya*. Yes. Circles. Spirals. The way a vine grows down the stem of another plant. Yes. That's how stories are twisting around. But English think stories travel like an arrow. *Gawiin*. Stories fly like the bee. *Amoog*. Stories twist and twirl around each other like vines. To the English, everything is separate. And square. Indian stories don't fit in their square books. Stories are not to be sold. That would be like selling our children. Or the trees." All the adult Indians in the wigwam said, "Mmmm," in agreement and in thought over her words. "Indian houses are round. Indian stories are round. *Eya*," she said, and fit her hand into the partially sewn mitten and examined it from all sides. "*Miiw*."

When she was five, the Antwatin sheriff grabbed her and other Indian children off the reservation and brought them in a wagon 189 miles to the Sisters of Mercy Morris Industrial School for Indians in west-central Minnesota. Gone for one year, her parent had not been told where she was or why she'd been taken. She had not been allowed to go home. Forced to kneel on rocks and pray for hours every day, her spirit simply floated up and out the top of her head, wandered over to the forest, and sat in tree branches until the nuns released the Indian children for their midday gruel. Why she was only gone a year, her family did not know. They also did not know the nuns had sold her to a farm in Fargo, which she ran from, and got a ride from a farmer back to Antwatin. One day, she ran down the path through the woods to their camp, the very day they'd begun boiling sap. "Protected," her elders said, about the six-year-old who, a year after disappearing, reappeared in a gray dress with her hair cut short, and immediately began picking up sticks to keep the fire burning.

Years later, the girls' great-grandmother sat cross-legged on the floor, stitching the right-hand rabbit mitten as her white friend stitched the left hand. She pointed her lips at Clarence, her youngest son, who sat on a blanket, carving short-stunted white men pipes they sold during summer tourist season. Her white friend said, "It's a pity they have your land and that fine house. I wish you could live in that house! It should be yours!" Her white friend tied off the end of sinew. "Had to once, not again," the girls' great-grandmother said about the time she lived in a square building at the Catholic boarding school and then the Fargo farmhouse. She thought of stories elders told her when she was a girl, out in the bush, learning to build round houses, wigwams, with willow branches and how if you didn't tie off the willow branch crossbars in a good way, they could fall on your head. That was how the beaver got its flat tail, from not listening good to directions and then its house fell on it, smashing its tail into the mud and flattening all beavers' tails thereafter as a reminder to listen.

Her eyes crinkled. She laughed, covering her mouth with her hand as she still sometimes did from being punished at the Catholic school for laughing or talking Indian. "*Gawain,*" she said, and pressed down the seams on her cotton dress as if her palm were an iron, that hot, heavy pointed thing they had taught her to use at the white school so the nuns and priests looked like straight black lines, hanging heavy to the floor—the way she thought of their spirits, dour and strict and cruel. Not a one of them had given her reason to think of them in any other manner. "No. *Gawiin geyaabe.* I won't live in one of them white houses," she said, mixing English and Indian, her mind jagging between Indian ways and white ways. "I will die out here, in trees and Indian house. Fine," she said in English, about the wigwam, thinking how her white friend described the farmhouse. "Wigwam. Fine. *Eya!*"

* * *

The girls walked a long loop east, then south, then west until they made their way back to Hennepin Avenue where Sher had seen the restaurants. They ate at The Broiler Cafe, sliding into the mammoth, cracked, pink vinyl booths as if they were the slick red fiberglass seats on a Tilt-A-Whirl ride. The girls devoured eggs and hash browns and thin white toast soaked in butter with loads of jam and ketchup smeared about on their plates like paint. As they ate, they glanced at the bums and dealers just long enough to be sure it was not the two men from the depot.

Sher pointed her fork at a white man with long curly brown side-burns, around twenty, she guessed, on the corner with his hands stuffed deep in a thick army green winter parka. "Anyone standing around in this heat in that is up to something," she said.

Kristin glanced at him. "He looks like one of those hippies from the farm. Remember them? The ones that used to come around in the summer asking for spare eggs and milk." She mopped up the rest of her eggs and ketchup and jam with the last piece of crust. Her back muscles twinged at the memory. Her uncle and grandparents gone. Em gone even longer. She couldn't name her emotions—just that at her core, she felt at times her life over. She would never again go to her grandparents' farm and listen to them talk around the kitchen table, their cigarette smoke turning the air into bluish oil rings. Or help her grandmother make red willow baskets to sell off the back of their rust bucket truck in the parking lot of the county fair. Or stay up half the night birthing calves with her uncle and grandfather and cousins, pulling blood and pus covered calves from inside their mothers and then wiping their eyes and noses and mouths as their mothers licked clean their bodies with gravelly tongues wide and thick as the rock bass they caught in the pond. Or have Em sneak her a cigarette. Gone. Since their deaths, she'd vacillated between caring about the war, smog killing the birds in Los Angeles, and the acid rain pouring down on cities. Kris imagined, while lying in bed in the dark, the acid rain dissolving houses and people and trees in the cities like water dissolving salt. Other times, she stared at the moon. A man on the moon! Who could imagine that?

"Maybe," Sher said, her mouth full, not thinking about tomorrow.

Sher wiped the plate clean with her finger and wished for another. Her stomach rumbled at the rush of food. She flashed to the time she and Auntie Em and Kris had been in town on an errand for their grandfather. The girls were five, waiting on the sidewalk for Em, who was inside Johnson's Meats delivering a note from her father asking for a few pounds of ground beef as payment for some work he'd done on their truck. They had not eaten in two days. Three white boys with brown crew cuts, including the oldest Johnson boy, fourteen at the time, appeared from behind the store. "Hey, girls," he said, wagging a white, grease-stained bag at Kris and Sher. "Hungry?" Sher and Kris didn't move. They stared at the bag, so hungry they felt they would faint.

The boys smiled. Sher thought their teeth big, like a horse's, and as white as their pressed T-shirts. "Come here." They motioned for the girls to go with them into the narrow space between the butcher shop and the firehouse. The girls stood stock still, knowing better than to trust white boys, but hunger overtook them. They wavered. Just as Kris jumped toward the boys and their bag like a startled calf, Em pushed through the front door, empty-handed. She saw the white waxy bag from the tavern, yellow grease stains swelling up the sides, took four steps and socked the Johnson boy in the face. He dropped the bag, blood dripping down his chin and splattering across his white shirt. "Piss!" he yelled, leaned over and spit out a line of blood. "She broke my nose." "Who's next?" Em asked, raising her fist. The boys ran. "Jeeesus H," one of the boys yelled, as they disappeared down a narrow alley. Em snatched the bag, grabbed the girls' hands, and cut east through town toward the farm, the three of them feasting on greasy salty fries and cheeseburgers with pickles the boys had meant to keep for themselves after they'd had their way with the girls.

Em knew what the bag meant because boys had done it to her. Alone and hungry at the jungle gym, at recess during her second day of sixth grade, a group of ninth grade white boys had lured her with a lard and sugar sandwich to a wooded area of the playground. They circled around her while taking turns shoving their fingers and a stick inside her. She shut her eyes. She did not cry out. "Tell anyone and we'll scalp you and your whole family, you stinking Indian," the boys threatened. Her fear and pain and confusion mixed with the threats until it became brackish and undrinkable. She buried it in a deep well and her silence became equivalent with her family's survival. There and then Em learned to hate.

Thad was playing with the Indian boys in the vacant lot on the other side of the school. Josie had left home to live with an older white farmer named Morgan. No one had been there to protect Em from the boys or the hate that took hold on her. Her anger settled on her older sister, Josie, who had always watched over her. Em felt abandoned. As Em hovered above her young body, her long black lashes like butterfly wings pressed together as the insect settles on a branch, she promised herself that she would never let this happen to anyone else. *Never,* she thought as she floated above it. *To anyone. She would stop it.*

* * *

"Bring an Indian girl a burger," was a common saying among white boys on the reservation. (More than 80 percent of the Goodhue reservation was owned by whites). Some of the boys thought it just talk, but others used their allowance money so that some Indian girls, half-starved, knew to meet them behind White's Pharmacy at seven in the summer and in the first recessed doorway in the alley between Fourth and Main right after school let out in the winter. At the rectory after Saturday morning prayers—in a turn of events, the priest who reigned for five decades listened to the boys and girls from behind a basement door, and then— miraculously—met the boys of his choice at the back door or in the hallway just after he'd dumped his greasy bag on a girl.

"Young man, imagine meeting you here on this fine day. Perhaps you could help me for a moment," the priest would say, never calling the boys by their names, although he'd known them their entire lives, having baptized them and their parents, and their parents' parents. Using their names made them too personal, too human-like. After a few weeks or months of manipulations (helping clean the boiler, reading the priest's favorite poems out loud, offering advice to the priest about one of the other boys, needing "special" altar boy training), the boys of his choosing were hand-jacking and going down on the priest in his office, at the altar, in the boiler room, and in the pews where the priest sat upright, his black robed arms spread on each side of him along the top of the pew, the robe hanging down like huge bat wings while the boys' heads bounced up and down beneath his robe as the priest's lips spread into a thin, pleasant smile.

The Indian girls found out what the priest was doing, or already knew, as he went after Indian boys too. Depending on their temperaments, some of the girls felt bad for the boys, others didn't care, and some were glad the boys who hurt them got what was coming to them. The girls and boys lived in a part of the world most adults did not see, or refused to see, or had been a part of, but now that they escaped it, they ignored it. Hunger is what it all boiled down to—the girls' stomachs folding into themselves like curling fetuses, releasing bone weakening, mind-erasing hunger while the white boys' spiritual starvation twisted them into rapists, or as Ojibwe elders said—cannibals. And then, at the rectory, fate twisted the white boys into being both the eater and the eaten. Consumed by their leader, the mouth of their God on earth—a man none of them could ever challenge—and never did. The priest's funeral, years later, was attended by over 1500 in a town with a population that never rose above 397. His page-and-a-half obituary made an unprecedented appearance just above the fold in the *Antwatin News Journal* and the commemoration of his life on WJJO 1400 AM Northwoods call-in show resulted in caller after caller avowing to his saintliness, his honor, his selflessness, his pure heart, his piety, his Godliness.

Despite five decades of the priest strutting about the town of Antwatin, and the rest of the reservation, like a bird pecking gravel on a road, few thought to look inside God's House for the black-winged creatures that swept across the sea with the ships to unite with their cannibal spiritual kin on Turtle Island, tilting the scale to the side of the Destroyers. The cannibals. The Old Time Indians knew. And those the priest diddled. And those who survived, who stayed alive despite their pain, so their bodies could go on, so the people would live on, so the next generation would curl where it should, *in utero*.

* * *

Sher and Kristin slept two streets over from Hennepin in the stairwell of The Holy Redeemer, a one-story brick church squatting on two blocks. The sun rose pink over the buildings as rain splattered pavement, thudded on canvas overhangs, and pinged off metal gutters. Sher woke. The earthy smell of the rain hit her. *We need this rain,* she thought, forgetting that she was over 200 miles away from the farm and corn crops and cows and the wooded pathways of her childhood. She fell back to sleep.

In her sleep, Sher hovered over a young girl. Sher did not know who the girl was, until, like a TV channel flipping to a new picture, her grandmother stood as an adult covering her mouth as she laughed, as so many Indians who'd gone through the boarding schools did. The girl reappeared. Sher stood next to her, protectively, as the girl looked behind Sher, beyond her, as if Sher were not present. The girl's face froze in fear. As Sher turned to see what threatened the girl, her feet were kicked from under her. She landed on her elbows and knees, and was unable to see. Pain as big and hot as the fire inside the earth ripped into Sher's anus. She screamed, on her belly, blinded. The broom her grandmother had used, that still sat in the corner of the farmhouse, flipped into her field of vision. As Sher wailed, she heard her grandmother saying "poopchute," the only word Sher had ever heard her use to refer to one's anus. Black, women's shoes without heels stood in Sher's face. "We shall teach you," a woman said, stern and clipped. The pain ripped a searing hole through Sher to her father to her grandmother. An open hole of pain that, if Sher had children, would pass to them like a marble bouncing down the steps of a spiral staircase.

Sher woke an hour later to the early morning noises of the city. She blinked in shock to be lying at the bottom of a block cement stairway. One of her boots was flipped on its side in the corner. How it got there, she did not know. She'd always done strange things in her sleep—waking to find herself stretched across her auntie's neck or in the corner of the hall closet wrapped in her grandmother's towel. Each family member had one towel apiece, worn through in places. When Sher sleep-walked at night or during a daytime nap, she always snatched her grandmother's towel, rolled up in it, and crawled into the closet. "My girl," her grandfather would say, patting her foot until she woke. "Bring her here," his wife would say, so she could rock the girl, both arms tight around her as if warding off something—her husband did not know what. "What's this about?" he'd ask Sher, just a babe the first time she'd done this. She simply looked at him, her braids fuzzy from the damp towel.

Her grandmother, for her part, knew exactly what it was about, as at night, when she was a girl, after the bad things happened at school, she would drag her sheet into a closet, spin herself in it like a cocoon so she could sleep, so she could regenerate herself for the morning chores which always began with Indian children kneeling on broomsticks up and down the hallways while the headmaster led them in the Lord's Prayer. Their bones on wood poles hurt so intensely their spirits rose into the air. For those who could see the others flying above the bodies, it was a sort of gathering. For those who could not see, their vision went dark. They felt even more lost and alone.

Whenever her husband raised his eyebrows about her grand-daughter's curious behavior, Ethel avoided his looks, busying herself with the task at hand—washing, cleaning, sorting, cooking, or simply stepping onto the porch to smoke, to forget the brooms, to forget the spirit gatherings, to forget the rest. She did not speak of her past. But as life is wont to do, experience—a form of knowledge—trickles down generations and then courses back into the world to become the next generation's behavior—unexplained, unrealized, unknown—unless someone follows it back through time to unravel themselves and the generations before them.

* * *

Sher stood up silently so as not to disturb Kristin. Birds sang morning greetings. Maybe being here would be okay. For a while. Sher stretched like a cat, reaching up toward the green and white striped awning that covered the stairwell. She cracked her knuckles. She stepped up onto the sidewalk and crouched on her haunches to watch the city wake itself under the low morning light like a dog shaking off water.

A garbage truck roared toward the girls, a Black man with an afro the size of the sun drove it. A brown man, straight hair down to his shoulders, hung off the back bumper. They worked together, dumping the cans—splattering bags, papers, milk cartons, broken records into the truck's maw—and then replacing the cans, and jumping back onto the truck. The men sang along to a radio duct-taped to the side of the truck.

The radio crackled "Maggie's Farm" by Bob Dylan, a singer from Hibbing, Minnesota who was making it big. "I'm not gonna work for Minneapolis no more," the men yelled, changing the words. The brown man grabbed the ears of the metal cans next to Sher, tossed garbage into the truck, and threw the bent can to the sidewalk. "Peace, sister," the Black driver saluted Sher. The dump truck screeched forward. She nodded as they drove off.

"Morning," Kristin popped up next to Sher. "Was that that singer from the Iron Range your brother likes?"

"Yah," Sher said.

"Yah." Kristin squinted down the street, watching the men run back and forth and listening to them yelling along to the radio. She combed her hair straight down over her face with her fingers. "Down with the man."

Antwatin Township, Goodhue Reservation, April 1956

The day Clarence's mother began her journey across the Milky Way to the Old Ones, Clarence, Ethel, their three children—Thaddeus, Jossetta, and Em—and various other relatives all lived in the wigwam on the edge of their land, now inhabited by the Finns. A week later the Finnish family in the farmhouse boarded their hay wagon, hitched up one of the three farm horses, and drove down the long drive they'd cleared decades earlier, their white straw heads bobbing out of sight of the Indian family living on the edge of the farm. Among the straw heads was an infant with a mop of black hair, black eyes, and chestnut-colored skin, the son of the eldest, unmarried girl. She held the baby tight to her chest. On their way to Duluth, no one would discuss the color in the family. Ever.

The Finns also took their clothes, two pots, the ornate plate and trunk they brought from Finland, two pails filled with food and covered with cheese cloth, and a horse and wagon. They left everything else—a complete working farm and farmhouse stocked with furniture, canning jars, blankets, pillows, seeded gardens, butter churner, and a full pantry. Most in the area thought it was the shame of the Indian baby that sent away the family. Others thought it the death of the patriarch a few months prior. Some thought they wished to return to their motherland—after all, why else would a family leave everything behind if not because they could not take it on a ship? Only Clarence knew the truth. Eventually, he would tell his wife and son, but otherwise, he took it to the grave as the true story imperiled many, including his family.

He did not have loose lips about how the patriarch's eldest grown son, Jalo, inherited the farm upon the death of his father. As a radical Socialist, and editor of Duluth's Socialist Finnish newspaper *The Industrialisti*, written in Finnish with a sizeable readership in Canada (and thus many contacts), and from a country occupied by others for centuries, he felt a kinship to the Ojibwe. Jalo was a friend of Olli Kinkkonen, who in 1918 had been tarred, feathered, and hung from a tree in Duluth by the Knights for Liberty for refusing to fight in World War I. Olli wished to return to his motherland, which had just won independence from Sweden the year before.

Jalo was the second on the scene to find his friend covered in black tar and crow feathers, his head lolling over his chest from when the rope snapped his neck. "Olli!" he had cried as he cut him down. Jalo felt such guilt and pain over the death of his fine, kind friend who wasn't even a Socialist, who just didn't want to fight. "He wanted to return to Finland," Jalo yelled in Finnish. He swore to the memory of Olli that he would work all his life to make things right in a devilish country filled with such hatred and lies. Two years later, Jalo witnessed three Negro carnival workers lynched in Duluth. "Stop! Stop!" he screamed, trapped in a sea of Russian and Swedish men, men from the very countries who had occupied Finland for centuries! "*Seis! Seis!*" he yelled, his ancestors' suffering and rage erupting through him. Unable to stop those brutish men from hanging the Negroes, and pressed in on all sides by thousands, his eyes rolled back in his head as he was overcome by his fear and hatred for Russian and Swedish men, the guilt he carried that his political work may have been the cause of Olli's lynching, and the terror and chaos of the mob as they were about to lynch three Negroes. Jalo was terrified he could be next, caught and hung by the same men who'd lynched a Finn for being a Finn, as they looped the ropes around the Negroes' necks, laughing and chanting, "String up the niggers!"

Two days after his father's death, Jalo made a deal with Clarence. He'd return the land, along with everything they'd need to operate the farm, as long as the Indians moved into the farmhouse, kept up the barn and gardens and a few crops and animals so it appeared as a working farm to outsiders and to the corrupt and contemptable government! Jalo's clincher was that Clarence become part of the underground network Jalo had joined after Olli's murder that hid people in barns across the Midwest as they made their way toward freedom in Canada. In his uncertain

English, Jalo said to Clarence, "Finns are outsiders here like you Ojibwe are on your land. Finns. Negroes, Indians. We must work together to overthrow the capitalist state that robs its workers of life and liberty and wages. We must assist those who must leave for their own liberty, like Olli. Long live his memory. Olli! And the Negroes! All innocents of this diabolical capitalist state that must be overthrown!"

Clarence, a World War II vet, didn't think too much about overthrowing anything, but he thought this could be the fulfillment of his mother's prayers. He knew some white ways now, after his few years at the boarding school in Carlisle, the day boarding school in Antwatin—not to mention the years he worked the farm alongside the Finns and fought in the army. He wished for the return of the land.

"What do you say? I will give you the papers," Jalo asked. Clarence nodded. "I show you the doors to the tunnel. We built it in case of too much snow. Now you hide people there." Clarence nodded. Now he understood all those years of watching the Finns enter the barn and then exit the house without ever leaving the barn. "*Kylla*. Yes?" Jalo said. "Sorry my English bad. I very happy you do this. The Swedes and Russians had tried to kill our language to conquer us just as the US government did to Indians. We are brothers. You and me." The men shook hands and the paper burned by Clarence's relatives so long ago, returned. And with it, the land. And with that, the trees as the Brauns would allow the forest to grow back across most of the fields, foot by foot. The Standing People returned, just as Clarence's mother said they would.

* * *

Across the street from the girls an old white man opened a steel cart, popped up a large red umbrella that said *Hotdogs! Pretzels! Pop!* in white cursive around the top. A siren swept through the streets.

"Sher," Kristin said, jolted by the siren.

"Yah."

"What are we gonna do?"

"Now?"

"Now."

"Eat."

"What?"

"What do you want?"

"Eggs. Bacon."

"Again?"

"Yah."

"Okay."

"Then what?"

"Call Carla. Got her number right here." Sher touched her pocket.

The old man arranged his items. Sher kept her eyes on him in between the cars and buses and cabs that drove by.

"We've got to get washed up," Sher said, as she watched the old man set a cooler next to the stand and pull out long-neck bottles of pop. "Kris, get me twenty cents."

Kristin dug around at the bottom of the pack and handed Sher two dimes. She tossed the crushed Coke can from the hunter's shack onto the sidewalk.

Sher crossed the street.

The old man narrowed his eyes. "Ain nothin' here for you."

Sher figured he acted that way because they were Indian. "How much for a pop, sir?"

"You got money?"

"Yes, sir. How much?"

"Twenty cents for the pop. Only Coke and Nehi today. Grape. Twenty-five cents a pretzel. Thirty for a dog."

The old man took her money, and handed her a Coke.

Sher crossed the street and gave the Coke to Kristin.

"Don't you want it?"

"Nope."

"Why'd you get it?"

"Wished to get us jobs."

Kristin drained the Coke.

Sher took the empty bottle from her and stuck her middle finger in the mouth to carry it. "Come on, Kris," she said, slinging the pack over one shoulder.

The old man was lacing a hot dog with mustard. He handed the hot dog to a man in a business suit. "Never too early to be eatin' a dog."

The man raised the dog in the air like a salute and walked north.

"Want it back?" Sher held the bottle toward him. "For the

deposit."

The old man looked at the girls. "What are ya a couple of hippie kids?"

"No sir," Sher had to keep from laughing never having had anyone ask if she were a hippie. She leaned on her good foot. "In town. Visiting."

"Uh huh." The old man tilted his head toward the sun. "I see." He took the bottle.

"Sher. This here's Kris."

"You're not hippies?" He squinted at Sher.

"No, sir," Sher said, confused, as she expected white people to distrust her for being Indian, not a hippie.

"You homeless kids?"

"No, sir. We have a home."

"You look plenty dirty."

"No, sir."

"Yes, ya do."

"No, sir, what I mean is we're out looking around for jobs and we've been sitting around waiting to talk to certain people."

"I see. Those hippie kids always takin from me."

"No, sir. We don't steal," Kristin said and bit her lip to be talking so nice to a man who insulted them.

"We're just looking for some work and we'd be glad if you would consider—"

"No, no, no. Git on outta here. I know what you kids are all about. Now git."

The girls crossed the street.

"Hey!" His papery voice followed them as they crossed the street. "You girls Indians?"

"Yah. Yah," they said, their voices layering over each other. They did not look back.

The girls cut to the left, heading south toward nowhere they knew.

When they reached Second Avenue they cut to west until they hit Third where Sher called Carla from a pay phone next to a pawnshop. No one answered. They walked the outskirts of Loring Park, poking their heads in the back doors of bars and restaurants asking for work as dishwashers and busboys, but they could not find anyone willing to employ two teenage Indian girls on the run. They found bread still wrapped in plastic in the trash of Moby's

Tavern, walked to Loring Park, and sat on a bench overlooking a pond. They shared the bread.

"I'm thirsty," Kris said. "Think we could drink from the pond?"

"Best not," Sher said. "It's pretty green." Her ankle hurt. She could barely put any weight on it.

Kristin balled up the bread bag. "Be right back."

Sher nodded. She picked up an acorn beneath the bench, popped the hat off it, and ate the nut, showing no outward sign when the bitterness of the nut hit her tongue. She'd grown eating roasted acorns, and ate a few unroasted ones as a young girl.

A squirrel ran the base of a gnarled oak. Sher removed her boots and socks and lay on the bench. The sun rode the tops of the trees and roofs of the buildings. Sher wondered what would become of her and Kris. *They could always move on*, Sher thought, and watched the squirrel chase itself around the tree, expending precious energy as it ran from predators Sher could not see.

"Nice boots."

Sher swung herself upright. A tawny-colored boy about her age in jeans and a tie-dye T-shirt stood with his back to the setting sun. His body was thin and angular as if it wanted to go in every direction at once.

The boy squatted. "Jacob. Nice to meet you." He ran a hand through his twiggy brown afro. His speech was quick and clipped, unlike the people Sher and Kristin spent their lives around.

Sher studied the boy from top to bottom. "Sher." She nodded.

The boy picked up a stick and drew a half circle in front of him. "Sher. That's a nice name," he said. "What are you? Where you from?" He looked off to the right where some other boys stood.

Sher studied the boys.

The boy grew impatient. "What are you?"

"Indian."

"Really?" the boy asked. His eyes flitted toward the boys, at Sher, and then behind her. "Like teepees and cowboys and stuff?"

Sher did not respond.

The boy became increasingly nervous, drawing more and more half circles and circles in the dirt. The squirrel was nowhere in sight. Sher edged closer to her boots in case the boy tried to run off with them.

"Me? Since you asked. I'm from Chicago," the boy said unable to bear the silence. He stood and stretched his arms behind his back, popping his small, bony shoulders forward like baseballs. He turned his back to Sher. The tallest boy with shaggy, strawberry blonde hair motioned at him. Jacob turned to Sher.

"Indian, huh. Where you from?" He moved his hands in circles.

"Your friends?" Sher placed her palms on the bench on either side of her hips.

"Yeah. Yeah. Sort of," the boy said. He stepped forward toward Sher. "You've got a hurt foot," he said tenderly as if he had just seen a wounded bird hidden in someone's sweatshirt.

"Ankle."

"Oh, wow. Man. Sorry." The boy began dancing on his feet like a boxer. "Sorry, that looks bad." He bent down next to Sher's ankle. He reached out to touch it.

"Don't touch me."

The boy jumped up. "Sorry, right. Don't touch you. Sorry."

Sher pushed her boots under her legs. "What do they want?" she asked, nodding toward the boys.

"Who? Them?" The boy ran his hand through his hair again and twirled the end of a curl. "Those guys," he said, turning his back to them and jerking his thumb at them. "Good. Guys. Nothing." He moved again, imitating Muhammed Ali.

"What do you want?" Sher tried to get a good look at his face in between his bobbing and the shade cast across his face.

"Me?" He sounded surprised. "I don't want a thing."

"What do they want?"

"They're wondering, um, where you're from."

"What do they want?"

"Nothing. Just said 'Jacob go find out where those girls are from.' So here I am." The boy stopped moving. "It isn't like they're going to beat me up if I don't do what they say." He struck a boxing pose, fists up.

Sher looked at the boy and no longer saw the softness she had seen a minute before when he was concerned about her ankle. "Tell them I'm not interested."

"I can't do that." Jacob slipped out a cigarette from his shirt pocket. "Got a light."

Sher shook her head no. "Sure you can."

"No." Jacob tugged at his pocket and pulled out a lighter. "No. I can't." His hands shook.

"Why not?"

"No reason."

"Sher?" Kristin stood behind Sher, staring at the funny-looking white boy with an afro. She raised her eyebrows as if to say *who is this guy?*

Sher nodded at her cousin.

Kris handed the bread bag filled with ice and water. "Drink."

Jacob lit his cigarette again, rounding his shoulders as if he were protecting the flame from the wind, even though there was no wind.

Sher drank water from the bag and then placed the ice on her raw skin. "Did you get it lit?" she said to Jacob.

"Damn. No."

"Give it to me," Sher said.

Jacob handed her the cigarette—an Embassy Filter—and lighter. Sher lit Jacob's cigarette.

Jacob held it like a joint and inhaled. He turned his back to the girls and waved at the strawberry blonde boy. The boy nodded and walked to the west, away from Jacob and the girls.

"Got another one?" Kristin asked.

Jacob slipped out a cigarette and handed the tip to her graciously like he was a gentleman pulling out a sword. "My name is Jacob, since you asked."

"Thanks. But I didn't. Embassy Filter," Kris said as she lit the cigarette.

"Best ciggies around." Jacob puffed from his and then blew a cloud of smoke toward Kris. "You like?"

"Em smoked Camel." A burst of grief came over Kris. "What do they want?" She pointed her cigarette at the group of white boys pushing each other and sprawling in the grass in jeans and white T-shirts.

"Not me," the boy said. "You, they want you, not me." Jacob tried to laugh as if what Kristin said was ridiculous.

"Why?" Kristin asked.

Jacob let out two quick sharp laughs to sound tough. Then he coughed into his armpit. "I'm here to bring you over to them." The boy glanced at the group of boys and turned back to the girls. "Come over to talk with them. They just want to talk. I swear. Please."

"We're leaving." Sher pulled on a sock.

"Nah, come on. Be cool, man. Just come over for one minute.

One minute, that's it. C'mon man. I promise nothing will happen."
The boy put his thumbs up. "Not one thing, man. It's cool."

"Doubt it," Kris said, ashing her cigarette.

"I think you need to come with us," Sher said.

The boy's face moved in a strange way.

Sher laced up her boots. Kristin strapped on their grandfather's
pack and the girls walked east toward the heart of downtown.

"Dumb chicks!" the boys yelled. "C'mon, ya kike!" One of
them ran a ways and threw something at them that wavered in the
air before dropping to the ground like a bird shot out of the sky.

A stick, Sher guessed, but was not sure because the fading light
turned everything a pale yellow or dark black. When the girls
reached the street around the edge of the park, Sher glanced back
again as the boys circled Jacob.

"Guess he got an F," Sher said.

"What's 'kike'?" Kris asked.

"Don't know."

The girls tromped off, carrying the pack and the half-melted bag
of ice.

"He should have come with us instead," Kristin said.

"Yah," Sher said. "He'd a been better off."

After walking a block, the girls had to wait at an intersection
for two cop cars as they wailed by, their red and blue lights
swinging in a wide arch over the pedestrians' heads like cowboys
swinging their ropes at a round up.

"Want to go back?"

"Yah."

The girls looped around to the west until they ended up on the
other side of the park where they had last seen the boy. The group
of boys milled about where the girls had been sitting.

"See him?"

"Nah."

The girls walked farther west, passing a woman pushing a
stroller draped with a sky-blue blanket. The girls cut behind one of
the apartment buildings and dropped down a short, steep hill to
the alley. The boy sat on the concrete steps of a four-story brick
apartment building.

"Hey," Kris said.

"You okay?" Sher asked.

"Real cool," Jacob said, his head down.

"They beat you?" Sher asked.

"Sure. Probably." He rocked.

A white man in a dark blue suit walked down the alley. He did not look at them, as if by not looking perhaps they would not actually be there.

The girls watched him, his pant legs flapping against his wing tip shoes. The boy studied the pebbles in the concrete.

"Got somewhere to go?" Sher looked at Kristin as if to ask her *is it okay to bring him along?*

Kris shrugged and nodded.

"No," he said.

"Want to go with us?" Sher asked.

The boy fiddled in his pocket, slipped out a cigarette, and lit it. He shrugged.

"Come on."

The boy took a drag on the cigarette. His face was swollen and bloody.

"You're going to need our face makeup," Sher said.

"Wash up." Kristin held the bag of water with a golf ball size chunk of ice.

"We're all in good shape," Sher said, propping her foot on a step.

Jacob splashed the water on his face and then held the ice over his eye.

After a while like that, the girls and the boy walked toward the heart of the city.

"Sorry about that," he said, flipping his hand. "What I did. I'm coming down. Acid."

"Acid," Kris said, her eyes as big and round as the moon. She felt the same way she did the times she'd heard Sasquatch stories— from her grandfather, uncles, and cousins about sightings on the reservation and in Canada. "I didn't believe it until I seen it," one of her cousins said. He'd seen Sasquatch on Antwatin as a boy, right before moving to the city. "Twice as big as a moose. All hairy. Little beady red eyes." His father said it was bull, just some old time Indian superstitions that modern Indians need to leave behind. His mother kept her mouth shut. She watched her boy. She'd heard the stories as a little girl, and believed them, but they were moving to the city the next day and she'd been told by her friends who were already there that it would be best for the children to leave the old ways on the reservation. "My boy," she'd said. "Come over here and help me with this box." When he stood next to her, she squeezed his shoulder to let him know she loved him. She didn't say I believe you. She wanted him to survive.

* * *

The girls and boy avoided the road next to the park and the main streets where there was a higher chance of running into cops or the boys.

"What are we going to do tomorrow?" Kristin asked as they turned down an alley whose sides angled down toward the middle, creating a gulley for runoff.

"Same as we did today," Sher said. She put her arm over Kristin's shoulder.

The boy wrapped his arms around his ribs as if he were in a straitjacket.

The sun disappeared over the girls and the boy, blanketing them in the gray down of dusk.

Virginia, Minnesota, July 1969

Em faced the door from which she heard the scratching. At first the scratching sounds confused and unnerved her. But after a while, it was hard to tell time in her condition, she realized the sound came from something small and desperate, but persistent. Like a secret language. Initially, she imagined a rodent, or baby raccoon, or even kitten, but what must have been hours later, she no longer imagined the sounds were being made by an animal. Another human? But who? What could she do? She would not talk. She'd learned that lesson on the drive here—had a cheek that looked like a burst tomato. The right side of her face was still burning and throbbing—to remind her that silence is golden, as the whites say, embroidered on their doilies and brass-framed wall hangings with spinning, curling metal flowers decorating the edges. Everything so hard and sharp. Who else, but the English, as Em's grandparents had called all whites, could take the softness of a flower and make it so hard and pointed?

Em knew—she'd watched white people plenty—that if silence were broken at the English dinner table or in the classroom, it would be followed by a fist or a palm or a snap of a ruler. Theirs was not the silence of respect but of fear. Of punishment. They hit their children. She'd seen it! No wonder their children were so afraid of them, so shut down and filled with shame or, on occasion, eruptive and openly defiant. And now this. She fought the fear in her belly. She could not birth that emotion, or she would not survive. Tied at her wrists and ankles, feet spread and belly down, she could not move her hands to talk back at whomever was making the noises. Her low back hurt and she had to keep her face to one side because of her cheek. How long had she been there, in that enormous gold house with carved wooden ornamentation hanging down from the eaves like stiff lace frozen in a winter storm and more rooms than Em could have imagined possible in one dwelling? Hours? Days?

Em was no fool. No Indian woman was. None could afford to be. She did not know the specifics of the garish gold house on the western edge of town, one and three quarters of a mile from an open mine pit. A Queen Anne built in 1894 by fifty-seven-year-old Giuseppe De Luca, an immigrant Italian mine owner who originally made his money in the garment district in New York City. The three-story house had once been referred to as The Grand Old Lady. Eighteen rooms, two sets of staircase (one for the servants—orphaned Indian girls and poor white girls De Luca purchased from the St. Scholastica Priory convent in Duluth), six fireplaces, a pantry, a formal dining room, two bathing rooms (one for each of the two bottom floors), a library made of imported African mahogany (even though De Luca was illiterate, he'd stood stroking with the tip of his pinky finger the spines of the books he could not read in his library), three sitting rooms, plain servants quarters in the attic, a wrap-around porch, and a root cellar. Oak and maple trim sawed, stripped, and dragged from the surrounding forest lined the floors, windows, door frames, baseboards, crown moldings, and fireplaces. In the ground-level sitting room two magnificent, hand-carved oaks sprang forth on each side of the main fireplace in bas relief, the mouth of the fireplace constructed of inlaid turquoise square one inch tile, the acorns tumbling from the trees' branches with such detail that their caps revealed each miniscule bump, the smooth meat of the nut, still shiny and bright beneath the lacquer.

Now no longer grand, largely unoccupied, the original cooking stove barely usable due to rust, mice nesting in the walls—their dead stacked in walls, ceilings stained with brown and yellow rings that bled outward like watercolor warts, wallpaper split down seams, Victorian pullout bathtub covered in mold, and grimy floors, the house's story included thirty years of neglect on the outer edge of a small northern Minnesota mining town. Virginia, Minnesota, where it regularly reached thirty below during the winter season. Virginia, Minnesota, one hour from Canada, dubbed the "Queen City," was a town no one in 1969 would suspect was a holding place for those who bought and sold Indians. No one needed to tell Em anything about the De Luca house's peculiar history. She knew the story. It was as old as America—the story writ in her ancestors' blood, the trees, and the land. The bones of the houses were, after all, trees. And trees, whether alive or dead, hold stories, as her father had always said.

Her mind, groggy, reached back, behind her to the time when she was small, her hair in two tight shining black bear-greased braids, listening, ear to the floor of her and her siblings' bedroom door, the iciness of the pocked wood floor against her cheek. That the farmhouse was theirs—an Indian family—was a miracle unto itself. Or a curse, depending on whom you asked. Her brother, the middle child. Thaddeus. Thad for short. A worker. Quiet. Good-natured. Funny. He did not seek out the stories not meant for young ears that his grandparents discussed at night, after the children had been sent to sleep, as Em did. But when stories were presented to him, each one as if it were a gift being unwrapped every time it was told, he listened and he remembered. Her sister Josetta, Josie for short, was the oldest, tough as moose hide, but also dreamy, easily airborne like the magpies that feast ticks off moose, which was why she did not get out from under the covers at night to listen. She disliked the night air that cracked like sheets of ice until the sun had been in the morning sky long enough, warming even the coldest, most remote room in her parents' farmhouse. Both girls were tough, their family Sturgeon Clan, but something in Josie's constitution made her flighty, made her not seek out and settle into the depths the way Em did. The unwillingness to hear the full truth made Josie more vulnerable, not less.

The afternoon the Finns left, the Brauns abruptly moved into the farmhouse. No reason was given to young Em, so she believed the move was due to her grandmother's passing. Although she would never know the true reason, the move turned Em's grief and loss over her grandmother into anger and then resentment. Then with the happenings at school, being taken from her family for months, her emotions turned to hatred and eventually rage and revenge. But at the core of all that were the girl's emotions over the loss of her beloved grandmother, an old timer who had no interest in white ways, especially their hard, cold, four-cornered dwellings with rooms that separated families. "Every room for something different. Eat. Sex. Sleep. Sitting. Making food. No wonder why they are the way they are," she said in Ojibwe. "They can't help it. In houses like that, it's how they grow." Em viewed their move into the farmhouse as a betrayal and dismissal of her and the old-time ways. Her unresolved grief was the seed that sprouted her bitterness and anger that propelled her away from her family, away from her teachings, and into the coldest and hardest aspects of the English house.

West

*In Ojibwe ways, the west direction is the place of
constant change, death, and loss.*

That night Sher, Kristin, and the boy found a place to sleep under a
bridge just southwest of Loring Park. They did not stay in the
stairwell of the church because the girls did not know if they could
trust him and they wanted to be able to go back to the stairwell if
they needed to. They huddled there in the tall grasses next to the
cement ramp that slanted downhill under highway 94. Despite the
gas fumes, the area smelled of the "happy grass" their grandmother
used to braid and burn. She had a patch out back, in the northeast
corner where the pasture met the government woods. She took
special care in the fall, keeping the seeds and a few roots in the
cellar.

"Smell that?" Kris asked, when an intense wave of sweet grass
enveloped her.

"Yah," Sher said. "Happy grass."

"I got some," Jacob said.

The girls laughed. Their spirits lifted. They were in the right
place.

Jacob pulled out a small purple velour pouch filled with
marijuana. He found an empty Tab can, pushed down one side
with his thumbs, and poked holes in the dents using a safety pin
that attached the pouch inside his shirt.

"Marijuana?" Kris asked, wide-eyed.

Jacob laughed. "Weed. Mary Jane. Only squares say marijuana."
He carved a small hole near the bottom of the can and mounded
marijuana over the pinholes. "Oh man," he said. "I need a light."

Kris lit the marijuana pile with the lighter Sher bought at the truck stop.

"Hey! You said you didn't have a light," Jacob said, as if he were a small child calling out injustice on an adult. "Why'dja do that?"

Sher shrugged.

He inhaled through the mouthpiece keeping his finger over the hole near the bottom that he had carved. He let his finger off and inhaled deeper until he could take in no more. Setting the can on the ground next to Kris, Jacob lay back holding his breath. The smoke drifted into the night air, disappearing as a spiral into the stars.

"Dig it, cat," Kristin said, nervous. She'd never smoked marijuana before.

Smoke shot out of the boy's mouth. He laughed, rolled over coughing and grabbing at his side. "Ow, shit," he said. "Dig it, cat. Where'd you hear that?"

"Mod..." She was about to say "squad" but realized he was making fun of her.

"Go'on, Indian girl. It won't hurt you."

Kris grabbed the can and lighter and sucked in the weed. She burst out coughing.

"Can't handle the happy grass, huh?"

Kris shook her head as she hacked. "Shut up."

"You gonna try?" Jacob asked Sher.

"Nah," Sher said.

"I don't feel nothing," Kris said, crinkling her eyes.

"Try it again, chickie." Jacob laughed.

"You're the chick," she said, pushing the burnt marijuana around. Kristin smoked again.

She handed the can to Sher and lay on her back with her arm crooked behind her head. "Can't barely see the stars here."

"Yah," Sher said, tossing the can into the weeds.

"Oooo la," Jacob said.

"What day is it?" Kris laughed.

The boy rolled over. "Who cares?" Car lights streaked through the evening. "Got somewhere to go?"

"Do you need to go to a doctor or something?" Kristin asked as she stared into the sky. "They're like eyes up there. Watching us."

"Oh, yeah. The hospital. So they can call my mom and dad. Stick me in jail."

"For what?" Kristin asked. "Who? The fuzz?"

"The fuzz?" Jacob snorted. "That's what you hicks say up there? Wherever you're from."

"The fuzz!" Kris jumped up, and pretended to point a gun. She sang the opening song of *The Mod Squad*. "Hey! I know! We could be the Minneapolis Mod Squad! Sher, you be Pete. I'm Linc. Jacob, you're Julie."

"Pete?" Sher asked. "How am I Pete?"

"Julie!" Jacob protested, but secretly that was who he wanted to be.

"Yah! Julie. You're Julie!" Kris yelled. "And what did you do that the fuzz would throw you in the slammer, man?" She stood over him as if she were Linc holding a gun on a suspect.

The boy tapped his fingers on his thigh, still twitchy from the acid and beating. "Okay. I'll be Julie."

"Solid," Kris said imitating what Linc said on the hippie TV cop show. "What did you do?" Kristin asked. The people she knew who'd been to jail had been tossed behind bars for fighting drunk in Antwatin, or when the sheriff tipped his whiskey jug at lunch, the people Kris knew had been tossed in jail just for being Indian in Antwatin.

"Hey," Sher growled. "Cool it."

"Having fun?" Two white boys walked up on them.

Kristin turned her pretend gun on the boys.

"Looks like it," the tall boy said.

"Smells like it," the short one said. They laughed, their hair nearly the length of girls'.

The tall one stopped over Sher's legs. "*Hola.*" He nodded. He handed a flyer to Kris. "It's cool," he said. "Don't shoot. *No dispares. Chido, muchachas.* Catch you Saturday."

The boys strode back where they came from, headed north toward downtown Minneapolis. Cars spun overhead and hummed down the road below them.

"What'd he say?" Kris asked.

"He thinks you're Mexicans." Jacob laughed. "What's it say?"

"Gimme a sec," Kristin said, tilting the paper toward a streetlight.

The boy stared into the black maw of the sky. "C'mon. You Indian girls are so slow."

"Anti-war rally," Kristin read. "Saturday, August 20th at Loring

Park, 10 a.m. Get the U.S. out of Vietnam now."

"Meh," Jacob said. "Who cares."

"You don't?" Kristin folded it and slid it into her back pocket.

"I've got more pressing concerns right here." He tapped his chest.

"I wanna go," Kristin said. "It could be our first undercover assignment as the Minneapolis Mod Squad!" She imagined them running down alleys, chasing some child molester like they did in the show.

"There's lots of pigs." Jacob pretended to smoke a joint. "Lots and lots and lots of them. Lots. Sueys! You better watch out because they'll grab you up and no one will hear from you again. Ever." He regarded the dark sky, a violet streak slashing the horizon. "People disappear."

Fear shot through Kristin. Her dad used to say that he'd make her disappear if she ever told anyone what he did to her. Said it was the easiest thing in the world he could do out there in the middle of this godforsaken nowhere goddamn reservation, just like he'd done to her.... Then he would stop, knowing what he said would hit her like a Mack truck. By not finishing the sentence with "mother" he kept his daughter in a terror she could not name.

"Well, you're a hippie," Kris shot back, afraid and angry he wouldn't play along with her Mod Squad fantasy.

"Nah, I'm not into peace. I'm a fighter." Jacob punched the air. "Just like Mr. Muhammed Ali!"

"You look like a hippie," Kristin said, "in that tie-dye shirt." Violence, the offspring of fear, surged through her. "You look like, like that singer. What's his name?" she asked. "Bill. Bob. Yah, Bob. All that curly hair." Her words came out mean, the way she felt.

"You're a big talker," Sher jumped in. "And big talkers always got something to hide."

"Nah. Not me," Jacob said, oblivious to their anger. He put his arms above his head like he was cheering. "I'm the champ."

Sher stared at him, his body a shadow. Kristin pressed her eyelids together, the way she did when her father was on top of her. She felt crazy, like there were too many emotions to make sense of. She contained herself that way, to stop the feelings flooding through her so strong and huge they had to come from somewhere else, from someone else, from long ago, passed down through her family. She rolled over rocks, through prickly bright weed beds, until she went under, hit the silty bottom. Sometimes, it takes generations for a feeling to emerge. And when it does, it is ten-fold stronger.

Virginia, Minnesota, July 1969

Em knew how to be still. She knew how not to cry out. In Virginia, the summer that the white men put dusty boot prints on the moon's face, Em waited for the scratchings. She studied the door and the narrow, tiny room with one small window face level, that is, if she were able to stand. Formerly a girl servant's bedroom. It had just enough room for a body to lie prone with a foot deep chest of drawers (the matron's gowns she'd worn to East Coast and Duluth political functions hung over the servant girl as she slept). The dowels were long since absent, but the metal racks were still drilled into the walls.

Em thought of her mother. How the only time she cried out was when the hardest stories were told. She cried about the one when six, squalling Indian babies taken from Fond du Lac on their way to an orphanage in Cincinnati were tossed overboard into Lake Superior, off a grain cargo headed to Toledo. So the story went, something went wrong, according to the breed who reported the story to his relatives. He had been working the ship. He didn't know why, just that the ship's captain ordered a first mate to throw the Indian babies into the icy waters two miles out from Duluth. "View for ship first," the Scottish captain had said in his broken English. "Be of upmost positive actions not viewed. Wait two miles." He held up two fingers. "Two. Then," and he made a dumping movement with his arms.

However, the Scottish captain told the one and only Slav working a ship in America, who knew virtually no English, and mistook his two fingers to mean two minutes. The Slav waited five minutes as he thought it strange to do this in full sight of the lighthouse. Yet orders were orders, was what he'd been taught and, still in view of the lighthouse on the rock, the Slav tossed the infants one by one into the frothy waters of Lake Superior, the lake the size of Austria whose temperatures never rose above 55 degrees at the surface. Across the way, the lighthouse attendant witnessed what appeared to be sacks of flower being tossed into the waters, but upon closer inspection with his government-issued binoculars he saw what he believed to be the bald head and arms of an infant whose sack came loose. He told his wife, who told her sister, who passed it down the generations until decades later, a descendant saw an article in the *Duluth Tribune* while sipping cold press coffee one sunny August morning in 2013 on The Screaming Gull's patio that overlooked the giant shimmering lake. The article said Indian women and babies had been sold on the ships for decades and, because growing up she'd heard the story of what her great-great-great-grandfather saw, she believed it.

The breed Indian on the ship did and said nothing when he'd realized they were going to throw the Indian babies into the icy lake. He pretended he did not understand, turned his back to the captain and first mate, and went on deck to smoke with the other breeds on board. Later, when he told other Indians, no one asked what he did. Everyone knew what would have happened—he would have joined the infants in their frothy death-bed, perhaps dragged to the bottom by the lake monster. A terrible way to die, because of the spirits in the great lake.

Em was young when she first heard that story, visiting relatives out in the bush. Her nieces, Sher and Kristin, just babies, lay sleeping next to her, their hot bodies tangled together, their breaths making soft, white clouds in the chilled room. Em's cry alerted her mother and auntie that she'd heard, her cry pushed their talk to a cousin's eighth-grade son who'd made Antwatin's high school track team. "That boy can run," Em's auntie said, and then moved to the blanket, quick as a shadow, and pulled it back a bit to look in on the girls. A wing of fire light flicked across the curved wall. Em shut her eyes but a moment before her auntie peered through the narrow opening. The babies stirred, but did not wake. Em's auntie returned to the bucket of potatoes they were peeling for the week. They shook their heads. "Six Indian babies," Em's mother said. Em's auntie shook her head no. There was no point to thinking on it. Em's auntie's thoughts on that subject ended. But Ethel's thoughts on it did not end. She did not know how to make them stop. She dropped her head and sucked back tears, as she did not want to show more emotion. The knife and yellow potato flesh blurred, and blood smudged the skin of the next potato she picked.

Em listened to Sher and Kris's sweet exhales, felt the innocence and love that surrounded them. She'd cared for them like a mother, a big sister, an auntie. Em turned onto her belly and wrapped one arm around the girls, listening to their breath, to the murmurings of her family in the other room, to the beat of her heart pounding through the thin blankets into the cold, hard earth.

On the floor in Virginia, years after the story about the six babies, her body pressed against the cold hard floor, Em thought of her people, shipped off, stolen, sold, traded. Their bodies poisoned by disease. So many dead. Em hardened herself. She must survive to get back to the girls, especially Kris, her sister's motherless child. She sealed off the pain of a broken cheek bone. She prepared herself to be sold off. She would not cry out.

* * *

The girls and boy huddled next to the cement outcropping. Sher lay on her side, the heat from the cement against her back. The stems of the grasses in front of her, all around her, were enlarged. They grew into trees in a forest, her perception altered from a contact high. She traveled among them—enormous white pines, whorled red oaks, slim cedars. Low slung ferns, each individual leaf moving like the smooth-skinned, neon-green caterpillars that dropped from the treetops every spring and summer back home. On the farm. The rez. Her family. Her people. Sher felt she was falling. She grabbed the weeds and pulled, cutting her hands. Kristin murmured and moved in her sleep, at odds with the demons her father planted in her. The boy made a yelping sound and then another low moan as he twisted too sharply in his sleep setting off the pain in his ribs. Sher listened to them as she studied her hands in the moonlight. She had her grandmother's fingers and thumbs—broad nails and double-jointed thumbs. Her grandmother was with her, in her, part of her. And her grandmother's grandmother. They lived in her, in Kris, through them both. The weeds were thick and tough and scaly like the ones on the farm. The memory of their grandmothers, the weeds, calmed her, rooted her.

Sher wiped her hands on her jeans, remembered her mother's advice about doing laundry, about how bloodstains are hard to get out so you should avoid washing them in warm water. Her mother, with whom she'd never been close. Her father said she'd changed drastically from being around those church people in Antwatin, but Sher never remembered her being any other way. Sher placed the palms of her hands on the slanted cement outcropping, leaving an outline of her hands in blood. Warm and flat is what Sher's mind registered. Warm and flat, the other two yelping in their sleeps like whelping pups and Sher's mother at home, on the farm, as she had returned after Sher's father died. Sher left a note under Sher's pillow so that her mother would not see it for a few days. Maybe think she was at Kris's. "I have to leave, Sher." She could imagine her mother telling her childhood friend, Wanda, or her cousins when she ran into them at the grocery store: "Cold. That girl was always cold. Nothing normal about a girl so cold toward her own mother. A girl so like a boy."

* * *

The listing, early morning rush hour traffic woke Sher. The shock of her surroundings hit her like a bucket of cold water. Kristin slept below her and the boy above her. One of Sher's boots lay on its side in the weeds. The sky was gray and sunless. Sher studied the large church to the right—its spire three stories high and tapered like a medieval sword—and the string of storefronts in front of her and the squat brick apartment buildings to the left. She had nothing to do and nowhere to go. No chores. No school. No home. No bed. Kristin stirred. Sher smelled her armpits and sank back down, stinking worse than after a day of baling in the hot sun.

"You get used to it," Jacob said behind her.

"Suppose."

"You Indians don't talk very much, do you?" Jacob yawned.

"Guess not," Sher said and thought of saying 'least not around you,' but decided to leave it at that.

Kristin woke.

"You're country girls, that's easy to see." Jacob sat up and twisted his ribs. "Ow. Shit." He grabbed at his side. "You're prime property out here, do you know that?"

Sher studied the scratches on her hands that had bled so ferociously the night before.

Her silence made Jacob angrier. "Youse dog meat out here," he blurted, lapsing into how his Brooklyn grandparents said "you."

"It's always good when your enemy underestimates you," Kristin said. She had read about wars and liked to imagine herself a warrior. Her grandfather encouraged her reading and flights of fantasy by telling wartime tales of his own. She would read about a general's strategy and then tell her grandfather. He would smoke, listen intently, adding in an "oh" and "ah" on occasion. When she finished, he'd say, "Oh, yah. Good story, my girl. Say, that reminds me. This one time twenty or even thirty Germans, but maybe even more as you know it was a long time ago, came up over the hill early one morning, smelling so bad like sauerkraut, stinky cabbage, their round little helmets too big on their heads and bobbing around so they looked like birds pecking at food. You know how that was. I jumped up, all alone, just me because the rest of the regiment were sound asleep. The sky there was all gray and there wasn't any green grass or trees for as far as you could see—just gray, everything was about death over there, no life at all, and then those Krauts were about to bayonet all of us, and since I didn't have time to wake anyone, I let out my secret Indian war whoop that I patented with the government right when I got called up to the army; I got the papers right here." And he'd pat the breast pocket of his cotton shirt. "That was the first thing I did because you know if you know how the government steals, maybe here," and he'd pat his back jean pocket. "Oh well, it's somewhere around here. Paper. You know how important that is. Anyway, when I find it, I will show you. So when I saw those bird heads coming my way, I yelled *Ai yai yai yai* and off those Krauts ran back where they came from probably all the way to Berlin 'cause we never seen them again."

He stuffed a corn-cob pipe with more tobacco and lit up, a white man's pipe, as he called them. "And then I became the US government's best kept secret weapon." He paused and puffed out smoke rings. "The government snuck me from camp to camp to let loose on enemy ear-drums my patented war whoop." He pointed the stem at Kris. "But you will never read about me in any book, my girl." He blew more smoke rings and studied his granddaughter, who was mesmerized by his story, her eyes glossy and distant from the scene she saw in her mind. "Top secret." He set the pipe on his knee. "Books, my girl, are okay. They tell good stories. But there's always more to it than what they got written in them."

* * *

"What's that supposed to mean?" Jacob's face twitched. "Huh?"
The girls said nothing.
"What's that supposed to mean?" Jacob's voice rose.
The girls said nothing.
"Shit." Jacob tossed a pebble.
A few minutes passed. Sher tugged on her boot.
"Why can't you talk more?" Jacob pulled on a curl.

"'Cause we're Indian," she said, her words wet with sarcasm. "What're you?"

"Who me?" Jacob asked. He jumped up and put his palms on his chest. "What do you mean what am I?"

The girls said nothing.

"What do you mean what am I?" Jacob repeated and tapped his chest with his fingers. "What? How can you tell?"

The girls said nothing.

"Oh," Jacob grabbed at his hair. "That's it. Well, I'm Dylan, *a* Dylan, that's what I am."

The girls said nothing.

"I'm Bob Dylan," Jacob said and sat down abruptly. "His cousin, really. Almost him. Yeah, I'm Bob Dylan's cousin." He turned sideways. "My profile. Same."

"Yah, sure," Sher said, double-tying her boot and watching a line of people walk into the church off to the right. "And I'm Cher."

"And I'm Sonny," Kristin said. *A* Sonny.

Kristin and Sher burst into laughter.

"You dumb Indians. I'm Jewish."

The girls stopped laughing. Neither had met a Jewish person. They just thought he was a funny-looking, curly-headed white boy.

"So that's why you say 'youse.'" Kri said. "I never heard any white person say 'youse' before."

"So's Dylan. Jews. We're Jews. Didn't you know?" he frowned. "*Goys*."

The girls and boy sat in silence, the boy holding his breath, his face set to anger to keep from crying.

"Did your family die?" Kristin hesitated. Her grandfather never talked straight about what he actually did in the war, but she knew, of course, they were fighting for the Jews. When Kristin asked him whether he'd seen any of the naked, starving people he immediately smelled war the way he knew it—gasoline and oil mostly. He'd been a mechanic, but he had also been close to the front on several occasions and twice smelled burning fat and flesh, the acrid overwhelm of gunpowder, and then like a tail whipping in at the end to protect him from the horror—the comforting whiff of *Lucky Strike!* the brand the government rationed to the soldiers. Then he adjusted himself to his granddaughter sitting in front of him, changed the subject, or made up another story.

"Gawd!" Jacob shouted. "My family is from Brooklyn. As in New York. U S of A. Hearda that before?" He slipped into a heavy New York accent. "I know nothing about those, those skinny Jews." And his mind glanced upon his two surviving grandparents, and their oddities—strange outbursts and Polish accents—and it skipped over the other two grandparents he'd never met because they died in the European camps until his mind settled comfortably on the lie he'd just told, perched there like a hawk grasping a struggling squirrel in one claw.

They sat in silence.

"You're going to drive me crazy," Jacob said, tossing guilt for disowning his family disguised as anger at the girls.

Sher was now intent on the people going into the church. The church door shut and no one entered for a few minutes. Then an old white lady laboriously pulled it open. Sher saw the door did not automatically lock.

The boy walked off into the weeds, his balance jagging to the right and left as he acclimated to his body after being high for days.

"Where's he going?" Kristin rolled on her side. The bruises on her face were smaller and mottled gray like the soft underbelly of the ducks on the farm.

"Don't know."

"Is he coming back?"

"Didn't say."

"That's sad about all those Jews who died."

"Yah." Sher rolled up her sweatshirt she used as a pillow and put it in the pack. "I've got to pee." Too many people were about for her to urinate crouched down in weeds or a bush.

"Starved and gassed."

"Yah." Sher wasn't one to set long on bad news. "Let's get some food." Sher nodded at Burch's Pharmacy as she slung on the pack. "Then use a bathroom over at the church." She pointed her lips toward the church.

They walked down the short grassy bank, crossed Hennepin Avenue, and cut south for a block. Sher opened the screen door that was cut across the corner of the building. She caught the door behind her back, holding it for Kris.

The middle-aged white man behind the counter looked up. "Going to be another blister today."

"Yes, sir," Sher said as she and Kristin stepped inside.

"Can I help you girls?"

"No sir. Just looking."

"All right then." The man glanced at Sher again—it was not common to see Indians that far west on Franklin. He bent down, searching the shelves below the counter for the key to his garage he'd misplaced a week ago.

Kris split off down a far aisle. Sher pointed at the white paper packages of hot peanuts stacked in neat rows in a glass fish tank under a bright light—the same kind of lights her dad had used to keep the chicks warm in the barn.

"I'll have one of these, sir," Sher said.

"Small or large?" the man asked as he stood on his creaky knees.

"How much?"

"Nickel for the small and nine for the large. Twice as big." The man lifted the lid in the back of the peanut machine. "Big one is the best deal."

Sher nodded. "Give me a small and two eggs."

The man pulled out a small white paper bag stuffed with hot salted peanuts, rolled the top of the bag over and placed that on the counter. He turned his back and picked out two hard boiled eggs from a red plastic basket lined with a cotton napkin. "From around here?" he asked.

"No," Sher said.

He nodded. "Antwatin?"

Sher nodded, despite her desire to not let anyone know where they came from. Didn't make sense to deny it here. He wasn't a threat.

He set the eggs on the counter. "Cloquet," he said. "Grew up on a farm there. Moved here in '53." He watched Kristin leave. "This it?" he said to Sher, tapping the peanuts.

"Yah."

The man rang up the sale. The numbers popped up on the cash register. Sher gave him a dollar.

"Good day." He handed Sher her change. "I always thought you Indians got the short end of the stick."

Sher nodded, grabbed the peanuts and the two hard boiled eggs, and pushed through the screen door cut across the corner of the building. She always wondered why they built doors like that.

"Set."

Kristin nodded. The girls walked toward the church. When they cleared the sight of Burch Pharmacy's pane glass window, Kristin pulled out two cans of RC.

Sher felt uneasy. The girls had been raised to never steal. They were taught to never even touch another person's things unless invited to do so.

"Here." Kris pushed the cola into Sher's arm. "I know. Look at how much he's got though."

Sher took the pop.

"We gotta do what we gotta do."

"Suppose," Sher said, but felt guilty.

The girls gulped the cola in between popping peanuts, and then ate the eggs in big bites.

"Feel better."

"Yah," Sher set her empty can on the ledge of a window to a hair salon. "Now I really got to pee."

"Surprise!" Kristin jumped in front of Sher. "Here." Kristin pulled out a toothbrush from the waist of her jeans and held it up in front of Sher's face.

"Okay," Sher said.

Kris pretended to brush her teeth. "I know, Sher," Kris said. "But we gotta brush our teeth."

"Suppose," Sher said.

"Never thought I'd be so happy to have a toothbrush." Kristin poked Sher's stomach with the toothbrush. "C'mon."

"Okay." Sher grabbed the toothbrush from her cousin. "It'll be good to get our teethies brushed," she said, using the word for 'teeth' their auntie Em used when they were little.

"Think we'll ever see her again?" Kris asked.

Sher shrugged. Her sadness prevented her from using words.

The girls headed toward the church with its promises of clean toilets and running water. They crossed Hennepin Avenue, jumped over the concrete outcropping, and then jogged under the freeway where they had slept the night before. They cut down a short slope under a row of tall pine trees. Sher lost her balance on a pine cone and slipped down the slope.

"Shoot," she said, as she regained her balance. A fresh shot of pain burned up her ankle.

"Okay?" Kristin asked.

"Yah." Sher stood on her good leg.

A white woman parked a red Mercury. The girls hurried to avoid interacting with her. In a matter of seconds, they were inside the cool dark church, trying to act as if they were not two vagrants on the lookout for a bathroom and a sink.

The girls peed and bathed using the powdered soap above the sink. Sher washed her jeans and draped them over the radiator. The jeans dripped through the radiator onto the floor, making two puddles the size of baseballs. A chalky film developed in patches on the blue denim.

"Kris," Sher said.

"Yah?" Kristin grimaced into the mirror. She'd brushed her teeth using the chalky soap.

"Do you miss the farm?"

"Sometimes."

"I'm trying to remember it. I'm afraid I'm going to forget it. The past, the farm, my dad, Grandpa and Grandma. Em."

"I wish I could. Not your dad, or Grandpa and Grandma and Em. Just the rest."

"I know what you mean. Not me, though. It's only been a few days," Sher pulled her knees to her chest. "And I feel like it's been a year."

"Yah." Kristin combed her hair with her fingers. She shrunk down in age, like she did sometimes with Sher, her big cousin who always protected her. "Know what I want to be maybe?"

"What?"

"A hippie. Like Bob Dylan. He's a hippie, right? I didn't know he was Jewish. Did you?" Kris smacked her lips. They were dry. She turned on the faucet and drank from it. "Those people from the war that Grandpa talked about sometimes. He said they did the same things to us. Only fifty or sixty years ago." She turned to look at Sher but didn't let her answer. "Remember how he said that. He was glad to fight because Americans did the same things to us that the Germans did to Jews? His grandpa had to hide his family in the woods from soldiers. Remember? Down at Mille Lacs." Kristin turned back to the mirror.

Sher watched her cousin. She reminded her of Auntie Em sometimes—their energy. Their anger. How sometimes their thoughts moved so fast. But then Kris became like this sometimes. A little girl. Little Kris.

Kris shook her hair. She sang a few lines from "Me and Bobby McGee," and then abruptly stopped singing, and stared at Sher in the mirror.

Sher was used to her changes in moods. "You sound just like her," Sher said.

Kris's face and eyes rounded.

Sher knew she was talking with 'Little Kris.' "Real good," Sher nodded.

Kris spun a full circle and took another drink from the sink. She sang "The Beat Goes On." "Remember all the times we watched Sonny and Cher with Grandma? The only Indian lady we seen beside the one on the butter." Kris sang a few more lines from the song. "It's just you and me now, kid." Kris found Sher's eyes in the mirror and grinned.

Sher nodded. It wasn't just the two of them, but it was best to give Kris space when she got like this. Sher assumed her mother had returned to the farm after her dad died because she, Sher, Jack, Kris, and Em—if still alive—inherited the farm. Thaddeus had not divorced her, still believing she would come back one day to her family, to being Indian. But the roots of shame were deep in Sher's mother. Having been raised by white foster parents outside Aitkin, she identified more with white people and the sliver of white ancestry in her own biological family than with being Indian. She'd been taught Indian ways were wrong. Sher never understood why she even married her dad. Now Sher's brother and the boys he hired right out of high school ran the farm. He'd pushed Sher out—forcing her to stay inside and cook with their mother. Sher did not like cooking and was not good at it. "We'll teach her," her mother said when her brother made a face over Sher's bad-tasting mac. "She'll become a proper girl soon enough." Sher didn't know how her brother turned out like many of the men around Antwatin and Goodhue, Indian and white and mixed, rude and spiteful and thinking women and girls inferior. Sher did not know why Jack was so different from her dad and papa. She felt a longing so deep for her father and grandfather that she thought she would cry.

"Sher."

"Huh."

"What do you think?"

Sher pushed her back into the wall. "About what."

"My singing. Do you think I can make it?"

"Sure Kris. Why not? Yah," she said and remembered that was what her father had said to her as a little girl when she told him she wanted to be a rodeo cowboy and her brother had laughed and said girls can't be cowboy rodeo riders. "My girl," he had said, "I don't see why not."

Kris sang Janis Joplin again. Sher sat bare bottom on the octagon tile floor. The girls had nowhere to go.

* * *

Virginia, Minnesota, July 1969

"Girl." A man's voice woke Em.

Her eyelids fluttered. Colors floated.

"Holay. She dead?" Another man's voice asked, his lyrical accent unmistakenly Indian.

Em's cheek was flat to the floor. As she regained consciousness, pain struck like lightning. The colors turned to shapes—the black tip of a man's loafer, dirty wood floor, scuffed walnut baseboard trim. She shut her eyes.

The black shoe nudged her hips.

Em made no sound, no movement.

"Sit her up," the first man said. "She's playing possum. Worth nothing if she chokes."

A white man, Em thought.

One of the men grabbed her armpits and propped her against the wall. She let her head loll despite the screaming pain. Her head felt like a melon dropped on concrete. He kicked her. For a moment, she was four and at the farm with her mother as they picked cantaloupe grown from seeds some Germans had given them for milk, only to find them smashed against the backside of the barn later that afternoon—their pinkish orange flesh split open and wet to the world. Three Indian brothers and their sister returned with their grandmother that evening to apologize for the children's prank and remove the burst cantaloupe flesh and rind to the woods where Em's mom said, "At least the critters will enjoy it."

"You sure she's alive?" the Indian asked.

"Let's see," the white man replied.

Water hit her chest. Em held her face still.

"Not gonna react, huh squaw?" The white man grasped her jaw

as if she were a dog about to get a pill, tipped her head back, and poured water down her throat.

Em gagged.

"Yeah." He laughed. "Still worth something."

* * *

The girls walked toward the Foshay Tower, the sun on them. At a pay phone outside a tavern Sher slid in her dime and dialed Carla's number. The line rang. And rang. No one answered. "She'll be home soon enough. Maybe tonight."

"Yah," Kristin said, and threw a small gray rock down the sidewalk as if she were skipping it across a pond. It settled in a crack.

The girls walked the sidewalks of Loring Park. The morning heat crept out of the cement. Sher's boot, hot and heavy, pressed the knife into her sore ankle. Kristin whistled the popular songs of the day over the rising and falling buzzsaw of the crickets, punctured occasionally by a slamming screen door, a woman yelling at her children, and the thrum of a passing car.

Kris sang "Spinning Wheel" by Blood, Sweat & Tears. She pointed at an imaginary crowd.

"Don't stay in the bad stuff," Sher said, in response to the lyrics.

Kris knew those were her grandfather's words. A bolt of jealousy shot through her. Sher lived his words. But Kris tended toward their auntie Em, who one day left for good. Kris and Sher were little then, but they knew something had happened in town to some Indian boys. Em came home fired up, wanting to take the truck and go after the white kids who hurt the boys. She jawed at her dad in the house as he moved from room to room, listening to her but not responding, until finally he trotted out to a car he'd been working on next to the barn's gray, paint-stripped maw.

Em, Sher, and Kris followed the old man. Sher and Kris stood in the shadow of the barn, watching. "Take it easy," Em's dad told her. He spit on the hood of a white man's car parked next to the barn. "We all feel it." He yanked a hanky from his back pocket and polished the smudge off the hood of the car. He'd fixed it last week. The motor hadn't idled right. Now he was waiting for the man to pick up the car, make good on his promise to pay "the old Indian mechanic," as the white men called him. Clarence served in World War II as a mechanic, eventually specializing in fixing Cushman Airborne scooters dropped by parachutes with Army troops behind enemy lines. He could fix anything with an engine, thanks to being a superior student at a boarding school, where superior young Indian boys, as the vicar referred to his "special boys," were taught mechanical skills. On Antwatin, men—white and Indian—came from all over, other counties even, to have him work on their vehicles.

Once, when the Antwatin white mechanic died unexpectedly in a hunting accident, the county hired Clarence to fix its fire engine and black and white squad car named Bessie until they could hire another mechanic—a white one. But he knew, one check-mark in the wrong box could stoke the engine that would end with him in jail, or hauled off to an asylum a state over, or the one in St. Peter, Minnesota, where they sent Indians from all over the state and Canada, too. Or maybe he would just disappear, his remains pushed over the edge of a fishing boat, weighted down with a concrete block or a rusty anchor tied to his waist. Indian trumped World War II vet, Indian trumped everything. But Clarence, he was always hedging being Indian, pushing a bit here and a bit there—fixing their machines, never drinking (not since he was twenty-two), sharing food with poor whites too, so as to appear occasionally on the edges of the white man's world in a good way. So they wouldn't suspect, so they wouldn't come looking for what ran underground, between the barn and the house, chilled and damp in the summer, frozen in the winter.

When the welfare ladies were on the farm, Clarence tossed hay at the edge of the barn or shoveled manure or puttered on an engine often just screwing on and off the oil cap or leaning down under the hood pretending to look at something, as he could not concentrate to do any real mechanical work while they were there. He tossed, shoveled, and puttered where they could see him and he could see them, always avoiding their eyes. He let them think whatever they thought about him. He did not care, just as long as they left without the children.

Once they left Clarence would say in English with his lilting Indian accent, "Those white ladies sure do know how to dress. Ho wah! Look at them! Give them some Indian shoes next time," he'd laugh, "so no one mistakes them for a goat." Of course, he had to ignore the fact that he stood in shoes with hard heels and laces made of cord, not soft brain tanned deer hide. But he joked anyway, knowing there wasn't much he could do to stop them, fearing them even, just a little, in the way one holds breath, because of what their pens could make happen. After all, they'd taken plenty of family. Clarence and his wife, included. They were the lucky ones because they returned after the boarding schools. But many had never been recovered, their families did not know where they were, if they were even still alive. They only spoke of this in Indian, among adults. They put tobacco out for the lost Indian children, in the woods, at the base of a pine tree tall as a silo, where no one would see—not whites, not even their own children.

The Brauns kept many things from their grandchildren—teaching only bits of Indian language and ceremonies to them. They didn't discuss their childhoods in the boarding schools, those who'd disappeared, and what ran underground between the farm and the barn. Their plan was to educate their children and grandchildren once they were out of school, and less likely to accidentally tell or be overheard by a teacher or student, and old enough to have established feeling good about being Indian as they could in a world that was against them. Then they would pass down their teachings so the link would not be broken, so Indians would not disappear, would not be Indian in name only.

But it wasn't just the children to be concerned about—an old Indian like him, Clarence knew, could also be dragged off. He'd heard of it—a Canadian Indian brought all the way down to St. Peter Asylum for the Criminally Insane in southern Minnesota. No one knew why they brought him there, across the white man's border and over all those miles, past all those other mental pens, or why they'd taken him in the first place. Clarence had seen it done. His uncle for getting hot with a white man over some used tires. A sleeping neighbor, dragged out of his tar shack in his underwear. No one even knew what he'd been accused of. An old drunk Ojibwe Indian at a powwow in a full feather Sioux headdress he'd won while on a gambling spree in South Dakota, yelling in Indian at the white men who'd walked on Indian land one too many times for the old man to keep silent. The BIA agents tore off the headdress in the ensuing fight to subdue the old man, throwing it on the ground where a Canadian Ojibwe Indian snatched it up, tucked it away in her blankets to get back across the border, and traded it for cigarettes with a mixed shopkeeper just off her reservation, which was how the Sioux headdress came to reside in a locked glass case at Beauchamps Dry Goods in Thunder Bay.

* * *

"Is he gonna even pay you for all your work?" Em yelled above the braying and shuffling of the horse, three cows, nine chickens, one rooster, and eleven pigs milling in and around the barn. She slapped the tail fin. "You let this white man take advantage of you. They owe us!" she shouted, pointing at her chest. "We don't owe them."

Her father wiped down the tail fin. "Maybe. But when people need help, it doesn't matter, the color of their skin. It's how they behave. That's how I was taught." He kept his head down, his eyes away from his daughter. His papa, his granddad, used to say angry people were crazy. Don't look at them. "That's how they thought, saw things. Those old Indians." He shook out his hanky, adjusted the brim of his old timey round hat, black with a wide rim all around. It had been his father's, and he preferred it over a baseball hat like most men—white and Indian—on the rez wore now. But he only wore it on the farm, in the sugar bush, and ricing.

Em's pain and rage over the way white people treated Indians collided with her pain about Josie's disappearance, and her guilt for being angry with Josie for leaving Em for a man who, they all knew, killed Josie. Em exploded. "Why didn't you stop him?" she yelled at her father. "Where were youse, where were all your old time Indians when Jo...." She glanced at Kris. "When she needed them?"

Clarence focused on the car. He found one small smudge on the taillight. He wiped it clean. "Get rid of the anger, my girl. Put it down and leave it, even if it is whites." Quick as a snap, his hands flew down his chest and thighs, brushing her anger off him. He fluttered the gray hanky like a bird wing over his body, mopped his forehead and neck. Clarence settled his eyes on a snippet of tan, winding road visible through the treetops and corn crops. "Have a hold on yourself." He glanced at Em, his daughter, a strong, young Indian woman, seething with hurt and anger next to the car, her fists tight to her sides. His granddaughters in the shadows, not moving, watching, and, he hoped, learning. "Don't let them take your spirit too. Then," he said, folding his hanky and slipping it in his back pocket, "they will have everything."

Em sucked her breath.

"Our way is hard. Harder than theirs." He rubbed his chin. "It's easy to get mad, let it run you. Like they do." He adjusted his hat. "Their feelings run them all over, like those chickens there." He pointed at two of their reddish-brown hens strutting through the tall grass next to the barn, hoping Em would see herself in them.

Em was infuriated that he polished the car, that he worked for white men, that half the time they didn't pay him for his work, or bartered, or promised to barter and then didn't give him anything at all. Even the poorest Indian who came to him with a broken-down car or run-over bicycle they'd found in the town dump gave him something in return, dressed rabbits or cooled cornbread wrapped in flour sack towels or their government cheese ration, which meant their family would go without. Indians never even visited other Indians without bringing some gift. They didn't take without giving.

"I'd rather starve," she spit. "Those kids hurt bad. I saw one. He's all cut up. Just for being Indian." She stayed with the anger so she would not sob.

Her father nodded.

Em looked at the girls, her beautiful beloved nieces, just little, now lined up along the barn wall, Kris's hands behind her back, Sher's head hanging toward the dirt. Thin white lines of sun shone through the cracks in the barn walls, casting soft stripes on and around the girls. "I'd rather spend every second hunting and fishing," she said, taking them into consideration. "I'd never let any white man take advantage of me. I'll never depend on them." She sputtered out of years of seeing whites humiliate Indians, out of years of pain and rage from the times a white janitor at Antwatin Elementary School pushed his fingers deep inside her in the mop closet.

She glanced at her father, who was looking off, away from her. Staring at the road. He would not look at her. She knew this was meant to give her space, meant to not embarrass her, meant to not take her emotions into him, but it enraged her further as if it highlighted her bad behavior, how she'd strayed from Indian ways, how "white" she and other Indians her age were becoming. She overheard the old ones say that, privately, to each other. "These young Indians might as well be white, the way they act. Just like them white kids."

Her anger and frustration rode over her. How could she be Indian if she had to go to school, live in the white world? She couldn't stay out in the bush like some who hid out there. How could she live Indian in a world that destroyed Indian? "Those days are gone." She lashed out with a rage far larger than what she felt over her father helping whites. Her anger rose like the water in the farm's well, dug by hand by the Finns so long ago.

Clarence turned his attention to the rooster strutting about the barn, pecking at pebbles. Em choked back a cry, those words hurting her more than they hurt him, because for him, those days were not gone. He still lived them. Even if he was on a farm, using white man's tools, giving his children and grandchildren raw cow milk every morning. In his heart and in his ways, he lived those days. They were alive in him. And he wanted, more than anything, to keep them alive in his children and grandchildren.

Em, overcome by her emotions and unable to think, stalked into the barn. She stomped through the barn, kicked a bucket, and decided to leave. "Outta here!" she yelled from the barn's wide-open double door, as it spit her out into the garish day. "I won't be back." She did not mean what she said. She figured she'd be home for a late supper her mom would leave cold on the kitchen table for her, but those were her words. When she said them, she'd forgotten what she'd been told by the old ones—words have power. Great power. Only say what you mean.

Their one-eyed Holstein, Ben, stomped her hind foot. Swished her tail. A hen clucked. Another pecked at a spider. A cat licked its hind leg. Em stomped across the dirt and grass. Slapped her hands together. Rage flooded her.

She will need all that anger, Clarence thought, for where she is going.

Em's intention was to scrounge up a few beers, find the other young Indians she hung with so they could give the white kids pay-back. What she did not know, could not know that spring day she set off on her own, intending to stay out late to scare her parents, was that by helping whites her father held onto not only the way he'd been taught, but also hedged the family's survival within the town and the reservation. Indians were not supposed to have farms. Few did. And whites wanted those few farms, too. Her family's survival meant others survived too—people Em did not know about—could not know about until she grew older and could control her emotions. Her father would not tell her until she was ready. When anger sparked in him, he did not allow it to flame or turn into a slow burn. Not ever. It was not the way he'd been taught, not the way he'd grown. Anger had raged inside him for a time, after the war—when he drank, but he controlled it so that his spirit returned to how it was born—dancing. For Em, the heat burned so hot it threatened to scorch what she most loved.

* * *

The girls passed the day in the shade of a stairwell near the church where they slept their first night in the city. The day turned into a blister. Sher's ankle swelled from the heat and the twist on the pine cone. Kristin fetched a bag of ice, tuna sandwich, pile of potato salad, and sweating bottle of Sunkist. Sher didn't ask how she got it. The girls split the food and drink, while watching the feet of those who passed by on the sidewalk. They played word games in the air, wishing they'd kept the pad of paper and pencil Kristin got on the bus trip into the city. They left once to go to the bathroom in a drugstore where Sher bought a dime's worth of Seven Up candy bars and filled up the bag Kris had found days ago with water. After the drugstore, they remained in the stairwell, occasionally making room for various men and one woman who descended off the sidewalk into the stairwell. They opened the heavy dark wood door behind the girls with a click of their keys.

Around two o'clock one of men who had entered the church returned to the stairwell. "Girls," he said, squinting at the street. "We need you to move on now." He jangled coins in his pant pocket, never meeting the eyes of the two homeless Indian girls sitting in his church's stairwell. He'd discussed this with the others inside. He'd said he didn't ask for money during the sermon every week to house stray Indians in the stairwell.

The girls moved a block down, descending into the damp stairwell of a three-story brick apartment building, chunks of mortar missing in spots where they could have slipped their hands in sideways. A white teenage boy, his hair shaggy like the Beatles, exited the building. Before he shut the door, Sher glimpsed wine-colored, matted carpeting, and yellowed walls with heavy black marks as if someone had dragged the corner of their sofa against the wall many times.

Kris licked chocolate off her fingers. "Look at that, Sher," she said, reading the package. "Made in St. Paul by Pearson's Candy Company. Maybe we could get a job there."

"Maybe."

They drank the water in the bag.

A scraggly elm sapling grew out of the sidewalk, struggling to produce a handful of leaves. The heat and the elm transported her to the woods she'd first run through when she was seven. Waking tangled in sheets on an unusually hot June morning, the girl stumbled onto the porch. Her spirit had not completely returned from another place. Seeing the backside of her grandma as she looked out over the farm, Sher ran. She sprinted barefoot over the dirt farmyard in the T-shirt and boxers she slept in. Sher did not know why she ran. She'd woke on fire from a dream she did not remember. Her grandma turned to watch her eldest grandchild run into the woods. She lit a cigarette and asked the *mishoomis*—the trees—to help the young girl with the burden of the past that she carried, passed down through blood. *Animoosh* raised from his place next to the barn. The girl and dog hit the narrow trail her family used for hundreds of years to find medicines among the oaks and pines and swamps.

The dirt path in the woods was cool and damp. The Indian girl and her dog ran and ran, dodging tree roots, cutting east and west. Jumping over rocks. The trees were thick and massive, part of the old growth forest that covered one billion acres before the English. Their straight tall trunks had been coveted by the English military for use as ship masts, which made it possible for the English to conquer half the world. Squirrels, sparrows and chickadees, mice, woodpeckers, and a bobcat peering from a hollow tree watched the girl and dog. The sun lit up patches of leaves, the sides of trunks, the edge of rocks, ferns, and the forest floor. Sher breathed hard. Her spirit lightened. Her legs became heavy, her feet covered in dirt. She stopped in a ray of sun, looked upward, and became blinded by the brightness. *Animoosh* panted beside her. He licked a spot where a cherry sucker had dried to her calf. The young girl's lungs heaved. In her moment of blindness, in the middle of the Standing People, the past fell off her. She remained balanced.

* * *

The day passed to evening.

"I'm bored," Kris said.

Sher nodded.

"I thought it would be...I don't know...different."

Eventually the sun dropped off and the moon rose, a half crescent illuminating the cheeks and foreheads of the girls with a pale white light.

"Think they really got there," Kris asked. "Or was it just a trick like grandma said?"

"Not a man up there," their grandfather would say. "See the ears. There?" His hand would move as if he were pulling on a long, slim rabbit ear from the base to the tip. But their grandmother would say it wasn't a rabbit, the moon was a woman, our grandmother. "That rabbit business from one of those other Indians at that school," she'd say to her husband. "Oh, yah maybe," he'd say. "But I still see it. The tail. There," he'd point with his lips. And then he'd smile, thinking of his friend from the picture Sher had found in the barn showing him the rabbit in the moon all those years ago. "Your grandmother is right," he'd concede to his wife. "Now I remember right. The moon is our grandmother. Rabbit was how their people saw it." But then, the next time they all sat together under the moon, he'd say the same thing over again. A rabbit.

"Dunno," Sher said, measuring the moon with her fingers. A million miles away, her grandfather always said, and big as a quarter tonight. Or a dime, or a half dollar depending on the month. "A nickel tonight," Sher said.

"Yah," Kris said. "It's berry moon, right? Or strawberry moon?"

"Berry. I think."

Around midnight a large white woman opened the door and stood in the stairwell, light shining from behind, her dark hair wrapped around Tab cans. "Ain't a good place for you girls to sit," she said, barefooted and wearing a baggy white men's T-shirt, and dark blue shorts, barely visible beneath the long T-shirt. An edge in her voice made them pick themselves up right off. The woman stood with her hands on her hips watching the girls walk away, the cans reflecting million-year-old moonlight across the streetscape.

Sher and Kristin headed north toward the section of Hennepin Avenue where they'd eaten their first night in the city.

"Where we going?" Kristin grabbed Sher's hand.

Sher paused. She felt Kris's panic. "Back to the church?"

"Which way?" Kristin stopped, surrounded by huge buildings, her breath short.

Sher's eyes settled on Kristin, the bruises now splotches beneath the moon, her chest heaving. She reminded Sher of the time she and her dad had seen a quarter horse after it was forced to run a mile race at the County Fairgrounds. The horse died, Sher remembered. "Run too hard," Sher's dad said, shaking his head. "A real pity."

"You won't leave me, right?"

"I won't."

"Sher?" Kris said, overcome by fear.

"Just you and me now, cuz," Sher said, wrapping her arm around Kris. "We got each other."

The girls cut east at Hennepin, their view of the street ahead of them obscured by a van. Two cop cars whistled past the girls, their lights flashing. An ambulance screamed behind it, lighting up the streets and buildings in revolving blues and reds so bright it was if as day had broke.

In seconds, the vehicles were on the next block and the girls were on the other side of the van. People shouted, huddled around something on the sidewalk—a dog, a deer—popped into the girls' minds, forgetting they were in the city. The cop car and ambulance settled in. Their wailing ended, but the lights continued to rotate between the buildings, swinging across the crowd's faces contorting with anger and fear, roping them all in tighter and tighter.

Bust his head and *I didn't do it, man—you gotta believe me* and *Lorraine! She alright?* and *It was someone else, man. He ran that way.*

A white woman lay on her back, blood pooling beneath her shoulders and hair. Her eyes were wild and desperate like a deer just before it died. A woman next to her screamed. Her wail rose up, overtaking the city and its sounds and smells and the noises of the crowd.

"Jessie," the woman sobbed as a cop pulled her away.

"Stand back," he ordered.

She fell onto the sidewalk.

A Black man yelled, "It wasn't me! Me and my chick just walked up on this!"

A white cop threw him to the ground while another whipped out his baton and cracked him on the head.

"Noooo!" His shout turned to a cry as one cop pressed his knee into his chest.

"It wasn't him!" someone yelled.

The cops hit and kicked the Black man. "It wasn't me," the

Black man yelled. The cops hoisted him to his feet and cuffed him.

A Black woman ran at them. "You got the wrong one! He was white!"

A cop swung around with his baton cocked. "Shut up, or you'll get it too."

"You shut up, you ugly white pig!" she yelled.

He swung, she ducked, and the crowd pulled back from the two, the way oil and water separate.

"Run!" the cuffed man yelled at his girlfriend.

The cop stepped toward her and swung again, connecting with her shoulder. She screamed, stumbled, and ran. Two cops threw the Black man in one of the police cruisers.

The paramedics lifted the woman onto a stretcher. She'd been sliced across her cheekbone and throat. As they wheeled her toward the ambulance, her arm flopped over the edge of the stretcher. The ambulance drove off without its lights. Two cops talked with a white man as the crowd drifted away.

Sher crouched on her haunches next to the woman who'd yelled "Jessie." Kristin leaned against the brick building behind them, trying not to vomit.

"Why not me?" the woman cried.

The cops glanced at the woman and Sher.

"The last one. Then we was going to the Poodle Club," the woman sobbed.

"Girls," a cop called.

"Kris," Sher stood. "Time to go."

The woman grabbed Sher's arm. "Don't leave me."

The cop car lights swept across the brick walls and windows.

Sher pulled the woman to her feet.

"Girls!"

"Run," Sher said.

The girls and woman ran.

"Stop!" the cop yelled.

They turned south down an alley. Halfway down the alley, seeing it was too long and the cop would spot them, Sher pushed open a door with a sign above it that read *The Red Rooster Inn.* "In," she commanded.

A flashlight beam cut through the alley just as Sher shut the door behind them. An acrid musty smell hit them. The room was dark as tar pitch except for two small high windows that cast a grayish tint across the ceiling.

"Girls?" the cop called, his flashlight bouncing off alley walls and windows.

The girls crouched, waiting.

"Don't see them. Over. Return now? Over. All right, boss. Over." The voice receded.

Once the sharp must receded, an overly sweet smell popped. Outlines emerged. Chairs were toppled over each other. A brass railing leaned against a jukebox. Boxes of glasses and papers and empty bottles of booze littered the room. A wood bar stretched across the back wall with a 150-pound mirror behind it, slanted to the right. Dust, disturbed by their presence, floated through the pale chutes of light.

Kristin tugged on a door in the back until it whooshed open. The three stepped through onto a landing with stairs going up and another set going down.

Sher nudged the other two down the steps, and then spread her hands on the door to shut it without sound. Discovering a latch above the doorknob, she flipped the hook into the eye. "Go," Sher whispered.

They stepped down, careful to not pop the dry, hundred-year-old wood steps, as their hands pressed onto the uneven limestone walls.

The crack at the top of the stairs lit.

"Girls," the cop called out. "I'm back."

All three froze.

The cop stomped. "I know you're in here," he lied.

"Sher," Kris whimpered.

Sher reached for Kris, scraping her boot across something on the landing. She pinched her cousin's lips. Sher kneeled and felt a rope.

The cop upstairs opened the door to the hall. "Girls, I know you're here." Since he'd been called back to the squad to help subdue another suspect, he was no longer sure they were in the building. "Girls," the cop turned the doorknob leading down to the girls.

Sher squeezed Kris's arm. The woman went limp. The latch caught the door.

"Dang." He rattled the door. Convinced they'd run outside when he went back to the squad, he exited the building, turning his attention to where he and his partner would eat on break that evening. Although he enjoyed frightening them, a few girls didn't matter to him much one way or another.

After what seemed an eternity, Sher tugged on the rope. The floor creaked and then pulled up. The smell of cold damp earth hit Sher full in the face. She swung her arm in the opening the way her grandmother kneeled next to the tub and tested the temperature of the water with her hand before her granddaughters climbed in. She lowered her legs into the opening, holding herself up by her forearms, until her feet found the steps. "Steps," she whispered.

As Sher dropped deeper into the earth, images and smells from the farmhouse popped in her mind. On her fourth birthday her father, the only one watching her that morning, chased the six remaining cows who'd broken through the fencing and wandered toward the road. "Stay put!" he yelled at Sher as he raced down the gray weathered porch steps two at a time, bent on saving their cows from the cars and semis that whizzed past their farm—the old two-lane highway being well-traveled because it was the least circuitous route between Duluth and Fargo. He charged across the dirt yard, racing after the cows' rears and flicking tails as they disappeared into a thicket of pine and cedar. They couldn't lose their remaining cows, as that spring, they'd sunk money into buying a herd as part of a failed government-sponsored venture to capitalize on the increased demand for red meat by city folks who'd been building second homes on foreclosed farmland and Indian-owned land on the rez. They'd butchered twenty-two cows with the hopes of making money, but ended up losing money after the program that promised to purchase the cattle at a certain rate reneged on the agreement, and cut the promised payment in half. What the Indians in the program didn't know was that the agent with the government program was on the board of the company that dropped the price. It had all been pre-arranged. Thaddeus's legs churned. They'd been counting on this money to pay their taxes. They could lose their land.

When the Brauns found out the prices had been slashed, Ethel said, "Somehow we forget, just for a second. They only want Indian land not nothing that might get us ahead in this world." Sitting on the couch, she scowled, and missed a stitch in her sewing. "And only if they can get our land for pennies on the dollar." Her husband, standing at the window, pushed his lips toward the kitchen, where Sher stood listening, out of her grandmother's view. "Come here, my girl," Sher's grandmother said. Sher trotted over. "See?" She held her stitching up to Sher who stood on her tiptoes. "This is why it's no good to stew." She pulled out her last stitch. "Understand?" Sher nodded. "Good," she said. "Get even instead. Nah!" She laughed and smiled at her husband and granddaughter, her eyes lit up the way they did when she teased those she loved. "We will figure it out, won't we, my girl?" Delighted with herself, she crossed her legs at the ankles and wiggled her toes, a habit she gleaned from one of her Canadian aunties. "Sit here, my girl." She patted the seat on the couch next to her. "Keep me company," she said, "and watch."

"Stay put," Sher's dad yelled again over his shoulder at his daughter, as he slid down an embankment. One of the cows had left the others and cut west. Sher, sweaty in the sweltering late-June heat, heard her father, paused at the top of the basement stairs, peered through the kitchen into the living room, the direction in which her father's voice had tailed off. The silver flash of a centipede drew her to the cool mouth of the basement. Clamoring down the cracked steps, Sher's fingers, sticky from the maple syrup candy her grandmother had given her that morning, grasped the hand rail. Her eyes followed the centipedes flashing their long pearlescent, fluttering bodies on the steps, walls, and dirt floor.

Sher squatted about the basement, dust and dirt sticking to her fingers. Fascinated by their swiveling, antennae-like legs she wondered why they ran so fast. As one darted into a crevice, a scuffling and creaking erupted from the walled off washroom where a concrete floor, double basin concrete sink, and wooden countertop had been installed by the Finns. Sher entered the room, just as the blue rag rug that covered the northwest corner of the floor raised up unleashing the pungent, damp smell of the earth. She stood rooted to the floor, thinking of her father. He'd told her to stay put.

"Knock it?" a man's voice emerged from the hole. Then a young Negro man's head popped out of the square hole. "Chief," he said low as he eyed Sher. He disappeared into the hole. Then Clarence's head popped out, locked eyes with Sher, surveyed the room, and disappeared again. A moment later, he climbed out, shook out his legs, patted his breast pockets, and smiled at Sher. "Happy birthday, my girl," he said. He handed her a quarter, knelt down, took her hands in his, brushed them off, and smiled. "Let's go upstairs," he said. Hand in hand, they walked up the stairs.

"Let's open one of them presents," Clarence sat his granddaughter on his lap in the living room. She tore off the newspaper wrapping and discovered a bridle big enough for a grown-up horse, a flower design stamped in the tan leather. She looked into her grandfather's broad face with ferocious love. "I made it, my girl," he said, his smile widening—wrinkling his forehead. "Someday we'll get youse a horse to go with it."

Sher's fingers stickied up the perfect leather as she leaned into her grandfather's chest. She forgot all about the Negro man and the hole beneath the big blue rug that had once kept the floor in front of the kitchen sink dry for many years before her birth.

Her grandfather set his head on the back of the chair. His heart calmed, knowing that if someone came knocking, Sher would not spill the beans about the Negro in the basement. And no social workers or sheriffs or anyone else would think to root through the barn, and find the Negroes, Indians, and whites he and his wife hid as they made their way to Canada via barns, tunnels, and buried under tarps and bundles of hay in the backs of trucks. Distracted by the quarter and the bridle, Sher would not remember it.

* * *

The woman and Kristin stared into the nothingness of the hole as a tattered blue rug, luminous bodies of centipedes, and a Black man's countenance spun in Sher's head. She blinked away the images, unsure what they were or where they'd come from. She had forgotten.

Kristin lowered herself into the hole.

"C'mon," Sher whispered to the woman.

The woman climbed into the hole.

Sher yanked the trap door, pulling the rope handle under with her. She caught the door just before it hit the wood frame, in case the cop was still around. Then she stayed still beneath the trap door, listening, in case he was standing still, listening. Convinced he had not doubled back, Sher stepped down the stairs, and the girls pushed forward, hands raised, unable to see anything at all, toward whatever lay ahead.

Virginia, Minnesota, July 1969

Em wanted to fly out the small window, like when she was young,

and lie on her back her hair twining about her head like tree
branches. She wanted to listen to stories that transported her spirit
into the wide dark, night sky through the wood stove's hole in the
ceiling. But Em wasn't going anywhere anytime soon. A day, days
passed. She drank the water they'd left in a bowl like a dog. Hands
tied with rope, she was unable to hold her hair back. Her hair fell
into the bowl. Strands curled around her tongue as she drank.
When she rolled away from the bowl to lay on her back, her hair
soaked her face and neck, creating rivulets that ran down her
shoulders and chest. She shivered in the fifty-degree house—
summers near the Canadian border dipped into the thirties and
forties at night and this house held cold, the wood floor as hard
and frigid as stone. *Whoever was doing this*, she thought, *would
pay*. She would get away and return to hunt him down.

Pain and hunger knocked her out. She slept and woke in starts,
her waking life and dream life twisting together. Technicolor
images overtook her, opening the doorways between her conscious
and unconscious worlds until she couldn't differentiate between the
two. In one life, she lapped water from a bowl in a cold,
abandoned house with a window sky-high. In another life, she split
in two, viewing herself at age three from the side. Her child-self ran
toward someone, laughing without restraint in an opening in the
woods, grasses face high, but her adult-self couldn't see whom she
ran toward. And then, she, the girl, jumped into the arms of a
man—her father, much older than she'd left him standing in the
barn. His hair long and white, not in the buzz cut he wore since he
returned from the war, his hat like those old-time black and white
photos of Indians in wide-brimmed hats and suits and moccasins,
holding their staffs. He swung her high, her long, dark hair
swirling about her head, as she laughed. The sky and clouds and
foliage were bright blue and peacock green.

What was happening? What was real? The elders had told her
all was real, dreams matter as much as waking life, but they hadn't
told her how it would be to experience it as one. Why hadn't they
told her, she wondered, in a child-like state of mind, blue sky
surrounding her as if she were a bird flying far above the trees. The
sun a sunflower. "It is not frightening—you only think it is" drifted
through her thoughts. She tumbled. Her mind spun like a Tilt-A-
Whirl, her favorite ride at the fair when she was a girl and later
too, when she began drinking as a teen. The ride gave her the same

feeling she had when she drank. It gave her the same feeling she had as a child, when her father swung her in circles through the air. Then, plain as day, as if her father stood before her, she heard him say, "Some of us do it to our own." She felt his breath on her cheeks and forehead as if his face were inches from her own. "Don't lose heart, my girl."

Em groaned, her eyelids fluttered, the small window now gray. Two quick scratches from across the hall, then silence. Em shut her eyes. She heard her father say something in Indian she could not decipher. She had mostly forgotten Indian, but her spirit held the words. Her shoulders burned. Her wrists were raw and bloodied. Two more quick scratches, and then faster—more urgent than the previous. Em shifted. Feet moved up the stairs.

* * *

The damp mineral smell of the earth enveloped the girls and woman, making it difficult to breathe. With only one direction to go, Kristin took the lead. Sher limped behind them. After walking for a few minutes, Sher stopped and pulled on the shirt of the woman in front of her who, in turn, pulled on Kristin's arm in front of her.

"Let's rest a minute." Sher leaned against the wall, unlaced her boot and pulled out the knife tucked away next to her ankle. She slid it into her jean pocket knowing that the woman would not be able to see it in the dark. Sher did not know if she would prove trustworthy.

"I'm Sher," she said, pressed against the tunnel wall. "This here is Kristin."

"Where the hell are we?" the woman asked.

"In a tunnel." Sher double-knotted her boot.

"Nah. Really?" the woman said.

"They've got tunnels like this on farms," Kristin said. "We had one. My dad," and her voice trailed off. She'd meant to say how he said farmers used tunnels to get to barns during blizzards and later to store whiskey and beer when they were illegal, but as soon as she'd said his name, she felt sick.

"Yah," Sher said to cover for Kristin. "We had one on our farm, too." She wondered about the images she'd seen of the man and her grandfather. Were they real? What did they mean?

"I never heard a that on a farm," the woman said.

"I've been in our grandparents' plenty of times," Kristin said.

"We used to play in it."

Sher straightened. Kris had not been in the tunnel plenty of times. They'd found it once and played in it, but decided it was too scary. She didn't know Kris to fib like this.

"Right, Sher?" Kris asked.

"We played in it," Sher said so as not to lie. She felt uneasy about this change in Kris, the way she exaggerated, and forced her thoughts away from this change in her cousin, the farm, her father, and the tunnel that he did not get to the night he died.

"Get this," the woman said, "a couple of farm girls showing me the city." She laughed.

The woman and girls continued with Kristin in the lead, her hands blind in front of her. Her fingers felt the end of the earth. "Stop," Kris whispered.

"Gotta get outta here," the woman panicked, sandwiched between the other two. "Turn around."

"Feel for a door," Sher said. "On the ceiling."

"You crazy?" the woman whispered.

Sher ignored her, found a ladder against the wall of the tunnel and climbed it. She pushed on a door in the ceiling from the second step. It whooshed open, flooding the tunnel with a soft gray light. She climbed up another step and pushed the door over on its hinges. The trap door banged on the floor. Sher pulled herself up to the edge of a dirty oak floor with a ceiling nearly as high as a barn. When she did not see or hear anyone, she swung her legs out of the hole. The woman and Kristin emerged.

Dust blanketed the woodwork, a hefty oak table, three matching oak dining room chairs, and an art deco slip shade hanging in front of a chestnut-colored built-in buffet. Along the north wall stood a chest-high gleaming wood bar with a brass foot rail along the bottom. Life-size framed photos of Betty Grable hung from the brick walls. Six dusty mattresses were strewn about the room.

The woman whistled between her teeth. "Flophouse? Whorehouse?" she asked, standing next to the trap door to have a quick escape if needed. "Heard about these tunnels in St. Paul. Knew an old bag who said she'd run a tunnel from the state capitol to a place two blocks away." She lit a cigarette and smiled. "If people knew the underground truth of their pretty cities. Their pretty lives." She dragged again and exhaled a plume of smoke while watching the girls. "Well, us working girls know it plenty well."

With her lanky dish water blond hair, black snowmobile boots, bell bottom blue jeans, an oversized blue men's pea coat frayed at the cuffs, Sher wondered if the woman really was city. She hobbled over to the door that appeared to be nailed shut and yanked to be sure.

Kristin read off a brass-plated placard on the wall next to the door. "Goodfellow and Eastman, 1878."

"The old Dayton's," the woman said. She pulled out a pack of Marlboro's. "Dry goods," she threw the pack on the table.

"How do you know?" Kris asked.

"I know a thing or two," the woman said between puffs. "Wasn't born yesterday."

"When were you born?" Kris asked. She looked old, Kris thought, at least in her twenties, but Kris wasn't sure because she acted like a teenager.

"Long before you." The woman blew a line of smoke toward Kristin. "But not in 1878." Laughter erupted from her that disappeared in a puff of smoke.

"What's the tunnel for?" Kristin asked.

Sher slid a brown drape to the side of one of the ceiling high windows revealing a black outline of a twenty-story building across the street.

"You don't know much about rich people, do you?" the woman yawned.

"No," Kris said.

"Yeah, why would you?" the woman said with the same level of haughtiness the whites on the reservation used with the girls. She ashed her cigarette on the floor while looking Kris up and down.

Kris felt the woman's attitude like a punch to her gut, taken off guard that this street woman would act superior to them. "Who do—"

"Look up." Sher pointed to the ceiling to avoid a confrontation. "Cobwebs like blankets. And dust on the floors and tables. No one has been in here in a long time. We could stay here. Rest up."

"Not for long," the woman said. "People can see straight down into here. They could watch us sleep. Shut it."

Sher ignored her. She seemed off.

The woman sensed Sher's attitude. "You don't know city life.

You got no space here. It's not like—" She stopped herself from telling the girls she was from Willmar. "Wherever you're from."

"What's the tunnel for?" Kris set her grandfather's pack on the plank floor.

"It's real obvious," the woman said, cracking her knuckles. "That place we came in was a bar, and you know how men are always running back and forth between their drinks and their women."

"No," Kris said.

"Whores, honey. This was a whorehouse." She popped a knuckle. "Girls'd be in here. Your age, maybe even younger." She popped another one. "Everyone'd think the men were in the bar, but they'd sneak off over here, do their thing, head back to the bar and no one was the wiser. Except the girls. And the cops."

"Oh," Kristin's face drew up blood.

"Yeah." The woman stared at the ceiling, allowing her cigarette to ash onto the table. "You'll learn," she said to Kristin. "All about people, men people, and their ways once you been on the streets longer."

Kris shot to anger. "I know about people, especially white—-"

"Okay, I get it," the woman said. "You're Indians. You got fucked over. A lot of us did. Not just you. I'm not impressed. I don't care one way or the other." She walked across the mattresses. Plumes of dust burst with each step. She crossed her arms and stared out the windows. "I grew up with plenty of you Indians." She pushed a mattress toward the windows. "White ones. Red ones. Apples. In between ones. The only thing you did wrong when you killed all those white people was you didn't kill my ancestors and thus I was born. Now here I am in this shitty life."

Sher and Kristin glanced at each other. Whorehouse? Indians killing white people?

The woman's voice softened. She'd been too harsh. They were just kids, after all. She pointed at a mattress. "If we move them here they couldn't see us sleeping. Maybe could stay awhile. There's plenty of abandoned buildings around here." She flipped a mattress over. "Not as dirty."

All three contemplated the room. The walls were brick, the mortar gray and crumbling. Every ninth row of brick, a thin cross section of wood was embedded in the mortar, to help hold the weight of the brick, to keep them straight. The three settled in.

"Name?" Sher ventured.

"J. H.," the woman said. "Jekyll and Hyde." She laughed mean. "That's what you got to be to get by on the streets. Jekyll and Hyde." She looked at the girls as if she were a telescope lens coming back in from far away. "It gets in here," she pointed to her chest. "And then it is you. And then you is fucked. You is fucked. Do you think I wanted my life to be like this?"

Sher and Kristin stood in the silver-lit room, not knowing what to say.

"Out here," the woman said, "one day you got something, the next day you don't. She looked at her boots. "If you can ever get anything." She lit up another cigarette. "Jessie," she said, but did not look up. "Here then gone." She exhaled a long plume of white smoke at the ceiling. "Like smoke, that's what our lives are." She took another drag, exhaled. "Disappear. No one knows. No one cares." She sucked on the cigarette. "Jackie is my name. Jackie. Like Jackie O. Only not quite."

* * *

Traffic woke Sher. She started off the mattress, not knowing where she was for a moment. The room was sullen. The sun fogged windows that hadn't been cleaned in thirty years. Jackie slept on a mattress across the room from Sher and Kristin, her mattress pulled next to the trap door so she could escape if need be.

Sher turned onto her side. Even though the mattress was old and dirty, it was good to have something beneath her hips and shoulders. She fell asleep again.

When Sher woke, the woman sat in the corner near a window smoking a cigarette. Her hands shook.

"I'm Tricia," the woman said, and put out the cigarette on the bottom of her shoe. "On the streets I'm Sticky. Like fingers. I need to eat. Got any food?" She smiled.

Sher ran her tongue over her teeth. Now this woman had two names. "Tricia?" Sher asked. "Not Jackie?"

"Jackie's come and gone. She's much crabbier than me. I look like heck," Tricia said. "I know it. Last night was hard."

Sher gathered her thoughts. Many Indians had more than one name. They had white names and Indian names they were not to speak of outside the family. Their grandparents might give them new nicknames when they went to school or obtained a new talent. Her grandparents each had their own name for Sher, as did her father. "Punkin" because she loved the pumpkin pies her grand-mother made every fall. "Ducky" because she followed Em like a duckling. "Little Elvis" which became "Elvis Junior" which became simply "EJ" because as a girl she sang along with every Elvis tune on WJO, the station her grandmother listened to while doing dishes or chopping carrots or grinding chunks of raw beef through the heavy metal meat grinder screwed to the kitchen counter. Having more than one name seemed normal to Sher, but this was not that.

"Sorry," Sher said, and sat on the mattress studying the cracks in the mortar because she did not want to invade the woman-girl-with-two-name's space. She was taught to stay out of people's space out of respect, but also especially when someone was unpredictable or mean like this.

"Up here," Ethel would say, tapping her forefinger on her temple, not to be mean, but to let her children and grandchildren know things were different, perhaps the person would need to be treated with more care than another. Sher could see her grand-mother clear as day—the tip of her finger pointing at her temple, the curls from the home perms her grandmother's one remaining sister—the rest had moved off to Portland and Los Angeles—sometimes gave her when she wore her hair short springing from her head. For a reason Sher never knew her, grandmother used pomade when her hair was short and permed, so her curls were stiff and shiny like the black metal springs Sher's grandfather used when he rigged up Indian trucks and cars so they'd sputter up and chug along another few months. "A little trick I learned in the army, eh EJ," he'd explain, smiling. He'd sing to himself, while puttering with a broken piston or warped cylinder. "Springs can take care of any little ill," a phrase he created based on a popular jingle for Ivory soap back in the '40s, and then he'd think of his wife's hair, and his love for her rose in his chest and made that day and every day a good day.

Tricia caught her breath. "Where is Jessie. Is she dead? Did St. Joe's get her? The insane asylum? You know my dad tried to put me there after all those bad things he did to me. That's why we ran away. Are they booking her?

"What's going on?" Kris sat up.

Sher shrugged.

"I'm hungry," Tricia said. "Anything. Got a candy bar in that bag?"

"No," Sher said. Her stomach pushed in on itself.

"I got to get some food." Tricia walked to the door. "You will let me in when I come back?"

Sher nodded.

Tricia wedged her fingers between the piece of wood and the door. She pulled until the nails creaked and the wood popped off the jamb. She disappeared down the hall.

Sher rubbed her leg just above her ankle.

"Any better?" Kristin asked.

"A little," Sher said.

The girls lay on the mattresses and stared at the ceiling.

"What's that lady's deal?" Kris asked.

"Dunno. She's kinda like a woman and a little kid at the same time."

"Oh."

The girls stared at the tin ceiling as the city thrummed.

"Sher. Is it always going to be like this?"

"Nope."

"How do you know?"

"Can't be. That's how I know."

Kristin leaned on her side and looked at Sher. "It could be like this forever."

"Nah." Sher observed her cousin lying on her side with her head propped up on one hand, her other fingers thrumming the mattress.

After most of Ethel's family had left over a handful of years, promised jobs by the government in Chicago and Minneapolis and LA and Portland, Ethel, who found her way home from the boarding school, would drum her fingers. Bite her lip. "They tear us apart. We find our way back. They tear us apart again." She'd wring out the gray dish cloth, drape it over the edge of the sink, smooth it. "Just when you think things are okay, might be okay, they're not." She'd turn to Sher, her hands balled in her apron pockets. "Never forget that, my girl," she'd say, her round face tense, her eyes a watery brown, "Things can always get worse. Don't let yourself forget that, ever." Sher often sat at the kitchen table, hulling corn or doing homework, feeling the pain that her grandmother couldn't hold back in the way the waves on the big lake couldn't be controlled when it stormed.

"There's always the state fair, if Carla doesn't work out. We could work there and save money," Sher kept on, her mind in two places, with Kristin and back home on the porch, hulling corn for hominy. And then, her mind in a third place—she'd seen an advertisement saying Dolly Parton would be at the fair.

"You sure?" Kris asked.

"Nah," Sher said. "I don't know. Just...." She trailed off, keeping her feelings far off, the way her grandmother had, the way many adults around her had, but she would not lie, as they had not lied to her.

Kristin studied the spiderweb-like cracks on the ceiling. She knew no one could say what would happen. She just felt so nervous. So scared.

Sher settled her feelings like dust in a corn bin. Once they'd found their places, she daydreamed a little of Dolly Parton. The strength of her personality. Her eyes. Her laugh. Her breasts.

The girls sat in silence for a while as they were accustomed.

"Sher," Kris said in a low voice. "What happened to that woman last night?"

"I figure she got stabbed."

"Things don't seem so real to me."

"Yah," Sher said, half-thinking of Dolly.

"Are we going to disappear," Kris asked. "Like my..."

Sher surveyed the bricks. Imagined setting them all those years ago. "Like your what?"

"Nothing," Kris said.

"Oh," Sher realized Kris was talking about her mom. She'd never heard Kris talk about her mom. "Nooo—" Sher's voice trailed off the way she used to run through the woods, three steps, a turn in the trail, and she would be gone from sight. Just her and the trees and the birds and whatever dog was around that year. When she was real little, the black-speckled dog, *Animoosh*, ran with her. "Part wolf," her grandfather said. Sher was just nine when a new dog loped into their lives, emerging one night, starved, from the county land. *Animoosh* and the new dog sniffed noses. The next morning *Animoosh* was gone and the new dog became the next *Animoosh*. "Went back to the wild," Clarence told his granddaughter. He patted Sher's shoulder. Sher dropped her eyes. Gulped down the sadness. "Here just long enough to keep watch over you when you needed it. He's where he belongs." Clarence smoked on the porch, his eyes distant, thinking about his boyhood friend in the photos. One night a man took him from the room the boys slept in at Carlisle. The next night, a girl disappeared from the girls' dorm. They never returned.

When the girl and boy came into Carlisle as five-year-olds, the nuns gave them Christian names to replace their "heathen" ones, scribbling each child's Christian appellation between the blue lines in the ledger. One from the southwest. The other from Oklahoma. They arrived three days apart. One cried for weeks. The other never shed a tear. One spoke Towa. The other spoke Tsalagi. If they spoke their languages both were whipped on their buttocks—preventing outsiders from seeing the welts—by the nuns in their robes, their heavy silver crosses swinging around their necks. One spoke her language in secret into her pillow at night. The other never spoke his language again. The night the politicians from Harrisburg visited the Indian school, the boy bled to death from the sexual assaults and the girl was accidentally strangled to death by the rope they used to tie her to the bed when they left the room to take a break from raping her. Both children disappeared from the school, from their families, and from their tribes. The children were never heard from again, not in Tsalagi, Towa, or English. It was as if they'd never existed.

Staff at Carlisle buried them on the grounds late that night, alongside the other hundred or so buried there over the years, their spirits caught between worlds, waiting for the day when ground-penetrating radar would photograph their luminous bones among the dirt and rocks. And those long-buried and disappeared Indian children would be found again, setting off collective grieving for the nameless children's bodies found six-feet deep.

However, these two Indian children did not disappear from Clarence's thoughts. When his wife bore a girl and then a boy, and they had to give them English names for the birth records, Clarence pleaded with his wife for these strange names to be passed along to their first two children, never telling her why. She said, "Whoever heard of an Indian named Josetta?" And when the boy was born years later, she said, "Whoever heard of an Indian named Thaddeus?" But she saw his head drop and she saw the look that came across his face, so she agreed to name her children those strange names. She did not need to ask her husband if these names were related to the boarding schools. She knew. *Anyway,* she thought, looking at her suckling newborn babies, *they will get their Indian names from a medicine man. That was what mattered to Gitchi Manidoo and the manidoog. That was what mattered to the Old Ones.*

* * *

"Sher." Kris swallowed. "Don't let that happen to me."

The girls' eyes met. The memory of the night before stood between them.

"Don't let me disappear."

"I won't Kris."

"Promise?"

"Yah." Sher turned her head, unable to get the picture of the woman on the sidewalk, cut and bloodied, out of her head. She bent her fingers. Her eyes skimmed her nails. Why did she say that? She knew better than to promise something like that.

"Pinky swear?"

"Pinky swear."

"You never know, kids," Jackie burst through the door. "No promises in this world. None. Zippo. When it's over, it's over."

Sher stood. She'd been listening to them through the door.

Jackie pulled two apples from her pocket and tossed them to Sher. "Jessie's time was up," she nearly shouted. "She's dead." She choked on dead.

Kris went blank. She stared at gray bulging brick mortar between two red bricks. She was nothing nowhere and had to be absent like that until the danger of feeling her buried emotions over her mother's murder ended.

"Damnit," Jackie groaned and sank to the floor.

Sher waited for her cousin to return. She polished her cousin's apple on her shirt.

The girls ate the apples. Cars honked. Church bells rang. Their thoughts spun from what they would do tomorrow to images of the dead woman to whether the woman in the room with them was safe to the farm where their aunties, uncles, infant cousin, grandparents, and Sher's father were buried.

As far as the rest of the family—the great-grandparents were in the Indian cemetery outside Antwatin. One great-auntie disappeared one sunny August day after selling her eggs in the unincorporated village of Meriden. No one ever discovered what happened to her—no whites, no Indians, no breeds. Speculations said she ran away to Duluth with a white lover, or hit her head while climbing rocks, or was abducted and murdered for sport by the gangsters who came up from the Cities in their big cars to hide from the law.

Other family were scattered across the reservation, some in Catholic boarding school cemeteries—their bodies in three-and-four-foot long unmarked graves, one in a Methodist boarding school, some in sanitorium cemeteries, others in no graves. One man—a third cousin to Clarence in the way whites thought and a cousin to Clarence in the way Indians thought—was murdered for going into Last Chance Saloon in Antwatin. He entered the establishment despite the hand-carved "No Indians Allowed" sign, his limp body ultimately shoveled off the bed of the murderer's '46 Ford pickup into a "mess of ferns" (what his murderer said when he bragged of the killing) near an old logging road in the state forest. His body had long since decomposed, but not the rumors of who had done it and why. Rumors no police officer would ever entertain, and so although Indians and whites knew Bob Benner beat him near death at the bar, loaded his still breathing, bloodied body onto the truck with the help of two white men, one the owner; they also knew Bob Benner wouldn't touch the Injun's body with his hands again, as he said he'd had enough of touching these wood niggers. He'd rinsed the man's blood off the shovel in the crick behind the bar where he'd killed him—not because he was afraid he'd get caught, but because he didn't want Indian blood dirtying up his things (as others suspected, and he himself knew, Indian blood was in him). "Strong Italian lines," he'd say drunk, at the bar. "Strong French Canadian." All the white men in the bar nodded in their beers, toasted the Wops, toasted the Froggers.

A handful knew he was a quarter or more Indian, grandson to Broderick Rice, a full-blood by Indian count, a half-breed by white count. Yet they raised their glasses along with the rest to placate their friend, accepted as white by whites. None were stupid enough to mess with Bob Benner's rage. The night Clarence's cousin walked into Last Chance Saloon and ordered a beer, he not only defied the sign hung on the door, but his presence challenged the whiteness of Bob Benner. "Cousin," he said to Benner. Benner looked into his face from the far end of the 1898 bar, with hand-carved boar heads along the edges, and saw a slightly darker version of his own countenance, sparking a murderous rage and self-hatred that would not be denied.

* * *

"Wonder where Uncle Leo and Auntie Rene are," Kris said. The girls had many aunts and uncles and cousins, some of whom were somehow biologically related to them and others whom were not but were considered relatives. The girls' thoughts fanned out to the unknown—cities they could not imagine where the rest of their aunties and cousins and uncles now resided, doing who knew what, who knew where. Living lives invisible to one another, their only connection with their tribe was the per caps and an occasional payment released from the government over some minor dispute filed twenty years earlier by a white farmer who believed his land extended into tribal land. When it was determined that actually some of his farm was reservation land, he had to pay to retain it. If the tribe had a good forwarding address, five dollars showed up at an apartment in Portland, the bridges in the sky city, bringing with it memories of a time and place that seemed a world apart, and that kept the lights on another month.

A car horn nickered. Sher studied the mattress's double-stitched floral design, darker than the rest of the mattress as the thread held dirt tighter. The stitches marched across the mattress in straight lines, wide looping bends, and curlicues, creating—as Sher counted—twenty-eight sets of a four-fern design. She ran her finger over one of the ferns, as if she were tracing a language her head did not understand, but her heart knew well.

The woman cried.

Kris faced the door that, with the board removed, could be broken into at any moment. "Sher?"

"Yah?" Sher pushed at black fuzz.

"What'll we do if someone comes?"

"Push him over and run out." Sher shut her eyes. "Drop through the trap door. It'll be okay."

"Yah?"

"Yah."

Sher dozed. Kristin stared at the ceiling, thinking small thoughts.

Three short raps on the door woke Sher. Kristin lunged toward the trap door. The hall door swung open, revealing a short round Indian woman in army fatigues. Sher stood.

"Girls." The woman leaned against the doorjamb holding a jug of orange juice and small bundles. "Shoot, Jackie." She shifted everything into one arm and slammed the door. "These them?" She nodded toward the girls.

"Nah. They're my long list kids." Jackie grabbed the juice and swigged.

"Not bad. Not bad." the army woman entered the room. "How did we miss this place?"

"Small. Hid by the alley."

"I suppose. Where's the trap door?"

Jackie continued to guzzle the juice, stepped to the trap door, and tapped it with her boot.

The army woman nodded. "Terry," she said and shook each girl's hand loosely.

Sher nodded, raising her head up slightly the way she addressed Indians rather than down the way she nodded to white people.

"Rosebud," Terry said. "Cheyenne on my mom's side." Terry squinted and rubbed the back of her head—her hair a black crew cut just like the girls' grandfather's before his turned white.

Normally, the girls would say they were Ojibwe from Goodhue but Sher did not want strangers to know where they were from. Kris was too taken by Terry's presence to respond.

"You in the army?" Kristin asked, wide-eyed thinking perhaps she'd been in Vietnam.

"Not the US Army." Terry laughed. "The Red Army." She held up her fist. "For our people."

"Indian power." Jackie licked her lips free of orange juice.

"Dig it." Terry smiled and lit up.

"Dig it," Kris said under her breath.

"Fight the power!" Jackie capped the orange juice.

Terry blew a smoke ring. "Whaddya think?" She nodded at Sher. "No more fighting for the white man."

"Yah," Kris said. "No more."

"You?" Terry asked Sher.

Sher shrugged. Her grandfather had been a vet. Lots of Indians were vets. None of the Indians back home talked like that, except Em—sometimes.

"Sisters?" Terry raised her eyebrows at the girls. "Lovers?"

"Fighters!" Kris shot back.

Terry and Jackie laughed.

"Nah," Terry said, "I mean, you two. How you related?"

"Cousins," Kris blurted. "Kris. Sher. Goodhue." She wanted to be liked by Terry, wanted to fight the white man. "Stop the war now."

"Yeah," Terry drawled. "I see. Cousins from Goodhue. Stop killing brown people, wherever we are." She took a drag, shot the smoke out in a straight line. "Starting in this country's own backyard."

Sher nearly groaned. Now these two women knew their names, relation, and where they were from.

"There's a march," Kris said, carried away by her emotions, by this masculine Indian woman.

"There's always a march." Jackie peered out a curtain.

"What?" Terry questioned Jackie.

"Garbage cans." Jackie lit a cigarette. "Rats."

Terry sized up Kristin, wondering if her luck could be so good as to have the light-skinned Indian girl be a dyke like her butchy cousin.

"Here." Terry tossed the packages on a mattress. Dust fluttered.

The girls did not move although they were hungry. Jackie cried. Terry embraced her from behind. "Talkin' about it on the street. Wasn't a thing you could do," she whispered.

The women looked sick. Dark crescents hung beneath their eyes. Jackie's hair straggled down her back, but it was more an overall feel of worn that made Kris unsure and Sher edgy.

Terry pointed at the packages, her arms still around Jackie. "Caramel rolls," she said. "Eat. They're not poisoned."

The girls ate.

* * *

Little Falls, Minnesota, May 1891

Although the Braun family would never know it, the night before Leonard arrived in Little Falls an article penned by L. Frank Baum, future author of *The Wonderful Wizard of Oz*, that had appeared two weeks earlier in the *Aberdeen Saturday Pioneer*, was recited just before closing by the owner of River Inn, the only man in the bar that night with an education beyond the third grade. The owner read from Baum's article, "The Whites, by law of conquest, by justice of civilization, are masters of the American continent, and the best safety of the frontier settlements will be secured by the total annihilation of the few remaining Indians. Why not annihilation? Their glory has fled, their spirit broken, their manhood effaced; better that they die than live the miserable wretches that they are."

The recitation motivated the drowning death of their relative, Leonard, as he traveled from the Goodhue Reservation to St. Cloud to retrieve a white man's horse in April 1891, the same year the smallpox epidemic took seventy-eight whites and more than three hundred tribal members, including his grandfather and father, leaving him, at fifteen, as the oldest male in the family. Money was needed to pay off his mother's land's back taxes, due to the state's (at the lumber barons' urging) passage of a lumber tax on all mature trees on Indian-owned land on the Goodhue Reservation. No one informed the Indians of the tax until it was due, and then each Indian, in the midst of an epidemic and kept out of white jobs, had a handful of weeks to come up with hundreds of dollars, as assessed by a government official who never once stepped on the actual land to figure the number of trees on each parcel. It was as if the government and the disease were collaborators in the theft of the 39 percent of reservation land still in Indian hands, as the epidemic and taxes were a one-two punch further decimating the tribe. The tax and disease dropped the Indian-owned percentage of the reservation to 11, still 11 percent too high for some whites.

Leonard took on a dangerous task for an Indian in those days—leaving the reservation to travel across the state—to save a pittance of his tribe's homeland, to keep what was left of his family, his mother, siblings and cousins, from becoming homeless. The money never made it to Goodhue. The boy never even made it to St. Cloud, instead, despite his precaution of taking Indian paths through the forest to avoid encounters with whites, three white men beat and then drowned him on the bank of the Mississippi in Little Falls. His skin, dark as an African's, moving through the trees converged with Baum's words and incited the men's hatred. "Indian," they nudged one another, still slightly intoxicated after sleeping off a binge in an alley behind the River Inn. The men were ex-farm hands hired away from farming by Little Falls' booming brick-making business that, a year earlier, had transformed the wooden storefronts along the wide dirt streets of Little Falls into simplistic but sturdy brick storefronts.

Springing upon him from the back and sides, they left Leonard with nowhere to run but forward. They knew the path. He didn't.

His double-soled, deer hide moccasins, slick from dew, and his legs weak from the rush of sudden fear, slipped on a matting of fallen leaves. He tumbled down a small embankment. It was only a matter of seconds before they tackled him, wrestling him down like a calf on the farm. "Prairie nigger!" they screamed, referencing the Sioux Indians (massacred nine days after Baum's words were published in the Aberdeen paper), not his people. They cracked his skull in three places against the gnarled feet of a hundred-year-old tree and then dragged him a short distance, semi-conscious, bleeding, tooth chipped, broken ribs, head split open, to the Mississippi River. "Meet your maker, Chief." They laughed and held him beneath the clear flowing water, pinning him at the edge of the river just three feet under, pressed against the silty bottom. Despite their hands on his body, the three white men watched him through the clear running liquid as if he were far from them, waiting for his eyelids and fingers to quit twitching.

Leonard was shocked and confused over the sudden brutality. He thought of his mother and cousins and siblings on Goodhue and his concern over what they would do without the horse-fetching money he was supposed to give them. Leonard's last sight was of two of the men's crotches, their brown buttoned cotton spun pants, one bulging with the stiffness of its member. Then his eyes rolled back and his favorite image of Goodhue overtook his field of vision: the golden sun fingering the tops of the white pines as night and day traded places. With his body succumbing, his thoughts settled like dropped pebbles on the unexpected silkiness of the river bottom, reminding him of the soft moss he'd helped his mother and aunties line cradle boards with, reminding him of the home he would never see again, of his family and his people who would never know what became of him.

The river flowed over Leonard's face, fluttering his long hair like seaweed. His lungs heavy with water, stilled his body, and the men let go. His spirit ascended with the early morning mist rising off the river, cradled briefly in the arms of the wide-reaching oaks along the bank as the current swept away his body, tumbling it like the agates in Lake Superior.

The three men who drowned Leonard emerged from the river, their pants and arms soaking wet. They climbed up onto the bridge that connected east Little Falls to west Little Falls. A young white boy, trudging to school down the path alongside the river, saw the

Indian boy's body and screamed, dropping his lunch pail. A green apple rolled out, settling in a bed of tall weeds, where its sweet white flesh would be gnawed on for two days by a family of squirrels until the copper-colored torpedo seeds scattered along the shoreline. A crowd of whites gathered along the east shore and on the bridge, yelling and pointing at the Indian's body snagged on a boulder. "Lookee there! What is it? A dead Indeean! Lookit the head! Smashed to bits! Look, ma, look!" And then the rock cut his body lose and the current tumbled Leonard into the boulders just south of the bridge, splitting apart his skull such that anyone who saw his body down river would not know his face. Cheers and clapping rose, until it all blew south into the sky and the city, just one-year-old, went about its day.

A few conversations across backyards and barstools and dirt roads were all that occurred in response to the drowning. Nothing appeared in the paper. No police report filled with the town's Sheriff's sixth grade chicken scratch. No relations informed, no body gathered and washed and dried, put back together, sat with for four days, fed, and buried as his spirit walked the path across the sky. No funeral services in Little Falls or elsewhere for the Indian boy, Leonard. No information given to his family about his disappearance, ever. He was just gone. His family would remember him by passing some form of his name on for generations: Leo, Lenny, L, Len, Leonella (for a baby girl) even though after two generations none of the proceeding generations knew who Leonard was or that one day he had left, never to return.

* * *

"Thanks." Sher finished the rolls.

Terry grunted. She pulled the morning edition of *The Minneapolis Star*—tucked into the back of her jeans—and handed the front page to Jackie. She leafed through Section A. "Nothing about last night."

"They don't list Jane Does," Jackie said.

Kristin's eyes widened.

"They're sending more troops, you know," Jackie said. "Just voted on it. Says so right here." She snapped the front page.

Sher took a swig of orange juice, set the carton down, and put on her boots. She felt naked without them. "Thirsty?" she asked Kristin, but Kristin did not respond.

"Hard on her?" Terry nodded toward Kristin.

"Yah." Sher opened the sports section to search for the score of the Twins game. She, her grandmother, and father had been fans, listening to WCCO during evening chores.

Terry took a swig of orange juice and said, "You quiet."

Sher nodded.

"Like an old timer." Terry studied Sher. A girl like her had to be broke different than the other one.

"Maybe."

Terry laughed. "Just like 'em."

Sher read the paper from front to end including the obituaries, paying special attention to the men's and women's classifieds for jobs she and Kris might be able to work.

"What are you doing?" Jackie asked.

"Looking for work."

"In the men's section too? Good luck. You can't do a man's job."

"Sure can." Sher folded the paper into quarters.

"You can up there," Terry said, noting Sher's narrow-hipped, broad-shouldered body. "This is the city. They don't hire girls to do men's work." She'd have to be a runner, Terry decided. And trapped good, because this girl had nothing in her for them to hook. Her only weakness was her love for her cousin.

Sher shrugged, grabbed the pack, and found the envelope with Carla's number on it. "Gonna make a call," she said. She nudged Kris's shoulder. Kris did not wake, so Sher limped down the hallway, propped open the door with a brick, and limped half a block to a pay phone.

"Carla, please," Sher said to the woman who answered the line. "Carla," Sher said when the line picked up.

"Speaking," Carla responded. "Who's this?"

"Sher. Sher Braun. Remember me from the state fair a couple of years back?"

"Sher?"

"Yah. The horse barns. And the barrels. Remember? I placed first. You were third."

"Oh," Carla said. "I guess so. Indian, right? You and your dad?"

Sher nodded her head as if Carla could see her even though they were miles apart. "Yah. That's me. My cousin and I are in town visiting and—-"

"I'll be out of town."

Sher nodded. She watched the cars speed down the street, felt the tremendous heat held in by miles of pavement and tall buildings.

"Sorry. You can always call another time. Okay, ah, Sher?"

"Sure." Sher hung up the phone. She wiped sweat from her brow, and set her jaw, steeling herself to the honking cars, the heat, the people hurrying by who did not look her way, and the ones who did look her way—two, three times—to double and triple check what they glimpsed on the streets of Minneapolis—an Indian.

* * *

Sher pushed open the door.

"What?" Kristin jumped to her feet.

Terry smoked as she leaned against the buffet, watching the girls, noting the light-skinned one's dependence. *The white in her makes her weak*, she thought, ashing her cigarette on the floor.

Sher shrugged. "She's going on vacation. Or something."

"And?" Kristin asked.

"We won't be meeting her."

"Where?" Jackie asked.

"The fair," Kris said.

"The state fair?"

"Yah," Kris said.

Sher grimaced.

"Fair starts soon," Jackie said.

Terry flicked her cigarette on the floor and stepped on it. She cleared her throat to get Jackie's attention. "How will the girls get in. Costs money."

"Oh yeah, that," Jackie said. "I can set you up, show you the ropes," she said to the girls. "For a little kick-back."

Terry lit another. "C'mon, Jackie. Leave these girls alone," she said to calm the girls, steer them toward trusting her. They'd be more likely to trust an Indian than a white.

The traffic hummed. A car horn blared. *For a little kick-back* rang through the girls' heads. The ropes? What did that mean?

Terry looped her thumbs in her jeans, deciding it would be best to separate the two. The white Indian would fold like a deck of cards without her cousin. But the butchy one, she was another story.

The sky turned light gray. Rain dropped on the people and cars and streets. Umbrellas popped open like black flowers. Some walked faster with newspapers held over their heads while others ducked under the overhangs of downtown Minneapolis to wait it out. Sher heard her grandmother's voice, *daylight in the swamp,* the way she'd woken her family every morning on Goodhue. Sher missed the wet earthy smell from rainy days in the country that made her feel solid. Connected.

Then heavy clouds rolled in. The sky became charcoal, sealing out the sun. Rain pounded the city. Sheets of water pleated windows and shined the dull, hot streets and sidewalks until they were dark and slick like snake skin. Sher flashed to the farm and the yellow glow that so often accompanied the sudden downpours in the country. As they watched, the sun met the gray sky, making a whole new color unlike anything that could be found elsewhere. Out there, on the reservation.

The girls and woman stayed like that all afternoon, bored, each lost in her thoughts, mesmerized by the city's sounds, or taken over by sleep. The wet dark day made time seem later than it was. Sher went through the paper once more looking for work. Jackie slept, paralyzed by what had happened the night before. Terry lay on a mattress for a while and then left, whispering something to Jackie first. Kristin alternately stared at the wall and ceiling and slept in the damp heat.

When it got going on five-thirty, Sher gave up on finding work and stood peering out onto the street. It was dark, an artificial dark the way it gets when a tornado is near, and the buildings and streets were shadows, blacker in some areas from soaking up the rain, the pores in the cement like the holes in a sponge. Men and women roamed the streets in black and yellow slickers, just leaving work or heading to Jax Café, Kramarczuk's East European Deli, 5-8 Club, and Nankin Cafe. The trees, evenly ordered in the midst of the concrete, lined the streets like soldiers at attention, donning leaves that flashed lime green, their trunks and branches slicked black from the rain.

"Going out to get food," Sher said absently. She'd forgotten about eating.

"Can rez farm girls steal, or do they have lots of money from selling chicken eggs?" Jackie asked. Terry had instructed Jackie to not let them both leave, but one was okay. They would not abandon each other.

Sher reached for the brass-plated doorknob, blackened from decades of oxidation and the sweat and grime of many hands.

"Steal me something," Jackie said. "Food preferably."

On the street, Sher kept her head down. Rain pelted her head and shoulders. She felt herself dropping away, daunted by the prospect of having to find a store nearby and stealing from its owners, keenly feeling her grandparents' disapproval as they'd taught her to not even touch another's belongings. A white woman in a plaid sleeveless dress and matching olive-green pumps looked at Sher like she was dirt. She felt the sting of humiliation. Was she truly a dirty Indian thief, the way she knew the woman thought of her—the way the whites had thought of all Indians up in Antwatin? She thought of her family. No. But what was happening to her? How would they eat with no job and soon no money?

Sher's hair hung dankly, weighted by the mist and humidity. She walked south two blocks and cut east on Hennepin where she spotted a bridge. She ran toward it as best she could on her ankle. She looked out over the river—raindrops making pockmarks on the Mighty Mississippi—knowing she was about to act against herself. At the east end, she spotted a huge sign for Grain Belt Beer. As she crossed the bridge, she saw a corner store named Polanski's Groceries. Sher trotted toward Northeast Minneapolis where Eastern European immigrants settled in the 1800s, and where more than a few heavily-accented Nazis let in by the government after World War II lived in the working-class neighborhoods whose churches still conducted Mass in Polish and Latin.

Her gait slowed as she neared the store. Guilt hit her. Maybe she could spend their money? Maybe she would find a job soon? Sher yanked Polanski's narrow glass door covered with black steel bars shimmering from the rain.

Smells slammed her —raw beef from the galley kitchen, the sweet rhubarb and cherry Polish *kompot* in an uncovered ceramic bowl on the counter, bleach swiped across the floor, and the lingering smell of piss from the bathroom in the back.

"Yah," an older, heavyset white woman said from behind the counter. Her gray hair was pulled up in a loose bun. She smiled widely at Sher and waved her hand around the store as if to tell Sher *shop here.*

A glass jar of brightly colored penny jaw breakers; one

crumbled piece of stale, blood-red cherry pie under a glass cover; and a greenish jar of pickled pig's feet rested on the counter in front of the woman. An immigrant, the woman had not absorbed the hatred of Indians as had so many other Americans. Since she had not found Americans to be very kind despite her minor success as a corner store owner—or perhaps because of her minor success—she disliked Americans and wished to return to the old country.

Sher nodded at the woman.

"Yah. Help yorself. Good!" The woman waved at a plate of *pierogis* she'd cooked that morning.

Sher dropped her eyes.

The woman reached behind her to a recently painted white shelf and picked up a pair of sharp-toothed tongs lying next to the glass jar. She pulled out a large dill pickle and resituated herself on the stool.

Sher slipped her hands in her jean pockets and shrugged her shoulders. She heard her grandmother's voice: *They say Indians steal, but it's the whites who stole from us.*

The woman bit into the pickle, the sound as loud as the snap of a chicken's neck. She chewed loudly—each mastication as sharp and loud as if she bit through another vertebrae.

Sher walked down the aisles packed with candy, crackers, and foods with names in languages she did not know. Nye's Polonaise bought wholesale from her. Eastern European Jews, Nazis-in-hiding, and Catholics alike schlepped and trolleyed and bused from north and northeast Minneapolis to her corner store to buy the woman's homemade *pierogi* and *racuchy* and imported *maslanka* that cost a pretty penny because it had to be refrigerated the whole, long journey on the boat and train from Poland to Minneapolis.

Sher kept an eye on the large round mirror mounted in a back corner. "So, so what," her grandmother would say as she canned or swept or sewed, as if someone else were in the room with her and her granddaughter. "You steal then you're as bad as them, you know. That's what the so, so what is about. Bad enough to lose our land and lives. Worse to lose being Indian. You don't touch other people's things. Indians DON'T DO THAT." Her thoughts would trail off, lost in the past, in some event from the boarding school—when they cut her hair or took her "Indian" clothes—or some other aggression committed by a priest or a brother or a nun against her or another Indian child. There'd been so many sometimes she got lost in them, as if she too were wandering through a store filled with foods and items created by someone else from another land, and packaged with words not her own, and sold on land they claimed was theirs. "Always, always Indian land," her grandmother would mutter. "Our ancestors' bones are here. Not theirs. Ours. We are of this land. We are in this land!"

Sher's memory of her grandmother's voice became so strong it was like there were three of them in the little store, one sitting, one scuffing her boots, and another soft-soling it across the worn-down, butter-smooth wood floors.

The pickle crunch was the only sound in the small store other than the scuffs of Sher's boots. "Bathroom?" Sher asked.

"Yah." The woman pointed a fat finger at the far corner.

Sher emptied her bladder, splashed cold water on her face, and stared at her visage in the small, hand mirror nailed to the wall. She was looking to steal a dollar or so of snacks, but felt she was about to commit murder. Her own.

Sher wandered the store. Two-thirds of the interior were visible in the mirror. The back third on the right side was not. Sher stopped in the back corner looking through bags of peanuts, Nut Goodies, Chiclets and packets containing plastic kerchiefs that women kept in their purses for when it rained. She hoped the storekeeper would lose interest in her.

The woman crackled a small radio, settling on a polka station. Sher glanced through the metal racks and saw her back turned to the store. She shoved a bag of sunflower seeds and three Nut Goodies in her left pocket. She grabbed a large bag of peanuts still in the shell and a box of saltine crackers, holding the crackers and the peanuts together as one item to the side of her thigh, shielding them from the woman's sight. She strode down the aisle plain as day, her grandmother's disapproval trailing after her like a dancer at a powwow. *I have to,* Sher thought, but she knew she lied. She'd hear the stories about her family. Her people. Dying from disease and starvation in the 1800s until only a handful survived deep in the bush, and the other handful disappeared into the TV sets and boxed foods in the surrounding towns, mixing with whites until the only way you knew they were Indian was through the facial features that looked white at first glance, but upon closer inspection the eyes, cheeks, and foreheads seemed stretched and angled in ways that made them look as if they were in a state of discomfort from never belonging anywhere.

The bells on the door handle tinkled. Sher had money in her pocket. The old woman turned and something small snapped in Sher, like a twig cracking underfoot, or the snap of a sapling broken in half. She hit the streets hoping she would not have to run. They had to keep the last bit of the money. The rain had subsided. She listened for commotion behind her, the woman yelling down the street after her. Sirens. Men giving chase. There was nothing but the buzz of the city. After a block, Sher glanced over her shoulder.

The woman sat inside her store listening to polkas, chomping pickles, and mulling over her daughter's recent engagement to a man not only not Polish but also not a Catholic—a blonde German Lutheran, of all things. After all they did to the Polish people— it was terrible, terrible, what they did. The woman viewed herself and all Polish people as survivors, as the real victims of the tall, square-faced Germans—never mind those Jews, they got what they deserved—and now her daughter would marry one of those lunkheaded blondes who'd forced her out of her own country. As Sher disappeared down the street, the woman set a half-eaten pickle on the counter, wiped her brow, her large breasts straining the threads of her gray cotton dress printed with small pink flowers. The woman sighed. What, oh, what would she do?

Sher turned the corner, keeping pace with the crowd, despite the pain in her ankle. The rain had subsided. She dodged two men talking loudly about the Lakers. She wanted off the streets. Car horns tooted as a light turned green and a car failed to move. Women clipped by in square-toed pumps. Sher focused on finding holes in the crowd cutting left then right then right again. She had food and wanted to get away from the looks and the cops and the horns and the lights flaring like fireworks red and yellow and green through the mist. The eyes of the woman who'd been knifed popped into Sher's mind. No matter where Sher looked, there they were. And her grandmother's eyes too.

* * *

"Hey. Indian farm girl back from foraging," Jackie said. She rubbed her eye. "Since when did Indians become farmers anyway?"

Sher tossed the Nut Goodies and nuts onto a mattress.

"What do you know," Jackie said.

Sher ripped open the bag of peanuts. She and Kris cracked peanut shells, making a mound at their feet the mice would enjoy once the girls vacated the room.

"Want some?" Sher asked.

"Nah," Jackie said. "Can't ever eat nuts without something to wash it down with. Whiskey, brandy, Schmidt's." She laughed. "Know what I mean?"

"Sure," Kristin said, thinking of her father's drinking. "I *know* what it's like," Kristin said, startled that she said that and not entirely sure what she meant by it.

"Thought you might," Jackie said. She jumped up and left.

The girls ate the nuts and Nut Goodies, digging the chocolate out of the wrappers and licking their fingers. Kristin grabbed Sher's wrapper and licked it. Sher grabbed it back. "Ick." She threw the wrapper at Kristin. The girls laughed.

The door flung open. Jackie burst in. "Why the hell didn't you lock it?" she hissed. "Oh hell, there's no lock. I forgot. What do I care anyway?"

The girls were silent, startled by her abrupt turn of emotions.

"Only thing Jessie drank," Jackie said, and lifted a bottle of Tab in the air as a toast. "Drinks," she said. "She's alive. Right?" Jackie set the other two bottles on the floor. "For Jessie," Jackie said. "We will never forget you, good friend."

The girls said nothing.

A cry cracked out of Jackie. "I think I got the "Subterranean Homesick Blues." She laughed at her joke about Dylan's song. Tears rolled off her chin.

The girls studied the floor.

"Good friend," Jackie cried. "Have one. Thing you'll learn on the streets is you can't live on stolen goods alone." Her face flushed as she fought off tears. "You have to find another way to get food and a place to sleep." She snapped off the cap and tossed it to the floor. She looked at the girls. "Winters get cold." She took a drink, swallowed, and then pushed the neck of the bottle into her mouth and pulled it out slowly. "Know what I mean?" she asked staring at the girls, both there and not there, seeing and not seeing. "Go home."

Kristin froze.

"Get away from here—before you can't." Tricia sat on the floor. Her eyes glazed over like marble, as if someone else had pushed the bottle into her mouth.

Kris's head spun.

Sher draped her arm around her cousin like she did when they walked the back roads on the reservation. "Shhh..." she said, the way Sher's father did for her when she was little and had been "bit by a bee" or lost her pet lamb to a coyote.

Tricia wrapped her arms around her shins and rocked, her curved backbone pushing against the wall. "Even you, butchy." She pointed at Sher. "They'll want you too. Break you in as a runner. Or," and she pressed her palms over her eyes as if she were trying to wipe out what she saw, what she knew. "Boys too. Got a hole? If you poop, you do. They'll stick it in."

Kris's emotions whipped her into the past, to a place where she had no words for what her father did to her. She had no idea what to do next—stand, sit, run, cry, yell. Panic shot through her like a drug. "We have to stop the war," she blurted.

"We are the war!" Jackie jumped up and stared into the mottled mirror. "We are what gets taken."

The girls lifted their eyebrows.

Jackie saw them in the mirror. "Get away!" Jackie yelled. "I don't hang out with stupid girls who ask for it."

Sher looked at the back of a chair, embarrassed for Tricia or Jackie or whoever she was at the moment.

Kris leaned into her cousin. "Let's..."

"Assholes!" Jackie shouted, flinging her empty Tab bottle against the wall. She opened the door, stared into the hall, glanced back through the windows at the alley, and then slammed the door behind her. She forgot about the girls, hitting the street full stride. No one would fuck with her that night.

Cars and cabbies tooted at one another or squealed to another part of town as the rain returned, falling around them in lines like long hair. The girls sat in the room as shadows moved in to replace the light of day. No one had thought to steal candles or a flashlight. Kristin grew despondent—her stomach a pit. She urinated into a dusty glass Bell jar she'd found in one of the buffet drawers. Sher became itchy from the silence and feeling trapped with nothing to do. She thrummed her fingers on the floor, matching the beat of the rain. Her thoughts strayed to the farm and the sound of the rain on the reservation and the feeling she had listening to the rain in the country, knowing that the crops would now grow and the cattle and deer and other wild animals would have full ponds to drink from. The garden would sprout fat bright red tomatoes and prickly cucumbers her grandmother would stuff into jars with onions and vinegar and dill and leave sit in the basement until they turned into sour pickles they'd eat when company visited.

As night drew around them, Sher's longing for her grandmother lay heavy at her feet like the enormous curved squash she and her grandmother discovered beneath leaves big as elephant ears. From the Minneapolis warehouse, Sher was transported two hundred miles north, ten years earlier, crouched in the garden next to her grandmother, digging through the clean, generous earth, gathered together in mounds. "Everything is round," Sher's grandmother said. "Not straight lines like their roads and houses that make corners and then someone is left out, in that corner, alone. With a circle everyone is the same distance apart." Ethel's long, brown, big-knuckled fingers moved swiftly under the leaves in search of zucchinis. Those green-skinned vegetables reminded Sher of a long fish, something about the vegetable's skin—shiny and dark green with cream-colored spots not much larger than pin pricks—and its curve like that of a fish flashing its lean, long body beneath the murky water. "I did this with *ninokomis*, my grandmother, yah," Ethel said, her eyes shiny and long-distanced, seeing the past before her again. She exuded joy, a lightness of energy when she spoke of her childhood—before they'd taken her. "And she with hers. Women nourish the people," she said, patting a mound of earth. She found a strong, well-formed zucchini, checked it for rot, flipped it without severing its tie to the mother plant, and set it back on the earth.

Ethel looked at Sher. Her face softened, radiating love for her granddaughter the way a squash plant flowers its golden petals, rejoicing in the beauty of being, before transforming to flesh. "Women are strong. Aren't we, my girl?" She cupped Sher's round face, pressing dirt onto her cheeks and chin. "You, in particular. My grandmother told me stories about old-time Indian women warriors, fighting alongside the men. Sometimes fighting the men, eh?" She laughed. "The Christians didn't like those stories to be told. They want their women to be obedient." She swiped dirt on the girl's nose. "That is you. The heart of a warrior." Her hands returned to the earth. "Remember, my girl. No matter what, not all is lost. Nothing is ever gone for good." And then, as swiftly as she'd focused on Sher, her intention returned to the task at hand so that her blooming family—all but Josie still at home at that time— would have sustenance come the howling winter winds. Despite living in the angled whites' house her parents so disliked, she would be sure none would be left out.

Virginia, Minnesota, July 1969

Em woke bleary. She turned her head toward the one small window. Early morning sun sparkled as if diamonds were cut into the window's glass. *Water drops*, Em thought. She noted her thirst, her tongue and throat swollen, dry as dust. The way she'd seen deer during a drought, she, her brother, and her dad took as many as they could to spare them the agony of choking on their own tongues. Em lay on her belly, in silence, arms twisted behind her back, face throbbing, her sight now on the walnut-stained baseboard, nearly a foot tall. It cost too much in pain to tilt her head toward the window. She lay that way for a while. Who knew how long? The only ones with her were the spirits, and neither they nor Em followed time. Then the scratchings began, faint, irregular sounds, as if something were being dragged across a surface, paused on one section longer than the rest, got caught up on the surface, and then finished with a swift flourish. She listened, moved her tongue in her mouth to make spit. She tilted her head at the jewels on the window for a moment, set her head to the floor, and listened for sound beyond the scratchings.

The tempo of the scratchings increased. Em knew not what or who it was, but she knew whatever it was—a squirrel or a mouse trapped by a piece of plaster that fell, blocking its hole, or whomever—a mute girl, a gagged woman, someone too frightened to speak locked in a nearby closet, or the spirit of a servant girl that stayed with the house—it was speaking to her. Could it be Josie's spirit, restless? Em quieted herself so she could hear, so she would be ready. The scratching ended. A screen door squeaked. A lock popped. A door scraped across the floor. Em swept her mind clear. Listened for how many. One set of feet, a pause, and then another, harder and heavier. The elaborately carved wood screen door slapped shut.

Em slackened her muscles. Let them think she was dead. Or

unconscious. *Is this what happened to Josie?* Em thought. Shoes slapped across the floor and up three flights of stairs. Em noted one slower than the other, pausing at each landing—out of shape. The men said nothing. Over-confident. Fearful. Or maybe they didn't know each other. Were they the same ones from before? Then they were outside her door. Em loosened the last fibers of her being as the handle clicked and the closet door swept open.

Rough fingers pressed into her neck. "Heart's beating." A white man's voice. He grasped Em's jaw, turned her face toward his. She played dead. He dropped her head, grabbed her wrists, pulled her into the hall. "She going to Minneapolis?" An Indian man asked. Em felt a surge of rage flash through her, hot and harder to control because of the betrayal. She squelched it, hoped they did not see or feel it. "I think they sold this one upstream. Thunder Bay. Maybe Toronto." The man dragged her by her armpits to the stairs. Em's head hung over the first step. Her hair fell off her face. "Grab her legs. She's not worth nothing dead." The Indian man wrapped his fingers around her ankles. He paused. She had his auntie's face. As he picked her up, her left leg slipped from his grasp. The white man looked at him. "This your first time? You moved furniture before, right? Same thing. No dings."

The men carried Em downstairs, maneuvering her limp body through a sitting room. She dared not even slit her eyes, lest they see she was conscious and hit her again or take extra precautions to keep her under their control. Plus, not being able to see helped her disconnect the pain—a trick she had learned at a young age in the schoolyard.

The Indian man banged the old stove with his hip as he backed the girl's body through the kitchen.

"Ugly one," the white man said.

"Yah," the Indian man said.

Em would get the Indian first. His betrayal hurt the worst. It always did.

If they got her to those ships, no one would see her again. Her best bet, she figured, was to get away from these two. The Indian was inexperienced. They hadn't worked together before.

They turned a corner into the living room. A man's voice boomed outside. The white man dropped Em. "Stay with her," he commanded and ran outside. The Indian man shifted his grip. Em slit her eyes, saw him craning his neck, his lanky black hair down to his shoulders. Behind him was a hallway to the kitchen door. Sun shone through the door's window. Outside, voices rose, at least three. Arguing. Glass shattered. "What the hell I told him! Stay the fuck!" More glass exploded. "Shoot," the Indian man whispered, glanced at Em's immobile body. He wondered if she was really alive. He dropped her legs. The way they smacked the floor, he didn't worry about her running off. "Greg!" The white man outside yelled. "Get out here!" Metal cracked. Greg bolted out the front door. *Greg*, Em thought. *Whoever heard of an Indian named Greg?*

A moment after the door shut, fearful they would see her through the front windows, Em crawled to the kitchen, scrabbled to her feet, and plunged out the back door. Her body didn't move right. Her eyes didn't see right. The sun shone hard on the tall grass around the house. The men screamed at each other. Em ran straight into the woods. As she entered the trees, she twisted her body to see behind her. No footprints to give away which direction she went. No men following her. Thirty feet in she cut to the left and disappeared. A towering canopy of white pine branches stood watch over her.

* * *

The girls lay on the bed until midmorning. Jackie and Terry were gone.

"Kris."

"Yah."

"I think we should leave here."

"Yah."

The girls didn't move. Their heads felt light from lack of food and water.

"Set then?" Sher asked.

"Yah."

"Leavin'?" Jackie burst into the room. She'd been listening again.

Kristin caught her breath.

Sher sat up.

"Where to?" Jackie asked.

"Don't know."

"Just stay then," Jackie said. "A little longer." She thumped shut the door. "Say another two hours." She lit a cigarette. "Or so."

Sher cleared her throat. She scuffed her boots on the floor, the way her grandfather had done when the social workers caught him on the porch—one blocked the door to the house and the other stood on the steps, or when they strutted out to the barn where he puttered, making it impossible for him to avoid them without making it obvious he was avoiding them.

"C'mon." Jackie tried to put forward the friendly part of her, but her eyes sparked. She tossed the morning paper on the floor: *Rally Today* across the top.

"Let's go," Kris said.

Sher shrugged.

"No," Jackie said, and twisted the doorknob as if she could lock it. "Just a couple of hours longer, I swear. It'll be worth your time. Promise." She tried to be friendly but her words and tone came out wrong.

Kris's pulse quickened.

Sher stepped toward the door.

Jackie and Sher sized up each other.

"Kris," Sher said. "Let's go."

Kristin grabbed the pack and stepped toward the door. Jackie blocked her.

"C'mon." Jackie invoked Tricia. "Stay with me," she whined. "Another coupla hours. Puhleaze. I—I don't feel so good. I don't want to be alone."

Kris hesitated.

Sher stepped beside Kris.

"I don't want to be alone," Tricia cried and grabbed Kris's hand.

Sher stepped around Tricia, yanked on the doorknob, springing the door from the frame. Jackie slapped the door with her palm to force it shut, but the door didn't budge in Sher's hand.

Jackie's eyes slid to Sher's forearm. The girl was strong. She could take Jackie. Jackie stepped back, and the girls sprang into the hall with such force it was as if they'd been thrown out of the room.

They hurried onto the street, cut to the right, and ran into the alley.

The girls stopped to breathe.

"Feel that?" Sher asked.

Kris nodded, bent over, her hands on her knees.

"You know what Grandma would say."

Kris nodded. "Yah. The spirit behind it."

The girls jogged a few blocks south to a stairwell. They

descended into the shade of the stairwell.

"I feel like I'm tripping," Kristin said. She squinted and covered her eyes with her hand like the bill of a cap.

"You never tripped," Sher said. The heat came off the sidewalk, hitting her face and chest like a wave.

"I can still feel like I am."

"Yah." Sher shuffled her boots on the step. "Didn't know it was this hot."

"Me either."

"How could we have?"

"Couldn't have."

The girls sat in silence. The heat circled their bodies like dogs looking for a place to settle.

A man dressed in a clown suit carrying a long string of yellow banana balloons behind him crossed the street. The girls watched him walk in floppy red shoes, white makeup, and a golden afro. He glanced at Kristin and Sher with a non-stop red smile painted on his white face, but his facial muscles were not smiling.

Kristin wiped sweat off her face. "Should we go to the rally now?" Kristin leaned over and spit.

"I don't know." Sher wanted to return to the farm, to the reservation. Maybe her mom and brother would leave again. Or just leave Sher alone. Let her be.

"C'mon. It could be fun." Kris tugged Sher's tank top. She smiled at Sher.

Sher draped her arm around her cousin. She couldn't leave Kris and Kris could not go back to Morgan. "I guess."

The girls took to the streets. They headed east in the general direction of the park.

"Should we have left her?" Kristin grabbed Sher's arm. "Why was she trying to get us to stay?"

"I dunno."

"Me neither."

"Wasn't good."

Kris nodded but pity tugged at her heart.

"The way she acted. Something weird."

Kris nodded. If Sher was sure, Kris would be too.

The girls heard a cacophony in front of them. They steered toward it. In a few blocks they encountered hippies smoking joints on the street, dancing, and yelling, "Down with the man!" and

"Peace, love and harmony, baby!" and "Make love not war!"

"A Indian," one young white man said to his friend. He held out his hand for Sher to grasp. "Sister!"

Sher ignored him.

The girls reached the corner of Hennepin and Lyndale. Waiting for the light to turn green, Sher glimpsed Loring Park. The light turned and the crowd moved, revealing a row of police. "Kris," Sher hissed. She grabbed for Kristin's arm but people streamed into the street, pulling Kris with them.

"Sher!" Kris yelled, as the crowd jostled her forward.

Sher found Kristin half a block away next to two barefoot hippies on a horse blanket in bell bottom jeans. Yarrow, Indian Hemp, and Purple-Stem Beggarticks sprang out of vases around them.

"Look," Kristin said, meeting Sher on the sidewalk. "They gave me these."

"Kris," Sher said, ignoring the flowers, "there's cops. People smoking weed on the streets." Sher pulled her close. "If we get arrested."

"Hey, little woman," the man said to Kristin, "is that your friend?"

"Yah," Kristin said.

"Hey, little woman's friend." He held a flower out to Sher. "I'm Darren."

Sher crossed her arms.

"No?" The man looked at the flower's face as if he were talking to it. He put the flower into a vase. Darren handed a pamphlet to a man passing by. "Drop by anytime." The man refused the pamphlet. "Dig it, brother," Darren said. "Did you see that? A real uptight brother."

Kristin held a pamphlet out for Sher to read. "It's their group." *Peaceniks a communal musical trip open to all* was written in gothic lettering across the top. *Join Us Anytime 3524 South Chicago Avenue.*

Sher nodded.

Kristin tucked the pamphlet into her jeans.

Darren grabbed the woman on the blanket and kissed her neck from behind.

"Stop by our pad sometime, little woman," he said to Kristin.

"Ah, I—" Red rose up Kris's neck and cheeks. She glanced at the woman and then at Darren.

He smiled.

"Kris." Sher pulled her away.

The heat bore down on that revolutionary day. The crowd thickened like cream shook from milk. Cops in sunglasses and round helmets appeared with their arms hooked. Drums pounded.

"Kris, we should leave."

"Yah," Kris said, but she was mesmerized by the energy building around them.

Cotton from the trees floated around the girls. The crowd began chanting, "No more war! No more war!"

"Girls!"

The girls twisted toward the voice.

"Girls, over here."

Sher squinted in the bright sun.

"Over here." Jacob waved. He stood next to Darren, who was talking to a man in bell bottom jeans and long brown side-burns.

"Jacob?" Kris asked.

Jacob bobbed between the crowd, now packed shoulder to shoulder, fists raised, shouting, "No more war!"

"Hi!" Jacob's smile was wide. He bopped up to the girls.

Sher motioned for them to move to the edge of the crowd. The girls and boy cut through the hippies until they were at the fringes of the rally.

"So," Jacob shouted. "Where'd you go? Why'da leave me?"

"You walked off," Sher said, her eyes following a sparrow as it disappeared into the shaking leaves of a cottonwood tree.

"No, no, no, no!" Jacob stomped the back of his heel on the dirt. "I came back and you were gone."

"We waited and you didn't come back and we went to the store and didn't see you," Kris burst out. "I even looked out the window for you and you weren't there."

"What window?" Jacob insisted.

"The church window." Kristin soft-punched him.

"What church window?" Jacob rubbed his arm. "What are you talking about?"

"Who cares?" Sher plucked a piece of lime green grass and chewed on the end nearest the root to get at the sweet white heart. She stared at a woman, her fist in the air, riding a man's shoulders.

"I care," Jacob said. "What church window? I thought we were going to hang out."

"Whaddya wanna know so bad for?" Kris asked.

"C'mon." Jacob followed Sher's gaze. "What are you looking at? That woman? Tell me where you were."

"In the church next to where we slept," Kris said.

"Across the street to the right under the freeway?" Jacob asked. "Or the other one to the left?"

"To the left," Sher lied. Sher's word was important to her. She'd been raised not to lie—ever—but she didn't like his insistence on knowing exactly where they'd been. She didn't want this boy knowing too much about them.

"Oh."

Kris didn't register Sher's lie. If she had, she would have been surprised. She'd never known Sher to lie.

High shrill whistles careened over the rally. "Run!" people yelled. Darren and his woman flew by. The woman turned sideways and yelled "Run!" at them. Her clog skittered across the dirt. She ran back to it, slipped it on, and then disappeared into the fray.

Men and women ran, shouting, "Run! Police brutality! The pigs are loose!" The police's dog whistles shrieked. From the east, police officers waded in to the crowd cracking the heads and shoulders of the protesters with bats.

The teens ran.

"This way!" Sher shouted. She ran half a block and slid headfirst under lilac bushes growing next to an apartment building.

Screams, whistles, and rocks flew overhead. The sound of the rocks ticking off brick buildings popped Sher's memory of her grandmother, telling her that the spirits always took four while her knife snapped carrots into medallion-shaped pieces for soup. Like the time the Rosseau infant died in a truck accident on Highway 79—his blanket-wrapped body sailed between two tall cedar trees the farmer had left to break the wind. People said it looked like a football the high school boys kicked through the uprights on crisp fall evenings in town. The baby landed with a thud in the soft, furrowed ground, his neck snapped. Two days later, three teenage boys drowned as they swam just ten feet offshore at Little Elbow River. All strong swimmers. No one could explain it. They families of those who died were Methodist and Episcopalian Indians—the funeral homes and Sher's grandparents' house were packed full of Indians from all over Minnesota, Wisconsin, North Dakota, and Canada for weeks.

As Sher pushed through the lilac bush, she thought *Grandpa. Grandma. Dad. Unless Em had died, there will be a fourth.* Sher smacked into a chain fence tangled with the bushes, saw a section where the fence flipped up like Batgirl's hair, and slid under it. The other two followed, scrambling under the fence. The teens crouched in a yard on the other side of the fence, catching their breath as people screamed, whistles screeched, and rocks and bricks flew in every direction. "All hell's breaking loose!" a man behind them yelled. "The cops are macing everyone!" The girls' eyes locked. Kris did not see in Sher what she usually saw—that it would be all right. Fear moved in. Something bent between the girls, snapped, bore down by too much weight—their losses, the chaos exploding around them, their pain, their ancestors' pain. Some *thing* moved in. Kris felt it, and shivered in the heat. Sher did not see the crow-like bat beast flapping about Kris or feel the air thrust out from beneath its wings, but Sher smelled it. Without thinking, she spit.

Her grandfather had told her. "If death gets near you, spit it out. Don't let it settle in you." And Sher did, on her runs, around the farm, through the woods, and in town—if she happened by dead animals, a squirrel smashed flat on the road, a ripped apart carcass in the woods, she spit. If she got a whiff of a rotting, rancid smell, she spit. And so, crouched in the yard, she spit. Without a thought.

Cops on horses lined the alley east of the girls and boy, cordoning off the yard where they hid. Cops cracked batons on heads. One yelled through a bullhorn, "Attention! Move north. Move north." The horses moved as one unit northward toward the cross street as their riders leaned and stretched to smash the heads and shoulders of protesters with their batons. Protesters screamed and ran. Residents hid in their basements.

"Pigs!" Kris screamed when she saw a cop whack a man. She wanted to throw herself into the chaos. She wanted to burn up in it.

One block away, hiding behind a garbage can cover used as a shield, a young Indian woman lobbed concrete chunks she'd gathered from a construction site at the police, her large, brown eyes visible above the rag tied over her nose and mouth. If she had known about the girls, one block west of her, or if the girls had known of her, the looming disaster may have been prevented. Instead, each fought as she could, not knowing, forty-five strides separated them from being reunited after she'd left the girls standing by the barn.

However, since the spirits have their ways, and fate has yet to be cheated, the girls and young woman missed one another in the amount of time it would have taken Sher to sprint thirty-eight sections of Portland cement sidewalk laid fifty years earlier by Lithuanian scabs, who merely stared at the throngs of German and Swedish day laborers, hurling insults at them in English, German, and Swedish, but not Lithuanian, Russian, or Polish, the languages they spoke. The Lithuanians mixed, measured, spread, and evened the concrete block after block, unsure why the Americans, who spoke multiple languages, screamed and marched around them as they worked; unsure why they stomped, spit, and tossed rocks at their heads and into the wet cement. And then, every Friday, the Lithuanians collected their pay, drank it gone at the neighborhood Russian tavern, where they could communicate well enough, returned to the flats they shared, and mounted their wives, sometimes hearing the unintelligible chants of the angry German and Swedish men as they thrust into their wives in three and four room apartments filled with sleeping and not sleeping family members and odd fellows from the old country.

* * *

A scream, like one of the lone big cats that occasionally passed through their farmland, wailed just north of the girls. Kristin lunged toward the alley. Sher grabbed her by the waist. Maybe, she thought, her brute strength could keep Kris with her. Jacob vomited in the bushes. Rubber bullets burst over the alley. People ran, yelled, "Honeywell's killing us all!" A line of blue pushed north, sticks cracking, clearing out the alley.

As Sher held tight to Kris, she saw her father half-buried in the snow, a calf in his arms, the bright morning sun gleaming off the sheet of a surprise late April snow so smooth and pristine, without blemishes, it looked unreal. "Dad!" Sher shouted from across the field, expecting he would stir, expecting he would say, "Thought I was goner, huh?" And then stand and move toward her with the calf he'd set out to find wriggling in his arms. He did not move. She thought he was teasing her. Pushing through the snow, she came closer to him. "Pops!" she yelled again. Her voice cracked, shooting out across the silent, icy land like buckshot. Deer, standing in snow midway up their bellies one quarter of a mile away, craned their necks. Mice nesting in the chicken coop twitched. A pack of wolves just north of the girl twitched their ears mid-leap hunting rabbits in the deep snow. The trees, their outstretched arms and fingers cradling delicate lines of snow, heard and saw all of it, and it became part of them, recorded in their beings, in their flesh. Ring after ring, year after year, the Standing People recorded the story of the land. They absorbed, held, witnessed. The Standing People. The libraries of the earth. The collectors of knowledge, their limbs arching over the land, over life. Holding. Bending. Protecting. "Dad! Dad!"

How many times had Sher and her father pushed through the snow-covered fields and woods in search of deer, grouse, moose, and squirrel in the harshest of winters? The snow brought silence with it, then and now, punctured by an eagle's far-off cry or the crack of a shell through a barrel, slung toward its target, to take a life so that Sher's family could eat beyond the block of government cheese, beyond what carrots and cucumbers and tomatoes suspended in water and salt lurked in the shadow of their basement on a cold, dark February night, when the world had gone barren, harsh and cruel, after her father and grandparents had given away their last winter reserves to families, Indian and white, with nothing left for themselves. That very thing—generosity—that the government had hoped to cure by stealing Indian lives, ways, and land and then giving the surviving Indians tar paper shacks, farms, and the white man's religion. How many memos they generated—*The Indian in his simplicity will give away the last of his clothing, food, and feathered trinkets that seem to have great value to him with no thought to how he will survive himself. This can be cured by teaching him ownership so that the Indian too can become civilized in the ways of the white man.*

When her father and the calf did not move after her second call, Sher knew. She froze, refused it—for a moment—and then darted forward, fell, straightened herself, and pushed steadily to him through the waist-high snow, her eyes on him and the calf, taking it in. Her father. Her pops. Her da-da. Her feelings, shut off. The only sound the expulsion of her breath and the crunch of the snow, the top layer a snapping sheet of thin ice. A red hawk circled in the treeless valley behind the barn, where they grew corn last year, and alfalfa the year before. The hawk searched for dark-colored rabbits and mice, and small, weakened barn cats, an easy snatch against the brightness of the land. If Sher had arrived the next morning, or perhaps later that day, long before she saw her father's body, she would have spotted the enormous black silhouettes of turkey vultures circling high overhead, as the birds took turns devouring the man and calf below.

At ten feet, Sher panicked. Perhaps she could still save him. If he could just get to him faster, to warm him, he would be fine, maybe lose a toe or two to a bit of frost-bite. Like that man in town last year. Spent a night in a snowbank, but he was okay. Only lost some toes and fingers. "Lucky son-of-a-bitch," some said. "Protected," others said. Sher pushed forward, swiping at the snow with her arms like she was like swimming. Certainly, he would jump up, laughing, wipe the frost from his face, shout "Gotcha! Ehhh!" and wrap his arm around her shoulder. They would trudge back to the house and sit at the kitchen table, play cards, listen to the evening WCCO on the radio. Fry up potatoes for dinner—in lard and salt with a handful of crumbled hamburger. After eating they'd stare out the dining room windows, over the land their people had been on for hundreds of years, their grief as heavy and suffocating as the snow—lost in their memories of Sher's grandparents. All the mornings Sher's grandmother stood in front of those same windows, announcing the new day by shouting, "Daylight in the swamp!" at sunrise as she looked out at the dirt driveway and rolling land beyond. Or her grandfather, perpetually tinkering at the cars and trucks and rusted-through farm tractors next to the barn or tossing a knotted-up rag with one of the many huge dog wolf crosses they'd had over the years, losing a few to bear, cougar, and wolf pack attacks. "Atta boy, atta girl," he'd say, scruffing their thick ruffs. *"Mino animoosh."*

At five feet she saw his face frozen blue, tiny ice crystals hung from his bottom lip and nose—the last of his breath. He'd died with his eyes open, his frost-covered eyelashes like white spider legs framing his dark eyes. The calf's red tongue, lolling out its mouth, blood clots frozen like berries from biting it in fear, and then beneath the tongue the frozen pinkish red pool on the crystal popping white of the snow, like the twinkling raspberry snow cones he'd bought her every year at the county fair. Her father's

hands and arms, stiff in his brown, wool-lined cow leather gloves
and jacket, clasped about the calf's midsection and neck. They'd
died together, as one, such that the coroner had to saw the calf in
three parts to remove it from the man's grasp.

Three feet from her dad's body, Sher's body slowed as her
thoughts bounced to the glossy photographs of Greek and Roman
statues from her school books. She remembered one of a man
holding a lamb. Or maybe that was Jesus. Or one of their other
saints. She'd looked at the pictures, trying to tell if the statues had
been carved from separate chunks of stone, then fitted together.
But they'd been carved from the same block of marble. That had
interested her—how things fit together. How things that look so
separate are actually one.

One foot away her mind stopped in shock. Then reeled with
questions: How could a day that pristine hold death? How could
her father die, so soon after her grandparents? How could she be
so alone in the world, at thirteen? Suddenly, utterly, alone. How
could this be? She sank to her knees a foot in front of her father,
her hands resting atop the frozen snow between them, the way
she'd rested them on the dining room table after she emptied her
hand in King in the Corner or the other card games she and her
family played night after night, and sometimes for days on end
during forty-below cold snaps.

Together, as one. That was how Sher had dragged them, on the
sled her dad had made to haul wood to the side of the house
during winter months. It took her five-and-a-half hours to get them
on the porch and then into the kitchen, where she'd laid down a
quilt in a pointless effort to contain the water and blood that
would soon melt off them. She covered them with the corners as if
she were wrapping a bundle to gift to someone, and then collapsed
at the dining room table, hoping, for a change, that her brother
would appear that night and help her figure out what to do, whom
to call first.

Once Sher's father and the calf had thawed, Sher and Tomas,
who worked the farm to the east, were able to move the calf some
despite the rigor mortis. They found a chunk torn from the calf's
hindquarters and gashes on the side of the calf and on Sher's dad's
thighs, back, and neck. A cougar, most likely. Possibly a bear. Her
father died trying to save the calf. "Something he would do,"
Tomas said upon seeing the gashes. His way of telling the girl her

father was a good man. He shook his head and kept his eyes away from the man's daughter, whose household had gone from six to two in a matter of months, if you counted that no good brother of hers. That and their girl who disappeared years ago. Presumed dead. He squeezed the girl's shoulder and trudged home through the snow to his evening chores.

* * *

"Pigs!" Kristin screamed, snapping Sher back to Minneapolis. Kris twisted, the way that calf must have tried to get away, its eyes wide and fiery, its tongue bloodied flesh. "Pigs!" The word erupted with such raw rage it felt as if it cut abrasions in her throat.

Sher felt Kris's hatred, so strong and shocking she almost lost her grip.

"Stop!" Kris yelled at Sher, the cops, her father, the whites on the reservation, the Indian kids who teased her for looking white.

Whistles blew. Cops boomed, "Disband immediately!" over a bullhorn. A hail of sticks on fire flew end-over-end down the alley at the cops. "Fuck you pigs! Fuck the state! Fuck the man!"

Sher pulled Kris past Jacob to the garage. They slid along the wall. On the other side of the garage waged war between the cops and crowd. Stones and fire flew. Batons cracked. The bullhorn shouted orders. Drums pounded. Men with bandanas pulled over their faces jumped off of a short concrete wall on the other side of the alley and pulled cops off the horses. "Free the people! Free the horses!" one yelled as he whacked a horse on its haunches, sending it into a frenzy that ended with it being hit by a car four blocks away, breaking a leg, and being shot dead in the street by the cop who'd been riding it.

Sher yanked Kristin toward an opening in the alley, shook her, and yelled, "Run!" The girls vaulted the short concrete fence behind a large stately white house, leaped over flat prickly bushes, and ducked under a tree, nearly running into two people leaning against the tree while rubbing their tearing eyes and swearing. Jacob followed. A white man popped out from behind the house, pointed at the girls, and said, "Watch this!" He lobbed a burning stick toward the cops in the alley. The fire stick arched through the air as if it were in slow motion. As the fire twirled, Kris wanted to hurl hurt through the air with a precision as beautiful as he did.

"Run!" Sher shouted at her cousin.

Kris stood staring at the fire stick spinning in the sky.

"Like that, chickie?" the man yelled at Kris. "Imma find you later!" He pulled out another stick, pointed it at Kris, yelled, "For you!" He lit the end and threw it high into the air.

"Run!" Sher pulled Kris.

The girls ran.

Virginia, Minnesota, July 1969

Em ran. Her breath ragged. When she could catch the sun through the forest roof she cut left or right to align herself toward the west. She was not sure, but thought if she stayed course toward the sun as it set, she would be moving in the opposite direction of the house. She was not fast, like her niece, who spent day after day running through the trees. She had not stayed true to the old ways, as her niece had. Em had turned her back on the old ways. Maybe the trees would have mercy on her, out of their allegiance to her family. Em needed help. She had no idea where she was. She had no idea where to go. She had nothing but her clothes. Her pride, as her father had warned her, would not get her out of this alive. Nevertheless, her parents, her grandparents, her ancestors had prepared her for this. Everyone, they'd taught, had their lessons to learn.

As she moved her mind regained its balance. Her body hurt. She could not stop. If they caught her, they would kill her on the spot, put a bullet in her head the way a sick cow is killed—dropping it to its front knees before the huge animal topples over. Her lungs ached. Her throat dry. She listened for running water, for the cries of water birds, but heard nothing except the crackling of twigs and dried leaves. Em was deep in the woods. No matter that it was June, it would get cold at nightfall. And her monthly was close. She felt it in the swell of her body. If she bled, she would be wet, cold. Without water to cleanse herself, dirt and leaves and insects would stick to her thighs and legs where her blood trailed. The voices of the old ladies at her grandparents' came around—"moon time"—and she recalled, they used moss, which lined the feet of the trees all around her. Did she remember how to start a fire with no match? Could her mind ring back to her childhood, when her father taught her Indian ways, taught her to survive a moment such as this?

Em moved her bruised body over the scrub, grabbing the roots of bushes and saplings to hoist herself over mounds and up small hills. "Please," she heard herself say. "Help me," she asked anyone or anything that might be present. The spirits. The animals. The trees. "Please." Desperate for water, her mind reared into her past. She remembered what the old ones said, when they prayed, when they taught. She thought it. Then knew she needed to say it. "I am a pitiful human being." Her father always told her she was too big for her britches, too proud. He said she needed to humble herself. The old men said, in Indian, "That one there," and they'd purse their lips, point at her, "she's going to..." and they'd lower their voices so she could not hear the rest. Or, "watch your girl, she's...." Her father, she recalled, as she stumbled among the trees, always looked down at the ground, spit. She didn't know what they were saying, but she didn't think it good as, even to her at that young age, his body seemed defeated, seemed sad, seemed to bend under some weight. "Please take pity on me," she shouted. The bodies of the Standing People vibrated around her, and, because she reached back into her childhood, into teachings that were forbidden by the white world, teachings that even some Indians, because of the churches, thought were devil talk, terror shot through her. Her foot struck the top of a buried rock. She fell. Grabbed the base of a large fern. "Please. I am pitiful human being."

She tried to propel her legs, but they would not move. Her breath was labored. She lay her head on her arm. Shut her eyes. Said "water" in English. Remembered it in Indian. Said it in Indian. "*Nibi.*" Said it again. "*Nibi.*" She didn't know she even remembered how to say it in Indian. *Help me*, she thought. "Help me," she said. She had not asked for help since the boys at school. Em had built a steel wall to keep the white boys at bay, relying only on herself from that time forward. Shutting out the spirits. Her parents and siblings. Anger was her fuel. Pride her horse. The old ones warned Em's father she would go down a tangled path. He could give her guidance, but the direction she went was her choice. She might be lost. She might never come back. Em's legs curled to her chest. A low whining emitted from her throat. She pulled her knees tighter to her chest, remembered something else about women and water. Her mind swam in her thirst, her body drying like a leaf. When was the last time she'd drank? She did not know. She stood, stumbled seventy yards to the west, down a hill and into an area of the forest covered in five-foot tall ferns. She crawled twenty more yards and collapsed. "*Nibi*," she called out.

* * *

The girls stopped in a backyard on the southeast skirt of downtown Minneapolis. Kris collapsed next to a garage shedding its gray paint in patches. Sher leaned against it, her lungs and legs built strong from running. Jacob flopped onto the ground. Sirens blared from the south, wound west, and then headed north as they made their way to the rally, now a full-blown riot.

"Cops," Sher said. She dropped to the ground.

Jacob froze. He felt he should run, yell, "Run, Nazis, *laufen, laufen*" the way his parents had in their sleep, their eyelids fluttering like pallid moth wings—hands and knees jerking in a suburb outside Chicago to ward off the SS men who grabbed them and their parents off the streets of Berlin thirty years earlier. "Run! Run!" Jacob's grandparents yelled to his parents. "*Laufen, laufen!*" But the children did not run. They could not move in such unimaginable fear, their feet rendered motionless at four and five. Then at thirty-five, in another country, their bare feet struggled to move beneath the twisted, white cotton sheets while their boy lay awake, eyes wide to the shadows, in the room across the hall. Their terror filled the house like smoke, engulfing their son, filling his lungs—the three of them were all that were left of two Jewish families that had once numbered in the hundreds.

Jacob grasped his legs to his chest, the way he lay in bed as a child while German words of death and disaster snapped about his room. He grabbed his head the way he was taught in elementary school nuclear bomb drills.

A young Black boy and girl appeared in the window. Their small faces pressed into the glass, peering at the girls and boy in their backyard. They disappeared behind a flutter of lace curtains.

"Jacob," Sher asked as the cops trundled by in trucks, "where can we go to be safe?"

"My friend's."

"Where's that?" Sher asked.

"No sé. No sé!"

An elderly white woman with a 1950s bouffant hairdo in the house next to the children's pulled the baby blue sheet she hung up as curtain just enough to see the girls and the boy pinned to the ground. Her face registered uncertainty and then surprise and then fear. She disappeared behind the sheet.

"What?" Sher asked.

"Um," Jacob said. "Let me think."

The trucks rumbled.

"Jacob," Kris hissed. "Where do we go?"

"The highway. 35W." Jacob's eyes fluttered, shocked by the bright blue sky. He felt, for a moment, like he did not know where he was, as often happened when he was a young boy, riding the roundabout on the playground at his elementary school, the world suddenly spun along with his consciousness, transporting him to a time and place far from where he stood, a country he had never been, but knew as if he'd lived it. A place he felt through the beating of his mother's heart when she gripped him with love and fear to her chest, the way her mother smothered her in the barracks as the smoke of their people wafted through chimneys and curled into charcoal skies, the ashes of their bodies breathed in by the neighboring town. And what he felt through his father's heart, pounding with excitement and rage, when he was on top of Jacob, ripping open his son's flesh with his own, as had happened to him in the Catholic orphanage after the war. "Jew, filthy Jewboy," releasing from the thin lips of the priest as he raped the young Jewish boy, pretending to be a Catholic boy, causing the boy's spirit to flee, opening space for a Gollum to take up residence where the boy once lived.

"Where near 35W?" Sher asked Jacob.

Jacob shut his eyes.

Kris wanted to punch him as if he were responsible for the imminent danger they were in, as if he were responsible for all the years of rape in her house and the murder of her mother which she could not remember or forget.

"Chicago," Jacob said, his voice disintegrating.

"Okay." Sher glanced at the trucks. "Take us there." She stood, pushed down the pain in her ankle, pulled the other two to their feet, and strode toward the alley, away from the trucks.

The girls and Jacob headed south through the alleys behind three-story Victorian houses that had been inhabited by Swedish and German lumber barons and bankers and politicians. This neighborhood was still as the wailing sirens whipped between the houses and gunfire at the rally popped like fireworks on the Fourth.

Only it was not the Fourth of July, it was the sixteenth of

August 1969, and two Indian girls and a Jewish boy on the run
from the past trudged along the edge of downtown trying to avoid
cops and clubs and hippies with too many hands and other men
who would get them to do things they would never be free from.
Things that, if they ever lived in a house again, and if they had
children, they would pass down to their children, and their
children to theirs, in one way or another. Maybe as violence.
Maybe as silence. Maybe as an absence of spirit and attention. And
maybe, as enormous, protective love for their offspring. Yet, even if
they didn't become what had hurt them, their heartbeats would
have shadows and their pain and fear would carry on, alongside
their love.

The girls and boy ran and trotted as best they could between
their hurt ankle and ribs and shoulder and drug haze, and
disappeared families. They stopped twice to drink from hoses left
coiled in side yards and piss in bushes. They crisscrossed through
backyards and alleys and over roads and under bypasses until they
reached the southern tip of downtown Minneapolis, a gutted-out
section of the city where drug dealers and porn theaters and litter
flipped through empty streets. Men in various levels of undress
leaned in doorways, their faces shaded and their arms folded across
their bare chests. Jacob kept his head down, stoned and coming
down off a trip, he had been in the neighborhood before and knew
the men in the doorways. Some didn't care if it was a boy or girl.
Others had their preferences.

The teens heard the far-off sound of a radio playing afternoon
rhythm and blues, the scratching of crushed aluminum caught by a
breeze, and the occasional abrupt cough of a man—black, brown,
red, and white. Most of the men were a mix of two or more. The
suffocating heat exploded on the teens without the cool green
shelter of elm-lined streets in the previous neighborhood. They
sweated. The girls felt as if they were walking through a ghost
town in an old western or a village in Vietnam recently bombed
overhead.

Jacob kept his head down, staring at his shoes as they made
their way over the cracked sidewalk peppered with scraggly green
weeds and dandelions sprouting through the cement. Sher's head
was up, making occasional eye contact with the men in the
doorways, but not enough to solicit an exchange and not too little
so as to come off as frightened. Kristin's shock receded with each

step she took through the strange and unbelievable city. No trees. No plants. No dirt. Kris knew the hurt from the men in the doorways—the hurt they wanted to inflict on others and the hurt they felt themselves. Jacob knew it too. But he tried to play the men in a game he could not win.

Thatcher's Trail, Goodhue Reservation, July 1969

Em dozed. Woke. Dozed. Woke. The forest had been awake for hours. Em took in a thicket of huge ferns, calm and still, next to her. She listened to squirrels. Birds. Insects. She didn't want to be seen. Desperate, she searched for moisture on the giant underside of the fern arching above her. She bent a frond to her mouth, licked the bottom, and then another, and another until her mouth was no longer bone dry. She listened for the men. Had they followed her? Did they get a dog to track her? Were they near? How far had she run from the house? *I must get up*, she thought, but her legs would not move. She lay on her side, her body curled like a fiddlehead when the earth births it. She stared through the green fronds at the scales on the trunk of a pine tree. She felt as if she could not rise again. She could not go on, not without water. She would die there, her body decompose into the black dirt, become moss, tree, fern, home to the insects rambling about her now.

Em closed her eyes, shutting out the green life around her. She prepared to die. Soon she would be with Josie. "I'm sorry for being mad at you, Josie," she said. She loosened her spirit, opened gates, let birds fly free, bees buzz, flowers twist through the shade of the undergrowth. She opened waterways she'd blocked long ago. Breathed air. Heard songs in Indian she'd heard as an infant. Felt the earth. Her heartbeat. The air off the wings of a horsefly. Sighed. Shouted "Li! Li! Li! Li! Li!" Rolled over. Threw off her shoes. Who needs shoes in the spirit world? She spit. She dug a hole with her fingers and buried a pine cone. She scraped together a pillow out of fallen pine needles and leaves, rested her head, closed her eyes, and listened to the singing in Indian, the songs of her childhood, her people, that she'd heard as a child, until she felt she was no more. She'd become one with all.

A scratching woke Em. She thought she was in the closet again, until the smell of the earth jolted her memory. Scritch. Scritch. Scritch. Her scalp prickled. She searched through the ferns. To her right, a Little Person stood on a rock. A few feet high, all in black, with a red and yellow beaded bandolier bag over his shoulder, he hopped off the rock and dragged a bent wire hanger across it. Em had heard the stories. She believed them as a girl, but left behind the Old Ones' stories. *What good,* she had thought, *would they do me now?* The Little Person continued to scratch the rock as if she were not there. Em did not move. The ferns waved around her. Then the Little Person tapped the hanger on the rock, looked straight ahead, and stared. He stood, putting one hand on a knee and pushing off to get to his feet. He slipped the hanger under his armpit and walked, with a slight limp, in the direction he had stared. Em did not move. He disappeared into the undergrowth. Still, Em did not move. Seeing him frightened, enlivened, and shocked her. Because she had turned away from the Old Ones, from their ways, her common sense had dulled. She should have known to follow him. She should have understood his cues, but she did not.

The ferns bounced gently around Em, despite a lack of wind. She took a deep breath. Images, thoughts, memories swirled about her. She felt frenzied and calm. She wanted to jump up and shout and run around in circles with her arms outstretched like airplane wings as she did when she was a girl. At the same time, she felt as if she stood in the center of a windstorm, like she'd been waiting for this moment all her life. Em moved one foot in the dirt. A sparrow darted past her. Next to her, an earthworm struggled to rise out of the earth. Behind her, an eagle sat high in a pine scanning the forest floor for food. The white pines and a stand of tamarack that grew in a dip in the forest floor stood over and around her. For a moment, Em felt like a child, a toddler, the young girl who'd heard the stories. A girl who'd sat in her grandparents' laps, listening, wide-eyed to their stories as they peeled bark, beaded, and drank swamp tea. Her sight was not in the woods, it was back in those days, an iron pot on an open fire cooking sap.

Then the Little Person appeared in front of her, bent over sideways. He looked into her eyes. Em returned to the forest. He turned, still bent, and crossed her sight again, continuing south, the direction he'd stared earlier. As he pushed apart the ferns again, Em realized what she was to do. She scrambled after him. Although he was only a few feet tall, and limped, he moved swiftly. Em's body did not work right, but she kept up. She made enough noise to wake a bear. They went that way for a while, until he cut up to the right, and then down a slope. Em lost her footing, and slid down the slope. At the bottom, she saw it: a lake! He hopped into it, wetting just his moccasins. He turned to watch the girl splash her face with water so clean the rose, tan, and bone-colored granules could be seen on the sandy bottom. The Little Person stood, his hurt leg bent at the knee, and stared southwest into the trees. Once he knew she'd seen him, he set off northwest into the forest. The ferns swallowed him whole.

Em reveled in the water and silky sand. She drank, and bathed, and splashed. Laughter burst out of her body, giving sound to the joy of being alive, of gratitude for having her most basic, physical needs met, the way the Old Ones had thanked the spirits for food, for water, for life. Em splashed. "Li! Li! Li! Li!" she sang to the trees, the water, the animals. Em put her lips to the lake and drank and drank, her body moving further and further from death with each mouthful of water. She cleansed her hair and body. Crouched in the water, she remembered what the Old Ones taught: women are the carriers of water. Women are the protectors of water. She settled herself, focused on the water singing with the rocks. The rustling of small animals. The caws and shrieks and stealth of those that hunted. One more drink. One more splash. And then, she replaced the moss and set out the direction the Little Person told her to go, her faith in the old ways, returning, running through her veins, as water runs through the earth.

Em pushed through ferns with her thighs and waist, catching long forgotten paths, then losing them. Spirits watched her search. Some loved her. Some did not. Some were still honored through food, song, tobacco, prayer by those who lived in the bush, and practiced the old ways. And by those who lived on farms and in cities and practiced the old ways. Other spirits, long forgotten, could only watch her, the ceremonies that connected these spirits to humans, that brought balance to creation, that allowed the spirits to intervene, had disappeared because the humans forgot, or the ceremonies were lost in the chaos and death the English brought, making the *Windigo* that some Indians revered before the English set foot on the land stronger. Still, the spirits watched her out of curiosity and care. Em's leg buckled. She fell into a thicket of dogwood. Her body, exhausted and weak from not having food in days, did not get up. She tried to move, but did not have the strength. She lay in the bush, breathing. She watched the sky above her through the massive boughs of a white pine thirty feet tall. She would not fret, as her mother used to say. "My girl, do not fret. I had to learn to not fret the hard way." Em never knew what that meant—I had to learn the hard way. Now she did. Em relaxed into the branches of the dogwood, thought *I won't fret*. Then she conked out, her body nestled in the belly of the woods.

* * *

A helicopter spun overhead, hovering just above the buildings.

Jacob flung his arms over his head as he darted under a staircase.

Sher and Kristin stood stock-still on the sidewalk, watching the helicopter, along with a few men from the doorways who stepped out into the sunlight with their hands shading their eyes.

"Air raid!" Jacob yelled as he crumpled into a ball of arms and legs in the shade of the stairway.

A man on the sidewalk watching the helicopter laughed and dropped his cigarette, snuffing it out with his loafer. "Ain't no air raid." He shook his head and stepped into the doorway.

As the helicopter whirred above them, sending trash and dirt into a whirling dervish half the size of a football field, some of the men slammed their doors. Jacob kept quiet under the stair, curled in his bomb-protection posture, as he'd been taught in elementary school in Winnetka. His father had laughed when he'd received a notice from the school about practice sessions wherein a siren would blare and children would dive beneath their desks, curling up like an egg. "Like this, like an egg," their teachers explained, with their hands clasped over their heads, their knees to their chests, their shoulders rounded. They'd been instructed to not say "fetal position" because it was too sexual and could cause students to have inappropriate thoughts. Jacob's father threw the notice across the table at his son. It cut through the air like a knife before dive bombing into Jacob's lap. "Twenty years late for that," he said in Yiddish, and for him, it was.

The girls' hair whipped their faces. The helicopter hovered over them and the barren road as the retired military pilots from World War II searched for rioters or an uprising of impoverished people—Indian, Black, mixed bloods, foreigners, and urban white trash—living precariously in that all-concrete land. Governor LeVander had sent the helicopter. If the poor people in that neighborhood joined the hippies, it would be more than they could suppress. They could lose control of segments of the city, and would have to call in for back up from outstate police and the National Guard. Although it would only last a few days, considerable embarrassment would ensue, and the police and the politicians and the businesses, especially Honeywell (that had already received its share of protests), did not want these disparate groups to taste that kind of power. For these reasons, the men in the helicopter looked closely, one using binoculars, but all they saw were a couple of street kids and some nondescript men smoking cigarettes and drinking booze. Mad Dog, the pilot guessed.

Kristin leaned forward to stay upright. She glared as the pilot turned toward the man with the radio and pointed at her and her cousin. Then all four men looked at the girls and laughed. At that moment, the helicopter lifted straight up. Kristin grabbed a flattened, faded Marlboro box under her foot and threw it at the men. The force of the helicopter's wind slammed it to the ground. The metal bird spun off farther down the street as it made a slow and impervious way toward the rioters in Loring Park.

Jacob emerged from the stairs punching the air. Sher adjusted the pack slung across her shoulders. Kristin stared as if her look could burn a hole into the sky where the helicopter had been.

"Got rid of them." Jacob tugged on his T-shirt, hoping the men in the doors had not seen him hide.

"Let's go." Sher jumped the pack off her hips.

"They're the ones, I'm telling you," Jacob said.

"Too bad I didn't have a rock." Kristin picked up a rock and skipped it down the sidewalk in one smooth motion like she did at the pond back home.

"They're going to lock everybody up," Jacob said. "And end with everybody locked in camps." Jacob's voice rose. "Like Pops said. He said they'd do it here too. In the U S of A." He shook his fist in the air at the helicopter now the size of an insect on the horizon. "Stinking pigs!" he yelled at the helicopter aware of the men in shining white tank tops standing just out of the sun.

Kris walked south. The knife rubbed Sher's ankle as she followed her cousin, the pack bouncing on her slim boyish hips. After a few blocks, Sher turned and scanned the streets for Jacob. Jacob stood in a doorway with one of the men. Sher limped after her cousin.

The girls crossed 94 on a bridge. Sher's thoughts flicked from sensations of hunger and thirst to her life back home. Kristin's thoughts were a carousel of painted horses circling her, closing her in, each one more demanding and faster and brightly colored than the one before. Red with the blood from the people cracked by bats at the rally and the blood left on her sheets when her dad broke her. Pink from the swirl of the laundry when she washed her sheets clean. Yellow, as glaring and unswerving as the summer sun, when Kris would step outside, after a morning of her father entering her. After his torture, the intensity of the sun made her feel she would crack wide open, like an egg, nothing but snot and yolk, the marrow of her bones exposed. The city released the frenzy pent up inside Kristin, propelling her forward, into the dog day heat of August.

Heat and hunger and dehydration slowed the girls' pace until they stopped. Neither spoke. They didn't know where to go. Despair, that dog, had picked up their scent that day but could not pounce as the girls' past still held strong. The girls stood protected under a massive elm on a boulevard for some time, as if they were back on the reservation walking with their grandparents among the sixty-foot pines and purple and yellow wildflowers growing in the shade, their heads delicate as snowflakes.

"Boo." Jacob popped up behind the girls. "My most favorite ladies."

Sher spit over her shoulder.

Jacob grinned. "What say we make our way to my friend's pad?" Pain cut through Jacob's ribs. He slid to the ground against the elm, fumbling with cigarette paper in his pocket.

The girls watched him, feeling unsure about him and dependent on him.

Jacob rolled a joint. He slid out a matchbook from his back pocket, broke off a match at its root, and struck it on the cement. The match died. Jacob ripped off another and then another until the book was empty except for two rows of gray, jagged, torn off teeth.

Sher pulled out the lighter from the diner just a week ago. It seemed like another lifetime. She pushed the metal wheel until a blue flame burst into the humid air.

Jacob scrambled to pull Sher's hand close to the joint hanging from his lips. He sucked in until his lungs filled with the sweet taste of Mary Jane. "Thanks." He slumped over. He held the joint out to Sher.

"Sure," Sher said, absentminded from hunger and lack of water. She did not take the joint.

He held it out to Kris.

"Nah," she said. "Too thirsty."

Jacob finished the joint and ground it out on the sidewalk. He licked the lit end and placed the stump in his back pocket, where he kept the charred remains of his joints. The pain under control, he asked, "Where should we go?"

Neither girl said anything.

He stood, looked at them expectantly. "Any ideas?"

"Your friend's?"

"Oh yeah." Jacob crammed his hands into his pocket, turned at the waist, and winced.

"You taking us to the friends who beat you?" Sher asked.

"Aw, no." Jacob glanced at Sher through his curls. "Naw, I got other, other friends." He brushed dirt off his rear. "These ones, they're not, not like that, they're groovy. Know?"

"No," Sher said.

"Will they have food?" Kristin asked. "Pop?"

Jacob reached toward Kris. "Food?" he said. "Soda?" She scared him less than Sher. "Sure." He put his arm on Kristin's back, practicing to become someone new—someone who sold instead of someone who was bought. "Big tables full of food. Cokes galore." He copped a smile.

Kris stepped away.

Sher watched his face. When he acquiesced, as he always did, Sher remained watchful, but not fearful. The girls had nowhere to go.

"Sure." Jacob smiled at the girls. "Sure thing. We'll eat like kings." He ran his fingers through his wild hair. "Or queens." He laughed, knowing the girls would think he was referring to them and not himself.

White Earth Reservation, 1891

On April 3, 1891, the girls' great-great-grandparents through Ethel, who only spoke Indian, and whose family had been relocated to White Earth from the Rabbit Band of the Ojibwe reservation where the mining towns of Cuyuna, Crosby, and Riverton sprang up after the Indians were cleared out, lost their forty acres on White Earth when a smiling Office of Indian Affairs agent pointed at two jugs of whiskey and then tapped a paper with the tip of a pen and made an X in the air. After their great-great-grandfather unknowingly signed away their allotment with an X and were escorted, at rifle point, off their homeland, some of those relations went to Antwatin, some went to family outside Grand Marais, others went to Cloquet, and a few wandered north to relatives in Canada.

After nine years, some of the girls' family walked from Cloquet to St. Paul, landed in West End Flats in 1900, the start of a new century, where they lived with Negroes, Jews, Mexicans, and poor whites—Irish and Italian—in a colony of tar paper shacks and rickety, crooked houses on the elbow of the Mississippi built out of discarded clapboards and found bent nails made straight by the hammer taps of West End Flat children. Despite the flooding every spring, they built a community, including Jewish merchants unable to run businesses or live in Gentile neighborhoods, united by poverty and marginalization and held together by the people's good hearts.

For four years, the girls' maternal relations survived, converted to Catholicism, and made friends in the Flats until the 1904 thunder and lightning storm with wind in excess of 180 mph took down the High Bridge—depositing seven wrought iron girders 100 yards downriver as if they were match-sticks. Like so many other Indians across the United States, the girls' male relatives were hired to scale and rivet steel girders, this time using "mild steel" to better avoid the rusting of wrought iron. The Indian men were trained on the cutting edge of bridge building technology. Literally climbing into the working class, they rebuilt the bridge, developed skills in the white world, were hired to build other bridges around the state, and in the process learned other construction jobs. This allowed them to rent and then eventually communally buy their own one-and-one-half story brick and stucco bungalow in near north Minneapolis, a middle-class and working-class Jewish community, due to a connection with a Kosher butcher on the Flats whose brother-in-law had a house for sale, whose family barely escaped the Russian pogroms, who knew what it was to be perpetually homeless, who wanted to be a mensch. In that way, although the girls' relations identified as Indians from White Earth if pressed, eventually they lost track of their ways, becoming more familiar with Catholic rituals, incense, menorahs, and matzo balls than drums and sage and sweetgrass.

One young female relative even married Jewish, sitting each Friday night in Mikro Kodesh Synagogue, 1000 Oliver Ave North, its oblong windows stretching three stories high to let in the setting sun. All the writing and speaking was in Hebrew, which comforted her even though she would never learn it. She was in an outsider culture, and it reminded her of home, her childhood in the bush, a distant and dim memory by the time she sat in the hard, smooth maple pews, searching for a memory of physical and cultural place so deeply buried she could not verbalize it. And so, her inability to speak of her deepest longings and pain were mirrored in the synagogue and gatherings at which Hebrew was the dominant language. Every Friday night, she listened to words she did not know. The Hebrew chanting like a pillow to her—soft and supportive, allowing her to recede to the deepest place inside her where she held such severe pain and loss that it startled her every time she allowed herself to experience it. This was the only time and place she could feel that part of herself, and although it was pain, it was still her, and holding that part of herself, caressing the misformed head of her agony, comforted her. She watched the setting light shine through the bejeweled glass windows, her brown skin and black hair unremarkable among the congregation. She felt among the Jews and their beliefs. Even though some in the congregation rejected her, others embraced her, taught her to make matzo ball soup, where to purchase Shabbot candles, and how to maintain a kosher home. All of them knew how it was to be without place, how quickly all could be lost.

Their ways were similar to the Indian ways she grew up with as a young girl. Yet—despite her trance-like melding with the chanting and the bright colors that she sometimes imagined to be melted beads in windows and the similarity between the release of Rosh Hashana manna into the stream just west of Mikro Kodesh and her grandfather's setting of tobacco, food, and prayers into the water up north—set in her, always, was a knife-like sense of despair. She'd lost her ways.

* * *

The last of the sun slipped away. The evening spirits filed in. Darkness slid over the pavement, wrapped around the light-posts and the hair and teeth and loose summer clothes of the women and children and men sitting on their couches watching television, listening to the radio, playing checkers at the kitchen table, showering under a cold stream, blowing smoke over porch railings, and staring up at the moon through windows, in wonderment that a man had walked on that pale light.

The girls and the boy knocked against each other like bones without enough muscle. They headed east toward Chicago Avenue past upside-down tricycles, metal garbage cans, and a child's turtleneck flattened in a front yard, ripped and muddied in a game begun yesterday morning, now a rag for the dog. The trio moved, listening to jumbled velveteen voices, the buzz of television sets, and the small puffs of lips wrapped around cigarettes and joints. The tips of which flashed red in the dark, marking the night air with red streaks.

Jacob's muscles and mind relaxed from the pot. He recognized the luminous pricks of light shining in the dark sky in patterns from when he was a boy. He recalled—Big Dipper, Little Dipper, the Northern Star—and felt connected to the young boy he once was, a boy who thought the sky was magic, filled with heroic tales and men on horses who would save him from his father's brutality and his mother's paralyzing fear.

Ruminating on the sky, he nearly missed the turn at 26th Street. His sight returned to the street just in time. Turning east, he bumped into Kris. Her shoulder, small but strong, set off his guilt as he remembered the girls' presence, where he was taking them, and what would happen to them. *I'm just the delivery man,* he thought as Darren had told him when they stood on the blanket at the rally. *Delivery man.* Jacob thought of the money. He ignored what he knew if he did not deliver—-Darren would find him and hurt him. He glanced at the stars one last time before returning to the street where he did things he would never have done when he was a young boy with wild hair and sad eyes who believed the night sky held the mystery of the universe.

The young group wound east through alleys with burnt-out street lights. They reached another freeway wide as the Mississippi with a sound barrier fence tall as the trees on the Goodhue State Forest, crossed it, and walked two blocks east. Then they jagged north.

They stopped at a busy intersection on a road wider than the others—a former busy thoroughfare built in 1864 to accommodate horse-drawn carriages and wagons. Up and down the once grand street, sprawling Victorians had fallen into disrepair—missing shingles and chipped scroll work—their paint dulled by eighty years of sun and snow and hail. Nevertheless, the ghost of their grandeur endured, if simply due to their massive stature. Immediately to the teens' right was a white stucco house the size of a barn; its west wall collecting the violet remnants of the sun under red Spanish tiles.

"Shoot," Kristin said, poking Sher. "Look at that. Lit up like a flower."

The light was strange—the house the only thing lit up like that so late at night. Lamplight flickered in a third-floor window. Kris caught the silhouette of a woman sitting down. A longing so strong for her mother, who oscillated through Kris's consciousness, overcame Kris that she would have believed Josie stood next to her on the still warm concrete sidewalk, bending over to smell the white, heavy-headed peonies that fell between the black steel bars of the fence surrounding the house.

Sher felt something enormous, something she couldn't keep Kris from, was near—pushing up against them. Bigger than what Kris's dad had done to her. Possibly bigger than anything Sher could do to keep her cousin safe. Sher pulled Kris across the street. Kris watched the woman's silhouette over her shoulder until Kris was across the street and unable to see the woman. Faint, elongated light from the window shone across the night grass. A small part of Kris recognized the spirit Sher had felt. That part of Kris settled in that spirit, waiting and unafraid.

"C'mon," Jacob said. "Let's be Fred Astaire." He twirled. "I'll be Ginger. You be Fred." He pointed at Sher. "C'mon," he pleaded with them, nervous about how they lagged, afraid of what the men would do to him if he didn't bring these two girls to the house on Chicago. The panic spun him faster and faster like the dreidels he and his mom played with when he was a boy. The dreidels they had to spin behind his father's back because they brought back bad memories.

Jacob had always wanted to be Ginger, not Fred. He'd always wanted to dance with a dashing man, like the 1930s black and white late—night movies he'd watched on the couch with his mom,

A *Damsel in Distress, Carefree,* and *Roberta,* in which Fred unknowingly sang "When Smoke Gets in Your Eyes" to a dreamy nine-year-old Jewish boy on a red and tan plaid couch in Illinois. Fred, the kind gentleman who would not hurt Jacob, who would hold him, spin with him to a place Jacob imagined, but had never seen. A place where boys loved boys, a place where he was not the only one.

Sher ignored him. They'd get away from him as soon as they could. Just get some food at this house, and then find a place to sleep. The girls were hungry. And thirsty.

Pain enveloped Kris like a wild vine. Too many parts of her were scattered across the land, like the deer fur that caught in tufts on barbed wire fences and tree branches when they leaped. Parts of Kris pinned to the beds and floors at her dad's house, sitting in grassy meadows and bathroom stalls at school. Or scattered across the back forty at her grandparents' farm, where she'd gone to find reprieve from her father, and left a bit of her spirit for safe-keeping under a rock on the farm, unable to bear the pain, unable to remain whole. Even though she'd run, there was no escape from him.

The young people walked three blocks.

"Here 'tis," Jacob bowed, sweeping his arm across the front of a narrow, purple Queen Anne. "Thirty-four seventy Chicago Avenue South. Home sweet home." He hopped up the steps and saluted.

Dread swept over Sher. As Kris stepped onto the stairs, Sher touched her arm to stop her. Focused on the thought of food and drink on big tables inside, Kris continued up the stairs. Sher's stomach growled. She acquiesced. They'd just get some food. Then find a park to sleep in.

Inside was dark except for light beneath a door down the hall. Muffled music and voices emerged from the back. To their right stairs ran up to the second story. At the bottom of the stairs a closed pocket door hid the living room from view. Jacob pulled the heavy door behind them with a thud.

Their eyes adjusted.

"Down there." Jacob's voice shrank. For a moment, he had the impulse to grab the girls and run. But where? They would have to leave town immediately. Even if they could get out of town without being caught, the men had connections everywhere—Chicago, Milwaukee, Duluth, Iowa, even New York City. They had grabbed him on the streets in Chicago and brought him here. They would track him down wherever he went. He'd seen them do it to others. Such a bold disregard for their authority would make him a liability and might mean death. This he knew. No matter how high he got, Jacob never forgot that. He steeled himself against what he knew was waiting for the girls. He had seen it before. He had *been* it before.

The hall was narrow and damp. Musty. Maroon velvet-striped wallpaper covered five other layers, the bottom, a floral pattern using Scheele's green made with copper arsenite, was original to the house. The arsenic in the wallpaper had killed the first four children of the Anderton family that built the house in 1872. The fifth and sixth children survived only because the mother, half-mad with grief, had made her husband cover "that putrid green paper," thus curtailing the absorption of the arsenic into the bloodstream.

Kris moved in a haze toward the voices, her spirit wandering among white peonies. She was hungry.

"Jacob?" Sher panicked. This was not safe.

Jacob snapped his palm with the back of his other hand. It kept him focused. He was afraid. He'd cleaned up the blood off the couch and bed sheets when the girls were virgins. He'd cleaned the blood off the walls when the girls fought back. He fixated on how good it was that the wallpaper in the room down the hall was not velvet like the wallpaper in the hallway because he would not be able to get all the blood out of the velvet, no matter how hard he scrubbed.

Kris was halfway down the hall. Sher had not gone deeper into the house.

"Sher," Jacob said, worried she would try to leave. "Food's this way."

"We should leave," Sher said, without conviction. She saw her cousin was not going to leave.

Jacob ran in front of Kris and knocked on the door. "Food's in here," he muttered, staring at the floor.

"Enter," a man's voice said above the bray of conversations and music.

Jacob opened the door. He stood in the doorway, the girls now behind him. He said nothing, waiting for Darren to notice him and his quarry.

White women and men sat Indian-style on cushions, or the bare floor smoking a water bong. A gold lamp with red glass beads cast a dim light. Jimi Hendrix was on the radio.

Darren sat with his back to the door, arms crossed, talking to a woman next to him. Jacob cleared his throat.

"Welcome, sisters and brother," said a woman wearing huge sunglasses. She patted the floor next to her.

"Where's the food?" Kris asked.

Jacob's throat caught.

Darren turned and smiled at Kris.

"Darren?" Kris asked. "I didn't know—"

"Ah, but you should have, little woman. You saw us together at the park." He watched the confusion on her face. "Food's coming, little woman," Darren said using a softer voice. "In the meantime, join our circle."

Sher eyed the others. She knew no good would come of this. She grabbed Kris's elbow to leave without making a scene, but Kris jerked away, drawn to the hippies, to Darren's attention, to the possibility of food.

"Right, my man," Darren stood up. "We always feed everyone well here."

Jacob nodded.

Darren pulled Jacob to his chest and whispered to him.

"Sure, man. No problem. Absolutely no problem." Jacob's eyes shifted away from the girls.

The hair on the back of Sher's neck stood up. Lightning quick, Darren grabbed Sher's knee and yanked, slamming her onto her tailbone.

"Oh man." Darren shrugged his shoulders. "Sorry." He turned back to the circle and lit a joint.

"Sher!" Kris yelled.

Startled, and in pain, Sher said nothing.

Darren turned to Kris and thumped her chest with his forearm. "Quiet, little woman, or you and your friend will regret it."

"What did you do that for?" A woman with big sunglasses jumped up, her skirt swirling at her bare ankles.

"Be cool, Irene," Darren said. "We're just having a little fun, right girls?"

Kris stared at Sher, afraid to move.

"Joe. Tommy," Darren commanded, snapping his fingers at Sher.

Two men in the circle got to their feet and stood next to Sher.

Darren snapped his fingers. "Jay, front door. No one in. No one out."

Jacob, his eyes on Darren, stepped to the side to allow Jay to leave.

Darren handed Jacob the joint. Jacob toked and then held it out to Sher, who sat between Joe and Tommy. She glared at him, tried to stand but lost her balance, and fell again. Jacob toked. Darren smiled at Jacob.

"Are you all right, hun?" Irene asked, kneeling next to Sher and spreading her skirt over her bare feet.

Kris stood frozen against the wall.

"I'm Irene," the woman said to Sher.

Sher nodded.

"It's her ankle," Kris said.

"Get some ice." Irene waved at the men. "Go."

Darren nodded. "Bring the girl to the kitchen."

"Don't be stupid," Irene said. "She's hurt. Bring the ice in here."

"Irene," Darren said. "Leave it alone."

"Don't tell me—" Irene said.

"Now," Darren raised his voice.

"Be cool," one of the men in the circle said. "Be cool, man." He held his hand out, palm up. "We're all, like, groovy."

Darren stepped toward the man who told him to be cool. He pulled a box of Camels from his shirt pocket, slid a cigarette between his lips, and lit it. He exhaled. "I make the fucking rules around here. My house, my rules."

The man put both hands out. "Cool. Right. Your pad, man."

"Joe," Darren said. He nodded toward the door.

The two men lifted Sher by her armpits and walked her down the hall to the kitchen.

She knew not to resist.

"Freaky bullshit." Irene slapped the wall. "I've had enough."

Darren laughed. "Oh, I've had enough," he said, mimicking the higher pitch of her voice. He sucked on his cigarette. "Whose turn on the bong?"

Irene glared at Darren. "I'm fucking out of here." She stood by the door like it was a dare. "This is shit. You come with me," she said to Kris and walked into the hall.

Darren twitched his cigarette toward the door. Two more men followed her into the hall.

"Let go of me!" Irene yelled.

Thudding echoed down the hall.

Jacob shrank against the wall next to Kris, his shoulders round, his breath shallow. The two stood there, trapped.

"Problems," Darren said, "are so easily disposed of." He saw the light-skinned girl was terrified and going nowhere. He gave the end of the bong to his girlfriend, who sucked hard to forget how quickly she could become the problem.

* * *

Sher and the two men stood in the moonlit kitchen.

"Ice." Joe slid a tray across the table at Sher. "I don't care what you do with this one," he said to Tommy. "Fun's in the other room."

"No!" Irene yelled from the hall.

"Stay with her," Joe said, jerking his thumb at Sher. He pushed through the door.

Sher did not move.

Tommy crossed his arms. He scratched the back of his head. He heard more thumping. He pushed the kitchen door, his long white fingers splayed across the wood, and watched the men drag Irene upstairs.

Sher did not move. Her had dad told her you always want your enemies to underestimate you. Thaddeus had prepared his daughter for this moment.

Tommy paced, chewed his thumbnail, glanced at Sher. Sher reached for the metal ice cube tray, releasing the ice cubes by lifting up on the bar on the top of the tray. The cubes popped like finger joints.

Sher slowed the world down, like she did when she ran through the woods. She heard but did not hear the woman being dragged upstairs, the grunting and the banging. She thought, but did not think about Kris in the next room, and she saw but did not see, the agitated man in the shadows. He was so close to her she could smell the whiskey on his breath and the pot on his clothes. She studied the three bolts on the door and the fourth lock, which needed a key to open from the inside.

Sher thought of her dad and his quick laugh and his praise of her strength and intelligence. She did not feel alone. She bent and unlaced her boot, moving slow. The slower she moved, the less likely she would distract him from what was happening upstairs. In one motion she pulled the knife out of her boot, stood up, and slid the knife between her thighs.

"Whadja do?" Tommy kicked one of the lower cupboards.

"Scratched." Sher lifted her hands.

Tommy walked to the window. He stared at the vacant lot. The moon shone off his cheeks and nose. The crickets rubbed their wings together, calling to each other in the dark. Sher transferred the knife to her front pocket.

"What do you think?" he asked Sher.

Sher said nothing.

"I said, what do you think?" He swung around, grabbed her chin and held her face up toward the moonlight. "Ugly girl."

Sher made her eyes dumb.

"You're not going to run off." He dropped her face. "Stupid."

Sher held her breath to keep the anger from crossing her face.

Glass shattered. Darren yelled, "Bitch! Joe!" Footsteps raced down the hall and out the front door. Sher's arm tensed. She did not allow herself to be afraid because, as her dad used to tell her when they rounded up cattle for the neighbors, frightened animals die first.

Tommy bolted out the door. Sher pushed up the window, opened the knife blade, and slit the screen down the sides and across the top and bottom. The center of the screen floated into the yard. She folded the blade into the beaded handle and slipped it into her front jean pocket. Footsteps pounded on the stairs. She placed her foot on the windowsill, wrapped the laces once around the boot, tied them in a double knot, moved her ankle in a circle to test it and then strode out the kitchen door into the hall.

"Jacob," a man in the room yelled. "Get the other girl!"

Sher ducked under the space beneath the staircase. As Jacob ran into the kitchen a man dragged Kris into the hall. The door slammed behind him and the music blared louder.

Jacob stood in the kitchen. *No Sher,* he thought. *Should I run?*

Sher jumped on the man. He hit her with his forearm, flinging her to her knees. "Your girlfriend?" He laughed. He pushed Kristin against the wall and held her by the throat with his forearm while he unbuckled his belt.

Kristin gurgled.

The man's mouth curled. "We're gonna do it in front of your girlfriend." He dropped Kristin onto the floor next to Sher, pressing his knee between Kris's thighs.

Jacob listened to the melee. The clock said ten to ten. His mind landed on a park in Chicago where he used to play before his family moved to Winnetka. He wondered if anyone was there playing in the dark, if the red ride that spun him and the other kids in circles was still there or if they'd torn it down along with the monkey bars that had begun to lean too far one way.

Sher slid out the knife. The man panted on top of Kristin. She was still as a mole with the top of its skull chewed open. The hippies yelled at each other. Jimi Hendrix's guitar wailed out the stereo. Blue-tinted moonlight streaked under the kitchen door. The man in the hall focused on hurting the girl beneath him. Sher dug her thumbnail into the knife's crevice, snapped the blade, and plunged it into the man's back, sideways. She sunk it deep between his ribs.

The man screamed. His legs buckled and his arms thrashed backward. Sher pulled the blade out and stabbed him two more times. She kicked him off Kristin, who scrambled to her feet. The man flopped to his belly, gasping for air.

"Run." Sher pointed the blood-covered knife toward the kitchen. Kristin scrambled down the hall into the kitchen. Sher wiped her blade off on the carpeting the way she did after she cut the throat of a deer before slaughtering it.

Darren called out, "You okay out there, man?"

Sher strode into the kitchen. Her body did not have any beginning or end. It moved on its own, connected to something much larger than herself that had begun long before she was born. She pushed through the door, saw Jacob and Kristin staring at each other. In two steps, she was next to Jacob and pushed the flat blade of the knife into Jacob's chest.

"Uh." Jacob gasped. His hands shot above his head.

Sher pointed with her lips to the hole in the screen. Kristin climbed out. Sher grabbed a fistful of Jacob's curls and wrapped them around her hand. She pushed the tip of the knife into his chest. "Keep quiet. Or I will come back for you, too."

Surprise popped in his eyes.

Sher snapped the blade into the handle, climbed through the window and disappeared.

Jacob heard "Goddamn!" and "Oh my fucking god" from the hall. He opened a drawer next to the refrigerator, took out a steak knife, and pulled up his shirt. He drew the blade across his belly. He watched as blood emerged in a thin line, beaded, and then rolled down his belly. "Ow!" he yelled. "Help! Help!"

Sher landed in the yard on her sore ankle but did not feel it. "That way." She pointed alongside the house toward the back alley.

Sher and Kristin ran to the alley, then cut north behind the tangle of vines. The girls heard shoes on gravel and knelt for cover. The vines had grown there for sixty years rallying through brutal winters to rejuvenate every summer, now providing cover for the two Indian girls on the run.

"See anything?" Darren asked.

"Fuck," Joe said. "I don't see a goddamned thing. Those little motherfuckers could be anywhere."

"Forget it," Darren said. A spray of rocks hit the street. "We need to deal with Jake. We'll get those bitches later."

Sher and Kristin did not move. The leaves' thin red veins tapered to pointed tips. Sher thought how similar it felt to gutting a deer when she pushed the tip into the man and an explosion traveled through her knife and settled in her neck. When she finished off a deer, it was always like that. The body revolted when struck that deeply.

The girls traveled all night long, walking down alleys, crouching behind garages and auto shops and garbage cans. Sometimes, they followed the moonlight, and other times, they walked away from it. Sher found a bucket of rain water from which they drank from. Then she rinsed the blood off her hands and arms, opened the knife blade and clean the crevices with leaves. She dried the blade on her tank top, closed it, and slid it back into her boot.

Two Miles Southeast of Thatcher's Trail, Goodhue Reservation, July 20, 1969

Em plunged out of the woods onto a single lane gravel road. Sunlight and a cloudless blue sky greeted her. To her left the tan road disappeared between thirty-foot white pines. The same to her right. She did not know when she'd last eaten. She didn't know where she was.

Em searched the sky. The sun to her right. The luminous outline of the moon to her left. She did not know what day it was, so she could not know that within hours the US space program, run by a Nazi who twenty years earlier worked Jews to death building rocket ships beneath a mountain, would float men onto the moon through space tethered to a ship. Em knew none of that. What she knew was she was starving. And thirsty. And bleeding into moss she'd fitted into her underwear. She stilled herself. She listened. Crows. Crickets. The rustling of squirrels. And then, just as she was to walk right, to the west, she heard a scratching to her left. She listened. Eyes shut. The scratching grew louder, so she set out, moss catching her moon, toward the east, toward she knew not what. As the men ate their space food and prepared to float in the vastness of the black sky, connected by an umbilical cord to the ship and the Nazis who built it, and all those who died in the caves of Germany, their bones crushed by the indifference of history, Em walked her earthly path, starving, as did her ancestors after the English landed their ships on the shores of Turtle Island.

* * *

As the girls wandered, the sun cast orange streaks in the eastern sky. Lights popped on in kitchens and bathrooms and narrow halls with gold and forest-green shag carpeting. Although neither would speak of it, if they had stopped, and reached inside themselves, they would have discovered a longing for their past and family—even the chores they once dreaded.

But those days were over. The girls would have to do the bulk of their walking by night now that Sher had stabbed a white man. In the gray, early morning light, they slid down a steep grassy embankment under a bridge until they were under it. They slept fitfully while cars spun tires twenty feet above them.

The girls woke late morning.

Kristin dug for money in the bag. "Is this all we got?"

"What?" Sher asked.

"Nine and change?" Kristin's voice rose up.

"Yah."

"Shoot," Kristin said and threw the bills toward the tracks. They settled on the grass.

A sparrow swooped down under the shadow of the bridge. After a moment, it flew into the sky and the world that went on above the girls.

They needed enough money to find their way out of town, maybe head to Milwaukee or up to Canada through Wisconsin.

They had family in Thunder Bay. Hitchhiking was too high profile. They needed money. Fast.

Neither girl said anything. They were tense from the night before. Hunger was taking over their ability to reason. Tan and brown sparrows flew among the concrete rafters behind them. Cars streamed overhead. The sun rose higher, inching the heat closer to the shade the girls sat in under the bridge. Neither knew what to say.

Sher stood. "Kris." She scuffed her boot on the grass, her hands on her hips, head down.

Kris did not look up.

Sher gathered the money, kicked her leg over a waist-high fence farther south than where she and Kris had hopped the night before. She stepped onto the sidewalk. Cars buzzed by in front of her, plumes of heat spinning off the tires. She felt naked and seen and paranoid she would be caught. She surveyed the street. To her left were bungalows and two-story stucco houses and to her right a Sinclair gas station, Zeke's Auto Body Shop, and an A & W.

She felt like she did in town when white people gawked at her and her family—pointing, whispering, staring, moving aside as if they would catch something from them. Like that time her grandparents had taken her and Kris to the St. Louis County Fair. Sher'd lost her family and while wandering spotted a tent, painted with an East Indian girl with four twirling arms. A red sign with yellow cursive read: *The Most Exotic Four-Armed Girl in the World! Watch This Beauty Eat! Watch Her Comb Her Hair and Dance! Limited Time! Only 25 Cents!* As Sher walked toward the cotton candy stand, two white boys exited the side of the tent. "Aw shoot," the bigger one said. "There was just somebody standing behind her. Prolly some nigger from Minneapolis." He flicked a booger at the tent. The younger boy ran to the bigger boy's side, jamming his hands deep into his jean pockets. His jeans were cuffed up over his black canvas tennis shoes. They trotted off toward a pronto pup booth, pushing each other. Sher felt a mix of sickness and fear and relief in her belly that they hadn't turned toward her, shouted one of the many names she'd been called over the years. "Tree nigger. Injun. Blackie. Pocahontas. Bulldyke."

Sher set out north along Snelling for the A & W, thinking about the food she would order: burgers with pickles and mustard and a big slice of tomato, fries, root beer, onion rings with ketchup, and a vanilla cone. She thought about spending all the money at A & W, bringing bags of food back to Kris. The two of them would sit under the bridge eating until they were full and happy. Sher imagined it, but then the scene took on its own life, ending with them vomiting beneath the bridge.

Sher bellied up to the order window at the A&W. *Did I kill that man?* She wondered. *Am I a thief? A murderer? We never should have left the reservation.* A siren blew behind her. She wanted to bolt, but steeled herself. She felt she was just about to be grabbed. The cops were here for someone else, not her, she told herself.

"Can I help you?" a dark-haired, white boy in a floppy orange and brown hat asked, sliding the window to the right.

"Two large root beers." Sher set the bills on the counter and stared at them to avoid allowing the boy see her panic.

"Sure thing," the boy said. He took a bill and strained to look through the window toward the siren.

Another cop car pitched a scream. Panic exploded in Sher's chest like a wild-eyed horse spooked by the caterwauling of a water cat—what whites called a cougar. One prowled the reservation a few times a year, so stealth no one would know of its presence except for the blood-curdling screams of a cat with paws as big as a human head and the ability to leap twenty feet horizontal. Sometimes Sher and her grandparents and father stood on the porch as the sun dropped blood red over the hills and the cat's scream echoed among the surrounding hills, making its call seem to come from the east, then west, then north. They could never tell where the cat was. That was its mystery.

The summer Sher turned eight, they never heard the cat again. Her dad told Sher and her grandparents his cousin Lenny said some white farmer had shot it, mounted its head. But Sher's grandmother said, "No. Animal like that can't be took down by a white man. Went up to Canada. I'm sure." Sher's grandfather stuck the tips of his fingers in his jean pockets and looked at the floor. He'd heard it too—there was talk in town. His wife could not accept certain things. The pain the white man made was too big.

* * *

In front of the A&W, Sher's legs went weak. Her thoughts, always steady, now tumbled. The cops or Darren's men were going to catch them. Sher would go to jail. Kris would go back to her father and what happened in the hall would keep happening. Sher would be locked up for life like when her brother used to trap her in the outhouse by dragging the barrel filled with chicken feed in front of the door when she was inside.

"Know what's going on over there?" the boy asked.

The sirens' screams spun through the sleepy neighborhood.

Sher smelled the rotting wood in the outhouse. "No," she snapped. Embarrassed, she pretended to wipe sweat off her face with her arm.

The boy stepped back, unsure of this girl. He'd never seen anyone like her.

"I'm hungry," she mumbled.

"Okay," the boy looked at a pile of napkins by the window.

The siren cut off.

"What do you got?" She felt crazy. "I mean, your menu?"

The boy leaned on one leg. He pointed his pencil at the menu on the wall behind him.

Sher nodded. "Two burgers with everything. Two fries. Onion ring." She drummed her fingers on the counter. "One." She nodded. She felt she would melt into the sidewalk, right there, in front of a white boy, the kind of person she most had to maintain control around.

The sirens spit two last times.

"All right." The boy nodded, jotting the order on a pad of paper. He adjusted his stained apron, turned his back and opened a waist-high freezer, releasing cold smoke. The boy set two raw hamburger patties on the grill.

Sher glanced over her shoulder at the police cruisers two blocks away, their lightbars flashing red, white, and blue like the lit-up swing ride at the county fair. She turned so they could not see her face, focusing on the bloody patties as they sizzled, popped fat, and turned gray on the grill. Some white girls had long dark hair. Sher wanted them to think she was white from behind, to leave her alone, especially if they'd heard *Indian girl wanted for killing white man* over the police scanner.

North

In Ojibwe ways, north is the place of pain and suffering. It is also where Ojibwe get strength, endurance, and gifts.

The girls set out north on a magenta sunset to avoid the heat and daytime stares and easy sight of cops. At the Sinclair station, the worker glanced up once at the girls but kept his attention on the 1956 Packard engine he was working on.

"Fifty-six?" Sher asked, one thumb hooked behind the strap of the pack. Her grandpa had fixed one for some Chicago gangsters who could not risk going into town. "On their way to a cabin in Ely," he said when telling the story of his brush with mobsters. "Only white men who ever paid me well."

"Know how we can get to the state fair?" Sher asked. "Nice sidewalls."

"That way." The mechanic jabbed his elbow north. The man was more interested in prepping his shop to close than he was in talking with two funny-looking street kids. Who knew where they came from or why the one knew about the car.

The early evening moonlight shone down on the girls as they pushed through the dirty glass door. They struck out north.

"Hope to get there tonight," Sher said.

"Yah." Kristin hitched up her sagging jeans as she and Sher made their way to miles of neon lights and fried foods.

* * *

The girls walked north on Snelling past four-square apartment buildings, under crabapple trees, and then across Summit Avenue lined with expansive well-manicured lawns belonging to the brick and stucco mansions sprawled beneath enormous elm trees. A line of people waited outside a Dairy Queen. The sun's fingertips shone over the barn red roof, turning it a wine red that made Sher think of the sunsets back home, when the deep red of the sun reflected off the flat tin roof of the chicken coop, until it covered the east wall of the dining room. Her ankle hurt. She was thirsty. But her fear lifted the more they moved toward the fair. She whistled. Then stopped abruptly, remembering her father telling her not to whistle in the dark. He never said why.

The sun sank to their left. Car lights popped on like fireflies. The girls plodded north on Snelling. The street was lined with red and yellow neon signs. Hardware Hank, Schwabe's Welding Supplies, Sam's TV Repair, and Johnson's Printing flashed in the darkening sky. The girls reached the sprawling, tree-filled campus of Hamline University and crossed an arching overpass. Ahead of them, and to their left, red and white lights flashed on a spire ten times higher than any house.

"The fair," Kristin said, looking westward at thousands of flashing carnival lights that burst upward, lightening the evening sky for miles. The near-full moon hung over the thousands of spinning, flashing light bulbs.

Fairgoers returning to their cars passed the girls, exhausted from the thousands of Minnesotans they'd bumped up against over the past five or ten hours jostling in line for the all-you-can-drink milk for a penny, climbing the tractors on Machinery Hill, ogling the 1261-pound boar in the Swine Barn, and perusing the thousands of quilts and preserves and krumkake in the Arts and Crafts building made by middle-aged white women from towns with populations of fifty-five that few had ever heard of before.

"Need tickets?" A scrawny white teenage boy held out two blue tickets ripped in half. He smiled.

Sher took them.

The boy walked off laughing, knowing the girls would need stamps on their wrists to get in with ripped tickets.

The girls set off for the east gate with two blue ticket stubs, their grandfather's World War II pack, two cups, a lighter, and a bit of cash. They smelled sour.

"That's it." Sher snapped her fingers.

"What?" Kris asked.

"You're not supposed to whistle in the dark. Grandma said it brought bad luck."

"Oh," Kris said, not knowing why Sher brought that up.

The girls reached the gate, *Minnesota State Fair* in wrought iron arching over six ticket booths. Agricultural societies held fairs throughout the territory in the 1850s, before statehood was granted, to showcase the productive farming and active social life in the territory so as to encourage immigrants to settle the land being opened by the removal of the Ojibwe and Dakota. The Minnesota State Fair, first held in 1859 in the area of downtown Minneapolis a year after the state was created, found its permanent home when Ramsey County donated a 210-acre poor farm to the state.

An attendant, a grizzled white man with hair down to his shoulders, who'd lost his farm in Litchfield to a land developer years before, glanced at the girls' tickets. "Reentry," he said but did not wait for a response. He nodded the girls through. What did he care the girls were supposed to have a red star stamp on their wrist to go along with the torn tickets? He hadn't cared about much since '54 when Meeker County plotted with Kreft Construction to get his land for their new elementary school.

The girls walked alongside a large, white building with a turret and state flag flopped over in the humid night air.

"Lucky we got those tickets."

Sher nodded.

"How'd you know we could get in with ripped tickets?"

"Didn't."

"Yah?"

"Yah."

The girls moved through the city within a city. People shouted, music blared, rides clanged, grease sizzled, and vendors shouted their wares: *The world's largest collection of live butterflies take some home for a penny, folks, one shiny copper penny starts your own collection of butterflies* and *Hot bratwurst with sauerkraut straight off the ship from Germany* and *Take a ride on the giant slide folks safe for the kids and fun for the adults biggest slide in all the world right here at the Minnesota State Fair best fair in all the world yessiree folks step right up right here take a ride on the giant slide.*

The girls passed between a three-story high wooden statue of a pilgrim woman outside Minnesota Territorial Pioneers' Hall and the shuttered booth of *Wendell R. Anderson Your Next Governor!*

"America the Beautiful" blared through a speaker from Wendell's booth:

> O beautiful for spacious skies
> For amber waves of grain
> For purple mountain majesties
> Above the fruited plain!
> America! America!
> God shed his grace on thee
> And crown they good with brotherhood
> From sea to shining sea!
>
> O beautiful for pilgrim feet
> Whose stern impassioned stress
> A thoroughfare of freedom beat
> Across the wilderness!
> America! America!
> God mend thine every flaw
> Confirm thy soul in self-control
> Thy liberty in law!

The tinny sound of the song, and its relentless repetition, pushed the girls across the street to a lit-up sign the size of a living room wall that read:

> *Welcome to the Minnesota State Fair*
> *The Largest Fair in the World:*
> *322 Acres of Fun and Fascination*
> *Nearly 1 Million Visitors Each Year*

A black-and-white photograph of past and current board members was featured beneath the words. Twelve smiling white men in short-sleeve dress shirts and ties surrounded an elderly white woman holding a blue ribbon and a pie. The photograph had been snapped in 1952, the year the board shipped in a V-2 Nazi rocket, displaying it at that year's fair on a plot of open land behind the oldest French fry stand at the fair, opened in 1932. Some on the board wondered about the wisdom of displaying a rocket that had killed thousands of Brits. Plus, news was leaking out about the 20,000 skeletal Jews who died building them in the subterranean tunnels of Mittelwerk in Nazi Germany.

Augustus, the boardman who suggested the Minnesota State

Fair host a Nazi rocket, responded to their hesitancy. "Think of the crowds we will draw being the only fair, no, not the only fair, but the only place in the world that can lay claim to hosting a German high propulsion rocket!" he exclaimed, careful to say "German" in lieu of "Nazi." He and the others in the so-called "German Heritage" group that met every Saturday evening at a New Ulm farm or a closed-to-the-public American Legion building had discussed this as a prudent strategy in light of the current political situation in America.

At the state fair board meeting, Augustus continued, "Imagine every small Minnesota boy being able to witness such technological wonder, inspiring him to aim for the stars!" He left his surroundings for a moment as he imagined a blonde boy eating cotton candy at the base of a V-2 rocket, one of hundreds of German rockets that had been identified, sorted, and reassembled in building 1538 at White Sands Proving Ground in New Mexico by Nazis the US government brought over after the war alongside General Electric employees contracted by the US government. Overcome by the profundity of the image of the boy, he shouted, "*Das Wunder Deutschtlands!*" in perfect German, shocking the rest of the Minnesota State Fair Board. Alarmed, he clapped his hands and stammered, "The wonder of America!" Hoping he had not blown his cover, he added, "The technology of the future!" The other men were unsure what to do or think. Ten minutes later, his enthusiasm overrode their reluctance and the board approved his motion to display a German V-2 rocket at that year's fair, unaware that Germany had been on the verge of perfecting a long-range V-3 rocket that most assuredly would have targeted Duluth due to its steel production for the American war effort.

At the next "German Heritage" meeting held at the Wilmar American Legion, the group opened the meeting, as they always did, with a rendition of Nazi Germany's National Anthem, based on a northern European folk song. The author, Horst Wessel, had joined the Nazi party in 1926 and was killed by Communists in 1930. Standing, arms outstretched toward the German Reich flag hung across the stage, they shouted in unison "*Sieg Heil!*" and then sang:

> Flag high, ranks closed,
> The S.A. marches with silent solid steps.
> Comrades shot by the red front and reaction

March in spirit with us in our ranks.

The street free for the brown battalions,
The street free for the Storm Troopers.
Millions, full of hope, look up at the swastika;
The day breaks for freedom and for bread.

For the last time the call will now be blown;
For the struggle now we all stand ready.
Soon will fly Hitler-flags over every street;
Slavery will last only a short time longer.

Flag high, ranks closed,
The S.A. marches with silent solid steps.
Comrades shot by the red front and reaction
March in spirit with us in our ranks.

The Nazis' arms slapped to their sides in unison. Then they sat in unison in the banged-up metal chairs used on other evenings for Bingo, wedding receptions, and veterans' meetings. Some veterans were also secret members of the "German Heritage" club, and some were not. When the issue of the rocket came up on the agenda, Augustus stood, pulled down on his SA jacket, and gave one curt nod to his comrades, indicating the fair board approved his request. Now the club's desire to bring the rocket to Minnesota from the White Sands Proving Grounds in New Mexico had a cover—the fair! "Who doesn't love a carnival?" his aged comrade thundered upon hearing the good news. "A place of such innocent fun!"

* * *

"The man!" Kris said, looking at the photo on the sign.

"Yah," Sher said. "A bunch of them. And I want some of that pie!"

The girls laughed from their bellies, now concave.

Included in the photograph was one D.T. Grussendorf, past President of the Minnesota State Fair Board, Duluth city council member, and Duluth-area forestry county agent. Grussendorf's personal crown jewel was his 1959 execution of a "grand vision" he had of a twenty-six-foot-high gold-colored fiberglass and "weather proof plastic component" Neptune statue to celebrate

Duluth's recent designation as a Foreign Trade Zone, which would bring in thousands of ocean-going ships. The Roman god of the sea held a trident in one hand and a replica of the *Ramon de Larrinaga* in the other. *The Ramon* was the first modern ocean ship to pass through the canal in Duluth after the opening of the St. Lawrence Seaway, which allowed ocean-going vessels to sail all the way to Duluth, creating an even bigger shipping market for the inland sea port, state, and region, including the increased export of Ojibwe women and children, although, of course, selling Ojibwe people would never be publicly discussed in any tourist pamphlets or AAA guide books.

Grussendorf was behind the push to relocate Neptune to Canal Park in Duluth. Mayor E Clifford Mork exclaimed it would be a "tremendous tourist attraction" for the city. Arriving in October of 1959, the statue stood for four years a few yards west from the 1860 carnival. Pockmarked by stones thrown by residents, one day the torch used by city employees to remove the statue from its base for cleaning ignited the King of the Sea. The magnificent vision by the mayor and a city council member of Neptune welcoming foreign ships to the shore of Duluth went up in flames, leaving just a pile of ash. The enormous statue burned in five minutes due to its insides being filled with papier-mâché.

* * *

The girls sat on a curb with a bucket of fries and a Coke. Faces merged into each other in the dark, lit up by the lights from the caramel apple carts, root beer stands, pretzel booths, foot-long hot dog booths, and the grandstand that read *State Fair Grandstand: Live Shows Daily*.

"Hey." Kris nudged Sher, pointing her lips toward a group of Indians in bell bottom jeans. "Sioux, I bet."

Sher nodded, absorbed by the food, her stomach releasing a knot of hunger.

"What are we gonna do?" Kristin asked, her mouth full of French fries.

"Find a place to sleep." Sher shifted her boots on the pavement.

Sher and Kristin licked the grease and salt off their fingers, drained the Coke, and tossed the cup in a barrel. Setting off west down Minnesota Avenue looking for a place to sleep, they passed the WCCO television station and the AM 1550 Talk Radio booth *Broadcast Live Every Day from the State Fair!* and *Hubert*

Humphrey's Fan Club boarded up for the evening and *Stephenson's Family-Owned Funnel Cakes* stand housing three tired family members: mom, dad, and daughter.

"Look," Sher said. "Horses." Two blocks away horses high stepped and wheeled in circles, their dark, thickly muscled haunches sweating and their ears pricked and twitching in the dusty street.

The girls dodged the crowd the two blocks to the horses and riders in their big cowboy hats and boots. The Coliseum, Cattle Barn, Horse Barn, and Poultry Barn sat on each corner of the intersection. Their Art Deco facades featured bas relief carvings of the animals inside the buildings. The girls leaned against the metal gate that separated the crowd from the horses and their riders.

"Arabian," Sher whispered.

"Dang," Kris's voice trailed.

The girls had only seen them in picture books. They watched every precise movement the elegant horses made—their wide foreheads, enormous and intelligent eyes, and high-tail carriage made the horses seem like royalty.

"So pretty," Kris said.

Sher's eyes glistened. She felt she might break down and cry right there in front of everyone for the beauty and love she felt for those horses—their hooves trimmed perfectly and manes and tails braided with red ribbon. Through them she felt the beauty of her childhood. Her family's love. The land. The trees she'd run through day after day, listening, as her grandfather had told her to do, for their stories.

The girls watched the horses until a hand opened the gate to the Coliseum. The Arabians strutted through, single file, stomping and snorting, and prancing sideways as the crowd inside clapped. Sher wanted to be with the horses and riders, stand in the dirt the horses had pranced on, breathe in the smell of the animals' sweat, the hay, the dirt, and the manure.

"Let's go in," Sher stepped toward the open gate.

"Girls," said an old man sitting on a stool at the gate, his skin as brown and worn as his chaps. "You got tickets?" He raised a bandaged hand at Sher.

Sher wheeled away from the man as the smell of blood from his wound triggered her to the smell of the man she had knifed. She leaned over a rail, breathing deep. She had to control herself the way she'd learned to change her physical response to the iron-tinged smell of deer blood at six, when her father had shown her how to slit the throat of a wounded, wide-eyed doe and then skin and gut it. Sher retched. She had to get back to herself, get the stink of the man she cut off her skin and out of her nostrils. Get the stink of the city out of her.

Kris joined her at the rail.

The old man's apparition broke from the girls and sped east to suss out a long-forgotten pleasure the old man had as a boy: fresh lemonade for a penny at a booth run by the Ancient Order of United Workmen (AOUW). Why, he'd never even seen a lemon until then, much less drank "lemon duice," as he called it at four. The AOUW, formerly located in the southeast corner of the fair, was razed in the spring of '69 along with all the other booths in that spot to make way for the installation of the Mexican Village (which would be open but not completed until 1970).

This was a change decreed by the State Agricultural Society during a meeting in February, 1968. At that meeting, Ada Pritchard, a fourteen-year member of the State Agricultural Society and great-great-granddaughter of the first pastor of Westminster Presbyterian (founded by political elites in 1860 in downtown Minneapolis), stated, "After all Hubert Humphrey ended Twin City banks from denying mortgages to Jews and Negroes in the fifties. It's time the fair catches up to the progressive race ways of state and national politics, instituted by this state's finest politician nearly two decades ago, by creating a location designated specifically for our darker skinned brethren to display their crafts." All those in attendance looked away from Ada. Few agreed, but she carried clout. "And, I might add," she said, knowing her idea would be instituted by the way they refused to look at her, "people have come to enjoy their food. Therefore, a Mexican Village is not only fair-minded, but financially beneficial." The old man heard about what she'd said. He would never forgive Mrs. Pritchard or Humphrey for ending the banks' ability to deny mortgages and the razing of the AOUW. To make way for Mexicans and their big hats, of all people!

* * *

The girls walked west past the Horse Barn.

"That's where Pops and I camped." Sher pointed at the trailers lined up in haphazard rows in a lot reserved for those showing animals at the fair.

"Yah."

Sher leaned into Kristin and pushed her into the Horse Barn. She was leery about going to the place where she and her dad had stayed. She did not want to reckon with how her life had changed when he died. She could not afford those feelings. She steeled herself like the rounded tips of her boots.

The scent of horses hit the girls. Hay, dirt, manure, horse piss, human body odors, perfumes, and smoke mingled in the cavernous barn, built in 1937 by the Franklin Delano Roosevelt's Works Progress Administration. The smell made some city folks nauseous and chased others back out onto the sidewalk, but to the girls it was home. The pale green walls and dark green painted woodwork surrounded 450 stalls, two bathrooms, three entryways on the south, west, and east sides, and a single copper water fountain. The girls breathed easier than they had since they'd landed downtown on the Greyhound. They walked up and down the wide aisles caressing the horses' noses and feeding them hay and alfalfa out of the buckets hanging at the front of the stables. "Pretty boy, pretty girl," they said. "Hey, Marshmallow. Hey, Sally's Knickers," they said, talking in low silky voices, reading their names off the cards taped to the stalls.

"Hi, girl," Sher said to an eighteen-hand gray mare with a black mane and tail. She looked like Patsy. "Bonnie," Sher said softly, reading her tag, and the horse swept its massive head toward the girl. Sher pushed her hand through the metal bars so the horse could eat the alfalfa hay off her flat palm. Bonnie nibbled at the hay, her big black eyes looking the girl over. "Pretty girl." Sher curved her hand over the horse's nose soft and fuzzy as the tops of the weeds waving on the farm.

Bonnie snorted. Horses neighed in the barn and the brown mare next to Bonnie stamped her feet and whinnied. Bonnie's eyes rolled. A child screamed a row over. The brown mare kicked the side of the stall connected to Bonnie's stall. Bonnie reared. Sher stepped into Bonnie's stall and grabbed her bridle. "Bonnie girl, you're okay. You're okay, pretty girl." The horse held her head high but did not scream or rear again.

"You handle that horse pretty good, girl," a man said behind Sher.

Sher continued to stroke Bonnie's cheek and talk to her low.

"Got horses here?" the man asked. The brown mare nickered. "Hey, there," he said to the horse as he leaned against the stall next to Bonnie's.

"Sure," Sher said. Immediately embarrassed by her lie. She wondered why she had lied. "In a few days, I mean," she said. "My dad," her voice faltered.

"Yeah." The man put out his hand. "Billie," he said. "Nice to make your acquaintance, young lady."

Sher shook his hand hard, the way she shook white people's hands, not lightly, fingers barely touching the way Indians shook hands, with deference, to show respect. "Sher," she said and motioned toward Kristin. "Kris."

The man nodded at Kristin and hung a rope over a nail protruding from the front of the stall.

"Been around horses a lot?" He looked Sher up and down, a strapping Indian girl, like the ones he'd grown up with on the White Earth reservation. Strong. Worked hard, knew their way around horses. Same as this one, he bet.

"All my life," Sher said.

"Where you from?"

"Goodhue."

"The up-north Goodhue?" he asked, although he knew the answer.

"Yah," Kristin said.

The man nodded, rubbing his thumb on his lip. "What're you doing the next few days?" He looped his thumbs through his belt loops and kicked one heel against the other, as was his habit. "While you're waiting on your dad," he added, figuring she had a good enough reason to lie.

Kris's eyes slid sideways at Sher.

"Don't know," Sher said, studying the toes of her boots.

"Hang around. Go on rides." Kris covered for her cousin.

"I see." He knocked his heels together again. "Would you girls like to help me out? My son had to go to Rochester. His old lady's about to pop." His eyes hit the hay covered floor then came back to the girls. "He'll be back in a few days but I sure could use some help in the meantime." He adjusted his hat. "Nothin' fancy, just cleaning the stalls, keeping the water clean, feeding and brushing them, exercising them out back. There's a ring. Five of them—two gray mares, one buckskin, two thoroughbreds. I'll be busy showing them. I sure could use the help."

"Yah," Sher said and looked at Kristin.

Kristin stared at Sher and realized Sher and Billie were waiting for her approval. Kristin nodded. Sher had lied about her dad.

They shook hands with Billie.

"Five dollars a day for each of you is the best I can do." He picked up the rope and slung it over his shoulder. "Times are tight. That okay?"

"Yah."

"Yah."

"All right," Billie said. "Be back here at six-thirty. You met Bonnie." He tapped his knuckles on the stall next to Bonnie. "Sally. All mine down to the end. Introduce yourselves." He turned on his heels, walked past his horses, and turned south out of the girls' sight.

The girls said hello to Billie's horses and then found a place to sleep against the west side of the Horse Barn. Sher figured people would assume the girls were with a family that had horses in the barn and, therefore, wouldn't question them. Here it helped that their clothes were not the kind city girls wore and their Indian accent was similar to a white rural Minnesota accent. Here they fit in better. Sher relaxed against the barn wall and watched the moon swing, full and ripe and white as the flesh of an apple, over the Horse Barn roof and then drop down into the tops of the elms and maples rooted between the girls and a parking lot filled with campers. She fell asleep and dreamed of Dolly Parton.

The dreams had begun after Sher saw Dolly sing on *The Ed Sullivan Show*, her smile and curvaceous body captivating six-year-old Sher, who sat Indian style, mouth-a-gap in front of the black and white Zenith. Sher's grandmother sat in the rocker stitching up her husband's favorite plaid shirt. She saw her granddaughter's face and nodded to herself. Her granddaughter took after one of her great aunts and two Canadian cousins, who'd been allowed to live as they pleased. Her family accepted that was who they were, and didn't question it. Sher didn't think much about it either. She'd always liked girls, and as long as she could remember, it seemed her family knew, and did not mind. Except, of course, her mother who was mixed up with those white church people, as Sher's grandmother used to say. Sher's mother had admonished Sher for her broad shoulders, her narrow hips, and wearing her brother's hand-me-downs, as if these oddities sprang from Sher alone, and did not come from the loins of her parents, from her family, from the Creator.

* * *

Sher woke to dozens of crows cawing in the elms. She jostled Kristin. "Daylight in the swamp."

"Ah hah." Kristin smiled at the memory of their grandmother.

The wine-colored daylight crept over the top of the Minnesota State Fair.

"Hup hup." A man barked to his family from the parking lot.

"Hear that," Sher said. "We got to get up."

Kristin stood and rubbed her eyes. They finally had jobs—what they had planned all along—and now all she wanted to do was lie down and sleep.

"Hup hup," he said again. "Get a move on."

The sun popped over the buildings and tree-tops. Sparrows hopped about the fairgrounds poking at plastic wrappers, popcorn, fried bits of bread and chunks of hot dogs spit out by small children. Owners opened the locks on their booths and placed cash in registers. They dumped ice into bins and flared the deep fryers and grills, readying for the hundreds of thousands who would hand their cash over that day.

The girls fed and watered Billie's horses and cleaned their stalls. After they finished, they pulled the curtain on the stall where horse owners were able to get water for their horses out of a hose and washed themselves. Billie shared his lunch with them, sitting on hay bales across from his horses—turkey sandwiches, chunks of rhubarb they dipped in a paper bag filled with sugar, cold corn on the cob, and milk he got from a friend with dairy cows across the street in the Cattle Barn.

"Thank you," the girls said, adding "sir," because they were unsure how to act with him.

"Call me Billie," he said and talked about his son and his daughter-in-law, how this was their second child in ten months and how he didn't know how they'd make it what with crop prices so low these days and so many farmers losing their farms. "I don't wanna end up cleaning toilets in the city," Billie added and brushed bread crumbs off his trousers.

The girls nodded and did not say much for fear he'd ask about them.

Billie regarded the girls a few times when they were eating. He figured something was going on. He had a personal policy of letting Indians be. He knew where his land came from, and he knew someone had lost it for it to be his. He figured the least he could do was to leave them alone. He did not want to hassle the girls, just have some help and some company until his son got back from the birthing.

"I got a show in a hour with Carmen, the buckskin," Billie said. He stood up and smoothed his trousers down to his knees. "Will you girls exercise the others? Take it easy on them. Just a few laps around the ring on the other side of the campers." He jerked his thumb toward where the girls had slept.

Sher nodded and set down the rest of her sandwich.

"If you need food that's not fried, go to Steichen's Grocery. Buy some bread and sandwich meat. Been there forever. Only workers go there cause it's in the alley across from us." He pointed east.

Kristin popped the last bit of rhubarb and chewed slow. "Yaaah," she said, thinking about how good it would be to eat rhubarb if she were stoned.

Sher and Billie looked at Kris.

"Okay, then," Billie said, slapped a knee, and walked off.

"Kris," Sher hissed. "What's going on?"

"Nothin'," Kris said, and returned to imagining being stoned, away from it all.

"We finally got a job," Sher whispered. "We can't blow it."

"Sure thing." Kristin laughed. But she felt bad. She couldn't explain how or why this happened—sometimes the bottom fell out of her, and her feelings switched up on her for no reason she could discern. When it happened, she couldn't stop it—it was like she sat at the bottom of a well, and watched herself above.

* * *

The day was a cooker. The girls exercised the horses in the ring behind the Horse Barn. When they were done, Sher and Kristin rested in Billie's stall. It was equipped with two coolers, blankets, and a little radio. A green and white sign that read *Schwartz's Family Farm* hung across the outside of the stall. The girls spent the afternoon and evening listening to AM 1130 *Minnesota's Only Real Country and Western Station*, the same station they received in Goodhue off of the busted-up radio Sher's dad fastened above the work bench in the barn when the girls were babies. The girls stared at the wide beat-up maple boards of the stall and their shoes and the ceiling covered with cobwebs. Kris chewed her nails. Sher put her arms behind her head and was back on the reservation, running through the thick trees, light dashing off rocks, branches, leaves. *Animoosh* by her side. The city people cooed, thrust their hands through the metal bars, and flicked their fingers at the horses' faces, sometimes patting the horses' haunches and shoulders.

On occasion, a waist-high white girl or boy would stare at the girls until the mother yanked the child away hissing, "What did I tell you about staring?" Sher would nod at the child and Kris would act as if she did not see the child. Neither felt much about it here. Anytime they'd left the reservation, they'd been gawked at in these ways. In the barn, the girls felt safe for the first time in a long while. Like they could relax. No one knew who they were, and no one knew where they were.

The girls lived that way for four days. They slept and ate and drank plenty of milk and played cards and twice got into the horse shows at the Coliseum for free as Billie's assistants. Billie bought them each a bag of mini-donuts every morning and made sandwiches for them at noon. Kristin felt the outside world no longer existed. They lived in a world that only consisted of horses, junk food, firework displays, and famous singers every night that they could hear from the Horse Barn.

Sher, too, became lost in the horses and entranced by the shows—the riders in their finest riding clothes sitting ramrod straight in the polished saddles and bowler hats and shiny knee-high boots. She'd competed here on Patsy. She missed her horse and her father, playing King in the Corner with him at night by the army green propane Coleman lamp in the front of the horse trailer. Twice, Sher left Kris and Billie when they were inside the Coliseum, making the long, steep climb up the narrow stairs to the top ring of the building where she sat against the wall with a view of the interior of the oval building—a giant, concrete wigwam. What her grandparents were raised in, what her great grandparents lived in until they died, and what her dad and aunties and uncles lived in for a while. The girls had cousins and other kin in the Canadian bush who still lived in wigwams.

There, in the Coliseum, a Roman invention she'd studied in school (it had taken the Italians decades to figure out how to build a convex ceiling out of brick), she let go. She floated, studying the enormous concrete blocks arching over them, melding the past with the present, the way she did when she ran through the woods, the trees lacing their bony fingers above her, connecting her with her ancestors, with her past, with the spirits of the trees. "My girl," her grandfather had said to her many times, "these old ones here, the Standing People, they hold knowledge. They are our grandfathers. They grow up out of the soil our ancestors turned into, as will we. Listen to them. They have stories. I'll bet, if you sliced them real thin, you could play them on a record player and hear the stories of the world!"

While studying the many tons of concrete and mortar arching over the green metal seats, the steep stairs, the dirt ring bigger than a hockey rink, Sher saw her grandfather again, putting tobacco at the base of the tree, his eyes working up the trunk out to the thinnest branches like fingers reaching into the air for sustenance the same way the tree's roots moved through the soil absorbing nutrients and moisture, communicating with other trees, providing stability and life for the gifts—maple candy, a balm for rashes, leaves for tea, branches for wigwams, nuts for food, wood for fire—that each tree brought to creation.

On the fourth morning Billie's son, Carl, returned to the Horse Barn and grimly took up where he had left off. The baby had been born underweight. Carl was exhausted and only seventeen and not yet prepared to be a father to two or to provide for a family. "Yep," and "Nope," and "Boy, five pounds one ounce," were all he said to his father. Carl's sinewy body seemed to strain at his every movement, no matter how small. To the girls, he said nothing.

Billie gave the girls $30 and a handshake apiece. He stepped back. "Good havin' you," he said, touching the bill of his John Deere baseball hat pulled down tight over his brow. Billie and Sher stuffed their hands in their pockets, studied the hay-covered floor.

"Sure thing," Kris said.

Sher nodded.

The girls put the sweaty bills in their pockets. They were glad to have so much money, but more than the money, they wanted to continue to work in the Horse Barn—to ignore the rest of the fair and the world. To stay in the barn that had become like a nest for them. The girls left the Art Deco Horse Barn, Billie, and the horses. Wandering out into the mix of the fair—the bright sun and the enormous crowds of bobbing blond heads, screaming toddlers, hawkers, and high school marching bands snaking through the streets—the girls were overwhelmed by the cacophony. They headed north along Lake Avenue toward the Midway with its rides and spinning neon lights.

After half a block, the girls stopped at the WCCO AM radio booth and stared into the glass-enclosed stand at the faces of those they had listened to as long as they could remember. Bob Daring rattled off the news: "Twins beat the Angels four to one. The spaghetti dinner at the ELKS club in Duluth changed to six on Friday. The revised hours at Antwatin library go into effect today. Don't forget the baseball fundraiser game between the Cloquet police squad and the Bemidji fire squad tonight seven-sharp. The drop in the price of corn threatens farmers. And now for the national news. There's a hurricane off the coast of Texas and a drought in the southeast and a string of bank robberies across the Midwest by a man wearing a red snowmobile mask. The protests against Vietnam have increased nationwide, which I predicted would bring about the moral decline of today's youth and the return of Commie politics. And that, folks," he winked at the people gathered around the booth, "is the news for the day."

The girls grew bored and left the booth. They headed north, cutting through a long line for Gary's Cheese Curds, curled like a pig's tail. They passed Granny's Caramel Apple, a booth owned by a family from Redwood Falls whose oldest son painted plywood cut like an apple with bright-green paint and screwed it to the top of the white lattice stand. "A real artist," the neighbor lady said about the boy's handwork. From there the girls passed a hay-covered hut selling *Tiki's Hawaiian Juices and Jems*, owned by a man from Neenah, Wisconsin who traveled the Midwest fair circuit. His booth featured rainbow-colored sugared drinks and plastic crystals hanging from the ceiling with fish line for sale at .10 cents per line, an idea that came to him the semester he attended college in Chicago.

The girls reached the end of the stands. The carnival grounds doglegged off to the left. They followed it without conversation or consent, their bodies turning west into the gullet of the Midway. The carnie lights were less garish in the daytime, splintering into the bright day, but they mingled, unseen, with the sunlight and the shouts of the carnie callers and children and clank of steel on steel

and the splish splash of Minnesota's Great Canoe Ride and the
spitting grease and the whir of the cotton candy machines and the
pounding of stakes and the ringing of basketballs off rubber rims
sprayed with a metallic-looking paint and the soft thudding of
softballs thrown into stuffed ducks weighted with lead and the
incessant shouting of the carnie callers at the jam-packed
Speedway stand. "Line up folks right here step right up every race
has a winner car number five coming in first six is second one is
third this is a tight one folks don't look away even for a split
second not to see your honey kiss someone else or your kid run off
to join the army no siree don't look away even for a split second
you'll miss the winner here it is folks looks like the fire engine red
five is going to pull it out but oh no here comes true blue six right
here folks!" The Speedway stand operator tap tap tapped his cane
on the counter. "Step right up six has won by a hair! Everyone can
race folks that's the beauty of the Speedway at the Fair!"

The bulbs lining the ticket booths blinked and the red and white
lights of the Ferris wheel spun unseen through the bright sky and
the green and yellow and red painted horses on the carousel—
Hand painted in the heart of Deutschland!—scattered blue light
into the mix each time the pistons thrust the horses and the
children they carried upward.

Sher and Kristin regarded the people and the carnie callers and
the games and prizes and food stands and fat men sitting in the
ticket booths and skinny half-breed brown men running the rides
and white teenagers serving up fried foods and the bands of yellow
electrical cords taped together big as a man's forearm, almost as
big as a South American snake, the size of the enormous silky pink
snakes with green eyes dangling from the ceiling at the *Toss A Ring
On A Bottle one ticket buys one toss six tickets buy a bucket of
twelve—best value!*

The girls struggled through the crowd, reaching the western-
most corner of the carnie where it blossomed into an enormous
circle. Around the outside of the circle were the attractions meant
for the teenagers and the adults—The Monster, The Whip, See
With Your Own Two Eyes: The Fattest Lady In The World, A Lady
With A Full Beard, A Man With The Skin Of A Leopard, A Boy
Who Looks 100-Years-Old, Snakes Galore, The Demon Rider, and
Injun Joe: A Real Live Savage who just so happened to be an
Italian man in a Plains Indian headdress. Bikers in leather chaps

and red bandannas strode around this end of the carnie and teenagers dressed in black, the boys in greased-back hair and smoking Marlboros dragged their heels in the dirt but were *Too cool, man* to ride the carnival's rides. Here no mothers with children or slicked down fathers from the suburbs, or wide-eyed, tow-headed four-year-olds, or babies in fringed carriages, or Grandmas and Grandpas holding hands like they were on their second honeymoons mingled among the deviants. The only outsiders who ended up in the belly of the carnie were "country punkins," the name the bikers and the fry kids—the druggies—had for the rural folks who wandered into their territory on accident. Like the girls.

The girls neared the *Injun Joe: Fierce, Proud, Uncivilized, Exterminated* trailer covered in images of Indians in war paint, riding ponies, scalping white men, chasing a white woman with a tomahawk, and raising spears at bisons. When the girls saw the trailer, their path swerved away from it, without conversation or verbal acknowledgment.

As they looped around the trailer, Kristin bumped into a man, *Minneapolis Hogs* writ in red cursive across the back of his leather vest. She recoiled.

The man grabbed her wrist and flung her arm at her chest. "Stupid chick," he said.

Sher pushed him.

The man leaned back, looked like he was afraid, and then laughed. He grabbed Sher's wrist and ripped her arm behind her back. Her shoulder popped.

"A hotheaded squaw." The man twisted her arm. "Did you escape Injun Joe's tent?"

His two buddies laughed.

The man leaned in, whispered in Sher's ear, "I'd fuck you for that if all these people weren't around." He rubbed against her from behind and then pushed her toward the Injun Joe trailer. "A dyke from the looks of *it*."

Sher landed on her belly in the dirt.

"Go back where you came from."

"Oopsie. Someone did a belly flop." One of his friends laughed.

The man who pushed Sher turned his back to her. "Raced at Sturgis this year. Just came back from Cally, ran nigger and white bitches from Sturgis to some Oakland One Percenters." He jabbed his thumb toward the girls. "Coulda used a coupla squaws to round it out."

"A whore from every race," the third man said. "We all like to dabble."

The men laughed.

Sher's hair covered her face.

"Let's go," Kris said.

Sher picked herself up. She loosened the laces of the boot with the knife.

"Please," Kris said.

Sher turned her eyes on the back of the man who had shoved her. She didn't consider what was best for her and her cousin, as she had in the past. Rage took over.

The man widened his stance, cutting his boots into the dirt and pulling his jeans tight over his thighs. Sher charged, caught him from behind, and shoved him the way she'd shoved cattle to get them moving. The man whiplashed forward into one of his buddies and let out an "Oomph." His buddy nearly fell with him in his arms.

"Shit." The third man jumped out of the way, dumping his beer on the three of them.

Quicker than fireworks popping at night, Sher reached into her boot and slipped out her knife. She flicked the blade and held it in front of her face.

The men were too surprised to do anything other than regain their feet.

"Go." Sher waved at Kristin behind her back.

Kristin did not move.

"Get," Sher said. "Now."

Kristin moved toward the thick of the fair, walking backward, her eyes on Sher and the men.

Sher turned toward Kris. "Run!" she yelled.

At that moment the man Sher pushed nodded at a younger man in a Hogs vest standing off to the side by a corn dog stand. The younger man nodded in return. Kris ran into the crowd. The younger man set off after her. The other bikers and fries in the area watched the melee out of curiosity. After all, it wasn't every day a girl went after a grown man, and a Hog at that. They continued drinking, smoking, and shooting the shit.

"If," Sher said to the man who had pushed her, "it wasn't

daylight, I'd kill you."

The man's face twisted. He couldn't nail her. Too many people outside the Hogs' gang were watching. His buddies stared. They'd always had their way with girls, until this one.

Sher folded the knife, turned, and strode east, the direction her cousin ran. She figured they would not follow. Too many people around. But just in case, she kept her eyes on the ground next to her, watching for their shadows.

Kris zigzagged through the carnie crowd until she hit Liggett Street and bolted north toward the Young America Center. She ran out of fear of the men and because she felt abandoned by Sher, by her risky behavior, but under those feelings was wide-eyed baby terror about her momma's murder, unacknowledged and screaming. She cut east on West Dan Patch Street and ran for blocks. The younger Hog had caught sight of her on the edge of the Midway and followed her as best he could through the mostly white crowd, which was less likely to move for a greasy biker than for a young, seemingly tanned white girl.

At the eastern edge of the fair, Kris cut south at the Food Building. She cut through a crowd of white hippies listening to a man on stage. "Woody Guthrie is my hero," the singer on stage said. "This next song is about how America is our land. The people's land! And the title is, of course, 'This Land is Your Land.'" "It was made for you and me," a man in the crowd yelled. "Yeah! Yes! Right on, cat!" the crowd yelled in response. Kris dodged elbows and sandals and whiffed the pot smoke lingering above them. She broke free of the crowd and looped around the grounds of the Horticulture Building with its towering elms and red tropical plants in pots. Spotting a group of brown people, she felt a burst of safety and veered toward them, her mind popping images of white peonies and cat-tail reeds that terrorized her for reasons she did not understand. She ran as if her existence depended on outpacing the images. Whirling past the group of brown people, she shot under a sign that read *Mexican Village—Open Now!—To Be Completed in 1970.* The Hogs' man turned the corner at the Horticulture Building in time to see her enter the village. Kris dashed down an aisle filled with sombreros and bright blankets like a colt fleeing the first time it heard a gunshot. Overwhelmed and exhausted, she bent over, gasping for air.

"Girl," an elderly woman whispered from a booth. "Come

here."

Kris looked up. The woman was the same penny-color as her grandma. *Marie Washington, Artist*, the sign on her booth read.

Marie nodded toward the entrance. "Hide."

The man in a Hogs vest stood at the entrance, scanning the crowd.

Marie lifted the striped Mexican wool blanket draped over her table.

Kris dove under the blanket.

"Don't move," Marie said, covering her mouth so no one would see she was speaking.

The man trotted down an aisle two over.

Kris pulled her knees up to her chest as Marie dropped the blanket around her.

"Hello, ma'am." Marie nodded at a customer.

"Do you paint these yourself?" a white woman asked.

"Yes."

"Mmmm hmmm. You have the most beautiful eyes," the white woman said. "Such a pretty green. If you don't mind me saying."

"I don't."

The woman moved on.

Marie painted scenes long gone of black and brown children, animals, and houses she recalled from her youth in South Carolina on slices of granite and petrified wood. She watched the man out of her peripheral vision.

He turned down her aisle. "Seen a girl run through here?" he asked an East Indian woman selling jewelry three booths down. "Long brown hair?"

Marie looked straight ahead. She did not hear her answer. This was not the first time she'd seen men pursuing young girls at the fair, and from the looks of the one under her table, a mixed Indian. Marie's grandmother, a fullblood Choctaw, with dark skin and straight black hair, had eighteen siblings and a family of hundreds of white, brown, and black Indians.

The man stepped toward her booth, glanced at her and then her paintings. She did not make eye contact, a way of surviving in the South that she still needed in the North. He stared at her hard, and she tensed inside as she did not know if the booth three down had told him a girl was hiding beneath her blanket. He grasped his bison-head belt buckle. She clasped her hands—her gaze unfixed and away from him. He thought she looked strange. Something was fishy. Then his attention popped to the entrance and he left at a fast clip.

"Stay put," Marie said, watching him turn west out the gate.

Kris remained folded beneath the table. She didn't hear the woman. She wasn't anywhere. She was floating in nothingness, a skill she'd developed the day of the peonies.

Marie waited more than twenty minutes, wanting to be sure he would not return. "Girl," Marie said.

Kris did not reply. Twenty minutes could be one minute or four hours to her when she was like that.

"Girl." Marie lifted the blanket the fair made all the vendors purchase to have a consistent and authentic-looking Mexican theme. She tapped Kris, who sat motionless, her arms wrapped around her knees.

Kris looked at Marie, her eyes unfocused and far away.

Marie knew the look. "Come back here. He's gone."

Kris crawled out. Stood.

"Be careful, young lady. There are dangerous men around here. You'd best know there's a world below the surface here, like everywhere. Go home. It's only a matter of time before they catch you. Do you have...."

As she spoke, Kris glanced across the table at a painting of a white farm house with two red chairs on the porch. "Where?" she asked, looking from the painting to Marie and back to the painting. Her grandparents' house. Exactly. It even had the garden and two brown people sitting in the chairs.

"Where, what?"

"Where you seen that house?"

"A dream. Know it?"

"No." Kris backed up. "I mean, yes. It's my grandparents."

"Ah," Marie said.

"I mean, it looks like my grandparents'. They're. Gone." Kris looked from the painting to the woman. "Just like it. Even the chairs." She took another step back. How did this woman know?

Marie grabbed Kris's wrist. "Be careful, my girl. You're in danger."

Kris turned and ran.

Marie watched her turn west at the gate and disappear.

* * *

"Where'd you go?" Sher poked Kris, curled in a fetal position in Bonnie's stall.

"Hmm?" Kris said, half-asleep.

"I been looking for you. Where'd you go?"

"Nowhere."

"You okay?" Sher asked.

"Yeah." Kris sat up. She pulled her hair back. She wasn't lying. She'd buried the memory of the house painted on rock and the woman's warning and the man who'd chased her in her mind's tunnels. Kris sat up.

"Okay," Sher said, unsure of what actually happened. She'd seen Kris do this before.

"Let's get some food, cuz," Kris said. "Walk around."

* * *

The girls headed north away from the Horse Barn and then cut east past the Sky Ride to a brick building painted light blue that housed the Minnesota Bureau of Criminal Apprehension. Sher turned her head away. Would someone in the Bureau of Criminal Apprehension building see her face and match it to one sent out on an APB? A runaway? A murderer? Had she become paranoid? Crazy? Sher tried to remember, had she given Jacob her last name? Fear took root in her stomach. It felt like every time she turned around, there was someone else trying to hurt them.

The girls approached the Grandstand. A four-story brick building built in 1894 to accommodate crowds in the hundreds of thousands to watch Dan Patch, the greatest harness race horse in the world. Never defeated, stabled in a palatial steam-heated barn called the Taj Mahal along the banks of the Minnesota River, his owner Marion Savage used the horse's likeness to sell everything from chewing tobacco to washing machines in Savage's International Stock Food Company. Along with harness racing, the Grandstand also featured locomotives smashing headlong in each other. On September 5, 1920, the "Gigantic Locomotive Collision" was held on the Grandstand's race track with the goal to break the previous year's World Fair Record Attendance. Two 160-pound train engines crashed into each other at 60 mph. Slated to be filmed by a "motion picture camera invented by the great American Thomas Edison who owns over 1,000 patents" (some of which he stole from the actual inventors), the rain that day kept the crash and the 55,117 attendees who broke through police barricades to storm the track after the crash from being filmed. The crowd rescued the two engineers, one of whom somersaulted three times and sprained his ankle on a boulder after jumping from the engine, and collected souvenirs from the wreckage.

The girls entered the Grandstand. Vendors and fair-goers stood shoulder-to-shoulder, covered in sweat. White men with crew cuts and calf-high white socks sat at the Minnesota Environmental Control Citizens Association (MECCA) booth, fighting to stop Reserve Mining from pumping tailings into Lake Superior. Grant Merritt, the grandson of the Merritt brothers from whom Rockefeller stole the Iron Range mines, looked up from a law case he was reading. He nodded at the girls. Two rows over, a skinny balding man hawked The Handy Dandy Little Ice Machine "See here! See here!" he shouted, his voice high and shrill. "Never worry for crushed ice again!" Kris wondered why someone would buy that when a person could use a hammer. "The most amazing miracle since sliced bread folks and men your little lady cannot be without this charmer everyone on the block will have one but her and what will that say about you?" Sher regarded the crowd watching him grind ice. "Perfect every time! Yes, every time folks, no more embarrassing moments at the dinner party when you realize you don't have crushed ice to impress your boss and his little lady this handy dandy little item crushes grinds and purees ha ha folks that last one is just a joke to see if you're listening but yessiree folks this handy dandy little item could not only save your marriage and your job but get you a raise as well!"

Sweat built on his forehead. He wiped at it frantically with his sleeve to keep it from dripping in the ice. *It would not look good for a man selling ice to lose his cool,* he thought, laughing to himself. After crushing a bag of cubes, he handed out Dixie cups of cherry Kool Aid and ice flecks. "It doubles as a snow cone maker! It'll make the little ones in the home happy too!"

The audience pushed nearer to him, as they became entranced by the hyper man with a nasally voice. He spoke so fast and with such enthusiasm that by the time the demonstration was over, three-quarters of the crowd lined up to purchase The Handy Dandy Little Ice Machine at five ninety-nine a pop. "C'mon, good folks of Minnesota. How many lakes is it that you have here? Ten thousand! This is the land of water and ice. You need The Handy Dandy Little Ice Machine! C'mon, folks, you don wanna be left out in the cold!" He pulled out a wad of bills as thick as the muscle off of a deer shoulder. "Step right up!"

Other booths sold welding equipment and winter car starters, "Hard to imagine now, folks, but we're in Minnie-snow-tah and winter will be back!" and rubber hoses, "Guaranteed for a life time!" and decks and plastic lawn chairs, "The future of outdoor entertainment!" and three sizes of dragons carved out of rock, "Hand carved in Malaysia! "and General Electric freezers, "The coolest in the world!" and drawing kits that would make you "An instant artist in one week or your money back!" and the new style Whirlpool washing machines, "The wave of the future!" and Oriental cookbooks, "Simply the best to be found!" and a Scientology booth, "Uniting God and science!"

The girls ate corn on the cob from a stand near the Grandstand. They drank milk from the Dairy Bar next to four feet tall chunks of butter carved like the heads of the ten white blond girls competing for Miss Minnesota 1969. The girls split a hamburger from Burgers Und Brats just east of the Horse Barn. To kill time, they leaned against the fence to watch the horses parade into the Coliseum for another show. Billie rode Bonnie, but he was focused on his horse and did not see them. The sun set like a fox, its bushy orange tail blazing above the trees.

"Where should we sleep?" Kris asked.

"I dunno," Sher said. She spat into the dry dirt.

A horse kicked up a clod of dirt. The rider flicked its neck with a short leather whip. The horse sidestepped and then spun its haunches in a circle. The man pulled back too hard on the reins and the horse reared. Sher wished she was the one riding the horse. She would do better.

Sher glanced at the fading fox tail in the sky. "Might as well sleep behind the barn."

The girls, their hands in their pockets, stepped around the piles of horse manure and made their way toward the other side of the Horse Barn where they'd slept the other nights. They fell asleep to the thrum of the insects and the horses' chuffing and stomping.

* * *

The next morning, the girls bathed in the Horse Barn bathroom, wetting their hair and splashing water under their arms, making gray Vs down the sides of their shirts. They rubbed their teeth with water and a dab of soap, rinsed and spit, rinsed and spit again.

Sher smelled the must and manure and sweat and oats and hay and that tangy horse smell she loved so much. She felt clean. "Dang," Sher said, her arm around Kris. "Let's find another job, cousin. Get some money. Maybe a bus to Wisconsin. Grandma's cousins' daughter in Milwaukee. We could find them. Just go to where the Indians are."

Kristin smiled. "Yah," she said, looking at the sorrel Percheron in the stall next to the washroom. Sher reminded her so much of her uncle.

"Fries for breakfast?" Sher grinned at Kristin. "It's a good day, eh?"

"Yah."

The girls headed east toward the fry stand across from the entrance to the carnie.

Fresh Cut Fries was bigger than three of the woodsheds on the farm combined, painted brown on the outside and white on the inside with enormous yellow and red letters proclaiming *Biggest Fries in the World!* with *as stated in the Guinness Book of World Records* in smaller letters.

Lines curled from three sides of the fry stand like pea tendrils. On the north side, teenage boys in bright yellow *Fresh Cut Fries!* T-shirts dragged garbage cans of potatoes from a storage shed to two metal tables where teenage girls in bright yellow *Fresh Cut Fries!* T-shirts peeled and pushed the white fleshy lumps through a slicer. Sher and Kristin sidled up to one of the lines. Flies buzzed and the carnie callers shouted from across the road. People sweated and milled about the grounds as the sun circled overhead.

The girls' line did not move.

People were hot and hungry and ornery. The *Fresh Cut Fries!* manager motioned the people in the girls' line to go to another. A man yelled, "Give me a break" and another yelled, "C'mon we been here near an hour," an exaggeration of forty minutes.

People trailed into other lines around the stand. Some left for the *Cream Puff Pastry Made with Real Whipped Cream!* booth while others headed east to the *Foot Long Hotdogs on a Stick* booth. Sher and Kristin stayed. They had no destination. The sun was hot and deepened the brown of their shoulders.

"What's going on?" a man asked a boy lugging a garbage can of potatoes from the shed to the stand.

The boy set his load down. "Four kids quit." He dragged the

potatoes across the dirt toward the stand.

"Hanson." The owner darted out from the stand into the sun. "I thought I told you not to drag those cans across the grass."

"There isn't any grass at all. It's all dirt." The boy pointed at the rutted dirt.

"My point, boy," the owner said.

The boy rolled his eyes.

The owner looked at the girls. "What're you doing?"

"Setting," Sher said.

"Setting?" the owner asked and put his hands on his hips and looked at the boy who dragged the can across the dirt toward the fryers. "What…"

"They don't work here," the boy said.

The owner looked at Sher and Kristin. "Well, why not?" he asked. "Need a job? Four kids quit on me this morning."

"Sure." Sher shrugged.

"Yah," Kristin said.

"Good," the owner said. "Then you're hired. Get two T-shirts from the storage shed. Cash at the end of each shift. You work ten to midnight two bucks an hour. You," he pointed at Kristin, "serve. And you," he pointed at Sher, "in the back with the boys."

"Told you it was a good day," Sher said.

"Yah," Kristin said, but she was angry about working up front. She would rather slice potato hunks in the back.

Sher grabbed two T-shirts and flung one at Kristin. She knuckled Kris's shoulder. "It's a job."

A girl told Kris the prices and how to salt the fries and scoop them into the tubs. "Take over that line," the girl said.

Sher went into the shed, grasped the handles of one of the garbage pails, and hauled it to a table.

"Hey," one of the boys said, "only guys do that. You peel."

Sher shook her head.

Another boy said, "Yeah, you peel. This ain't a woman's lib thing. There's too many of us hauling right now. You gotta peel."

Sher grasped a paring knife and cut into a potato.

The girls were drenched in sweat within ten minutes, working only a few feet from deep fryers. Kristin felt safe inside the stand. Sher focused on the nubbly potatoes and the skin that clung to the flesh. She thought the potatoes were too green but did her best not to take out chunks of flesh with the skin. As she peeled and as the heat overtook her, she found herself drifting back to her grandparents' land when they had one of their gatherings—the ricing and the feasts when they roasted deer over a bonfire and fried pats of bread in lard, sprinkling them with sugar and blueberry sauce made from berries picked on county-owned land. "It's our damned land!" someone would say as they divvied up buckets among family. Sher remembered the laughing and the jokes funnier than *The Ed Sullivan Show* about someone's Indian name being Two-Legged Moose. Or their auntie who married a half Ho Chunk and said, "What's the Ho Chunk war cry? Help!" Or the wry comments about how the government agents were trying to get Indians to eat canned and processed food that Sher's grandparents called "casket cans" because the food was dead and would "send you to your casket early." Or sugar in gas tanks and fights over girlfriends or money owed or what was the right way to rice. Or the especially painful fights about how the old-timers did things and why. But what Sher remembered most of all was the love the children received from everyone: the hugs and cheek kisses and hands grasping the sides of the face. They'd say, "Oh you are a beautiful one," and "You do well by me, my girl," and "Never forget who your people are. What we been through."

The girls worked that way covered in potato juice, dirt, and grease until midnight when they and the all-teenage crew cleaned-up and collected their money. The girls went back to the Horse Barn, falling asleep with the crickets ringing in their ears and greasy dollar bills burning holes in their pockets.

The girls worked that way for four long days—selling and peeling and frying white spuds grown just east of the White Earth reservation. Four days of watching day turn into night on carnival land, of watching the fireworks and the red and blue neon lights of the carnie spin off into the night sky, their lights joining the stars a billion miles away. The silhouettes of the Ferris wheel and roller coaster and the gigantic spider ride replaced Sher and Kris's memory of a skyline with rounded treetops without twirling lights.

Kristin did not think about getting high. Sher did not plan for the future. The fair intoxicated them. The heat and the grease and the monotony and the never-ending crowds and the carnie callers bellowing through megaphones and the royal blue and red and white quilt depicting the head of a bald eagle made by Rose Myers from Rice, Minnesota (population 84); and the stained glass window made by Art Corscadden from International Falls, Minnesota (population 4,983); and the blanket crocheted out of yellow and white yarn with royal blue ties by ninety-two-year-old Mabel Duncan from Dent, Minnesota (population 113), who also entered the senior baker competition and won first for her spicy baked apple pie and her banana bread.

All that created a world that suspended the outside one, the life the attendees and workers went back to, but the girls did not. During their free time, the girls viewed the 4-H top hog and cow and sheep and French lop-eared rabbit and the Premium Prize Blue Ribbon apple streusel and rum cake and pickled tomatoes and loom woven rugs and log stools with hand carved seats and porch swings welded out of leftover oil barrels made by a twelfth-grade boy from Big Lake along with everything else that made up the spirit of the fair.

They worked that way until they felt they'd known nothing else, until they felt their past was a dream. The things in the Chicago house had never happened. This world would last forever. Once, in a dream, they had lived on a reservation. Once they'd had family. Once they went to school; milked cows; plucked and fried chickens; identified bear, lion, and bobcat scat. Ran through woods. Now they drank cola like it was water, as if the pop their uncles and grandfather had used to remove rust from car engines would not eat away at their insides.

And then, on the fifth night, Sher stepped outside to get a break from the fryers. The rides spun neon sparks into the dark sky. Just past them, a nearly full moon shone steady. Sher rubbed her eyes and set her hands on her hips. She did not feel the eyes upon her, watching her from the dark space behind the shed.

On the sixth morning, Sher woke before the sun, her heart beating fast, holding fear from a dream her mind did not remember. She stared at the grainy gray sky. The dread said she and Kristin should flee before the day began. But what could one more day bring? Her grandfather had told her never to doubt her gut, what the spirits were telling her. "Listen," he'd say. "You can't always understand, see what they see." Sher knew to trust her feelings and her body as much as her mind but she could not bring herself to tell Kristin about her feelings or even to try to convince herself that they should get up and leave immediately. One more day at the fair. If they left now, where would they go? They could use the money. And they had no plans once the fair closed down. Nothing out of the ordinary had occurred to cause Sher alarm. Here, they were safer. Plus, they might be able to work on the clean-up crew—she'd overheard two boys at the stand discuss it— which would extend their stay at the fair by another week or so, she guessed, but did not know for certain. Enough to save for two bus tickets to somewhere. Maybe back home. In a matter of a minute, she talked herself out of the feeling beating in her body.

A rosy gray crawled across the sky from the east and then turned to a pink blush.

Kristin woke, stretched one arm over her head, and yawned. "Whatter ya doin?" Kristin asked in that sleepy daze that took her hours to leave each morning.

Sher tapped her fingertips on the rock-hard dirt. "Nothing." The dread spread into her chest and arms.

Kristin walked into the Horse Barn half-asleep. She returned from the bathroom and slumped against the wall. "What's going on?"

Sher rolled over onto her belly and lay there looking at the few remaining trailers and campers and tents. An adolescent of indeterminate sex rolled a pile of blankets and tucked them into a canvas bag. Sher pretended the feelings from the dream were those blankets, rolled up and tucked away.

"Dunno." Sher sat up and reached for her boots. "Should we ask about doing clean up?"

"Uh, huh," Kristin said, watching Sher and wondering why she had ever decided that leaving her home—no matter what her father was doing to her—was a good idea. "I shouldn't have made you leave."

"Nah." Sher fiddled with her boot laces. "I had to leave too."

Sher pushed her foot into her boot and laced it halfway because of the heat. Kristin poked with her tongue at a piece of potato caught between her back molars. A squirrel dropped a wrapper, raced down the trunk, and scampered into the area where the campers and trailers were parked. The space was fast becoming a field again as fairgoers packed their belongings, loaded their animals, and headed back to their farms.

"You know," Sher said. "Not too many squirrels here. Think that's the first one I seen."

Kris nodded. "Think they kill them or something?"

"Maybe."

The girls sat that way for some time. They shared a caramel apple and cherry slushee for breakfast until it was time for them to wind their way through the crowds to the stand.

"Hup, hup, hup," Jerry said when he saw the girls. "Let's go; let's go." He tapped the face of his watch. "No slacking off. Today's one of the busiest."

Sher said nothing. Kristin scowled. They were ten minutes early.

Jerry smiled at Kristin. "Labor Day, girls. Big crowd. Perk up."

Kristin's frown deepened. The way he smiled at her when she was mad reminded her of her father. Sher began peeling. Kristin stepped to her place behind the counter. Jerry stuck a key into an army green cash box and sprung the lid.

He winked. "Now let's see that pretty smile of yours."

Kristin set her teeth.

A woman held out a five to Kristin. "Large."

Kristin grabbed a tray of fries hot out of the fryer, jerked the salt shaker over them, and scooped up the steaming fries until she filled a large red tub.

"Heard it's going to be over 100 today," the woman said. "You kids are really going to be hot in there."

A young boy, his face bright red, peered up over the counter next to her. "Do you know when the fireworks are?"

"No," Kristin lied thinking the woman and boy must really be stupid. She took her money, and accidentally gave her less change by a dollar. Kris realized it but did not acknowledge it. She looked over the top of her head at the next customer. *We need it more than she does*, she thought. *I'm sick of these white people.*

The woman took her change, picked up the tub of fries, and stepped to the side of the line. The next person ordered. Someone dumped a basket of fries in the grease. It popped and sizzled. The din of the fair rose and swelled.

The woman returned. "Excuse me, miss. You gave me the wrong change."

Barkers shouted and kids cried.

Kristin popped inside. Her fear and her anger wrestled until Kristin snapped, "Get out of the way."

The woman's eyes popped. The fryers spurted grease.

Kris's chest crackled. She slammed the cash box on the countertop. The people in line stepped back. The woman dragged her son away from the counter.

Kristin slammed the cash box again. "Stupid. You stupid idiot!" she yelled. As soon as the words were out of her mouth, she heard her father calling her *stupid idiot*. She ran to the shed.

Sher went after Kris.

Kristin gulped air.

"Set," Sher said.

"Girls!" Jerry yelled. He turned the corner by the shed. "No running off on me. Not today."

Dread flooded Sher. She wanted to pull Kristin up and run.

"You," Jerry pointed at Sher, "up front pronto." A muscle on his jaw popped. "And you," he pointed at Kristin, "peel." He stepped toward the stand, stopped, and looked back at the girls. "No more outbursts. I mean it. Back to work," he bellowed at the other kids.

Sher felt the pull of his anger. It tripped something inside that made her feel he was not talking about being upset at the thought of being left shorthanded.

"Creep," Kristin coughed.

One of the boys stuck his head around the side of the shed. "Hurry up, country bumpkins. We're waiting on you." He disappeared.

"You okay?" Sher asked.

Kristin's scowl deepened. "Yah."

"Yah?"

"Yah."

"Want to go? Let's just leave."

"Where to?"

"Dunno."

"But what about the money?"

"Dunno," Sher said. "Leave it."

"But," Kristin said. She couldn't let him keep their money even if it was only a few bucks. "No. We need that money. It's ours."

"Not worth it."

"It's mine," Kristin said. She stood, turned the corner of the shed, and ran into the boy. Fear lit in her. He had been listening to them.

The boy stood over Kris. His eyes narrowed. A smile flickered like a flame and was gone.

Sher stepped up to them. Something caught in her throat.

"Girls," he said, without feeling. His face went blank, like a mask of white gauze had been pressed across his forehead, sealing his eye sockets, lips, and chin.

Sher grabbed at Kris's arm. Kris pulled away.

The boy turned to Sher, his face normal now. "Get up front Indian gal." He moved toward the stand.

"Indian gal?" Sher said, following him. "Who you calling—"

He stepped into her shoulder.

"Hustle up!" Jerry yelled, working Kristin's line. "Or you won't get nothing from me today."

"Sher," Kris warned. She wanted her money. Why let another white man take from them?

Sher pushed past the boy. "White boy," she said.

"Indian—" he said.

"Get up here." Jerry slid a burning hot tray of fries onto the counter, motioned to Sher that they were hers. Sher glanced at Kris, who had her back to her at the peeling station.

People fidgeted in line. Rides whirled across Cosgrove, adults clutching metal bars locked into place across their laps, screaming like children. Barkers sold hot dogs for a quarter and beer for two. Raw mini-donuts plopped in grease, sizzled, and then were sugared and bagged—ten for a quarter. Plastic balls lit up yellow and red when squeezed. A line snaked at the caricature booth. Stuffed alligators swung in the Midway as consolation prizes. Horses snorted. Sheep bleated, tethered and sheered. Roosters screamed. Rabbits nickered. Money and germs and food and gadgets and paper cups for the All You Can Drink Milk For A Nickel exchanged hands. Sher took Kris's place, shoveled fries, gave change. Nodded. The feeling they should run grew, but every time she turned to Kris, Kris ignored her, cutting and peeling and slicing white fleshy potatoes hand-picked for Jerry's stand by Mexicans near White Earth working for fifty-cents a day on a farm co-owned by the city of Mahnomen's mayor.

The fair spun that way. Then that way. Then another way.

The girls worked that way for hours, the heat of the day, and the fryers loosening their bodies' hold on their spirits such that the girls floated beyond the carnival to other places and times.

Jerry tapped Sher on the shoulder. "Break," he said. "Ten. Not a second more."

He took over her line, scooped a small fry, and handed it to her.

"Thanks," Sher mumbled and then felt stupid for being polite to a jerk. What was happening to her? She poured a Coke. Kristin was still working so Sher walked to the east side of the shed. The only shaded spot. Sher sat, dug her heels into the dirt, and ate the fries while looking out over an empty, cleared area where, unknown to Sher and largely forgotten by those who had seen it, fourteen years earlier a V-2 rocket had been displayed, tethered to the ground with nylon ropes; a Swastika painted just above the back fins by Jewish slaves in the caves of Mittelwerk concentration camp. Sher watched four teenage girls cut through the clearing, laughing, and leaning into each other. She gulped the Coke as if she were out in the fields haying and had to eat fast to finish before the sun went down.

Little Falls, Minnesota, 1955

Four blocks east of Leonard's drowning, forgotten even by the man who dropped his pail when he was a boy, a German-born widow with long, gray hair worn in a bun lived in a white Victorian with green trim, its interior updated in '50s pink and turquoise, including a Formica turquoise and white swirled kitchen table and chairs, purchased at Falls Furniture, thanks to a hefty savings from her late husband's business dealings with Friedrich Krupp AG, a German manufacturer of munitions, propaganda leaflet rifle launching grenades, and Luftwaffe airfield lights. He'd worked there before and during the war. Every chance she got, the widow publicly bemoaned the anti-Semitism of the town's cherished son, Charles Augustus Lindbergh—the first man to fly an airplane solo across the Atlantic. She hoped others would believe her and never suspect that her house, new furniture, and remodel were bought with coins that she and her husband had taken off dead Jews and Gypsies, or received from prisoners for favors and as Christmas gifts from Krupps' owner, who filled former potato bins at his farmhouse in Germany with gold coins once owned by Jews. She was paranoid that the cardboard boxes stuffed full of shiny gold Weimar, Prussian, Nazi, and Polish coins in her house in Little Falls would one day be discovered by a local, and her past as a Nazi would be found out, and then all would be taken from her.

Upon settling in Little Falls, where she and her husband moved because of their admiration for the Lindbergh family and because it was sufficiently removed from the cities along the eastern seaboard teeming with Jews and other Darkies, the widow's husband hid his four boxes of stolen gold in the attic walls the very day he bought the house. He then promptly wire-transferred his hefty savings from Switzerland to Old National Bank, one of three banks at Bank Square. His money was obtained from his '30s and '40s business operations in Essen, Germany and Switzerland where he assisted the higher ups at Krupps in opening a front to hide the company's sales of arms in Finland, Spain, and Turkey. The widow had met him when they were both employed at Krupps—he working his way off the factory floor up to managerial level, and she staying where she began—a cook and guard for the Jewish and Slavic female slaves the company imported from Auschwitz to do textile work.

The widow feared losing everything, but she also felt a bit guilty. Under her breath during household chores, she'd think—*I am a bit guilty, ja*—but she had also cooked for them, she reminded herself (ignoring what she had cooked: maggot-infested gruel), and so did not feel guilty enough to do something to amend the wrongs of her and her husband's ways.

The widow felt as if she never had enough of anything, as if everything were about to be stolen from her—vaguely, she blamed the Jews, even though she'd had nothing to do with a single member of the Hebrew tribe in decades. She did not know two seemingly gentile families in Little Falls were Jewish, pre-war escapees from Germany and Austria who attended church weekly so as to never fear dying for being Jewish again. Originally, the families attended St. Xavier—the French-Canadian Catholic congregation formed in 1868. Although they spoke German, they felt they could pass as gentiles since they did not speak French, thereby their lack of knowledge about Christianity could be better hidden than if they attended Sacred Heart, the German Catholic congregation in Little Falls founded in 1886, comprised of German immigrants who had followed a group of Benedictine monks and nuns to St. Cloud in the mid-1850s. All that became obsolete by the time the widow reached Little Falls, as in 1943 the two local Catholic congregations converged to form one—St. Mary's Catholic Church—in an attempt to bridge the ethnic differences by invoking Mary, the patron of American Catholics. The widow did business with the Jews almost every day—one the owner of the Ollendorf's Butcher Shop of Little Falls and the other a gas station manager at Eich Bros., one hundred yards due east of where Leonard died in 1891.

Never mind she had enough money from her husband's doings to live on comfortably for three consecutive lifetimes, not counting the cache of gold upstairs. Nonetheless, she pilfered the gold coins on occasion, driving to St. Cloud in her husband's black 1939 Borgward 200 that he'd shipped over from Germany after the war due to his nostalgia of having driven the company's *Bliztkarren*, a small, three-wheeled transport van used by the *Reichspost*, where he'd worked as a postal carrier before joining Krupps. The car was an ostentatious purchase the widow abhorred and kept locked in her garage, just as she kept her house locked at all times—aberrant behavior for anyone to lock anything, ever, in Little Falls. Out of sight, out of mind, she told herself, turning over the key after driving to St. Cloud to sell a few coins at a bank owned by a German American member of the National Socialist Party who paid her the cost of the gold and then sold them to his brethren who desired authentic Nazi-era mementos such that the gold coins became talismans at the American Bundt gatherings in St. Cloud, New Ulm, Willmar, and St. Peter, Minnesota, with one ending up in the hands of a professor at Gustavus Adolphus College who passed it around her classroom when she did presentations on Nazi Germany with no thought for her Jewish, Indian, and Black students who might be harmed by the spirit that manufactured that gold coin.

The widow exchanged the coins of her past for cold, hard cash an hour south of Little Falls so as not to raise suspicion in Little Falls, but she never returned them, or donated any of the money to a useful cause—not even a Pennsylvania-based German orphanage she received pamphlets about in the mail every Christmas. Instead, she let the coins sit in the attic walls—still divvied up and stashed in two locations just as her husband had hid them—in case someone found two of the boxes, there would be two others. There they would stay, after her death and through seven resales of the house until finally, eighty-eight years after she died, her beloved Victorian house was demolished due to an uncared-for, tree-damaged roof that rotted walls and eventually crumbled the foundation. As the jaws of the machinery crushed what was left of the house, toppling the brick fireplace and roof onto the gold coins, and then scooping up the bricks, coin, plaster, and fractured, molded wood and dropping all of it into a dump-bound refuse pile, her spirit, muddling about the gold and house, left the rubble and wandered the city, still easily recognizable with its wide horse and carriage accessible streets and restored storefronts from 1890, the year the city turned to brick. No gold coins escaped the jaws of the wrecking machines, and the widow and her husband's ways remained hidden from the townspeople, and from history. The European and Nazi metal burnished in the earth, burrowing under the weight of refuse until it almost became one with the dirt.

Kitty-corner across the alley from the widow's detached garage lived a young, mixed Irish, French, and Ojibwe woman, only twenty-years-old herself, with olive skin and black hair and almond-shaped eyes, whose husband drove truck across country for weeks on end. Her mother, a line worker at Larson Boat factory, would not speak of being Indian and her father, a gentle white man, thought it best to emphasize his wife's French ancestry to explain away their coloring and eyes. Therefore, the girl knew nothing.

"It's not back in the day," he'd say to his wife over the years. "You and Casey aren't liable to get lynched like." He paused. "Like those Negroes down south, but still best to be cautious." *It's been done before*, he thought. He'd never spoken of the conversation he'd overhead when he was a boy. His grandfather, a first generation Norwegian, who'd grown up on the Iron Range, thinking he and his brother were alone in the barn, said, "You remember when we were boys and those Indians from Little Creek went missing. I seen what happened. Ya. Dey hung dem from trees for going into town. Pa took me to watch." He stopped drawing milk out the teats, and adjusted his stool. His brother said nothing, nodded his head ever so slightly, just enough to tell his brother he'd heard. "I seen dem swinging. The moon right over the tops of the trees. Mr. Johnson. His boys." He pushed a piece of hay off the teat he held. "The Fjelds. Some others. Danced under the bodies. Their necks snapped and everybody yelling, you know, like Indians under dem. Celebrating. War whoops. You know, ya, you know how they are." And he blew a few pulls of milk onto the hard ground for the cats to lap up. "Ya. You know how dey are."

Casey's father, when talking with his wife, would putter with something before him, a fork or salt shaker and then add, without looking at his wife, "You know how they are," having lost the "ya" of the generation before him to better blend with the Anglo-Saxon culture. He knew the ways of those white men as did his wife, bothered by the men at her work the first years she was there. She outlasted them, with the protection of her white husband who'd fist-fought two of them, but she and he always knew what men like that were capable of, should they change their minds.

Sometimes, when her husband felt safe with someone, usually a female, and especially if there had been a big storm, or someone's barn burned, or a freak accident killed ten horses, or an unexplained illness took out half a man's herd of cows, he would relay the story of the Ojibwe Chief's Curse. For he also knew that a hundred years ago an Ojibwe chief had died near Little Falls, and been buried in the bluffs. Hole-in-the-Day had been traveling from St. Paul to his home at Gull Lake. Drunk on whiskey, he'd fallen out of his wagon, hit his head, and died later that night. No white knew exactly where he'd been buried, but out of respect, ignorance, and fear, some white people had begun a rumor supposedly passed on by Hole-in-the-Day's son, who visited him on his death-bed, that Hole-In-the-Day had placed a curse on the land around Little Falls. This was untrue, but it traveled down through the decades, twisting and turning, like a river, like a coiling vine, like a snake, taking on a life of its own until the story some believed included certain weather-related calamities, such as tornados and floods and other catastrophes. These catastrophes were blamed upon the Indian chief buried on the bluffs, and the wrongs the white man had done to him and his people, causing him to cast a curse on the area with his last breath, even though Hole-In-The-Day had been drunk by his own doing, a friend to the white man in some ways, and hated by many Indians.

On days when Casey's father reminded his wife of the importance of silence, his wife nodded, didn't speak of it—it being her Indianness—worked hard, and pushed her tore up feelings, like grasshopper ravaged leaves, deeper and deeper until they were so chewed she did not recognize them anymore. What he said to her was what her parents had done to survive—they taught their daughter silence with their own muted lips so that when her husband told her to be silent, she did not have to learn that lesson. For her part, she figured she was doing what was best for her husband and daughter and then her granddaughter, who, though a toddler in '57, looked just like the woman's grandmother, skin like cream-tinted coffee, black eyes as big and soft and wide spread as a deer's.

Casey, before the birth of her daughter, alone for weeks at a time, took long walks through town, imagined kissing her husband under the moon in the little park along the river just south of the bridge, imagined him swinging high into the air the children she was sure God would bless them with one day. Despite generations of silence and hiding, when Casey became pregnant with her daughter, she began avoiding the section of the river where Leonard had caught his last breath—the oak trees and the willows and one lone surviving apple tree held the memory of his murder in their fiber. As Casey's spirit opened during her pregnancy, her body bearing a child whose looks were undeniably Indian, from blood coursing through her, Leonard's fear and the terror of the times caught her, hurrying her away from that place and the knowledge it held. Although she knew nothing in her head, for the conscious line of knowledge had been severed, her Indian ancestors were strong in her, and preparing her and her child for the prophecy of the Seventh Generation—that generations removed from their people would return through a dream or a series of events white people understood as coincidence, as fanciful thinking, but which were anything but. The grief of her people lived within her and was a way of knowing, with or without her conscious understanding. Casey, a descendent by the rolls, a mixed Indian woman by society, an Ojibwe woman according to the elders, was barely twenty-years herself; and had only vestigial facial features from her Indian ancestry. But inside her were the seeds of being, more than 20,000 years of a people, a knowledge of the experiences and knowing of the Old Ways. She would pass by that place where Leonard died, his murder held in the trees and the singing of the river currents over rock. That same oak, but a sapling when Leonard died, now stood thick as four barrels laced together, along the shore next to willows with lime leaves dangling over the water. Some spring days the water would curl over into the shape of Leonard's face again, just for a moment until it slipped away downstream, undetected by humans, never forgotten by land, water, and trees, by place.

Despite the beauty to the eyes of that spot Casey felt a grief and terror of loss—for even the stones, and the seemingly negative space of air held the memory of the white men's deed. This knowledge reached her, despite the severing of ways, conscious removal of the Old Ones, loss of language, and the schools and science and white thinking ways that said nothing like that could happen—once a deed is done in the white religion, now this young woman's religion, it flows away into time. Once a deed is forgotten by the people who witnessed it or heard of it, or spoke of it, or a man in black with a loon collar listened and crossed himself, it is over. But not in Indian ways and not in the ways of the world—deeds live on. Deeds have consequences that do not end. For place holds memory, not time.

* * *

Tens of thousands of white people in shorts and tube tops and T-shirts milled about in the heat licking ice cream cones, sucking slushees, slurping pop, and nibbling cotton candy fuzz off their fingers. Sher sweated in the shade of the shed. The heat burned the blue out of the sky. All she saw was a hazy white and yellow above her. Sher's dream came to her with a jolt—she and Kris were driving along the back roads on Antwatin. Their car quit. In it were baby turtles and a fox and puppies and kittens. Sher got out to see if she could fix it when a pickup drove at them. Sher yelled at Kris to move out of the car, to get out of the way, to run into the woods with her, but Kris wouldn't move. Sher pounded on the windows. "Move, move, move!" Kris wanted to save the animals. Sher yelled, "Leave them!" Kris would not. The pickup hit their car. Everything disappeared. But Sher. She stood in her boots in the woods alone. And then, she ran.

"Girl!" Jerry yelled at Sher. "Hustle!"

He sounded far off. She felt confused. She was lost in that space between dreaming and being awake. Sher had a vague idea that she was homeless and trapped. That she did not know where to go or what to do.

"Girl!" Jerry yelled.

She looked at her boots. The scuff marks on the toes. They were not in tall grass on the edge of a flock of trees but on bare dirt. In some abysmal place.

"Hey, Pocahontas!" Jerry had not learned her name.

Sher snapped to, stood, and returned to the fry stand. She glared at the overweight white man. Kris was gone. A paring knife lay on the table next to a pile of potatoes.

Sher pointed at the mound of spuds at Kris's station. She was still dazed. Like the sky, she felt like something had been burned out of her too.

Jerry frowned, looking at the peeling table. "You serve." He shoved an empty tray at her.

Sher grabbed it, slid it to a fryer boy who jiggled a basket in the fryer.

The boy couldn't stop thinking how the fries looked like white floating fingers. He raised three fingers.

Sher nodded at the boy and looked for Kris in the crowd. She was gone. Just like in the dream. Jerry said she was on break, but a dream like that was real. Kris was gone.

A man held his fingers up like a peace sign. For a moment Sher thought he was signaling peace. Then she realized he was ordering. It was her job to get him two fries.

He shifted the baby on his shoulders. "Tub." The baby kicked his chest.

Sher picked up another empty pan, tilted it toward him. She carried it to the fryer, set it down, turned, her intention to walk out of the stand. She had to find Kris. She'd been taught—a dream like that—she turned to leave.

"Hey," Kris said and tossed a naked potato into a bin. "Where you going?"

Sher did not flinch. "Nowhere." She turned back to the pan she'd set down, picked it up. Set it down. Waited for fries. Had she gone crazy? She'd been taught to believe dreams like that. Kris was back and the day was more than half over. Soon they would be done frying potatoes. Nothing bad had happened. Had she misinterpreted the dream? Were dreams just dreams, like the white people said?

The sun dropped from four to five to six to seven. Sher and Kristin were dog-tired. The fair neared its run. The fireworks crew set up. The 4-H kids dismantled their artwork and science projects and packed away their ribbons and the scarves they crocheted. The grounds crew doubled in size and the booth owners in the far-flung corners of the fair began packing, ignoring the contracts with the fair, stating they would not do so until nine. Some on Machinery Hill drove their cars and tractors and trailers and combos out the northwest gate but the stands in the heart of the fair and the carnie games stayed intact. They would run until eleven. Sher and Kristin had a few hours until they hit the streets or slept another night in the Horse Barn, sticking around for the clean-up crew.

The sun corkscrewed over the fair. Sher was jumpy. The dream and what she'd done to that man twisted in her head. She worried. She stopped thanking the customers, and then she stopped speaking to them. She hid a Coke under the counter to keep her going. She sweated. Kristin peeled and tossed potatoes. Jerry disappeared without a word. The white kids snuck fries, slipped dollar bills and coins into their pockets. Sher pocketed a dollar. Kris devoured fries, worried about when they would eat again.

The sun popped behind the Ferris wheel, casting pie-shaped patterns across the ground. Sher concentrated on the shadows as they curved and spun across the dirt and concrete, ignoring the "Excuse me, girl," and "Honey, hurry up," and "Hey, miss" until a boy poked her.

"Country," he said. "Wake up."

Sher stepped forward to get away from his touch. Her belly hit the countertop, jumping her attention to the Tilt-A-Whirl ride with its red hunchbacked seats. Her eyes settled on a dark figure facing the fry stand. Her body prickled. The man turned sideways, the sun behind him. He lit a cigarette. He faced the fry stand again, the cigarette between his fingers. Dread flooded Sher.

"Medium," an old man said, his fist on the counter.

"Medium." Sher pulled her gaze away from the man by the Tilt-A-Whirl, stared at the old man's dirty, chipped nails and broad thumb. "Medium."

His hand unfolded, dropping two crumpled bills on the counter the way a dog's jaw dropped wounded birds.

Sher's heart cascaded dread through her bloodstream. Something terrible was going to happen.

Over the next hour, her hands scooped fries, collected money, and gave change. She kept her eyes off Kris, her head down, but snuck looks at the man by the Tilt-A-Whirl. When he took a drag, his face lit up enough for her to see his visage. She could not place him but had seen before. In a dream? Another lifetime? Many years ago? The sun dropped over the horizon, casting shadows. The lime-green octopus ride's tentacles sent shadows lunging across the dirt next to the man and oversized hunchbacked Tilt-A-Whirl shadows spun across his body. He did not budge. Then Sher remembered the dream with the man in spinning shadows. It was a warning. She and Kris should have left immediately, but she did not heed the dream. Now he was here.

Sher glanced at Kris, who peeled and cut, her head down. Suddenly, Kris looked up, directly at the man. Then at Sher. Their eyes met. They didn't need to speak. They knew eyes were upon them.

Instinctively, the girls reacted as if they did not know. Sher collected money, scooped fries, handed out fries and change. Kris put her head down, peeled, cut. Trembled.

"Girl," a man's voice cut through Sher's fog.

"Yah," she said, as if she were answering a long-awaited call. She looked up. The man who'd stood next to the Tilt-A-Whirl studied her. Sher's heart stopped. The dread stopped. Everything stopped. She did not move.

His blond Vaseline-slicked hair shone under the stand's lights. The pock marks on his face were dark because of the light's angle. "Sher. That's a pretty name."

She flinched.

The man's smile grew.

He flicked a five onto the counter. "Small." He used his chin like a finger to point at Kris. "I see Kris likes it better back there. Yes?"

"Ah," Sher said. Her thoughts turned abruptly to Em. She wished for her to appear. To protect them, as she'd done so often before she disappeared.

Was he a cop? Or one of the men from Jacob's group? Or one of the men from the carnie? Someone from her past? She scooped a small fry. She tried not to let her face give her away.

"Thank you," the man said. "I sure do appreciate you and all you've done." And he made a point to politely step around the people behind him. He walked a few yards, turned, stared at the fry stand, and ate his fries, one by one. Occasionally, he ran his tongue across his teeth.

Sher could barely breathe. What did that mean? Did he know she'd stabbed that man? Was he going to arrest her? She wanted to run, move her body under the sun as it traveled over the railroad ties, as it played among the leaves above her until bits and pieces of it settled on the grasses, ferns, and stones.

"You two. Bag in back." Jerry pointed at two fry boys.

"Geez." One of them walked around the front of the stand, cutting off Sher's view of the man. "Why's it always me?"

Then Sher saw the man's shoes splayed outward under long dirty jeans. *We'll find them sooner or later* floated through her mind. The man from the bus depot. Her energy left her body the way her dogs had worked the marrow out of lamb bones, and then gulped the white lump of fatty tissue that popped out. She'd made a terrible mistake.

She had not heeded her feelings, her dreams.

Sher scooped fries and took money and made change. She tried to formulate a plan, but every time her thoughts skipped to *run* and panic overtook her. How long had they been watching? How'd they know the girls' names? The man finished his fries, flipped the container in a garbage can and returned to his spot, feet splayed with his arms across his chest.

The line dwindled. Sher and Kris worked until fireworks popped like sparkling dust over the Grandstand. Sher moved next to Kris. "That man is from the alley," she said in her ear. "At the bus station."

Kris gripped the paring knife. She shot a look at Sher, over her shoulder toward the man.

"Don't look." Sher grabbed Kris's arm.

"Nah. Can't be. How could they have found us here?"

Sher grabbed Kristin's arm. "I'm sure of it."

Kris wore fear on her face.

"We need to leave now. Grab the pack. Run."

"What can he do?" Kris asked. She did not want to lose a day's pay. She didn't want him to take her money. And she didn't want it to be true. "Maybe it just looks like him." She piled potatoes high on the table. Despite her words, fear overtook her.

"Kris," Sher pleaded.

Kris dug out eyes. What she couldn't say to Sher, didn't understand herself, was how the dollar bills her father had left in her sock drawer after he raped her grew into rage and shame that bound her to the money Jerry owed her.

Sher turned back to the counter. There was nothing she could do but go back to work.

The neon Ferris wheel spun light like a web into the night air. Fireworks popped and boomed red and white flowers in the sky. People ohhed and ahhed. The girls worked. The man watched the girls, his cigarette dancing like a red eye in the dark.

* * *

"Wrap it up!" Jerry yelled. "Nineteen-sixty-nine is over." He dog whistled.

Sher shot a sideway look at the man from the depot, dropped her tray in a sink, wiped down her section of the counter, counted out her drawer, and paper-clipped a note with the total around the wad of bills. She handed it to Jerry.

"Done girl," he grunted, and counted out her wages for the day. He turned to the next bleary-eyed girl waiting for her pay.

That's it, Sher thought. She grabbed the pack that she'd shoved under her station.

Kristin collected her pay from Jerry, folded the bills into a tight wad, and shoved them in her front pocket where no one could get it. "See. He's gone." She pointed with her lips.

Sher scanned the shadows. The man was gone. She pulled the pack over her shoulder and the girls walked off into the night.

Most of the fair disappeared in the snap of a finger. They hit Liggett Street going south, passing straggling, exhausted workers and a few fairgoers who closed down every fair. The moonlight spit off the metal rides, now empty and motionless. The girls stopped at the Coliseum intersection. The girls stood in the intersection. Their breathing uneven. Such rapid barrenness. Neither could think. Sher shifted the pack slung across her shoulder. Kristin watched a lone person lead a Guernsey out of the Cattle Barn. Lights flickered. Sher shifted to the west. Kris turned south. A Cattle Barn door rattled from the inside. Someone shouted behind the girls. The light above the entrance to the Sheep and Poultry Barn popped off. It was over.

"That way." Kris nodded toward the Midway, toward the fry stand and the cream puff stand. She fingered her wad of money. "I want a cream puff."

Sher shifted. She felt like she was running in slow motion beneath the trees on the reservation, face up, sunlight shifting through the leaves. She meant to say *we need to leave* but instead she nodded.

The clock struck eleven. Carnie workers pounded plywood over windows and locked doors. Unsold donuts and popcorn and pizza were bagged, twist-tied, and dumped in the yellow barrels. The carnie workers would return in the morning to dismantle, pack, and load the apparatuses, and then aim their trucks toward the Dakotas, Iowa, or California. The girls passed the Octopus's giant, twisted limbs, dismantled in pieces on the ground. A stringy carnie man leaned on the sledgehammer used to ring the bell of The

Strongest Man in the World game. Another man popped balloons pinned to a cork board with his pocket-knife. Down from him Fred Barnes snapped a lock on Freddy's Ring Toss—Everyone's A Winner booth to get to Matt's Bar in south Minneapolis for a couple of burgers stuffed with cheese, his ritual at the end of every Minnesota State Fair before heading out to the carnies on the West Coast for the winter.

The girls walked up a slight incline to the Real Whipped Cream Puff stand—the owners, two junior high school teachers from Maplewood, had gone round and round whether to have "cream" appear twice in the name. Kris knocked on the shuttered stand. The booth was empty, hollow as a carcass. Above them the Skyride's teal blue cars swayed in a breeze.

"Let's go," Sher said. The hollow sound of Kris's knuckles on the wood made her nervous. "Let's get outta—" She stepped backward into a man's chest.

He grabbed her. "You didn't think you were going to get away, did you?" the Tilt-A-Whirl man from the bus depot said. He twisted her arm. "The street always finds you."

A second man covered Kris's mouth. "Quiet," he whispered.

The Tilt-A-Whirl man stuck a knife into Sher half an inch to the right of her spine. "We heard about you, girl."

Sher stood stock still. The knife tip a tooth in her back.

"Sher?" Kris's voice wavered.

Blood trickled like a slow-moving river down Sher's back.

"Shut," the other man whispered. "Don't make a noise, or your sister gets it."

Cousin. Kris wanted to tell him. *Cousin.* And then her thoughts shut down like the rides at the Midway—bing bing bing—until she was as shuttered and boarded as the rides and stands.

The Tilt-A-Whirl man said to the other man, "They start cleaning in the carnie and barns. Nobody on Machinery Hill. Larry said to meet him there."

Kris froze. Sher loosened. The men breathed, excited.

The breeze curled around the four, fingering their skin, lifting locks of hair. They were suspended in time and place. Power, strength, hatred, superiority, inferiority, strategies, vulnerability— all disintegrated. They were as spirits. Others joined them. Ancestors. European. Indian. The earth. The water. The Star People. Two shy Little People because a stream once ran through where the fair now stood. Leonard. His head put back together. An Ox Cart driver. A St. Paul furrier. The Indian who hunted beaver for Astor who sold beaver top hats overseas to English gentlemen. A white housewife from down the road, dead in 1954, with the salmon-colored kerchief she wore around her neck to hide the red streaks left by her husband's fingers. A Filipina grandmother, who as a teenager escaped a ship in 1884 in the Duluth harbor, hopped a wagon to St. Paul with an Indian man she fell in love with, married, had eight children, and learned to pick Indian medicines on the land before it became a carnival. A Dakota *winkte* who played in the stream as a child, before the square buildings, before the city, before the fair, before the whites, before the Ojibwe.

The wind curled and wound and wove around them like ribbons. Then the wind stalled as they all paused before this thing, writ in books and on stones and bit into birchbark, this thing dreamed of and schemed over by generations. Their ancestors knew it was coming, would happen, no matter what, it was dreamed. Writ. Told. This point in time and place when a decision would have to be made and that decision would determine whether Creation would be destroyed or whether Creation would flower again. All Kris and Sher's people could do for generations was hold steady to earth in the winds of change, of death, of destruction, of the imbalance the English brought with them, the imbalance that would spread and join with those on this side of the great water, the *windigo*, who held to destruction, too. Together, the destroyers from all sides would join. Together, they would tip the balance so far over that this would happen, again and again and again, near brooks, on water, on ships, beneath the earth in the tunnels they dug to disembowel rock and sand and minerals from the earth. Girls and women, mostly, especially, targeted for their sacredness, for their power, for their generation of life, but boys and babies as well. The trees moved imperceptibly toward the moon's light, pulled by the reflection of the sun. Then the wind whipped around them one final time and it was gone. And so it began.

For a reason unknown to the two men, they paused, looked at the girls, as if for a moment they had the choice to realize the Indian girls existed on their own, beyond what the white men wanted. They did not understand it, why they'd turned to the girls the way they had. They would not reflect on it, that moment when their spirits stepped forward, became naked, had a choice, and chance to change what they were about to do. The men would not wonder why they'd suddenly both turned to the girls—young, Indian, female. One a looker, the other like a boy. Their captives. As strange as their momentary change in perception was, the men would not think of it again. They did not have to consider it.

The men made their choice.

"Walk," the man holding Kristin ordered. "Anyone asks, we're your big brothers. You yelp, and your sister gets cut." He uncovered her mouth. "This time all the way through."

Help, Kris wanted to yell, but saw, as they passed a lone lit streetlight, the dark stain growing on Sher's shirt.

The men pushed the girls east, past Lillie's Old-Timey Cookies on the left and Cyndi's Cotton Candy on the right. They paused at the Grandstand, facing a track that once hosted harness racing and locomotives that raced headlong into each other, exploding into dust and bits and pieces of metal and debris scavenged afterward, illegally, by those in the stands. Scraps of blown-up trains that now hung on nails in paneled rec rooms next to pool tables or in frames in hallways, or were tossed into tool-boxes in garages such that few knew where the twisted pieces of metal originated.

"Look at those bazooms, would ya?" The man pushing Kris stood in front of half-a-story-tall poster of Dolly Parton *Tonight! Live at 7:00pm!* written across the bottom. Her blond hair shone platinum in the black and white photograph.

"Bet you'd like her." The Tilta-Whirl-man pushed Sher's face in front of Dolly's breasts. "Huh?" He pushed the knife tip deeper.

Sher did not cringe, the way he'd expected.

"I asked you a question, girl."

Sher said nothing. Her T-shirt grew heavier with blood. It stuck to her skin.

He pressed Sher's face into Dolly's breasts.

"Huh?" He squeezed her neck.

Sher stared at the crack in the singer's cleavage. Dolly's skin looked like cream. Like her dream.

"I asked you a question," the man said.

The other man laughed. "C'mon, Jer."

"Yer ugly as a dog." Jer grabbed Sher's long bangs and pulled her head back as if he was grabbing the forelock of a horse.

She shut her eyes.

"Maybe you're not all that ugly." Jer pulled up her right eyelid with his thumb. "After I fuck the boy out of you, I will put you in some proper clothes. You'll be a good ride." He ground his crotch on her.

Shame burned Sher, hotter than the pain the knife made or the blood soaking her T-shirt, now the shape of one of the gigantic, deformed tomatoes she and her grandmother used to find. "Big as a dog's head," her grandmother would say, setting them on the kitchen windowsill to ripen.

"Don't," Kris pleaded.

The man holding Kris slapped her.

Sher's muscles tensed.

Jer laughed. "Warrior here." He smashed her cheekbone into the poster. "I asked you a question." He pinned her to the brick with his groin. "I ain't joking."

"Jer," the man warned. "Not here. Wait."

Jer, the Tilt-A-Whirl-man, stuck the knife lower on Sher's back. He shifted his weight, causing the knife to slide, cutting a tiny, moon-shaped crescent into her skin, deep enough to scar. "Soon enough," he whispered to Sher. He pushed her east toward Hamline Dining Hall, the Root Beer Barrel, the World's Best Mini-Donuts, and then to Underwood Street that would take them north to Machinery Hill.

As they trudged through the deserted fairgrounds, the moon shone between the leaves on the trees along the boulevard, floating shadows across the dirt, the pavement, their arms and legs and faces. The squirrels and birds, if any were present, were silent.

They neared the northern edge of the fair. An eight-foot-high chain link fence divided the fairground from Larpenter Street.

"Larry here?" Jer asked.

"Right where he said he'd be." The man nodded at a white van idling on Larpenter.

"Larry'll be real glad to see you two." Jer poked Sher's back. He wasn't worried about her getting away, but he wasn't taking chances either. "Remember us," he said, sneering in her face. "We heard about what you did. Did you think we wouldn't find you? Think the street wouldn't notice two new Indian girls in town?" He felt her pockets and her bag for her knife. "Nothing."

"Keep an eye on her," the other man said. "We'll need to find her knife."

"You don't look all that tough." Jer slapped Sher's head. "Are you?" He slapped her again. "Huh?"

Sher dropped her head. She stayed loose. She would play it that way, get their guard to fall.

"Of course, you're not. You got in a lucky. He can't wait to see you again, you know. He's got a present for you."

The two men laughed. They pushed the girls toward the gate and the van—its lights off.

Sher figured they were about one hundred yards from the fence. She needed to do something soon. Jer tightened his grip on her arm.

She let the pack slide.

"Leave it on," Jer said.

"It's too heavy," Sher lied. "It's hurting my arm."

He jabbed her. "No."

Sher let the pack slip down to her elbow.

"Why do you drag that old bag around?" Jer asked.

"It was our grandfathers." She whipped the pack into his face.

"Fuck!" he yelled, dropping his knife.

She kicked him in the crotch.

"Ow," he screamed and crumpled to the ground. "Dan!" He alerted the man holding Kris.

Sher swung the pack into Dan's face.

He caught it.

She kicked his knee backward.

"Shit!" Dan tripped and lost his hold on Kris.

"Run Kris!" Sher yelled.

Kris ran toward the gate, right at the idling van.

"Not that way!" Sher yelled. She dropped their grandfather's pack and ran.

Kristin had not been paying attention.

Dan regained his balance, flung the pack into some bushes, and ran after Kris. He didn't yell or wait for Jer. He hoped Larry would jump out and help him corral the girls like a couple of loose cows. He'd grown up on a farm. Rounded up loose animals all his life, even worked the fair as a boy a few years. These two girls were no more valuable than the heifers he'd chased down as a boy on his family's farm in Walnut Grove. A hundred a piece, tops. Maybe more for the light one. He'd been paid to round these girls up, and that's what he would do. After, he'd throw down a few beers and watch some titties at The Lamplighter, get up in the morning, and find a way to blow the wad of cash Larry promised him.

Kristin reached the gate and pushed it open. Larry had cut the lock. "Sher," Kris said, her voice a whisper, her mind shut down from fear, just barely aware of her surroundings.

"Go the other way!" Sher waved her arm away from the van. The pain shooting through her ankle and back muffled her voice.

Kristin slipped sideways through the gate, took two steps toward the van, turned the other way, and ran west down Larpenter toward a grove of pines and stunted cedar trees on the boulevard across the street.

Sher ran as best she could. She had not yet reached the gate. Dan would be next to Sher in a few more steps. Jer struggled to his feet behind them, barely able to walk.

Sher called out, "Cousin." But the word barely left her lips.

Dan reached Sher and with one swift punch to her shoulder, sent her flying.

Sher slid belly first on the pavement. Pain flushed through her body like hives, her palms, chin, and elbows skinned raw. Her jeans tore at the knees.

Dan ran past Sher. He wanted the light one, bolting like a deer into the scraggly trees.

From her belly, Sher looked up. Bits of glass sparked across the pavement like the Milky Way, the road the spirits followed to the spirit world. Sher gathered herself and pushed off the pavement into the midnight air of August dog days for the last leg of the journey she and her cousin had embarked on three weeks earlier.

Kristin's shadow disappeared into the trees. Dan cut west toward Kris, his shoes *tap tap tapping* in the sultry evening air. The back van doors swung open, pushed from inside by Larry. Sher ran through the gate as best she could with her hurt ankle, imagining she was back home sprinting through the woods and fields in the snow, in the heat, in the gales cutting across the culled fields of the reservation. Larry joined Dan in the chase for Kris. As five bodies moved beneath the trees, the only sounds among the shadows cast by the moon were the breathing of the girls and men and the tapping of their shoes.

All else was silent. Watching. Waiting. The Standing People and the land absorbed the story as it unfolded, like leaves off a branch in the spring. Maybe one day a human being with the gift would encounter this story in flashes of emotion and images. Maybe one day the trees would be cut down and turned into a table and someone who'd fallen asleep in a recliner next to the table watching reruns of *I Love Lucy* would have a strange dream of being chased. But in that moment, the trees and the land absorbed the heat cast off from those who chased, and were chased. All else watched from above, from below, and from all around the humans in their life and death pursuits. Some watched with curiosity. Others with compassion. Others with sadness. And others, with anger and vengeance.

Headlights turned onto Larpenter from the east until they shone down Larpenter, two hundred yards from the van. Larry and Dan closed in on Kris. Jer was behind Sher. Sher knew if she ran into the trees, it would be easier for the men to grab them both. So she pivoted, and ran east onto Larpenter, hoping the car would stop to help her or scare them off. Dan ran northwest, across the road toward the trees. He was after Kris.

"She'd pass as white, sell for a pretty penny. Or we could sell her as an Indian Princess," Jer had said, as he and his men discussed business while shooting pool in the basement of his Minneapolis bungalow on Eleventh and Irving North. "Plus, she's been primed. At the pump, if you know what I mean." The men had nodded, their focus on the table, mentally lining up the shots. They could tell who'd been done up by a father or a brother or a neighbor. Kids like that oozed blood the men could smell.

The car barely slowed, forcing Sher off the street. Its taillights disappeared to the west.

Kris hid behind a pine. Larry ran past the trees up to a chain-link fence erected twenty years ago to keep fairgoers off the property. Upon turning, he spotted Kris.

Now there was no side for Kris to stand where she would not be seen. She froze. The rough scales from the pine bit into her back and shoulders. Above her, the needles grew in clumps like fists. She faced Larry. Dan grabbed her from behind.

"No!" Kris yelled as his dirty, tobacco-smelling hand slid across her mouth.

"Get the van," Dan said to Larry.

Another car approached. The beams flared across tree trunks and the fronts of houses vacated by occupants to avoid the fair crowds until the headlights settled west on Larpenter. Sher stepped into the street. The car stopped twenty feet short of Sher. Larry walked to the van. He whistled to appear calm, normal. Dan pulled Kris behind a tree.

"Help!" Sher shouted at the car. She tried to run to the car. Her ankle gave way. She fell, landing on her forearms and chest.

"Our little sister!" Jer yelled at the car from the gate. "Out of control." He was out of breath. "Taking them home." He smiled at the woman in the passenger seat and the man leaning out the driver's window. "Drinking, you know." He waved toward Sher, indicating she was Indian.

Sher wanted to yell but the pavement had knocked the air out of her.

The man in the car nodded, not because the smile reassured him but because something was not right and he did not want to get involved. He pulled away. A white husband and wife continued about their business. "Kid stuff," the man said to his wife, pretending to believe the man on the street. The woman was not convinced, but she never challenged her husband. Glancing out the back window at the commotion—silhouettes of trees and shades of humans in a pewter sky, she wondered what was happening, if they should stop or find a phone booth to call the police, but told herself her husband was probably right. She turned in her seat toward the lights of downtown Minneapolis, four miles ahead of them.

Kris twisted. Tried to yell. But Dan had her. He was strong.

Sher struggled to breathe. Her ankle burned like lightning. The cuts on her back crazed her. She gritted her teeth, unlaced her boot, and pulled out her knife. Laces undone, her grandmother's knife in her hand, Sher stood.

Dan emerged from the trees dragging Kris, one hand clamped on her mouth and the other wrapped around her chest, as the van, silent, headlights off, pulled up next to the trees.

"Get her," Dan said to Jer, about Sher.

Jer, his groin still hurting, limped toward Sher.

Sher flicked open the blade behind her back. If the girls were going down, Sher was taking someone with them. Stink from her leather boots mingled with the smell of pine needles and cedar and gas fumes.

The red glow from the van's brakes lit up the night like a nebula. Wind murmured. A clump of needles bounced. A bird swooped through the dark sky.

"In the back!" Larry yelled through the open passenger window. He pulled forward. Kept the van in drive, his foot on the brakes.

Dan dragged Kris to the back of the van.

She kicked and twisted.

Jer and Sher limped toward each other. He grabbed her arm. She stepped into him, slashing the knife at his face. She meant to put out an eye, but he ducked and sent her sprawling onto the boulevard. She landed sideways on a bed of rusty pine needles that covered bare dirt, baked rock solid in the sun. Her head whiplashed. He stepped toward her.

Kris planted her feet on the back of the van. "Sher!" She twisted away from Dan, and ran toward her cousin.

"Jer!" Dan shouted.

Jer turned toward Kris. He grabbed her. The two men shoved her into the van's maw.

"Leave the other one," Larry said, watching the men in the rearview mirror. Dan pinned Kris down on a mattress in the van. Jer jumped in. Just then lights, like spinning suns on a hazy day, sped toward the van.

Sher got to her knees. The grove of trees and van to her right.

"Shut the doors!" Larry yelled at Jer.

Jer slammed the back doors.

Kris screamed, "Sher!"

"Kris." Sher meant to shout, but her cousin's name came out as a whisper.

The van lurched forward, flinging open the back doors. The latch had not caught. Jer reached to pull them shut again, lost his balance, and fell out of the van. The headlights stopped, shining straight into the van.

Sher regained her feet.

The car horn blared.

Sher lurched toward Jer, jabbing his hand.

"Bitch!" he screamed as she pulled the blade out. It had gone all the way through. He knocked the knife from her grip. The driver of the car honked his horn.

"What the heck," Larry said to himself, stunned and too afraid to exit the van.

"Get in!" Dan yelled.

Jer reared back and punched Sher's face as hard as he'd ever hit any man in any bar brawl. She flew into the road. The man in the car drove forward, flashing his brights and honking.

"Leave her!" Larry yelled.

Jer shut the van doors. The latch clicked. He climbed over Dan, who lay on top of Kris, and into the passenger seat. "Fuuuuck," he said, blood spraying the dashboard. "I'ma kill that bitch."

"Later," Larry said to Jer, dropping his head to look in the side mirror at the car and the girl laid out in the street. "We'll get her in the morning. If she's still alive."

"Cousin!" Kris managed to yell through Dan's fingers. "Run!"

Cousin? Dan thought, sealing off her mouth with his palm. He'd thought they were sisters.

Larry threw the van into drive and drove evenly toward the Minneapolis skyline, the buildings lit up like the rides at the Midway. He did not want more attention. Some of the police were on his boss's payroll. Some were not.

The car lights beamed over Sher. The nebula of taillights from the van receded. She muttered, "Cousin." She'd heard Kris. She'd said to run. The beams flicked, and then veered into the middle of the street as the car drove around her and stopped next to her.

Sher attempted to stand but collapsed. She noticed her sock, rolled around her arch. "Cousin," she muttered again, as she watched the van taillights wind toward Minneapolis.

"Girl?" The man in the car leaned across the front seat.

Sher looked up at him through the car's passenger window, unable to process what he said.

He could not see her well, but now that the moon shone on her just so, he saw she was dark-skinned. Perhaps some kind of Negro. He did not want to get involved in those people's business.

Sher did not answer. She shifted her gaze to the jagged teeth of the Minneapolis skyline. The van's taillights seemed like pinpricks, like the sun as it shone through the cardboard their teachers had them poke holes in with a needle and hold up to the sun, for some reason, Sher could not remember. Could not think. Some lesson. What was it? Science?

"Girl?" the man repeated, lingering out of guilt.

The lesson, Sher thought. *What was it?*

The man hesitated. And then drove away.

Sher set down her head on the street. The headlights pointed at the pavement like long fingers. Science. The day the sun darkened, she remembered. The day the moon covered the sun. Something about a rabbit, she remembered. And then her vision went black, her body settled into the dog day heat radiating out of the pavement, and her spirit floated toward the stars.

SS *Werner Von Braun*, Lake Superior, September 1, 1969

As Sher's spirit left for the stars, an Indian girl, who had just turned thirteen, lifted her head to the round window on the port side of the SS *Werner Von Braun*, a US ore ship named after the Nazi who invented the V-2 Rocket. As the current head of NASA, Von Braun had, just that summer, become a national US hero as the orchestrator of a rocket ship that shot men to the moon and back. Five men had already raped the girl that evening, so her eyesight and mind were ragged, but she could have sworn, had she anyone to talk with, that she saw a spinning wheel in the charcoal sky across the bay on the Duluth shoreline. Pressing her cheek into the cool glass, she blinked repeatedly until her eyesight cleared and only the shoreline and sky existed where she'd just seen the bright wheel. The Indian girl dropped her head and wrapped herself in a dirty blanket before the next sailor entered the closet where they kept her. She had disappeared four months earlier while walking down Mission Road to visit her cousins on the Fort Williams reserve, just south of Thunder Bay. Her family, part of the band that officials called "the pagan branch," put out tobacco and food every day, praying to the Creator for her safe return one day, wherever she may land.

St. Paul, Minnesota, September 2, 1969

As the sun rose, a young Indian woman climbed the ten-foot chain-link fence on the southwest side of the Minnesota State Fair. No one saw her. She ran, unheeded, between the Cattle Barn and the Coliseum. The garbage stank. The crews wouldn't arrive to haul it away for another three hours. Seeing the Horse Barn, she veered east, circled the building, and yanked on each locked door. The woman stopped in the middle of the street, breathing heavily. She'd heard the girls were at the fair, sleeping in the Horse Barn. She'd spent the night running from where she'd been staying for a week under a bridge that separated the Near North neighborhood of

Minneapolis from the Bryn Mawr neighborhood of Minneapolis. And now they were not here. She was too late.

She caught her breath and took off running, dodging the horse, cow, and sheep dung piles drying out on the pavement. She didn't know where to go. She ran east, in beige canvas tennis shoes two sizes too big that she'd found in a church parking lot, and then north, and then west for two blocks until she hit the western perimeter and turned east again.

Her long black hair flowed down her back. Her arms pumped like an Olympic sprinter. She ran to the French fry stand the girls had worked at, slowed, scanned the dismantled Midway, and decided to run each south-north street like a grid. She cut east, and turned south at the corner of the DNR log building. A DNR agent from New Brighton, who'd arrived early to begin preparing the fish for their trip back to Lake Mille Lacs, witnessed a pretty, yet tough-looking Indian woman running down a deserted street on the fairgrounds. He squinted, saw her jag to the right, her hair flying. He thought her a vision in the early morning light. Why he saw that, he didn't know. He wouldn't mention it to anyone. He'd had dealings with Indians on Mille Lacs and, although he would never admit it, both feared and admired their ways. He'd seen too many spooky things on that lake and thought Em yet another unexplained vision. Who'd ever heard of an Indian girl on the streets of the fair the day after it closed? No one. He turned his back to her and stared at the murky pond. He put on his waders and rubbers, deciding to catch the sturgeon first this year—a prehistoric-looking species that had been around since the age of the dinosaurs and were revered by the old Indians at Mille Lacs.

The young Indian woman ran. And ran. The sun rose to quarter after seven in the morning. She'd covered the entire fairgrounds. Seen no one. She collapsed on a bench on Machinery Hill. She stared at the tractors, and thought of her pops. *Please help me*, she thought. These girls were all she had left, and now they too were gone. She'd heard through the Moccasin Telegraph—how Indians on the rez and in urban areas kept track of each other—that her parents and brother were gone. And from others on the streets, she'd heard two Indians girls from Goodhue were at the fair. Staying at the Horse Barn. Working a fry stand. What she didn't know was whether her pop's spirit would help her just yet, given how she'd left him. She had not set things right. She didn't know if she ever could.

She sat on the bench for another half hour, her spirit drooping. A Little Person, passing through the fairgrounds looking for shiny metal objects he could use, saw her and knew what to do. Carrying a bent wire he'd found inside a hot dog stand, he approached the young Indian woman, who could not see him. He stood in front of her, his bandolier bag across his shoulder, and studied her face. Then he tapped the metal bench she sat on. She didn't respond, so he dragged the wire along the concrete. She sat up. The same noise she'd heard in the Virginia house. He scratched again, in the direction he wished her to go. Em followed the scratching across the road, alongside a building to another road. Then the scratching turned north on the same road her cousins had run on the night before. The Little Person scratched right up to the gate.

As she pushed through it, she saw a body across the street curled on its side beneath some trees. She ran. The Little Person studied the bend in the wire. Deciding it was not quite what he needed, he tossed the wire onto the grass where a state fair employee would find it two days later and wonder where it came from. He glanced at the body across the street, sighed, and returned to the fair to go on with his business. He found shiny, metal objects to be quite useful, and there were many to be found at the fair.

Sher's body was curled in a fetal position, her neck crooked against an exposed tree root. The night before, her spirit, not wanting to leave but having been dislodged from her body by violence, snagged on the needles of a white pine on its way to the stars—the Old Ones. The Ancestors. The tree held her there, cradling her high above the hounds the Spanish had released on Turtle Island long ago. The spirits of the Spanish hounds still roamed the land in search of the Indian blood their masters had attuned them to when they set them on the people. The cedar trees' medicine kept them from climbing up the pine after her spirit, forcing them to snap at her from below.

"Sher," Em cried. Kneeling, she cradled her niece's head. Sher's face was bruised and bloodied. One eye swollen shut. "Where's Kris?" She scanned the trees and street for her other niece. "Sher." She felt the dried blood on her shirt. "My girl. What happened? Who did this? Are you still here?"

Em calmed herself. She put her cheek against Sher's cheek like she did when the girls were babies. "My girl. Are you still here? Where's Kris? Am I too late?" Em felt Sher's breath, like a whisper from her lips.

Sher moaned.

"My girl," Em said, wiping tree sap and dirt from Sher's forehead.

Sher's eye squinted. "Em?"

"Yes. It's me."

"Auntie. Did I die?"

"No."

"Oh." Sher closed her eye.

"Where's Kris?" Em whispered.

"Where are we?"

"At the fair," Em replied.

"The fair?"

"You're all bloody. What happened? Where's Kris?"

"Auntie," Sher whispered.

"I'm here. I love you, my girl. Your eye. I've been looking for you—-" Em paused. She hoped Kris had gone for help. Would she come running down the road with a bag of ice for Sher's eye? That was something she would do. "Where's Kris?"

"Kris?" Sher tried to sit, but didn't have the strength. "They got her."

"What? Who got her?"

"Who got her?" Sher repeated. She stared at a smooth red root of a cedar curving out of the earth. "The carnival lights. The men. They took my cousin." Tears streamed down her cheeks.

Em's pain flared and burned deep, catching the pain of murdered and missing ancestors she'd never known, creating a fire as large as a forest in the young Indian woman's blood.

A pine bough fluttered in the still morning as the carnival workers arrived to start their day.

The Four Directions

In Ojibwe ways, the four directions comprise the medicine wheel in which all of life's cycles—sadness and joy, life and death—are one. There is life in death, and death in life. Beauty itself resides within the balance of the whole circle.

Minnesota Point, Duluth, Minnesota, May 1994

Unknown to the men who ordered the removal of the Indian graveyard on the Village of Park Point in 1860, but foretold by an Indian doctor at the time of the first carnival, the Ojibwe Indians' bones began returning to the shores of their spiritual home on *Onigamiinsing*, the spit of land the French named Minnesota Point. The digging of the channel, which severed the strip of land so that ships could pass into the harbor, along with the rerouting of part of the river that altered the flow of water, led to an erosion of the new site of the Indian bones. Slowly, one by one, the bones returned, moving upstream, against the current, back to *Onigamiinsing*, their home.

Minneapolis, Minnesota, October 2019

The Ojibwe woman ran through the Bryn Mawr neighborhood to avoid the circus that had arrived in town. Between the bare branches to the east, she glimpsed the city's skyline, where a white revolving light flashed atop a spire on the tallest building and red and blue lights burned atop glass skyscrapers that dwarfed those of 1969. It began to rain. She continued running, her thick dark brown braid the length of her backbone. To get farther from where the leader with the white rings around his eyes would draw 80,000 screaming white people, she cut south over a bridge. As she did so, a cop car stopped traffic on the bridge over freeway 394. The chief with the orange hair would soon pass beneath. Under that same bridge, in 2011 and 2015, two teenage Native women had been murdered, and left to rot. There were no protests. Only silence. The woman knew about the bodies, but not about the motorcade. A cop car's lights shone through the rain over the slick, empty bridge. He had set up road blocks. He had his orders. She sprinted across the bridge before he could stop her. "Girl!" he yelled. "Stop!"

Running north, back toward Bryn Mawr, her clothes beat flat by the rain, she was stopped from crossing by a different cop. "What's going on?" she asked, as she'd meant to run away from the heart of the beast.

"Someone important's in town," he said, as if she should have known the President's motorcade would pass under the running path she chose precisely to avoid him. He pushed her backwards.

She stood in the pouring rain, watching black SUVs parade by as a helicopter hummed overhead. She figured he was in one, but she and the line of people in their cars popping their lights on in the fading light did not know exactly which one. After thirty minutes the police allowed her and the bug-eyed cars to cross the bridge.

Ten minutes later, she was on the eastern edge of Bryn Mawr, near a semi-trailer parking lot. A man took elderly Native homeless women there, parked between the trailers, and raped them with a machete. Their blood soaked everything, including the bottoms of their Pendleton purses. He drove a red car and told them they were lucky. He'd already killed two. She knew this as well. As she turned back to the west, crossing a foot bridge under which a creek trickled, she looked over at the skyline, where sirens blared as the English clashed over their clown chief. A finger of white light from a helicopter roved through the sky, as if searching for something lost long ago. As she ran, the Ojibwe woman took one last look at the city. Rain made the air hazy. The lights bloomed into an orange brume, as if fire were consuming the city. She thought of the elders' prophecies: how one day many would die and those who survived would return to Indian ways. She thought of the dreams she'd had as a girl, where the whole world turned charcoal. And she kept running.

About the Author

Chris Stark (Ojibwe & Cherokee) is an award-winning writer, researcher, visual artist, and national and international speaker. Her first novel, *Nickels: A Tale of Dissociation,* was a Lambda Literary Finalist. Her essays, poems, academic writing, and creative non-fiction have appeared in numerous publications, including *The Palgrave International Handbook on Trafficking; University of Pennsylvania Law Review; Dignity Journal; The WIP; Florida Review; The Chalk Circle: Intercultural Prize-Winning Essays; When We Became Weavers: Queer Female Poets on the Midwest Experience; Hawk and Handsaw: The Journal of Creative Sustainability;* and many others. Her poem, "Momma's Song," was recorded by Fred Ho and the Afro Asian Music Ensemble as a double manga CD. She is also a co-editor of *Not for Sale: Feminists Resisting Prostitution and Pornography;* and a co-author of the ground-breaking research "Garden of Truth: The Prostitution and Trafficking of Native Women in Minnesota." Primary research she conducted with Native women survivors of prostitution and trafficking on the ships in Duluth, Minnesota is included in her article "Strategies to Restore Justice for Sex Trafficked Native Women." She is also co-author and co-researcher of "Evidence of Survivor, Agency, and Researcher Collaboration: An Example of an Emerging Model of Survivor Wellbeing."

Stark's writing has been nominated twice for a Pushcart Prize. In 2012, she was named a "Changemaker" by the *Women's Press* and she was a Loft Series Mentor Finalist. In 2019, she received the International Social Justice Citizen Award from the International Leadership Institute. She has appeared in numerous media, including NPR, MPR, PBS, Justice Talking, and Robin Morgan's radio show. She has spoken at law schools, conferences, rallies, and at the United Nations (four times). She has taught writing and humanity courses at universities and community colleges for twenty years and she was the Two-Spirit program director at Minnesota Indian Women's Resource Center. Currently, she facilitates art and writing groups at Breaking Free in St. Paul, consults with a variety of local and national organizations, and teaches writing and literature at Central Lakes Community College in Brainerd, Minnesota. She is a member of the Minnesota Missing and Murdered Indigenous Women's Taskforce. She has an MFA in Writing and a Master's in Social Work. For more information, visit: www.christinestark.com

Acknowledgements

Twenty years ago, the seed for this book was planted during a ten-page classroom exercise at the University of Central Florida. The professor, whose name I've forgotten, said, "You owe it to Sher and Kris to finish their story." Since then, it has gone through hundreds of iterations until it settled into the story on these pages. I'm grateful to the professor at UCF, as his words stirred a sense of responsibility in me to this story and its characters.

Many have supported and guided me along the way as I have worked for healing, identity, and belonging. Many years ago, Sam Emory brought me back to White Earth Reservation during a snowstorm to get my Indian name, which was the beginning of my return to *Anishinaabeg*. Earl Hoaglund gave me my *Anishinaabe* name along with a life-long connection through his kindness and patience. Both have passed on now, but I'll always remember Sam's crazy-fun sense of humor and Earl's pancakes. I try not to miss them too much. I also especially want to acknowledge Skip and Babette Sandman, Tommy Saros and Becca Countryman, Sheila and Terry Lamb, Terry Forliti, Jessica Smith (both of them), Patti Larson, Deb Foster, Michelle Noor, Amy Arndt, Eileen Hudon, Brenda Hill, Mysti Babineau, Sherri Dougherty and Cyndi Carlson, April Posner, Romona and Lisa Abrazo, Melinda Masi, Catharine MacKinnon, Marie Caples, Maggie Kazel, Trina Porte, and Rene Simon. And, in loving memory and with gratitude for our friendship, Andrea Dworkin. I want to thank Dora Ammann, and all the elders, whose presence in our community is a quiet, steadfast source of spiritual support for so many, me included.

Many thanks to Sherry Quan Lee, Deb Blake, and Amy Foster for their comments on the manuscript. I have much appreciation for Victor Volkman at Modern History Press, especially for his extreme patience with this book.

Most especially, I want to thank my grandmothers, now in the spirit world, who passed down everything I needed to live a good life. And much love for *niiyawen'enyag Daanis* and *Zhoni,* as their young lives provide much hope that our ways will carry on.

It would be incomplete to not express my gratitude and love for the land and water, especially the woods and lakes of Northern Minnesota where I spent much of my childhood, and where I go to now whenever I have the opportunity. My heart resides in that particular place on earth. There's nowhere else I'd rather be. When I look at the stars in the night sky, I know I am exactly where I should be—among the same trees and water that saved me as a girl. *Miigwetch, mishoomis.* I am most grateful.

"...a perfect genius that makes the impossible in expression, possible; the unknowable in experience, knowable"
--Anya Achtenberg, author of *The Stories of Devil-Girl*

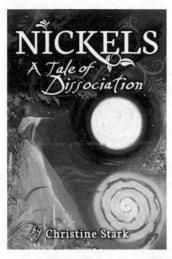

Nickels follows a biracial girl named "Little Miss So and So", from age 4-1/2 into adulthood. Told in a series of prose poems, *Nickels'* lyrical and inventive language conveys the dissociative states born of a world formed by persistent and brutal incest and homophobia. The dissociative states enable the child's survival and, ultimately, the adult's healing. The story is both heartbreaking and triumphant. *Nickels* is the groundbreaking debut of Minneapolis-area author and artist Christine Stark.

"Christine Stark has crafted a language and a diction commensurate with the shredding of consciousness that is a consequence of childhood sexual abuse. She brings us a wholly original voice in a riveting novel of desperation and love. Every sentence vibrates with a terrible beauty. Every sentence brings the news."
--Patricia Weaver Francisco,
author of *Telling: A Memoir of Rape and Recovery*

"To be taken into the mind of a child can be an enchanting adventure, but to be taken into the mind of a child who is abused, confused, and taken for granted is a lingering, livid journey. I applaud her fortitude to bring an olden--too long ignored-- truth out of the darkness with blazing, innovative light."
--MariJo Moore, author of *The Diamond Doorknob*

"In *Nickels*, Christine Stark, powerfully portrays the story of abuse and its impact on our lives. When this beautifully written and compelling story leaves, you are left wanting more. It's riveting; a book that will capture you from the beginning and carry you through the end. Everyone should read this book."
--Olga Trujillo, author of *The Sum of My Parts*

Modern History Press